The pistol had to have been a hundred years old, a Colt Army model, single action six-shooter, universally known as the Peacemaker. The handle was cherry, well worn, but well kept.

Captain picked up the gun and went over to a picture on the wall beside the bar. In an ornate frame was an engraving of downtown Clearwater dated 1921. He poked the barrel under the bottom edge, lifting the picture. Hinged at the top it rose, revealing a box recessed into the wall. Artie peered inside. There was nothing in the box.

"How'd you know the gun was in there?" Artie asked.

The old man smiled, silent for a moment as he remembered. "Because I was the one who put it there," he admitted. "Back in 1938. After the gunfight." He hoisted his skinny shanks back onto the stool and looked at the faces surrounding him. "You all do know about the gunfight on Clearwater Beach, don't you?"

"Gunfight? What gunfight?" Artie said. "I never heard anything about a gunfight around here."

"Well, it happened just the same. And I know 'cause I was there." He paused for a long minute. "I'd a been 'bout thirteen back then …"

Chris and Dave Manley are back, and once again neck deep in a mystery!

GUNFIGHT ON CLEARWATER BEACH vividly transports the reader to another time in America ... an uncomfortable, but definitely interesting time. Kafrissen weaves murder, politics, greed, and the racism of 1938 with friendship, honor, family, and dogged determination. Then ties it all together with familiar characters from previous novels for a great weekend read. Marlene Becker, author of The Deacon & the Demon

Some other books by Don Kafrissen

BROTHERS BEYOND BLOOD

Book One of the Holocaust Trilogy:

"The plot is skillfully developed, and the characters are genuine The narrative style is different from most novels, and it is an approach that fits the story. The novel is interesting and entertaining. A good read." *Robert Krueger, author*

LONG LOST BROTHER

Book Two of the Holocaust Trilogy:

"An exciting new chapter to the Rothberg saga! Kafrissen makes you feel as if you are there, experiencing the horrors of the concentration camps and the desperate efforts of the people there to survive. Being forced to experience such inhuman atrocities would be enough to make even the most peaceful man consider revenge. But at the same time, Kafrissen makes you face the morality of such a decision. A powerful story!"
JM Bolton, author of Heirs to the Empire

NOT MY BLOOD

Book Three of the Holocaust Trilogy:

Beginning in 1938, the Roma or European Gypsies were rounded up and interned along with Jews, homosexuals, and other people deemed unfit to live by the Nazis. NOT MY BLOOD is the tale of Luca the Gypsy who escaped from Auschwitz, the Nazi's largest death camp in eastern Poland. Nearly 1,000,000 men, women and children were killed there during the 4 years it was in existence.

MISSING PIECES

A Chris & Dave Manley Mystery

What could go wrong? It's a simple job, right? Drive a custom Lincoln Continental Convertible to Las Vegas, all expenses paid. That's what Dave Manley and his wife, Chris, thought. Until a simple car delivery turns into days of terror. But you can always count on your friends when things get just a little bit too hot!

WHITE EMERALDS

A Chris & Dave Manley Mystery

They're like diamonds, but much rarer. The large diamond companies don't like this and are determined to close this mine once and for all. Dave Manley, his friend Tom Novak and their friends are there to help. They steal an experimental helicopter and fly it down to Central America to help the family who discovered them. Lots of action!

THE BLACK MADONNA & OTHER STORIES

A grand collection of 33 tightly written short stories to keep you laughing, crying and on the edge of your seat! You're sure to find a few you'll never forget.

Gunfight on Clearwater Beach

An Old Tale & a Modern Tale Combined

DON KAFRISSEN

IDBPI
International Digital Book Publishing Industries
Brooksville, Florida, USA

For information, visit our website at
www.idbpi.com

ISBN: 978-1-57550-097-3

Electronic books and paper books are published by
International Digital Book Publishing Industries
Brooksville, Florida 34601, USA

PRINTED IN THE UNITED STATES OF AMERICA

10 9 8 7 6 5 4 3 2 1

Acknowledgements

Many people helped me write this book.
First and foremost, I would like to thank

Johanna M. Bolton. My formatter,
organizer and most of all, my good friend.

To My Cover Artist and friend **Karen Heidler**,
a world-renowned artist.

To my esteemed colleague, **Jill Svoboda**, my editor, who is instrumental in helping me pare this book down to a reasonable length and understandable prose.

To **Marlene Becker** who manages to toss out unnecessary verbiage without making me feel like a total idiot.

To my wife, **Diane**, who I dare not let her read a word until I am finished. However, we discuss all aspects, and she gives me invaluable ideas for direction. Many, many thanks, dear!

Dedication

This novel is dedicated to my friend
JIM PETRONE
We've certainly had some good times together!

Author’s Note

The basis for this book is purported to be a true story. It was told to me by an old gentleman I met years ago while living on Clearwater Beach on Florida’s West Coast. I searched old newspaper reports but never found another word about the “gunfight,” or the ‘drifter’ who shot the police chief.

But it’s still a good story!

PROLOGUE

The Gun

Brooke expertly topped off the beer and twirled the chilled mug down the bar, landing it exactly in front of Tom, handle to the right. She cocked an eyebrow, standing a little taller. Tom nodded slightly, a small grin on his face.

Next to him, Dave shook his head. "Will you two cut it out?"

"What?" Tom and Brooke chorused.

Chris teased, "If her old man catches you, Thomas, he'll gut you like a fish."

"Worse," said Dave. "He'll call in your bar tab."

"I don't know what you two guys are talking about. It's just some harmless flirting." Tom took a sip from his beer. "Besides, I'm meeting Bobbie here later." Tom Novak sat hunched on the barstool, beefy forearms resting on the padded edge. He was heavy-set, solid, 58-year-old, with a military style crewcut beginning to gray at the temples. His navy T-shirt stretched tightly across his broad shoulders. Idly twirling his glass, he glared at Dave from under bushy eyebrows.

Chris stuck a fat pretzel stick in the corner of her mouth and said in her best Groucho Marx imitation, “Is this Bobbie the nurse, or Bobbie the ladies room inspector?”

They were sitting at the bar of Harrington’s Grill & Bar on a warm summer afternoon. Harrington’s was a funny place. It sat opposite the big old pile of constantly-under-construction courthouse. After opening around ten, the bar was usually full of lawyers and clients huddled over pre-trial or pre-sentencing drinks, a usually unsuccessful attempt to calm frayed nerves. The after-lunch crowd was generally composed of judges and lawyers, both prosecutors and defense, hashing over the day’s courtroom antics and planning next weekend’s golf games. What started out as a neighborhood diner had become a hangout, a home away from home. Newcomers received the best service in town, great food and an unusual amount of good-natured harassment from the waiters and waitresses. At its core was an old stainless-steel railway dining car which had once squatted on the Clearwater Beach. Years before it had been moved to its present location, been remodeled several times so that all that was left of the old car were some curved oak rafters, a few mementos from faded glory days gone by, and just a few stainless panels peppered with what looked like bullet holes of long forgotten origins.

Chris and Brooke had just come from a joint meeting between the County Commission and the county Bar and Restaurant Owner's Association concerning a new sign ordinance.

Christine Manley and her husband Dave lived on a beautiful 40' sailboat and owned a big, barnlike bar and restaurant called Chesney's just outside of the town of Clearwater.

They were still steaming about the perceived unfairness of the new ordnance. The county had recently lost a large court case against a local religious cult known as the Brotherhood, that had been buying up businesses and land in the city and county and yanking them off the tax rolls. The county was now desperately seeking new sources of revenue. Naturally, every attempt at adding new or increasing taxes was met by a protest from the targeted group, be it fishermen, homeowners, cab drivers or, in their case, restaurant owners. The mayor was due to go on TV that evening and make the announcement.

Chris and Brooke had their heads together and were angrily denouncing the cult, the City Council, the federal government and anything else that came up. Tom and Dave tried to stay out of it as best they could, especially when the ladies were angry. Just then the door opened and two of the cult's "security guards" came in. They were obviously in high spirits, slapping each other on the back and talking loudly.

The taller of the two shoved a barstool casually aside and leaned his elbows on the dark mahogany bar. The shorter and stockier of the two shoved in between his partner and Tom, jostling Tom's elbow.

"Sorry, pop," he apologized.

Tom turned his head slowly and glowered at him, taking in the tan uniform shirt, sharply creased dark brown slacks, spit-shined shoes, and wide leather belt festooned with the normal paraphernalia of cops everywhere – 2 way radio, handcuffs, night stick and, in his case, a short sword. The short sword was another point of contention between the City of Clearwater Police and the Brotherhood. According to the teachings of their prophet, all male members must wear the sword as a symbol of their loyalty to the prophet and defense of the faith. The fact that the sword had metamorphosed from a purely decorative ornament to an actual fighting instrument was a real sore spot also between the police and the Brotherhood. Several arrests and trials later, the Brotherhood's lawyers had won the right for the members to wear the swords, all based on similar cases in Canada with the Sikhs.

"I'll give you Pop, you skinny asshole," Tom growled.

The two guards ignored him and ordered beers. Brooke reluctantly drew the beers and placed them in front of them on gaily-printed napkins.

"That'll be $2.50. Each." She smiled but was guarded.

"Aw, honey, just run a tab, will you?" the tall one reached a long arm across the bar and patted her on the cheek. She recoiled instantly, putting up a hand and slapping his wrist. Brooke was a willowy woman in her late twenties with shoulder-length dark brown hair. She was usually found with a smile on her face, deepening her dimples and bringing out the sparkle in her eyes.

"Hey, baby, no offense." He put his hands up in mock surrender. "After what happened this week in court, this is our town now."

Brooke frowned, "Maybe so, but this is still my place. So keep your hands to yourself."

"Hey, what about it, Grandpaw?" The smaller one chortled. He was turned toward a slim black man in his late 70's, ill fitting blue suit, skinny wrists sticking out of his cuffs and wrinkled hands wrapped around a squat glass. "Ain't you the city lawyer whose ass we just whipped?"

The black man looked up at his accuser through the mirror behind the bar. "Son, you couldn't whip me with that club and that sissy boy toad sticker there in your belt." He smiled sleepily and shook his head, twirling his drink in the wet circles on the bar.

"Hey, old man, who the fuck you think you're talking to?" The guard was standing now with hands on hips. His shirt had two buttons undone and a nest of chest hair peeked out. The man was in his mid-twenties, stocky, probably a former football linebacker in high school. His hair was cut in the expected white sidewalls and what looked like a short circular toupee on top. He was chewing a toothpick and his cheeks were just a little sunburned.

"Watch your language, asshole. There are ladies present." Tom swung around on his stool facing the two guards.

Dave reached out a hand and gripped Tom's shoulder. "Easy, big fella. These guys have more lawyers that you've got pimples on your ass." He was muttering this under his breath.

The tall guard eased to his feet and glared down at Tom.

He was easily six inches taller than Tom and, though slim, appeared to be in excellent physical condition. His uniform shirt clung tightly to his upper arms and was stretched snugly across his back. “Sit, Pop. This ain’t any of your business.”

Meanwhile, Shorty was leaning close to the black gentleman and talked sneeringly in low tones to him. He had his hand on his back and suddenly reached up and gripped the fellow by the back of the neck, shaking him. The black man tried to turn his head against the iron grip but couldn’t. Shorty barked a harsh laugh in his face.

The old man reached shakily for his drink and with a flip of his wrist, threw it in Shorty’s face. The guard just stopped, stunned. “Why, you old geezer,” he gasped. With unexpected force, he slammed the black man’s face on the bar. It happened so fast that neither Tom nor Dave could move. Brooke gave a shriek that brought several of the waiters and waitresses running. Shorty held the back of the old man’s skinny neck, watching the blood flow from his nose and pool on the bar.

Tom slid off the stool and with one swift motion jabbed at Shorty. The tall guard slapped his hand down and backhanded Tom, sending him crashing against a table, knocking the cutlery to the floor.

Dave leaned toward Chris after sipping from his beer. “Do you think he needs help?” He gestured toward Tom who was now on his feet shaking his head.

Chris surveyed the situation, “Give him a few minutes. There are only two of them, and besides, you’re wearing a new shirt." She turned to Brooke, who was loudly calling for Artie, her husband. As Artie came running from the kitchen, Chris held up a hand, stopping him.

Dave turned on his stool, back to the bar, ready to slip off the stool if needed.

Tom slipped sideways toward the tall guard and faked a jab to the head. As the tall guard blocked the jab and swung at Tom's head, Tom ducked and slipped inside, striking him rapidly in the stomach and kidney with his fist and elbow. The guard grunted and bent over, only to meet a spinning kick from Tom's pointy cowboy boot to the side of his face. His eyes glazed and Tom caught him as his legs began to fold. He eased him to the floor and started to prop him against the wall. Just then Shorty swung a roundhouse at Tom who hunched a shoulder and partially deflected the blow off the back of his head.

Chris hunched her shoulders and said, "Ow, that had to have hurt."

"No kidding. That poor guy's hand," Dave chuckled. He and Tom had been in a few fights together over the years. The first in a bar in Saigon where they'd met. They'd been fast friends since.

Just then, the tall guard woke up enough to grab the front of Tom's shirt, catching him off guard. Shorty hit him hard behind the ear and again in the shoulder. Tom jabbed an elbow back, catching Shorty in the stomach, expelling his air in a whoosh. As the tall guard struggled to regain his feet still clutching Tom's shirt, Tom grabbed his head between his meaty hands, grinned and kissed him on the forehead. The startled guard stopped for a second. It was all the time

Tom needed. His hands tightened on the guard's ears and he head butted him, again sending the guard into sleepy time.

Shorty was on Tom's back in an instant sending him to the floor and was reaching for his short sword. Before the sword could be pulled clear, a loud click was heard, and Shorty felt the cold hardness of a gun barrel against the side of his head.

"You move that fucking pig sticker one more inch and I'm going to decorate this here bar with white boy brains, if you've got any." The black man hissed loud enough for everyone nearby to hear. His blood steadily dripped onto Shorty's uniform shirt.

Shorty slowly let the sword slip back into his sheath. The gun barrel didn't waver, didn't move. "Stand up, fat boy. Take out the trash." He nudged the fallen guard with his shoe.

Tom struggled to his feet and pulled the groggy guard upright, draping his long arm over Shorty's shoulder. The black man kept the long revolver trained on Shorty. The two guards staggered out into the sun, glaring back at the stunned tableau.

Tom broke the silence. He shoved a paw at the old man. "Much obliged, pard. How's the shnozz?"

The black man swapped the heavy gun to his left hand, took Tom's proffered hand, and replied, "I'll live." He pressed a napkin to his face tilting his head back. "Octavio Toffelmeyer. My friends call me Captain." He paused, surveying the man standing before him. He obviously liked what he saw, giving the hand a final shake. He pulled a large, red bandana out of his pants pocket and held it to his nose, attempting to staunch the blood. Out of the corner of his eye he glanced at Tom, noting an abrasion over his ear. "Looks like you could use a mop up, too."

"Here, old timer, why don't you let me have that gun?" Dave reached out and took the old six-shooter out of the bony hand. "So where in that suit of yours did you hide this?" The pistol was a long, heavy revolver, obviously old and well-used. Dave identified it as a Colt Army model, single action six-shooter, universally known as the Peacemaker. Dave hefted it and looked at the cylinder. It wasn't loaded. It must have been a hundred years old, though. The handle was wood, cherry, he guessed, well worn but also well made. Stamped into the handle was an inscription, two Rs entwined and beneath it a scripted T.R. and 1889.

Captain barked a laugh. "Me carry a gun? Un, uh. Nossir. It's been here all along."

Shelly, a pretty waitress, was dipping a napkin in a glass of water and swabbing the blood off the bar. She offered a damp napkin to the black gentleman. "Here? Where?"

Artie chimed in, "Yeah, I don't keep a gun here." He looked around and shrugged. "After those two guys, maybe I should." He wrapped a handful of ice cubes in a white cotton bar towel and handed them to the black gentleman.

Captain picked up the gun in his free hand and pointed the long barrel at an antique plaque hanging on the wall beside the bar. The plaque was actually an ornate frame containing an engraving depicting a view of downtown Clearwater dated 1921.

Brooke looked puzzled. She walked over to it and stood on tiptoes reading it. Tom casually leaned over the bar to get a good look at her rear encased in skintight brown slacks. Chris kicked him and glared, shaking her head a fraction. Tom looked at her innocently.

Brooke tapped the plaque, running her slim fingers around the edge.

Captain shook his head and poked the barrel under the bottom edge. The plaque was hinged at the top and, as he lifted it, revealed a box recessed into the wall. A string was attached to the bottom edge and disappeared behind the wall, attached to a weight to keep it closed. Artie smiled and held the trapdoor open, peering inside. There was nothing else in the box.

"How'd you know it was there, Mr. Toffelmeyer?" Dave asked?

The old man smiled, a far-away look on his face. He was silent a minute, thinking about the past. "Why, I put it there. In 1938. After the gunfight." He hoisted his skinny shanks back onto the stool. The blood was just about stopped now, and he tilted his head forward and looked at the faces surrounding him. "You do know about the gunfight on the Beach, don't you?"

"Gunfight? What gunfight?" Artie asked. He looked around, "Any of you ever heard about a gunfight?"

Artie and Brooke were originally from Detroit, the children of Albanian immigrants. They were self-taught and had purchased the restaurant and bar several years earlier. Their hard work and determination had pulled the old diner from a hangout for bums and down and outers to a classy hangout for lawyers and criminals, in other words, a different breed of bums and down and outers. A step up or sideways?

No one had ever heard about the "gunfight."

"There was a gunfight in my bar?" asked Brooke. She leaned across the bar, her tan, silk top stretched tightly. Chris kicked Tom before he could move his head.

"Oh, yess'm. Fact is, it is the only gunfight ever reported on Clearwater Beach." He shook his curly gray-haired head, grinning, his teeth gleaming in the early afternoon light. Then he was silent, staring off into the distance again.

"Well, you can't just leave us there," complained Tom. "So who shot who?"

Just then a voice was heard from the door, "Shot? Was somebody shot? Should I get my bag?" A well-turned-out woman of medium height and weight, dressed in a gray pleated skirt and a sleeveless yellow sweater ankled over to the bar. She was definitely a stunner with a generous figure, billowy deep red hair, wide set blue eyes and a no- nonsense, take charge look on her face.

Tom hurriedly stood up and introduced her. "Bobbie, this is Chris and Dave, I told you about them." She shook hands with Chris and gave Dave a serious smile. When she smiled, her lips turned up at the corners. Dave noted that the smile didn't quite reach her eyes. "And this is Artie and Brooke. They own this joint." They how do you do'd.

"This chubby little twerp is Shelly," Tom gestured with his beer at the dimpled waitress whose short hair was caught up fetchingly with a pair of clips. She waved a blood-spattered hand, bringing an alarmed look to Bobbie's face.

Shelly noted the look and hurriedly said, "Oh, its okay, it's not mine. It's his." She pointed to Captain Toffelmeyer.

"And this is Captain Octavious Toffelminer," Tom offered.

Captain shook his head and mumbled something about white folks. "It's Octavio Toffelmeyer, madam. Please call me Captain." He took her smooth hand and bowed gallantly over it, a small drop of blood dripped on it. "Oops, sorry."

"That's okay," she replied. "I'm Barbara Young. Please call me Bobbie. What are you captain of?"

"Nothin', ma'am, just a nickname."

"Yep, that's right everybody, this is Bobbie, my friend and she's a nurse...."

"Nurse Practitioner," finished Bobbie. "So, what's going on? Why do you two have blood on you?" She surveyed the two men with a practiced eye. "Thomas, have you been fighting with this nice man?"

"No, no, no, Miss Bobbie. Tom actually helped me out." Captain turned to Tom and said, "For which I'll be forever grateful." They shook hands again.

Hurriedly, Chris and Brooke recounted the events of the past half-hour for her, finishing with, "The Captain was just about to tell us about the gunfight on Clearwater Beach."

She snorted, "Yeah, right, a gunfight on the Beach? When was that, last week?" Her skepticism was obvious.

"No," piped in Brooke, "in 1938. Right, Captain?"

"Yep, that's right, Ma'am. Nineteen hundred and thirty-eight." He paused for a long minute. "I'd a been 'bout thirteen then and..."

"Wait a minute, Captain," interrupted Artie "Why don't we move into the big booth in the corner? That is, if you've got the time."

"Got nuthin' but time, son. I'm handing in my resignation tomorrow. You sure you all want to hear this story?"

"Oh, yes. Un-huh. Yep, Sure do," they all chorused.

Tom leaned over the bar and refilled his glass from the tap. "Put it on my tab," he grinned as Brooke glared at him.

"Shelly, would you please get drinks for everybody?" asked Brooke.

"Okay, but don't start 'til I get back." She took their orders and scampered away while the group settled themselves in the comfortable, semi-circular booth. It was just after lunch, the tables were clear. The only customers were courthouse regulars busy sipping their twentieth draft beer of the day. The dinner crowd wouldn't be in for another couple of hours.

"Let's see, where to start, where to start?" He thought for a minute then looked around the table. "I guess I'd better start with the murder of Bob Brightwater by the Chief of Police of the City of Clearwater."

CHAPTER 1

1937: The Murder

Bob Brightwater sat at his desk, going over the figures for the third time. His office was on the third floor of the old city hall building on Osceola Street, overlooking the bay. Of course, he had to stand up and peer around the edge of the window frame to see it, but it was still an inspiring view. He was a mild man, forty-one years old with a full head of sandy hair. He was married to a lovely woman, Martha, had a son Bob Junior whom everybody called BB, and lived in a small house on the Beach. All right, it was the south end of the Beach, but it was the Beach, nevertheless. The time was early spring in 1938. Hitler had just met with Mussolini and solidified the Axis pact. The Depression, though deep and wide, seemed to have a minimal effect on the small community of Clearwater. The federal government, through the

WPA, the Works Progress Administration, had recently approved a grant to the city for the construction of a water and sewage system to the Beach that would run alongside the new causeway. This would bring money, jobs and, most of all, hope for the future to the city. After all, why would the federal government spend the estimated two hundred thousand dollars in a city of little more than twelve thousand inhabitants? Bob had hope for America. He had dreams for his wife and son. He had hopes for Clearwater. He also had one thing a lot of Americans didn't have. He had a job.

Now he was troubled. Since the federal money had come into the city treasury, several contracts had been let. Only the week before, ground had been broken on the west end of Cleveland Street almost where the freshwater wells had been that first attracted Spanish explorers to the area. Bob was an accountant for the city and had reviewed many contracts since taking on the job. These numbers didn't seem right. They were too high, and some of the contractors were unfamiliar. Bob thought he knew just about everyone for miles around. After all, he'd grown up here, spent his life roaming the coast, the orange groves, the nearby towns.

Well, he'd talk to his wife, Martha, about it tonight. Meanwhile, he'd show the figures to Avery Gibbons, the city attorney. He glanced at the old regulator clock noisily ticking away the minutes to quitting time. Bob pulled a fresh piece of paper out of the drawer of the old wooden desk and set out to convert his notes to a logical sequence and readable figures. In a few minutes he was done. He calmly folded the paper and slipped it in his jacket pocket, then ran a hand through his sandy hair and lit a cigarette. The cigarette was a little on the lumpy side, and he hoped no one would notice. When they'd cut his pay for the third time, he'd been forced to give up the habit. After a week, he was jittery and nervous, irritable and cranky. Martha had suggested that they hand roll some for him and put them in a Camels pack so no one would notice. This seemed to satisfy the craving, but now he was ashamed and afraid someone would ask to borrow one. After all, he didn't want to look like some dime store cowboy.

Just then, a young fellow in a policeman's uniform came in and headed toward Bob's desk. It was Chick Warner, the kid brother of an old friend of his from high school.

"Hullo, Chick, what brings you all the way up here?" Bob had been a senior when Chick was just in grade school. From a skinny kid with reddish hair and a raft of freckles, Chick had turned into a solid, beefy, dour individual. He wore round spectacles and kept his hair short as per police regulations. Cecil McBride, the Chief, wore his hair almost shoulder length and rarely wore his uniform, which only served to set him apart from the majority of townsfolk and certainly from the other officers. Chick hated McBride yet envied him his power and freedom.

"Hey, Bob. I'm just dropping off some papers for Mr. Gibbons. What's new here in city hall? Any new secretaries?" Chick grinned, exposing a missing tooth just off center.

Bob looked over his shoulder at Avery's closed door. "Looks like he's busy right now. Leave them with me, Chick. I've got to see him before I go home tonight anyway."

Chick looked doubtful. His wide rear was perched on a corner of Bob's desk and he was rhythmically slapping the envelope against his leg. "I don't know, Bob. The chief told me to make sure I gave this just to Mr. Gibbons."

Bob shrugged and ground out the last of his cigarette. "Suit yourself, but there's a new girl in building inspections, one of the Sheck girls, Doris, I think."

"Jeepers, the Scheck girls were always a load of fun, Bob. Remember Mary-Ann at the beach party that time? She went skinny dipping!" His eyes were glazed just remembering. "Boy, she was beautiful!"

"Chick, you were what, fourteen then? And she couldn't have been more'n twelve or thirteen." Bob snorted at the picture he remembered of a skinny Mary-Ann Scheck running down the beach naked. Of course she did have the beginnings of small high breasts and already a thatch of dark hair between her legs.

"Yeah, but them were good times, huh Bob?" He grinned a boyish grin. "Tell you what, you give these here papers to Mr. Gibbons. But don't show 'em to nobody else, okay?"

"Fine, Chick. Just leave 'em on the desk." Bob gestured at the IN basket, now nearly emptied.

As soon as Chick's retreating back disappeared around the corner, Bob slipped the envelope out of the basket and undid the clasp. With a glance at Avery's still closed door, Bob peered in at the thick sheaf of documents. They seemed to be several contracts for more construction work on the water system to the old Clearwater Hotel on the Beach, though what the Chief of Police was doing with them Bob couldn't figure out. He rapidly flipped through them and noted a contract for gravel, fill, welding of pipe, and haulage. Two of the contractors Bob recognized, Kellinger Welding, an old firm in the area, and McMullen Sand and Gravel, an even older name that went back to the founding of Clearwater and the neighboring townships. Both reputable and the figures sounded reasonable. He flipped back and forth to a third name, Hoffmann Haulage. Bob frowned. He'd never heard of that one. He slipped the papers back into the envelope and redid the clasp, pulling a black hair from it as he did.

Avery Gibbons was just opening his door and ushering out a thin, nervous man with Avery's large hand on his back. "That's right, Mr. Childers, don't you worry about anything. You just leave it to me."

The thin man turned, seeming to shrink from the hand on his back. His blue suit was shiny and frayed at the cuffs. "Well, if that's the case, Mr. Gibbons, I surely would have to thank you." He offered a slim hand that had seen its share of hard work. "But if you don't mind, I'll just wait until I see what's going to happen." His back went noticeably straighter and he looked Avery Gibbons in the eye for a long minute. He withdrew his hand and let it fall to his side, absently wiping it on his pant leg. Then he turned and stalked from the room, following in Chick's path toward the stairway.

Avery Gibbons had been the attorney for the City of Clearwater for well on twenty years, slightly longer than Llewellen Teague had been mayor. Gibbons was a large man in his early sixties with a great shock of white hair and bushy eyebrows. His teeth were tobacco stained as were the first two fingers on his left hand. He was a cigar smoker, coughed a lot, and tended to speak out of one side of his mouth, the opposite one from his cigar side. He also tended to wear double-breasted blue pinstripe suits with stiffly starched white shirts and blue and red striped ties. In fact, thought Bob, appraising him, his nominal boss and supervisor, it seemed that Avery either wore the same suit and tie for weeks on end or he had a closet full of identical garments. Bob stood and hefted the envelope.

"Problems, Avery?" Bob inquired at the retreating back of Mr. Childers.

Avery raised an eyebrow. "No, no, I don't think so. Man's got a grove and the city and some of the county want to push a road through it. Electric wires and telephone lines, too." He stood deep in thought. "Came to me for help. 'Course, there's nothing I can do. Nothing I want to do. Council voted on it a month or so ago."

"So, why'd you tell him to leave it to you; you'd take care of it?" Bob asked.

"Son," Avery turned and laid a hand on Bob's shoulder. "Sometimes even when you know there's nothing you can do, you hold out a little hope. Then in a week or two, I'll go see him and tell him I tried, but he and I are in the same boat, just little guys against the system. We'll have a drink, curse the government, Wall Street, Niggers, Jews, and next time we have a problem, him and me'll be bosom buddies." Avery gave Bob's shoulder a squeeze and indicated the envelope with his cigar. "What you got there, son?"

"Oh, sorry, sir. This was sent over from the Police

Chief's office for you." He held out the bulky envelope.

"Did you look at it, Bob?"

Something told Bob this was not a time to be truthful. "Nossir. I was told it was for your eyes only." He smiled disarmingly and turned back to his desk.

Avery stood looking at him for another few seconds, lips pursed, cigar in his hand. He tapped a finger on the envelope and slowly turned and went back into his office, quietly closing the door.

Bob rose, slipped on his jacket and hat, an older, light gray fedora. As he left, he stopped at the desk of Ann-Marie Knightington, the secretary for the accounting department. "I'll see you in the morning, Ann-Marie. If anyone is looking for me, just take a message. I have some city business to take care of that will take me past five o'clock."

"Good night, Mr. Brightwater." Ann-Marie said without looking up from her typewriter.

Bob hurried down the stairs and out the large oak doors that opened between the gleaming columns. It was a beautiful spring day, a light breeze off the Gulf, the sky a deep blue with huge, fluffy clouds out toward the west. Bob squinted at them. Nope, not rain clouds. Maybe he'd take the boys for a swim and dig up some clams or catch some stone crabs tonight. They could cook them in a pot on the spit of sand pointed at Sand Key and watch the sun go down. He skipped down the wide steps and headed for the Arcade at the corner of Cleveland and Ft. Harrison. The traffic was light and, as he came alongside the Arcade, a small man in a dazzling white uniform and cap whipped around the side of a car stopped at the curb, nearly colliding with Bob.

"Whoops, sorry Bob, didn't see you!" Johnny Livingston was a fixture on the corner, bringing drinks and eats to customers in their cars from the Dutch Kitchen.

"It's all right, Johnny, my fault." Bob smiled and walked with him back inside. The dim confines of the Scranton Arcade gave out onto shops on both sides of the main hallway. It was patterned on the old English Mews. The Dutch Kitchen was a small four-booth eatery with a row of stools alongside a counter. Beside it were a dress shop, children's toyshop, barbershop, the Clearwater Times newspaper office, and the Postal Telegraph office, where Bob now headed. Also in the Arcade were two pay telephones. Bob stopped and fished a nickel out of his pants pocket. He dialed a number from memory.

"Hello, may I speak to Mr. Kellinger, please." He waited until a familiar voice came on the other end. Gerald Kellinger was an old schoolmate. They'd played football together in Gerald's senior year, and had become friendly, though not close. Bob hoped Gerald would remember him.

"Hi, Gerald, it's Bob Brightwater."

"Oh, hullo, Bob. What can I do for you? Long time, eh?"

Bob tried to read the voice, detect caution, fear, anger, friendship; but the voice was neutral, controlled, and just like Bob remembered of Gerald when they played. No wasted motions, very organized and deliberate.

"Gerald, I just heard about your contract for welding on the water and sewer mains to the beach. I, uh, just wanted to clarify your timetable." He waited.

Gerald was quiet for a full minute. Bob could hear him shuffling papers on his desk. "Sorry, Bob, I don't know what you're talking about. Not only didn't I receive a bid on the mains, but they're all concrete with tar sealing. Nothing for us to do until it gets to the houses and buildings. Then it's all out to bids from the owners." He was quiet again and cautiously asked, "Why, was there a bid?"

Hastily, Bob said, "No, no, I guess I got the name wrong. Sorry to bother you, Gerald. Goodbye for now." And hung up the phone.

Bob paused and lit another cigarette. That was odd. He was sure he'd seen the Kellinger name on the contract. Maybe it just hadn't been let yet. He turned and dialed another number on the wall-hung phone after looking it up in the hanging book.

"Hello, is this McMullen Sand and Gravel?" Bob asked politely. The phone had been answered just "McMullens", by a rough female voice.

"Yeah. What's it to ya?" The voice answered.

"Sorry to bother you. This is Bob Brightwater from the City of Clearwater Attorney's office. I'm just checking on the contracts for the water and sewer work on the Memorial Causeway. I believe work is to start next week. Is that right?"

"Yeah. I guess so. I think that's what the paper's said." She paused. "Hey, are you Sally Brightwater's boy?"

Bob replied in the affirmative. His mother had died several months earlier and, though they'd never been very close, Bob missed her hectoring and lectures. She'd been a grade schoolteacher at the school on North Ft. Harrison St.

"Sorry to hear about your Ma. Tell your Pa that Elsie McMullen was payin' her respects." And the phone went dead.

Bob tried to place Elsie McMullen but failed. His mother taught school as long as Bob could remember, right up to the day before she died. Bob knew that the McMullens were one of the founding families and were quite prolific, but still didn't see his mother travelling in the same social circles as the McMullens. Bob's father was a builder, a carpenter. He'd built several of the "cottages" out at the Bellevue Biltmore Hotel. Mr. Laplant had liked his work and had named the last and most ornate cottage "Brightwater House". Every time he'd taken a drive with his father, the old man had insisted on driving near the grounds of the huge old hotel and always pointed out the cottages he'd built and the ones built by other carpenters – and their defects.

His father had a big ten-year-old Buick Touring Car with a ratty top that he kept sewing together as it fell apart more and more. He had insisted on a Sunday drive when Bob and his kid sister Sarah were youngsters, but the Depression had curtailed these activities except for the occasional instance when Bob would treat the old man to a gallon or two of gas. Then they'd travel up to Dunedin or Tarpon Springs for a lime rickey or a sarsaparilla. Once they went all the way out to Oldsmar, but the roads were terrible, so they came right back.

Bob looked in the telephone book for Hoffman Haulage but couldn't find a listing. Stranger still. The contracts were supposed to go to local firms to provide local jobs. Bob strolled down to the Clearwater Times office in the back of the Arcade. At the desk he asked a young harried, disheveled man for Arthur Perkins, the editor of the local paper. The young man just pointed to a glass enclosed office in the corner. Arthur J. Perkins, Editor, was neatly lettered on the door front and through it Bob could see a head of white hair bobbing up and down as the editor gestured with his left hand while cradling one of the new telephone handsets under his chin. A cigarette was clutched between the fingers of the flailing hand, almost burned down to the skin. Bob smiled and pushed through the swinging gate. He tentatively opened the door a crack and stuck his head in just as the thin editor slammed the phone handset onto its cradle, muttering, "Stupid bastard!"

"What do you want, Brightwater?" Arthur barked.

Bob didn't mind. Arthur Perkins barked at everyone. He smiled and shook hands with the florid man. "Howdy, Mr. Perkins." Bob gestured at a chair. "Mind?"

"Naw, just make it snappy, will you?"

"Tell me about the water and sewer project to the Beach, will you?" Bob leaned forward expectantly, his hat clutched in his hands.

Perkins leaned back and drew in a great glowing breath on his cigarette and stubbed it out in the enormous, overflowing glass ashtray on a corner of his desk. "Why, you got something for me, Bob?"

"No, Mr. Perkins, I'm just trying to get a grasp on the whole picture. I usually just see the odds and ends that come through my office. I figure you could give me a better idea of the, you know, scope of the project."

Perkins shrugged then swung his feet up on the desk. "What's to tell? Wall Street is in the shitter since the crash in '29. The country is at a standstill. Franklin fucking Roosevelt gets elected, and he's giving money around the country for municipal projects to get people working. It's called the WPA and they're approving projects left and right, from new post offices to courthouses to roads and now, a water and sewer line out to the Beach. Personally, I think it's a waste of money but those rich bastards out on the Beach convinced the Mayor and council that it's the thing to do."

Bob frowned. He lived on the Beach and he wasn't one of "those rich bastards" by a long shot. Perkins was known far and wide for his rough language, having come up from that squalid, seamy little island of Key West a few years ago.

"Well, what kind of work goes into building the lines and how is the money disbursed?"

"Jesus, Bob, you know as well as I do. They dig a ditch, lay some pipes in it, build a couple of pump houses, hook it all to the main system and dump the shit out in the gulf somewhere. What's the big deal?" Perkins swung his feet down, leaned over the desk and stared at Bob for a long minute. Slowly he said, "The work is contracted by the mayor and council. When the job is done or when the contractors submit a bill, the paymaster writes a check after the city attorney looks at the invoice. What's going on, Bob? I haven't told you anything you don't already know."

"Nothing, as far as I know, Mr. Perkins. However, if something comes up, you'll be the first to know." Bob hurriedly gathered up his hat and jammed it on his head, making for the door, a deep frown on his face.

Outside on the sidewalk, Bob studied the imposing façade of the Bank of Clearwater. That's where the money is, he supposed.

Just then a firm hand gripped his arm above the elbow. "Would youse come wit me please, Mista Brightwatta?" Bob turned and looked right into the washed-out blue eyes of Arnie Brodsky, a policeman, but today dressed in a plain suit. The plainclothes cop gripped Bob's arm tighter and urged him toward a dark sedan stopped at the curb, its rear door open, another figure reaching for him.

"Why, what's going on?" Bob asked, attempting to pull his arm out of the viselike grip.

"Nuttin, nuttin's wrong. The Chief just wants ta see ya, is all." Brodsky urged him towards the sedan. The other hand reached out and pulled him into the back seat. Just as the door closed, Bob saw Johnny Livingston staring at him, puzzled. Bob was about to put his hand up to wave to him when Brodsky hit him in the stomach with a quick, hard jab. He doubled over, head between his knees as the car sped off.

Bob gasped, seeing red, nearly passing out. The sedan sped away from the curb with a squeal and almost immediately turned a corner. A couple more corners and the car slowed, bumped over a lintel and turned into a narrow courtyard. Bob was still trying to get his breath back and tried to lift his head. He looked out at the gray walls for just a second before Brodsky gripped the back of his neck forcing his head down onto his knees. "Youse just wait a minit, bub. Da Chief wants ta talk wit youse." His iron grip was causing

Bob's vision to blur.

"Arnie," Bob croaked. "Ease up, will ya? You're hurting me. I'll keep my head down, for Chrissakes." His voice was muffled even to his own ears.

Brodsky eased his grip slightly, patting Bob on the back of his head. Suddenly, a dark shadow fell across the window, blocking out the daylight. A guttural voice muttered, "Get him up, Arnie."

Bob felt his head snap back, Arnie's big hand gripping his hair. Outside the car, a lanky figure leaned against the window, one foot cocked on the running board. It was Cecil McBride, Clearwater's police chief. He wore a black frock coat, string tie and twin pearl-handled revolvers. His pocked face sported a droopy mustache under a thin sharp nose, lipless mouth and a broad wrinkled forehead. He wore his thinning, lank black hair pushed back under his black Stetson. But fear grew in Bob's belly as he gazed into a pair of close set, coal black eyes. Dead eyes.

"Robert Brightwater. What am I going to do with you?" McBride shook his head mournfully, scratching his chin.

"Chief." Bob tried to nod but his hair was still knotted in Arnie Brodsky's big fist, "What do you want?"

Instead of answering, McBride jerked his head to one side and disappeared. Brodsky opened the door and pulled Bob after him, easily. Bob looked around. He didn't recognize the courtyard, but he could see the top floors of the Ft. Harrison hotel off to his right. He thought he was behind the police station but wasn't sure. Arnie jerked him through a narrow doorway into a damp cement corridor, down a short flight of stairs and shoved him into a small room.

Bob stumbled and almost fell, but his hand touched and then managed to grip the back of a wooden chair. He ran his hand over his face. "What the hell's going on, Chief?" He stood glaring at the tall lawman.

McBride was lighting a thin, black cheroot, his head cocked to one side. Brodsky stood with his back to the door, hands clasped in front of him. His face was impassive as if he'd witnessed scenes like this many times before.

"Shut up and sit down, Brightwater." The chief gestured at the chair, the only piece of furniture in the room. Dim yellow light came from a small bulb dangling from the ceiling. The corners were dark and Bob thought he could see something in one, but couldn't make it out clearly.

Bob slowly took a seat. "You have no right to bring me here. No right at all. When I get back to City Hall…"

He never finished. With two swift steps, the Chief strode in front of Bob and hit him a hard backhand blow, knocking him off his chair, breaking his nose and sending a bright gout of blood dribbling onto his shirt.

"Didn't I tell you to shut the fuck up?"

Bob just nodded, scared now. More scared than any time in his life. But why was this happening? What had he done? The blow had hurt but Bob had suffered worse playing football many years ago. He pushed himself to his knees and then back into the chair. He just sat attempting to stem the flow of blood with his shirtsleeve. He couldn't help but think, my last good shirt, too. Won't Martha be angry?

McBride was speaking again. "You had to stick your fucking nose into my business didn't you? You had to read private papers, didn't you?" He drew on his cigar, the smoke trickling out of his nostrils like a smoldering dragon. He was walking now, back in forth in front of Bob, his polished black cowboy boots clicking on the rough concrete floor.

"Avery said to just scare you, give you a little something to keep you in line, but I know guys like you. First you tell your wife, then a close friend, pretty soon you're blabbing all around City Hall." He shook his head, rubbing a hand on the back of his neck. With a flick of his wrist, he gestured to Brodsky. The big man strode to the darkened corner and turned on a faucet.

After a few minutes he said, "Go wash your face in the tub in the corner." He gestured with the stub of the cigar.

Bob warily slid to his feet and groped his way to the indicated corner, avoiding Brodsky. His knees hit the edge of a steel tub and then his shaking hands found it. He let the water run and as he kneeled down to wash the gore from his front, two pairs of hands gripped him like iron, forcing him down, down into the steadily growing pool. He fought like a madman, bucking and trying to get to his feet. At one point he managed to get a foot under him, but a swift kick crumpled his knee. Bob held his breath as long as he could but eventually he tried to draw a breath. All he got was water flooding his lungs, Arnie's big hands on the back of his neck. Now his lungs wouldn't process air even if he could get it. A calm settled over him, his body beginning to go limp. With a flash, his wife's face filled his vision. He'd be late for dinner, he absently thought. It may have been his last thought. Like a large beam of light it glowed in his mind's eye, narrowing to a pinpoint and finally flickering out.

Arnie kept him under until he'd stopped squirming, then a moment longer, finally loosening his grip. Bob hung on the side of the tub. McBride checked his pulse in his neck. There was none. Bob Brightwater was unequivocally, irrevocably dead.

The Chief and Arnie stood up. "Get rid of him. Drop him in the Gulf. Pile his stuff on shore. If his body's found, it'll look like he went for a swim and drowned."

Arnie nodded once and followed the Chief through the door, locking it behind him. As they trudged up the stairs, Arnie muttered, "I'll wait 'til dark. Nobody see me den."

A few minutes later McBride picked up the phone in his office and dialed a number. "It's me. We won't have trouble with him anymore." He listened another minute. "Okay," And hung up.

Chapter 2

Tom's Arrest: Present Day

The old black man continued his narrative. "The next day a fisherman found Bob's body floating in the Gulf. His clothes were found in a pile just south of the big grove used to be out on the Beach. The coroner at the time was Doc Hoskins. He reported that Bob was drowned, but Hoskins was a weak man, prone to drink and on the city's payroll. He'd have put down that Bob had been abducted by aliens if they wanted him to." He took a sip of his iced tea and looked around at the quiet circle.

Dave asked, "So who goes after the police chief? Who guards the guardians?"

"Yeah," piped in Artie. "Did they catch him?" He found it vaguely alarming that a murder had been committed by the police.

Tom chuckled and fiddled with his drink, spinning it on the shiny tabletop. "Nope, he wasn't caught. That's who got killed in the gunfight, right, Captain?"

The old man chuckled, "You'll just have to wait and see, Thomas."

"If all this stuff happened to Bob Brightwater in the cellar of the police station, how do you know? How did anybody find out?"

"Well, now, I…" Captain started, but a policeman appeared at his elbow. Behind him was the taller of the two security guards.

"That's the one. That's the asshole who attacked us!" The guard pointed a skinny finger at Tom. He was now sporting a large bandage across the bridge of his nose and strips of plaster on his knuckles and brow ridges.

"Who, this one?" the uniformed officer indicated Tom Novak.

The guard nodded, keeping the policeman between himself and Tom.

"That's not the way it happened, officer," Brooke protested. She tried to push her way out of the booth. Dave held up a hand, wordlessly restraining her.

"Excuse me, Ma'am, but this fellow and his partner want to press charges for assault. The other fellow is in the hospital, pretty beat up." He gripped Tom's arm and hoisted him out of the booth. Before the others could say a word, the officer held up his hand. "I have to take him in if this guy and his partner want to press charges. By the way, they also say you pulled a gun on them." He glared at Tom. "Is that true?"

Tom looked at Captain Toffelmeyer and imperceptibly shook his head. "Well you see, officer, fat boy, this guy's partner, started to pull his pig sticker and, well, I kind of dissuaded him."

"So you are armed, Mr. ...?"

"Novak, Tom Novak." Tom reached into his rear pocket as the officer quickly drew his pistol.

"Easy, son." Tom smiled and slowly drew out his wallet. "Here's my I.D. and my Concealed Weapons Permit." He handed the two cards over to the policeman.

The cop eyed Tom narrowly. "Just keep your hands where I can see them. He edged around until he was behind Tom and ordered him to put his hands on the table. After he did, the cop patted him down, finding a Walther PPK automatic tucked into a small holster in the small of Tom's back under his shirt. He carefully removed it and with one hand ejected the clip.

"Mr. Novak, you're in violation of a city ordinance prohibiting firearms in places where alcohol is served. Plus the Brotherhood is filing assault and battery charges along with attempted murder charges against you. I'm afraid you'll have to come with me." He handed Tom back his ID and Tom replaced them in his wallet and the wallet in his pants.

"Doesn't hardly seem fair, officer. Those two assholes attacked the old man and Tom just tried to help him. Now you're taking Tom in and the bad guys go free." Dave was slowly sliding around the booth.

The policeman still had his gun out and gestured with it toward Dave. "Nobody was talking to you and if you've got a complaint, you can take it to the DA. I'm just doing my job. His office brings charges. Meanwhile, Mr.Novak, you'll have to come with me." He tucked Tom's gun and clip into his belt and cuffed Tom's hands behind his back.

Tom turned to Chris, "Would you please call Sy Goldberg, my lawyer, and see if he can meet us at the police station?"

"Sure, anybody else?"

Tom shrugged and grinned, "Nope. See ya later."

They all watched as the officer put Tom into the back of the cruiser and drove away. The tall security guard looked around him at the crowd of faces.

Brooke jumped up and would have slapped him if Artie hadn't caught her arm. "You bastard, don't you ever come in here again, you or that fat friend of yours." Her face was flushed, high spots on her cheeks.

The guard beat a hasty retreat.

"Well," Dave broke the ice, "that certainly was an interesting turn of events." Chris was busily dialing their friend, Sy Goldberg, on her cell phone. A minute later she reported that Goldberg was playing golf and that his office would try to get in touch with him and free Tom.

Captain leaned back in his seat and said wearily, "You know, ever since the Brotherhood came to town, it's been all downhill. I'm just tired of fighting them."

"Well, since there isn't much we can do right now, why don't you tell us more about the gunfight, Mr. Toffelmeyer?" asked Chris.

Chapter 3

Suspicion of Murder: Present Day

"Well, at the time me and my family were living out on the Beach, too. We had a little ol' place not far from Brightwaters. Me an' BB, that was Bob and Martha's boy, used to go fishin' and crabbin' an' all. BB was a little younger'n me. Daddy had a fishin' boat him an' my Uncle Lester'd built. Bob Brightwater had helped them get an ol' Ford T-model engine for it, an' if I remember right, Martha's brother, Abel, had helped, too." He took a small sip of his drink, hand slightly trembling.

"You see, after Bob's body was discovered, nobody did anythin' about it."

"What do you mean? Didn't anybody investigate? Didn't they do an autopsy?" asked Chris.

"Young lady, you got to remember, this was the Depression. It seems like there wasn't money for hardly anything. The city wasn't going to spend a dime on what was obviously a drowning." He pronounced depression like it was an event, a big deal deserving of a capital D, a slight lowering of his voice, respect in the inflection.

Dave shook his head, "Somebody must have missed him, must have had a clue?"

"Oh, sure, he had lots of friends, but everybody assumed Bob'd gone for a swim after work and just up an' drowned. That is, everyone 'cept Martha. She knew he was a good swimmer and on a nice summer evening, he woulda come home and got BB an' me. She raised holy hell, but nobody official would do anything a'tall." He stopped to loosen his tie a bit.

"So who's this Abel character?" asked Shelly, her fine smooth brow furrowed in frustration.

"Ah ha, so you picked up on that, eh child?" He grinned, smothering a chuckle. "Ol' Abel is the next part of the story."

Chapter 4

The Telegram: 1938

Abel Landis leaned over the table and speared a slice of bread with his fork. His yellow hair fell in a mop over his forehead, his brow pink from the sun. His flannel shirt was rolled up over his forearms, freckled and dusted with a fine spray of golden fuzz.

"Oh, for gosh sakes, Abel, you could ask." Mrs. Hartmann harumpped. She was a large, matronly woman, with dark hair, braided going to gray. She usually wore the braids tightly wrapped around her head, but today a single fat braid hung down her back to her waist. Her blue and white checked gingham dress was freshly pressed and a dusty white apron was wrapped around her ample middle.

"Yes'm, sorry." Abel grinned at her while slathering the slice of bread with homemade blackberry jam.

"Mind your manners, Abel, or I'll take you out behind the barn and kick your butt." Otto Hartmann grumbled around a mouthful of oatmeal. Abel knew this was just talk because he could take the little man with one arm tied behind his back. He also knew that this was code for, "I'll meet you behind the barn after breakfast for a snort of homemade moonshine."

But Abel was in a particularly feisty mood this morning, so he answered, "Do you want me to go out and cut a switch, Dad?"

Otto Hartman nearly dropped his spoon; he was so perplexed at this reply. What in the world had come over this young lad?

He just looked at Abel bewildered, spoon poised halfway to his mouth.

"Sorry, sir. I'm just feeling so good today. I was in town last night and won almost $50 playing cards. And I filled the tank on the truck with gasoline!"

Mrs. Hartmann clucked at him, shaking her head in mock disapproval while collecting his plate.

Mr. Hartmann grinned a toothless grin at him and asked. "Who'd you win it off? Was it one of them Carper lads?

Abel nodded, "Yup, it was Ikey Carper, you know, the oldest one."

"Be careful around that one, sonny, he's a mean one. Like his daddy." Otto resumed eating his oatmeal.

Abel sat back his hands clasped over his stomach, feet spread out in front of him. Otto had found him wandering their road one gray day in a snowstorm nearly two years ago. Abel couldn't remember how he'd got there or where he'd come from. The last thing he remembered was being in a fight in a bar and being tossed into the back of a truck full of pipes and chain. Next thing he knew he woke up in a soft bed in a high ceilinged room and a large lady bent over him wiping his forehead with a warm rag.

Abel had run away from his home in Florida after a shouting match with his father and joined the Army just before it went overseas in 1916. He'd become a daring dispatch rider on his motorcycle, being posted under Captain Dwight Eisenhower. He'd even met General Black Jack Pershing a time or two. Toward the end of the war he'd managed to familiarize himself with the Harley-Davidson and Indian cycles, which were common at the time. There were a few Excelsior-Hendersons but they weren't as reliable or as surefooted as the Davidson's. He didn't particularly care for the British cycles either.

After being mustered out he tried going back to his home in Clearwater, Florida but his old man had become a mean drunk, his Momma had died in the great influenza epidemic of 1917, and his sweet sister Martha had married Bobby Brightwater and already had a little boy of her own. He lived out on the Beach for a while, hanging out with a rowdy bunch, but after the excitement of the war, he found Clearwater too restrictive. He'd fixed up an old cycle much like the wartime bikes and had drifted west, working odd jobs, not settling in one place for too long. Abel was adept at painting and drawing, so often he would set up a small shop to do portrait work or drawings of prize bulls or horses.

By nineteen twenty-seven he'd saved up some money and married a woman named Ellen Fitch in a small town near Waco, Texas. Ellen had inherited a large house from her daddy, so they started renting out rooms. After a year, Abel converted part of the ground floor into a saloon and restaurant. They prospered, and Abel strutted around town in a dark suit and a bowler hat, a thin cheroot clenched between his strong teeth. His only failing was that he was short and had a big mouth. In very large individuals, this doesn't usually present a problem, but like as not, Saturday nights would see him in a fight in his own bar and often thrown out by men who'd been his drinking companions just an hour before.

Ellen endured his drinking and carousing for about as long as a woman could and finally asked him to leave. Times were tougher than they had been a few years before, and she couldn't afford to continuously replace the broken tables and chairs, not to mention the glassware. Abel begged and pleaded, as he had so many times before, but this time was different. One of their boarders was a tall, thin fellow with a narrow mustache named McBride. He worked for one of the oil companies. One night Abel and Ellen were going at it hammer and tongs when McBride interceded.

"The lady is mine now, runt. Pack your stuff and git."

When Abel protested, McBride drew a long revolver from under his frock coat and hit him on the side of his head, hard. Next thing Abel knew he was in a boxcar, clothes strewn about him and a welt on the side of his head. He accepted his fate philosophically and drifted from town to town, drawing, painting, playing cards and even working in an oilfield outside Tulsa, Oklahoma for almost a year. At one time or another, he could be seen, his runty, bowlegged figure either trudging through town or hanging from a rope on the side of a barn, painting murals; in a restaurant decorating the wall beside a booth in exchange for a meal or even daubing a scrolly name of a town on a water tower. When the depression sunk in, it really didn't mean much to him; he'd been on the road drifting for so long. In a short letter from an old friend from Waco, he'd learned that McBride had beaten Ellen to death in a drunken rage a year before. By the time he was Abel to hitchhike back to Waco, McBride was long gone, nobody knew where. A year later, Otto Hartmann found Abel. The work was hard, but the grub was fine and the Hartmann's treated him like a son.

The ranch was only twenty miles from Lander, Wyoming, and Abel went in most weekends, weather permitting. It boasted a couple of saloons, a fine whorehouse run by a Swedish woman named Gerta, two automobile garages, and even a motorcycle dealership and garage. Abel was content to work on the ranch, play cards and carouse, avail himself of a whore now and then and save for a motorcycle of his own. Life had dwindled down to a matter of a week at a time. Ambition had flown the coop. He was thirty-seven years old and content. Occasionally he drew a picture for Mrs. Hartmann or one of the whores, but his massive mural days were done. He barely remembered them, though years later tourists would see his work from Mobile to Denver, sometimes overwhelmingly plastered on the entire side of a building or in a small drawing stuck up on the wall of a bar-room on a pin. His distinctive "by Abel" visible in the lower left-hand corner.

Now he slid out of his chair, slipped into a long dark, waxed cotton duster and a wide-brimmed Stetson. "Good day, then, Mrs. Hartmann. See you at lunchtime." He turned to his boss, pulling a pair of leather gloves out of his pocket, and slapping them against his palm. "I'm going to ride out toward the northeast. We've got a couple of cows that should have calved by now. If they have, I'll bring them in, and if not, I'll find out why, okay Otto?"

Otto grunted an assent and noisily slurped his coffee from the saucer.

He would ride out too, after a little nip behind the barn.

Abel saddled a piebald mare and rode out toward the snowcapped peaks at a slow trot. The Hartmanns' ranch was in the foothills of the Tetons, always an impressive background, and Abel loved the rolling prairie, clumps of trees beside gurgling streams and the feel of the rippling horse muscles between his legs. Growing up in Clearwater, Florida, he'd seen and been around horses some but never actually ridden one until he'd come west. At first he was apprehensive but grew more confident with practice. Now he was as one with the little mare beneath him and steered her with his knees, when she needed any guidance at all.

The day was spring warm and the dust rose behind him. He paused to wipe his brow with a big red bandana he'd tied around his neck. His mind drifted and he thought of his former wife, Ellen, his sister Martha and their little boy BB. He guessed BB'd be about eleven or twelve now. Gosh, he hadn't seen the kid since he was a baby. He wondered if his old man had kicked the bucket yet, and he missed his Mama. But Mrs. Hartmann made up for it and Otto just got happy and giggled when he had a wee bit of a load on.

Overhead a hawk circled, riding the thermals, looking for an elusive fieldmouse or small snake. And so his days went, one by one, nothing much of anything happening. Sometimes sitting around the parlor listening to the radio with 'Fibber McGee and Molly', 'Amos 'n' Andy' or 'My Gal Sal'.

On Saturday Abel washed and slicked back his unruly yellow hair. He and Otto took the old Ford A-Model truck and, with a list from Mrs. Hartmann, drove into town, Abel at the wheel. The previous night it had rained and the track was muddy until he came to the gravel and tar road. Even that was only marginally better, the gravel hammering like birdshot on the underside of the old pick-up. Abel eased the throttle open, and the truck rattled along at a teeth jarring forty-five miles an hour. "Yahoo," Abel yelled, bouncing around on the cracked leather. Otto grimly held onto his hat and clutched at the door.

Abel had forty of his fifty-dollar winnings from the previous week in his pocket, which in those days made him a fairly wealthy man. He planned to help Otto get his shopping done, pay a little visit to Miss Gerta's, and have a steak at the Lander House Hotel before wandering over to Lefty's Club for a few hands at cards. They agreed to meet back at the general store at five o'clock.

They secured the boxes and cans in the back of the truck and spread a tarp over them to keep prying fingers and eyes away. Abel'd bought a dime's worth of hard candies in a twist of newspaper for the gals at Miss Gerta's and walked to the edge of town where the modest two-story house stood, shielded by a high thick hedge. Miss Gerta met him on the porch.

"Ah, Abel, my friend. So good to see you. Sit, sit." Gerta indicated a pair of white painted wicker chairs and a low table.

Abel removed his Stetson and tossed it on the table on top of a pile of newspapers. He slouched into a chair.

Gerta turned and bellowed, "Lottie, tea please!" Then she turned to Abel, "Haf you seen the newspapers this week?" She moved his hat and pulled a Denver Post out and thrust it toward him. The headline read "Adolph Hitler hailed as Nazis take Austria". Shaking her elaborately coifed head, she said, "I have heard from some of my countrymen that the Nazis are taking all things away from the Jews, and they fear that soon a war will come."

"Nonsense," Abel declared, "The last war was more than most people could stand. It will never happen again." He fidgeted in his seat, anxious to get upstairs.

"I hope you are right but if you are not, would you have to go? I hope not."

Abel grinned, "Why, afraid of losing a good customer?"

"Ach, no, young man." She patted him warmly on the knee. "Not many people in this town speak to me openly the way you do, and I would miss our chats greatly."

Abel leaned over the table and took her hands in his. "Try not to worry, Gerta. If it comes, there isn't much we can do about it and if it doesn't, well, all the worry is for nothing." He thought for a minute. "Say, why are you worried about the Jews? What are they to you?"

"Why, Abel, I am Jewish. Didn't you know?" Before he could answer, she said, "No, I don't suppose you would. I do not believe it ever came up in our conversation."

He eyed her thoughtfully, "You don't look Jewish. I mean your hair is fair, you're Swedish," he turned her face so that it was in profile, "Nope, not a Jewish nose either. I think you're making it up," he grinned and kissed her impulsively on the cheek.

She slapped at him playfully, "Oh, you rogue. Off you go. Who will it be today? April or Lottie or perhaps the new girl, Fiona? She's Italian, you know."

He pretended thought, stroking his chin, "I think April. We were embroiled in a discussion over the plays of Eugene O'Neill."

"Oh, Abel, you are such a liar. I know why you always want April. Go, go dear boy. We'll talk in ten minutes when you are finished."

"Ten minutes," he sputtered, "more like two hours. Maybe more!" Abel spun on his heel indignantly. In a matter of minutes Gerta heard the rhythmic squeaking of the bed in the front room and the squeals of pleasure from her April.

She settled back with her tea, and was remembering when she had been younger and squealed with pleasure in a large fluffy bed, a man sweating above her and she giving as good as she got. These Americans were so funny about sex. She thought that the activities in the twenties would loosen them up a bit, but when the crash came, then the depressed times, social mores became even more puritanical than ever. However little her business had slipped, the men still found her, willing dollars clutched in dirty hands. She made them wash before going upstairs with her girls and had trained the ladies to watch for the more obvious signs of the syphilis and gonorrhea sores. When they detected these, she made the men use a French sheath or one of the rubber condoms. Sometimes the men became angry, but there were always other men to subdue the more belligerent fellows.

Just then a small man on a bicycle stopped before her porch. She recognized Walter Frolich from the Western Union office.

"Good day, Walter. Have you something for me?"

"Ah, no, Miss Gerta." He held out his hand displaying an envelope. "I've got a telegram for Abel from some lady in Florida. It says…"

She held up a hand. "That's enough, Walter. That is a private communication between Mr. Landis and the sender. You have no right to read it and certainly no right to broadcast it to the entire world." She snatched it out of his hand and placed it on the table. "I will see to it that he receives it as soon as his business is completed." She reached into a pocket of her skirt and handed him a dime.

Walter, looking properly chastised, touched the brim of his hat and greedily put the dime into his waistcoat pocket. "Thank you, Ma'am." And he rode off back to town.

A short time later Abel was down and sitting in the wicker chair, drinking a cup of mint tea, a satisfied smile on his face.

"This came for you, Abel." Gerta handed over the telegram.

Abel took it and held it in both hands staring at the envelope. A sense of dread fell over him. The only time in his life he'd ever received a telegram was when he was in France, notifying him that his mother had died. He didn't want to open it.

"Would you open it for me? I can't, Gerta."

"Yah, give it here." She carefully pried the flap up and folded it back, her exquisite nails lightly fingering the folded paper. She read, "Mr. Abel Landis, Lander, Wyoming. My husband Bob is dead. Stop. Suspicious circumstances. Stop. Police doing nothing. Stop. Please help. Stop. Martha." She looked curiously at Abel who had turned pale.

"Is this an old, ah, girlfriend?"

Abel, startled out of his own world, said, "No. Nothing like that. It's from my sister in Florida. She has a little boy about ten or eleven." He shook his head. "I haven't heard from her in, must be more than a year." He lapsed into his own reverie again, staring at the yellow paper.

"Abel, my friend, can I help in any way?" She sat with a crease of concern on her brow, hands knotted in her lap.

He suddenly jumped up and, with a bewildered look on his face, looked down at her. "I'm sorry, Gerta, I have to go. I have to telegram my sister that I'll be coming. I mean I have to go, don't I?"

"Yah, Abel, she is your sister. You have to go. Have you money, a way to get there?"

"Uh, yeah, I have money but I don't have a clue how to get from here to Florida. Maybe a train to Chicago, then

New York, then down to Miami and somehow over to Tampa. Jesus, I don't know." He ran a work-hardened hand through his hair. "Look, I need a drink. I'll be over at Lucky's, okay?" Abel turned, then came back. "Uh, Gerta, I don't know when I'll see you again, but thanks, thanks for everything." He leaned down and impulsively kissed her on the mouth.

She gently touched his cheek and gazed intently into his deep blue eyes. This boy, this man meant more to her than she thought. She would miss him terribly. "Goodbye, my boy, and please be careful. Write to me if you need anything, please."

"Yeah, sure," he replied, but his mind was elsewhere. He turned and strode away from her, his bandy legs pumping in his jerky, quirky style. She'd know that walk, arms pumping away from his sides, head thrust forward.

"Goodbye," she whispered, a tiny tear slipping down her cheek.

CHAPTER 5

The Motorcycle: 1938

Abel entered the saloon, striding across the wooden porch and pushing open the wooden screen door. Inside it was dim, lazy ceiling fans turning like silent propellers. There were only a few patrons here in the middle of the afternoon. Abel nodded to those he knew and stepped up to the bar.

"Gimme a whiskey, will you, Tilly?"

"Why sure, Abel. Sure you don't wanna start off with a beer?"

"Nope. I had some bad news today, and I need something stronger. Don't give me any of that bar shit either. Pour me something good, will you?" He took his hat off and placed it on the bar next to him.

"Hey, Landis," called a voice from the dim rear.

Abel recognized the voice of Ike Carper. Ike was a large man a few years younger than Abel. He wore dirty blue overalls and scuffed work boots. His face was a mass of black bristles and acne below narrow dark eyes sunk below a prominent brow ridge. He chewed tobacco and seemed to have a permanent dribble of juice from the corner of his mouth. He shambled over and placed a large hand on Abel's shoulder.

"You gonna give me a chance to win back my money, Abel?" His fetid breath stung Abel's eyes.

Abel turned and looked up at the big man. "Look, Ike, I got a lot on my mind right now. Leave me alone." He shrugged the big hand off his shoulder and brushed where it had been.

"Look, you little asshole, that was my money that you took and I wanna chance to win it back." He gripped the back of Abel's neck in a dirty mitt.

Abel sighed. He'd been in enough bar fights to know when one was coming. A series of scenarios ran through his mind. He slashed at the big arm, eliciting a grunt of pain from Carper and allowing Abel to twist away. Before Ike could recover, Abel stepped in and thrust a hard finger into his chest. "Look, Ike, I won that money fair and square. It's now my money, not yours but if you want to win it back, let's go. I've only got about an hour then I have to git." He pulled himself up to his full five foot six inch height, jammed his hat on and grabbed Ike by the arm, dragging him toward the poker table in the back. "Tilly, bring me my whiskey and a beer, will you?"

"Sure, Abel." Tilly gulped and slid the baseball bat back beneath the counter, careful to make no noise.

Abel shoved the big man into a chair and grabbed a fresh deck of cards off a side table. He leaned over until his face was only inches from Carper's. "Now look, Ike, I got no time. I'll give you one hour," he held up one callused finger. "At that time I am leaving. Win, lose or draw. You understand?" Ike nodded, mouth hanging open. Abel went on, "If that's not suitable to you, then let's duke it out right now." He clenched a hard fist in Ike's face.

Ike nodded again and reached into his pocket and pulled out some grubby bills.

Abel split the seal open on the deck with a thumbnail and shook out the cards. He shuffled rapidly after pulling the jokers out and slammed the deck down on the table in front of Ike. "Cut 'em."

Ike was in awe. Nobody ever treated him like this, especially a runt like Abel Landis. But he saw the cold fury in his eyes and for a moment wasn't sure he could whip the little bugger. He shrugged his massive shoulders as the few patrons gathered around. Tilly silently put the two glasses down beside Abel and slid a beer in front of Carper.

Abel grabbed the cards from Ike and snapped them on the table. "Draw poker, no wild cards, nothing fancy. Winner deals." Ike grunted an assent.

The hands went back and forth, mostly in Abel's favor. Then Ike had a string of close winning hands. Abel was down to ten dollars. He was almost ready to throw in his last ten and call it a day. He was depressed enough. The anger had worn off and he was feeling low. Outside he heard a raucous motor roar up, then screech to a halt. A few rumbles and it was silent. The door flew open and Ike's brother, Amos flew in. He was shorter than Ike, but just as heavy and dirty. They lived with their father, A.J. on a hardscrabble dirt farm on the south side of town.

Amos strode over to the table and said in a loud whisper, "Ike, Pa wants you home." He stood uncertainly, eyeing the pile of money in front of his brother.

"Pa kin wait. I'm gonna clean this runt out. I'm almost done."

"But, Ike, Pa'll skin ye if'n…"

Ike turned his murderous gaze on his brother. "I said wait, goddammit. Sit down an' shut up." He shoved his brother hard in the stomach pushing him into a vacant chair. The chair tilted back momentarily, teetered, and then righted itself with a thump.

"Deal," Abel muttered. And deal Ike did. Abel recklessly bet and the hand was his. He was up to seventeen dollars now. Five minutes later he won his fourth hand in a row. Up to sixty bucks now, twenty better than he'd come in with. The clock was almost five now. "Last hand, Ike. How much money you got left?"

The big man looked down in front of him. Two dollar bills and a few coins lay there. "Jist what you see, Abel."

Abel considered, "Fair enough, Ike. Play what you got." He slid the cards across the shiny table one at a time.

Amos slid his chair behind Ike and looked over the massive shoulder. One by one Ike put the cards into his paw. One ace, an eight of clubs, an ace of hearts, a deuce of spades and a nine of diamonds. Ike looked up under his brow, dirty black hair over his forehead. Slowly he slid the paper and coins into the center of the table.

Abel counted the money in his head and slid the same money into the pile. Ike threw two cards onto the table. Abel threw three, and then dealt Ike his two and himself three.

Ike put the cards into his hand. Two aces, three eights. Amos looked at him. Ike muttered, "Shut up."

Abel slid his pile of bills into the center. "There's sixty bucks there, Ike. What've you got to match it?" The crowd was silent. Abel took a sip of his beer.

Ike showed his cards to Amos. Amos' eyebrows went up. "How much money you got, Amos?"

Amos was taken aback. His brow furrowed. He reached into his pocket and spilled out a few coins onto the table top. "I on'y got about a buck, Ike." He gulped expecting a swat from the older brother.

"Gimme the keys to the cycle."

Amos gulped. "But Ike …"

"Don't gimme that but Ike shit, gimme the goddamn keys. Look at what I got." He crammed the cards into his brother's face.

Amos gulped again and dropped the grubby key onto the table.

"That about even things up, Landis?" Ike grinned a yellow-toothed grin and spit a glob of tobacco juice in the direction of a spittoon against the wall. He missed.

Abel frowned. He hadn't expected the brothers to come up with enough money to match his bet. Finally he shrugged. "I guess. What kinda cycle?"

"What kind is it, Amos?" Ike asked his brother over his shoulder.

"It's one of them Harvey-Davidson's. I believe it's a '27 model. I won it off'en a guy from Cheyenne a month ago," he said brightly.

And it suddenly dawned on Abel how he was going to get to Florida. "Okay, Ike, what you got?"

Ike laid his cards down, the aces on top, the three eights slightly separated. Ike crossed his arms, a smug grin on his face.

Abel laid his cards down one at a time. A queen, a jack, a ten, a nine and, he held the last card in his hand before tossing it down onto the pile of money. Ike grabbed it. It was a four. A four!

Ike grinned and reached for the pile. Before he could scoop it in, Abel laid a hand on his arm. "Hold on, Ike. Look at them cards a little closer." He put them all together. They were all spades. "It's a flush, Ike." He waited a beat. "Flush beats a house. Sorry." Abel scooped the money and keys into his hat and pushed back from the table. Ike sat there stunned. Before he could move, Abel fished out the cycle key, clapped the hat on his head and ran for the door, pushing his way through the crowd as he did. In a flash he had the key in, kicked the cycle into life and thundered down the street and around back of the general store.

Otto was sitting on the loading dock smoking a cigarette, his skinny back propped against a four inch peeling porch post. He jumped to his feet as Abel skidded to a stop.

"Otto, can you make it back with the truck okay? I just

won this cycle playing poker." Before Otto could reply, Abel gunned the motorcycle in a sweeping arc and tore off out of town, a dust cloud hanging over the street.

Otto stood contemplating the eager youngster. "Yep, I guess so," he muttered.

When Abel reached the ranch, Mrs. Hartmann was just finishing hanging out the wash.

Wordlessly, he handed her the telegram. Quickly she scanned it and nodded. "I'll fix you some food and give you an extra pair of socks. Come inside."

"Otto's on his way. Should be here in a half-hour or so. I'll be upstairs packing." Abel dashed up the stairs and threw an armload of clothes into an old military style duffel bag. He dug around in a drawer and found his old leather riding helmet and a pair of goggles. Taking a last look around the room he'd come to call home, he carefully shut the door.

Downstairs, Mrs. Hartmann placed a loaf of homebaked bread; a small jar of jam and some smoked meat in a large handkerchief and tied it up. Abel opened the duffel bag and jammed it in. She also twisted a pair of wool socks into a ball and handed them to him. Abel closed the bag and stood shifting his weight from foot to foot.

"I don't quite know what to say, Ma'am. You and the Mister have been like family. Mor'n family, but this is my sister and I guess I owe her and the young lad something. I know she wouldn't of wrote if it wasn't important." He stopped trying to think of something else to say.

"Abel, lad. You go do for your kin. Me'n Pa will do all right. If you get back before harvest time, we'd be much obliged. In fact," she brightened, "if you want, you bring your sister and the boy with you. They'd be welcome." She walked with him to the door. "Fill up that contraption with gasoline from the tin and be careful drivin'. And if you want to send us a note that you arrived safe, we'd appreciate it." With a small shove, she admonished, "Now, get along with ye."

A few minutes to top off the gasoline tank, another to tie on his bundle and he was ready. Mrs. Hartmann stood in the door drying her hands on her apron. Abel settled his old leather helmet on his head, goggles over his eyes, and tightened the long duster at his throat. With a shy wave, he was off, off on a cycle he was marginally familiar with. It was a 1927 Model JD Harley-Davidson. The sleek machine had a 74 cu. in. V-twin engine, a side shift transmission and no front brake. The elaborate graphics on the teardrop tank were pretty much worn off and the footboards were scuffed and cracked. Abel had read the cycle magazines from time to time when in town and at the barbershop. He knew that he ought to baby the beast because the transmission was unreliable and the clutch was undersized, the whole being initially made for a one-cylinder machine, and only at the last minute was the big two-cylinder engine installed to help flagging sales. He wished he had a fatter butt, too, because the old cycle had no rear springs. It was known as a 'hard tail,' and he sure knew why.

Chapter 6

Captain's Tale Continues: Present Day

"Wait a minute, Captain, how do you know all this?" asked Chris.

"Yeah, you weren't there," chimed in Brooke.

"Hold on, now. I was just about to tell you," the old man chuckled. When the crowd was silent, he went on. "Once Abel got to Clearwater, me and him and BB used to go out on my daddy's boat. Oh that Abel could tell a tale." He took another sip of his drink. "I can still see him standing on the deck of Daddy's boat, his hair goin' all which way, them bow-legs looking like they just unwrapped themselves from a bronc, his arms waving in the air and those blue eyes all big an' round. Yessir, when Abel Landis got into a tale, you just sat spellbound and took it all in. 'Course, I was just a young sprout then." He trailed off, looking out at nothing for a minute.

"Well, what happened then? Did Abel just fly in from, where did you say he was working, Wyoming?" prompted Artie.

"Oh, you think it was easy like just jumping on a plane or the freeway is now?" He chuckled that deep bass laugh of his. "Sheet, it weren't an easy ride. Oops, pardon my French, ladies."

Chris, Brooke and Shelly looked at each other and grinned. They probably swore as much as the guys these days and were unaccustomed to a man apologizing for his language. "That's okay, Mr. Toffelmeyer," Shelly chided.

"So what was the big deal about this trip? He was just riding a motorcycle, wasn't he?" queried Artie.

"Son, do you know what the roads were like in those days? Or gas stations? Or cops? Sheee-oot, it was mor'n 2,000 miles, that trip." The Captain looked around uneasily. "Why, do you know that right around that time, the Klan had a rally on the steps of the Court House right across the street," he gestured over his shoulder with his thumb, "and over five hundred people attended?"

Dave and the others were shocked. After all, except for the Brotherhood, Clearwater was a pretty cosmopolitan place.

"I'll tell you about that ride that Abel took on that ol' Harley-Davidson. He almost didn't make it!"

CHAPTER 7

The Ride: 1938

When Abel reached the highway, he looked west expecting to see Otto and the old A-Model truck, but nothing was to be seen on the horizon. Abel wanted to wait, but there was no telling how long Otto might be and if the Carpers would be looking for their cycle. With a sad shake of his head, he pulled his goggles once again over his eyes and turned the cycle south and east.

The road was pretty good until he reached Jeffrey City, which was just a crossroads. He was able to buy three gallons of gas there, but at a price of ten cents a gallon; he'd have to watch his money pretty carefully. He tore out of Jeffrey on the dirt track heading for Rawlins, on the other side of the mountains. Abel felt that this was going to be a long ride if all the roads were like this one. He'd be lucky to make

40 or 50 miles a day.

The rolling hills gave way to increasingly steeper slopes; the track grew narrower and rougher. It took three days to get over the hills. He didn't pass many other vehicles, once or twice a truck carrying a farmer or rancher, once a big steel-sided bus, and late one day a convoy of three old cars with a bunch of people in each one, daddies, mamas and young 'uns and lots of stuff tied on the roof, running boards and back bumpers.

Abel gave them a wave but rode on hunched over the wide handlebars, black duster flying out behind him like some great bat on wheels. It was just getting on toward dark when he reached the outskirts of Rawlins. It sat in the mountains, cupped in a little depression between two peaks.

That night Abel bedded down just on the other side of town in his blankets, cooked up some beans in a can and ate the last of his bread.

The next morning dawned bright and chilly. He awoke shivering, his breath a cloud in the crystalline mountain air. There was a mockingbird trilling in the stand of trees surrounding him and a squirrel scampered past his head, cheeks full of nuts. Abel pulled his head down under the blanket and blew on his hands. With a mighty effort, he hopped out of the warmth and danced around smacking his palms and singing an old campaign song. He sat on a low rock and pulled on his boots and a pair of socks on his hands.

"Damn, if this keeps up," he thought, "I'll need a third sock for my pizzel." In a few moments he'd collected a few twigs and had a fire started with a wooden match scratched against the metal button on his fly. The water got hot enough to drop a teabag in and a few minutes later was warming his innards. Not much of a breakfast. He felt he could squeeze a second cup out of the teabag. It was weak but hot was hot. Need to pick up some oatmeal and cane sugar in the next town.

The next big town was Laramie, then Cheyenne, the capital, about 75 or more miles. He hoped he could get a map and some warm clothes there.

He kicked the Harley over three or four times, but it was cold, too. "Well, Harley, old sport, are you gonna take me to Martha's or not?" Two more kicks and the old cycle muttered to life, complaining and coughing, finally settling down to a smooth purr. Abel tied his gear bag on the rear bar and swung a leg over the worn leather saddle. "Hi yup, giddyap old sport!" With a growl, then a whine, they were off, sliding down the eastern slope of the Rockies, snow-capped peaks visible now off to his right and over his shoulder. Stretched out before him were foothills and scree slopes. Far below prairies stretched out in an indistinct sea.

The days wore on with a studied monotony. The old cycle proved fairly reliable, requiring only steady fill-ups of gasoline and oil. Once in Springfield, Missouri, he had to buy a rear tire at a greasy cycle shop. He'd been on the road for more than three weeks by now and decided to head south and make the rest of the run along the Gulf of Mexico. The roads were in poor condition and when it rained, he'd hole up beside a saloon or in a barn where he bartered his labor for food and an occasional bed.

Late one fine day he was puttering along just south of

Pine Bluff, Arkansas when he came upon a black man walking by the side of the road, stiff legged, carrying a blanket roll over one shoulder. He had a battered cowboy hat on his dusty head and a red bandana tucked in his rear pocket. Abel slowed the cycle down and pulled off the dirt road just ahead. He sat with one leg curled up on the tank and waited.

The black man glanced at him as he got abreast. He nodded curtly.

"Where you headed?" Abel asked.

The man stopped. "Why, officer?" He regarded Abel sitting on the big cycle, goggles pushed up on his forehead, black coat streamed out behind him. He was a little taller than Abel, a stubble of beard showed on his chin, a grass straw stuck in the corner of his mouth. He shifted the weight of the pack so it rode lower on his back.

"Officer?" Abel looked over his shoulder, first one side, then the other. "Who, me?" He snorted. "Take it easy, son, I ain't no copper."

"Then what you wanna know fer?" He slouched toward Abel, stopping a few feet away. He slid the roll off his thin shoulder and eased it to the ground at his feet. A little puff of dust rose from the hot ground and settled on his scuffed shoes.

"Just wondering if you wanted a ride, is all. I'm headed for the Gulf or near and it's been kinda lonely the last coupla weeks." Abel slid off the cycle and held out his hand. "Abel Landis, formerly of Wyoming and soon of Florida."

The black man looked at Abel's grinning face, then down at the proffered hand. "What for you stickin' yo' hand out to me, white boy? Don' you know where you at?" He shook his head mournfully. "Suppose some other white man come along and seen us shakin'. You an' me'd be in a world of shit. You in the south now, man." He angrily kicked at the dry earth. "Sho I kin use a ride, but how'n hell is a white man an' a nigger gonna ride on the same cycle?"

Abel pondered this for a moment. "Tell you what, its getting late and I was gonna find a place to camp. Why don't we make up some grub and talk about this. I guess I don't remember all the rules." Abel turned and wheeled the cycle back off the road and down a slight rise and into some scraggly trees alongside a trickling stream. He didn't look back but thought he heard the shuffling footsteps behind him.

In a few minutes he'd unpacked his bedroll and laid it out on a smooth piece of ground. He reached into his duffel and pulled out a slab of salted beef, two cans of chili and half a loaf of rye bread. Beside him, the black man unrolled his blankets and added a greasy package with some home-made sausage.

Abel grinned and went to the creek to wash his hands and face. When he came back, his guest had a smokeless fire going and an old cast iron fry pan spitting and popping on top of some stones on either side of the blaze. He rubbed the sausages on the bottom until the grease coated the pan with a slick layer, then cut the sausages into pieces on a black book he pulled out of his roll. They were soon crackling as he shook the pan back and forth, flipping the pieces over to coat them thoroughly. Abel set to work with his folding jack-knife, prying the lids off the cans of chili. Soon, the chili was bubbling, the pieces of sausage bobbing to the surface as the black man stirred them with a twisted spoon.

"My name's Cuddy Fowlette," he muttered. He pronounced his last name as two drawn out syllables. Fow-let.

"What's that?" Abel asked innocently. "Did you say something?" The liquid brown eyes met his, the lips pulled back exposing the teeth.

"I said, my name's Cuddy Fowlette. I'm goin' to Calvert in Alabama. It's a little town just north of Mobile"

"What you going there for, Cuddy Fowlette?" asked Abel, wiping his spoon on his shirttail.

"I got me a letter from my Mam. My daddy went an' got hisself killed. She got nobody to take care of her." He busied himself stirring the stew, head bowed.

"How'd he get killed?" asked Abel carefully, watching the tired black face.

"Klan." A tear rolled down his cheek and dripped into the chili.

When Cuddy didn't elaborate, Abel kept silent. In a minute, Cuddy snuffled, wiping his nose on his shirtsleeve. "He was a good and decent man who never hurt nobody. He raised three of us kids and ain't none of us never took nothin' without workin' fer it."

"I'm sorry," Abel said quietly, spooning some of the chili into his bowl and some into a chipped and cracked bowl Cuddy produced.

They sat back and ate in silence, occasionally breaking off a piece of bread in the twilight. Up on the road, they saw a car's headlights sweep past, the hum of the motor fading like the light.

"What you goin' to Florida fer, Mista Landis?" Cuddy asked after a while.

Abel thought for a minute. He'd been on the road for so long, he'd nearly forgotten. "My sister's husband got himself killed or drowned. I don't know which. She cabled me pretty upset so I'm going to her and her boy." Again they sat in silence.

"I don't know how much help I'm going to be to my Mam. I got me the cancer in my bones. The doc I saw said I got maybe a year, no more. Maybe less." He expelled a great breath of air. "Thought maybe I like to meet my maker in my old bed with my Mam standin' over me."

"That why you walking so stiff?"

"Mos'ly. That an' this." He pulled up his baggy pant leg and showed Abel a neatly wrapped bandage that covered his right leg from knee to just above his ankle.

"Ouch," said Abel. "That sure looks like it hurts." The bandage was securely tied but there was a crust of blood on the top third and underneath was a series of uneven lumps and bumps.

"Yeah, sho looks like it, don't it?" He grinned a wide grin. "It don't hurt much no mo'. My Mam's gonna take care of it soon." He pulled the ragged pant leg down and rolled over on his side facing the fire.

"I guess it's best that we turn in, Cuddy. Good night." Abel was quiet, contemplating the mess that was Cuddy's leg. The night thickened and a weary little breeze blew into the hollow, barely ruffling the hair on Abel's cheek. The fire dimmed down to just glowing embers, the crickets fell silent and the moon crawled out of the trees and rose laboriously into the muddy sky. The silence was like a thick canvas shroud. Not an insect, not a bird, not a night animal sound. Abel slipped into sleep without being aware of having been awake. The next sensation was of a gentle kick in the ribs.

"Git up, man. We gots to make time. I ain't feelin' too good." Cuddy sat clutching his stomach. His face was an unpleasant shade of gray and a thin trickle of sweat ran down the side of his face.

Abel was up in an instant, throwing his blankets and their cooking gear in his duffel. He ran to the water and filled a cup and brought it back to the sick man. "Here, drink this." He thrust the cup into Cuddy's shaking hands. Some spilled over and onto his lap but he managed to get the balance down.

In a few minutes Cuddy had stopped shaking and the bout was over. "Shee-it, it's sometimes worse than others."

"How long has this been going on?" Abel helped the gaunt man to his feet and rolled his kit into the folded blanket, tying it with a piece of frayed rope.

"'Bout a month or so. Mayhap we kin get some laudanum in the next town," Cuddy looked hopeful. He watched Abel carefully. "I'll have to go to the colored part of town fer it."

"Crap," angrily answered Abel. "We'll find an apothecary and I'll git it for you." In a few minutes they were putting down the dirt road in a sunshiny day. "I saw a sign a ways back. Next town's going to be Dumas," he hollered over his shoulder.

Cuddy just nodded against his shoulder. An hour later they were rumbling down the main street of a small town, dusty cars and trucks parked on an angle in front of the weather-beaten stores that lined the only road through town. On their way in a decrepit sign greeted them. Welcome to Dumas, Arkansas, home of the Dumas Cottonseeds. Whatever the Cottonseeds were, they were a long time ago. The town was nearly deserted. Abel found the apothecary in the town's Rexall store. He parked the cycle at the edge of the wooden sidewalk and turned it off. The sign on the front said James Robinson, Proprietor.

"Now you wait here, Cuddy Fowlette. Keep guard on the cycle, eh?"

"Sho, sho, Abel Landis." Cuddy sat on the edge of the wooden step and leaned against the rail.

Abel entered the tired old store and headed for a man in the rear behind a long counter. The store had sparsely stocked shelves, some canned goods, a few boxes and bags of foodstuffs and in the rear some cans of baby powder, bandages and bottles of iodine. He approached a high shelf that was painted an off white. On top were three mortars and pestles, neatly arranged. A face peered over the top of the shelf. The druggist had a round face, a fringe of white hair around a pink bald head, a small flat nose, and close set deep blue eyes. He was in his forties or maybe early fifties. A tinny radio was playing Doris Day singing 'This Can't Be Love'.

"Can I help you, young feller?" The man's eyebrows crept upward, mouth scrunched up like he was smelling something foul.

"Yes," replied Abel. "I need something for pain. In the stomach." He patted his belt.

He looked shrewdly at Abel. "You just looking for a pint of hooch, young feller? Or what?"

"N-no, sir." Abel replied confused. "I'm seriously in need of some medicine, like laudanum or something like it." He pulled himself up to his full five-feet and six inches.

The storeowner leaned over the counter and looked down at Abel carefully. "You don't look sick to me. What's ailing you?"

"I told you, my gut." He patted his stomach again. "It comes and goes. But when it's ailing, it hurts like hell."

Robinson grunted and disappeared under the counter. Abel could hear him rattling some bottles around. Finally he stood up and reached a skinny arm over the counter. In his hand was a dusty bottle half filled with white tablets, a cork in its top. He tossed it over, "Here. Put a half-teaspoon in a cup of coffee or tea before you go to bed and after a meal. It'll help for a while but you need to see a doctor. Sounds like you've got an ulcer or some such."

"Much obliged. What do I owe you?"

"Ah, gimme a buck. It's old. My Pa used to take it before he died." He snickered. "Don't worry, it isn't what killed him, just eased the way."

Abel handed over the greenback and asked, "Say, where is everybody? Town seems deserted."

"Down at Tom Avery's place just south of town. They're having a sheriff's sale. Folks are pretty mad about it. Talk is, they'll try to stop it but Judge Terwilliger's going to be there to see it don't happen." He chuckled again and shook his head.

"Why's that?" Abel was curious now.

Robinson leaned his forearms on the counter and inclined his head in a conspiratorial manner, "Personally, I think the Judge wants that farm for his good-for-nothing brother-in-law. Otherwise, the idiot would have to live with the Judge since his wife died. The brother-in-law's, not the Judge's."

Abel nodded as if he understood. "Well, thank you Mr. Robinson. Good-bye." He turned and strode for the door.

"One more thing, son. Don't stop there. The Judge's nephew is Gordy Terwilliger, the sheriff, and he don't like niggers too much."

Abel nodded again. This time he knew what Robinson was talking about.

"Come on, Cuddy, on your feet. I got your medicine." He hoisted the black man to his feet and edged him toward the cycle. Cuddy gulped down two of the tablets.

By the time Abel had his goggles over his eyes and the cycle humming, Cuddy'd settled in behind him. Abel eased the clutch out and smoothly shifted the long lever through the gears, gathering speed. Three or four miles south of town, they came upon a large gathering of cars and trucks pulled off the edge of the road. A large florid man with a big, floppy black hat was peeing against the wheel of a battered Ford A-Model flatbed truck while two little girls watched him. He paid them no mind and, as Abel tried to ease around him, he looked up. His dour expression turned to meanness. He held up a meaty palm.

"Hold on there, boy!" He stuffed himself back into his fly and did up the buttons while coming toward them. His starred badge glinted in the sun. His fat legs rubbed against each other as he waddled their way. A gun rode on his hip and the belt disappeared under his protruding belly.

He stopped with his hands on his hips as Abel dismounted. Cuddy stayed in place, holding the cycle upright, his head hanging low.

"Where all you taking this nigger, mister?"

"What nigger?" Abel answered.

"What nigger? Why, that one right there." He poked Cuddy in the arm with a sausage-like finger.

"Who? Why this piece of crap?" Abel looked around as if not understanding.

"Yeah, him." The sheriff poked Cuddy again. Abel saw Cuddy stiffen and his nostrils widen just a bit. He'd have to do something and quickly.

"Why, that's no nigger, sheriff. That's my manservant."

"Your what?"

"My manservant. He washes my clothes, cooks for me, cleans and takes care of my cycle. You know, my manservant. My daddy, the Colonel, gave him to me for this trip. He also told me not to hurt him or he'd tan my hide. Yes sir, Jethro here, he's a good 'un." He patted Cuddy gently on the back. Cuddy looked up at him in what he hoped was an adoring way. He slowly closed one eye, the one the sheriff couldn't see.

"A manservant, huh? Well, you keep him away from the white women now, y'heah?"

"Oh, not to worry, sheriff, my daddy had him gelded when he was a sprout. He don't even know what it's for no more."

"No shit? Well I'll be goddamned." He stuck out his left hand for a shake. Abel knew this was the Klan shake and he just as naturally gave it a spastic wriggle. The sheriff's grin widened. "My uncle, the Judge, is the Grand Dragon 'round heah. I'm his Night Hawk. You an officer from where you from?"

"Naw," replied Abel, "I'm just a klavalier." He looked toward the back of the crowd about 50 feet away. "Say, what's going on over there?"

The sheriff turned and spat over his shoulder, "Nuthin', jist a farm auction. The ol' boy couldn't keep up with the bank payments so they foreclosed on 'im." He spat again. "Happens all the time around heah. This'n's supposed to be quiet but I'm still s'posed to keep order." He hitched up his pants and patted his revolver tucked in a holster on his fat hip. "C'mon over, maybe you'll see some shit you need." He eyed the motorcycle. "'Course, you won't be able to put much on that ol' cycle."

He pronounced it sickle. Abel hated the Klan. He'd almost become a member back in the twenties when it seemed everyone was joining, but when some of the more violent elements started night riding, lynching and burning, it had sickened him. He also remembered some of the kind colored folks back in Florida when he'd been growing up. He'd been in far enough to know the organization layout, handshake and some of the passwords and phrases but that was all. If he'd had to give the Klavern name and number of his local, he doubted if these local yokels would be Abel to trace it. He'd have called it the Nathan Bedford Forrest Klavern #1 or 2 Realm of Wyoming or Oregon or something. Hell, half the Klaverns were named after the Klan's founder. Even ol' Nathan Bedford Forrest had been disgusted by the violence and had quit or disbanded it a couple of years after forming it up in Tennessee after the Civil War, or as Southerners liked to call it, the War for Southern Independence.

The sheriff walked away and Abel followed. Cuddy stood by the cooling cycle scowling, arms crossed. Abel gestured a sign to relax at him and caught up to the sheriff as they entered the loose crowd. The auctioneer/judge was standing on a wagon and arguing with a gaunt man. The man's equally gaunt and weather-beaten wife stood beside him pulling on his sleeve.

"Leave it, Harry. Just let's us just go." She pitifully argued in a resigned voice.

"I'll be damned all to Jesus if I jist let it go," he yelled, shrugging off her hand and menacing the judge.

The judge was a florid, well-fed man like the sheriff. He was wearing a rumpled gray fedora and had a string tie around his gleaming neck. He wiped his brow with a red bandana and pointed at the man. "Harry, you git your stuff and high-tail it out o' heah. I'm conductin' an auction of this property and you don't have nothin' mo' to say about it." He turned back to the crowd and once more demanded a bid.

"The bid stands at five cents. Ain't nobody gonna raise that?" No one stirred. He glared at the closed-faced crowd. They were all local farmers and their wives, friends of the owner and his wife. "Hell, I'll bid five dollars myself."

A well-dressed man spoke up, "Y'all can't do that, Judge." The crowd looked around at him. He was the lawyer from town, Bob Wilkins. "Anybody's got a hand in these legal proceedings can't bid. That goes for your fat nephew there, too," he indicated the sheriff, standing next to Abel. "Nor can Mr. Farley, there, from the bank. Since this is an open auction, y'all have to accept the bid."

"The hell I do, Bob. Hell, they'll just give it back to Harry here."

"Law's the law, Judge." Wilkins was firm and the crowd nodded in unison, starting to crowd the wagon.

The judge looked a little panicky. "Gordy," he said to the sheriff, "do something. Arrest this man." He pointed to Harry.

The sheriff elbowed his way toward the wagon, Abel right behind him. This was better than a picture show! "You folks go on home. This show is over." He turned toward Harry and said, "I'm placing you under arrest for threatening a, uh, county judge."

Harry pushed the sheriff's hand away and shoved the big man in the chest, "I'll be goddamned if you are." He backed away, fire in his eyes, pushing his wife behind him. The sheriff made a lunge for Harry and as Harry twisted to the side, accidentally grabbed Harry's wife, tearing her dress. Harry threw a wild punch and caught the sheriff on the side of the face, bruising his cheek and nose.

The sheriff reached back for his gun but Abel had deftly slipped it out of his holster and dropped it on the ground, then backed into the crowd. When some of the men saw what the sheriff was up to, they produced several shotguns and the air was filled with clicking and cocking. The sheriff and the judge froze.

“Hold on now, folks. There’s no call for gunplay.” Bob Wilkins shouldered his way to the front of the crowd. He looked up at the judge. “I think you’d better tell your nephew here to maybe not try to arrest anybody today and you’d better finish off this auction. Legally.” He handed the judge his gavel, which had slipped from his fingers and fallen to the bed of the wagon.

Shakily, he muttered, “Five cents once, twice, sold to Angus Moorhead.” He banged the gavel down on the wagon seat.

“Just sign the deed back to Harry, there, Judge,” Angus boomed. “And you tell that damn bank, there better not be no more foreclosure auctions around here ‘til things get better.” A number of men muttered assent, nodding their heads.

The sheriff scrambled around in the dust until he located his gun and jammed it back in his holster. “Uncle Joe, I mean Judge, you still want me to arrest him?”

“No, no. It’s all over, Gordy.” He sighed. “C’mon, let’s get back to town.” The two of them trudged out to the road and climbed into a four-passenger A-Model sedan, ‘Sheriff, Dumas, Lincoln County, Arkansas’, emblazoned in faded yellow paint on the front door. The car u-turned on the powder dry dirt road and sped off trailing a white cloud of fine dust.

Abel felt a strong hand on his shoulder. He turned and saw it was the smiling bearded face of Angus Moorhead. He thrust his broad face near and said, "Say, ain't you the feller came in with the sheriff?"

Abel rounded on him, shrugging the thick hand off, "Yeah, what about it?"

"I seen you come riding up on that moto sickle with that nigger there." He waved a sweat-stained arm at the row of cars. "You with him?"

"Yeah, I mean no. He's with me." Abel looked around at the crowd, a tiny bit of panic starting way down in his gut. "He's my mechanic and cook."

"Easy, Angus," a thin man in overalls said. "I seen him slip the sheriff's pistol out'n his belt and drop it on the ground."

After regarding Abel for a long moment, he stuck his hand out and grinned. "Any man that ain't with the judge or that nitwit nephew of his, cain't be all bad." Several of the men shook hands with Abel, mumbling their names as they did. "You're welcome to stay the night, friend." Angus offered.

"Many thanks, Mr. Moorhead, but I've got a long way to go and I'd be hoping to make the Louisiana state line by nightfall."

"Hah, good luck. That's more'n sixty, seventy miles. There ain't nuthin' 'tween here'n there and onct you cross, there ain't nothin' 'til you get to Vicksburg, maybe another's day ride." He turned to one of the men, "Hey, you there, Charlie, can you lend this feller a can o'gas?"

In a few minutes, a small gas can was produced, a shoulder strap rigged up out of an old piece of harness and Abel and Cuddy were on their way.

The next several days were uneventful except for Cuddy chastising Abel about his remarks to the sheriff. He groused about it across Louisiana and into Mississippi. They were about a week away from Mobile, Alabama, sitting around a campfire one night. Abel had pulled off into a grove of trees just south of the crummy track that passed for a road in these parts. He'd managed to purchase some gristly meat from a farmer that morning, and Cuddy had picked some poke salad greens. They had a little bottle of vinegar and some lard in a twist of newspaper. Cuddy had filled their water bottle in a rain barrel a few miles back. Abel sat swigging from his tin cup and telling Cuddy about his Klan adventures.

Cuddy was silent and just stared off into the night. Finally he said, "I hate those white sheeted cowards." He said this so quietly, Abel had to ask him to repeat himself.

"Why, Cuddy? Because of your Pa?"

"Naw, long before that. The Klan's always been strong in Washington and Clarke counties. That's where I'm from. Why, back in the 20's, if you was white and not a member of the Klan, you was either a Jew or a Catholic." He snorted, "Or a nigger." He took a long pull at the water bottle. "My uncle Mo was a woodcutter, ran a small mill and lumberyard back then. One of the local boys thought he overcharged him for a load of pine so one night the Klan come a'callin'. They lynched Uncle Mo and burned him out. My Aunt Minnie and their two kids got all burned up, too." He snorted again. "Now the Klan is sore 'cause they don't have no lumber for more'n twenty miles!" He was quiet for a minute. "You know, them Klanners should've lived in that town we come through in Arkansas."

"Which one was that, Cuddy?"

"Dumas." He pronounced it 'dumb ass.'

’

CHAPTER 8

The Klan: Present Day

Tom lay back on the thin mattress in the holding cell. He’d been printed and had his pictures taken. The officer told him not to smile, but Tom did anyway. They finally got tired of telling him and just took the mug shots. He knew his lawyer, Sy, would be with him soon. Why get upset about it?

Back at Harrington’s restaurant, the small group hung onto the old man’s words with rapt attention.

Shelly knelt at one end of the booth, “So what does all this have to do with the gunfight, Mr. Toffelmeyer?”

“Yeah, who cares about the trip? I want to know what happened.” Brooke waved her arm in dismissal.

The Captain chuckled, “I’m just trying to give you an idea what the times and especially the South was like back then. It wasn't like it is now, you know. I, or Cuddy, couldn't be seen sitting down with a bunch of white folks like you; like we are now." He sipped his iced tea. "Lawd, that's real good tea, Miss Brooke, what's in it?"

"I put some raspberry syrup in it. Do you like it?" She swiftly refilled the old gentleman's glass.

"Yes'm, it's right tasty." He swigged the amber liquid.

"So the Klan was big out there in Mississippi and Alabama, huh?" Dave asked.

"Why, Mr. Dave, it was huge. Also, here in Clearwater." He pointed a shaky finger at the courthouse. "Why, there was a rally right there on those steps that filled this road and the whole grounds. My daddy saw it. Said there were 'bout a thousand of them white-suited devils there. And their women and kids, too. All dressed up like Casper the Ghost. You didn't get elected to nothing, not even dogcatcher, without the Klan backing. It went into decline after the scandal in Indiana in the mid-twenties but, here in Florida, nothing goes away very long or very deep." He shook his head sorrowfully. "They say the mayor and the police chief was in the Klan back then, the thirties, I mean."

"Yeah, okay, so get on with the story. I want to hear about the gunfight – and how that pistol got into my bar," Artie urged.

CHAPTER 9

Cuddy's Revenge: 1938

On a warm afternoon a week later, Abel and Cuddy putted into the small town of Calvert, Alabama. It wasn't so much a town as a collection of wooden stores leaning against each other on one side of a two-block street and an old brick courthouse, police and fire station on the other. There was a shuttered two-story department store next to the fire station and a poolroom and bar next to that. On the south side of town was the white section, ten or twelve houses, and north of town, the black section, more houses but slightly more dilapidated. They trickled out into the country where some of the black folks sharecropped. Cuddy directed Abel through the black section and into the country a little more than a half-mile. They turned into a fenced yard. A forlorn wood shack sat in the yard, up off the ground on what looked like old railroad ties, chickens picking around the tidy yard. A porch ran across the front and a sagging roof covered it supported by peeled and grayed pine poles. The woods ran up to about fifty feet behind the house. At the sound of the motorcycle, the front door opened and a gray-haired black woman came out, a broom in her hand. She stopped at the front of the porch, her face closed as she looked at Abel. She didn't see Cuddy mounted behind until he swung his leg off and said, "Hello, Mama."

"Is that you, Cuddy?"

"Yes, Mama, I heard about Daddy and I came home."

She dropped her broom and rushed down the stairs, arms open and enfolded him. She was almost as tall as the sparse Negro and hugged him fiercely, tears trickling down her wrinkled face. Abel looked away, embarrassed. Softly he switched the cycle off. It was quiet on a hot Alabama afternoon, the only sound the clucking of the chickens and the ticking of the cooling metal. When she opened her eyes again, she looked at Abel and stiffened.

"Who's dat white man?" She held Cuddy at arm's length, keeping him between herself and Abel.

"He's all right, Mama. That's Abel. Abel Landis. He gave me a ride the last million miles." He turned and gestured to Abel to come forward.

Abel slid his helmet and goggles off and placed them on the seat. He held out his hand, "Howdy, Ma'am, Mrs. Fowlette." She just looked at his hand. White folks didn't shake hands with black women, at least not here in Alabama.

"Aw, Mama, I told you Abel was all right." He turned to Abel. "You'd best get that cycle out back before somebody sees it. Then come on in and we'll have a wash and some grub." With that, they turned and, arm in arm, Cuddy and his mother stepped up on the porch and went inside. In a minute Abel parked the cycle and threw a couple of old burlap feed bags over it. He rapped at the back door and entered.

Cuddy sat in an old armless chair and his mother was on her knees unwrapping the filthy bandage from his leg. Abel went to the counter, pumped the rusty handpump and filled a bowl with water. He took out his handkerchief, pushed it into the cool water and laid it on the floor next to Mrs. Fowlette. She looked up at him, face still blank, though Abel thought he saw a hint of gratitude. Abel looked for another chair but all he saw was an upended wooden feed box. He pulled it over and hovered over Mrs. Fowlette's shoulder. As the bandage came away, the lumps became evident. They were sticks of dynamite. Cuddy grinned up at Abel. As the old woman kept unwinding she revealed a yellowed and bluish puffiness to the flesh. The smell was awful. Abel wanted to vomit but since Mrs. Fowlette didn't seem to mind, he held his gore. At last it was all off, revealing several weeping open sores.

"Land sakes, son, what happened to you?" She sat back on her knees and started to wring out the cloth. Gently she wiped the putrid flesh, pausing to wring out the bloody rag.

Cuddy looked at his mother's head bent over his leg. "Well, Mama, I was working for a short time out west on the railroad. I learned to do some dynamiting and one day the white men sent me in to blow a hole in a tunnel we was digging. They didn't tell me they'd already rigged a charge.

They blew it when I got in that tunnel. It was only a small charge and I wasn't up to the face yet, so I just got a slice of rock in my leg. They were all laughing when I came out. 'Course the Doc wouldn't treat me, so me and some of the boys pulled the sliver out and washed it as best we could. One of them had some whiskey so we poured it in. Hurt like the devil's own hand. I tried keeping it clean, but doing that kinda work, it wasn't always possible. So now I'm going to die. But not for a while yet." He patted her shoulder. "Don't worry, Mama, I'll take care of you as long as I'm able."

"On hush, son," she sniffled. "You ain't takin' care of me. I'm movin' out anyway. Mr. Lawton, the landlord, is throwin' me out, now that your Daddy's gone anyway." Cuddy started to protest but his mother hushed him again. "That's all right, son, I'm going up north to Philadelphia tomorrow to live with my cousin Lavinia. I don't want to stay around here nohow." She sat back against the old wood stove, exhausted.

Abel cleared his throat, "Uh, Ma'am, would you have something we can use for a bandage for Cuddy's leg?"

"Land sakes, where's my mind?" She hauled herself to her feet and went rummaging in a drawer. In a minute she was back with a piece of threadbare sheet. Abel took it and tore it into strips. One he made into a pad and tied it into place with another. The rest he just wound around and around until the wound was covered. He expertly tore the end and twisted it into a flat knot.

"Where'd you learn to do such a good job of bandaging, Abel?" Cuddy asked.

"The Great War. I was a dispatch rider. But if you were

in it, you learned something about dressings. You never knew when you needed it!" He grinned at Cuddy, gently slapping the leg. "Man, that must hurt."

"Nah, not much. It's kind of a dull ache. I feel it most in my belly, or," he hesitated and looked at his mother's back, now busy at the kitchen counter, "down here." He patted his groin.

Abel pulled the feed box up next to Cuddy and whispered, "What's with the dynamite?" indicating the seven sticks on the floor next to the water bowl.

"Abel, my friend," he hesitated and asked, "you are my friend, aren't you?"

Abel nodded again.

"Well, I reckon that before I leave this good earth, I'm going to take a few Klanners with me. If possible, I'm going to send them on ahead!" He shook his head positively and chuckled. "You know, when I was growing up around here, I was friends with a white boy. We used to go fishin' and swimming and roaming these woods around here a lot. 'Course that was before I turned twelve. Around here, when you turned twelve, whites and niggers stopped hanging out together. Lord, I missed that boy." He chuckled again, remembering.

"Go on, man, go on."

"Okay, my friend. One of the things we used to do was spy on the grown ups, you know, like most kids do." Sure, Abel knew what he meant. He'd done the same. "Anyway, we found a nice little cabin in the woods near the river and one night we followed this feller's daddy. He was all dressed in white, and we thought it was neat. He walked back in that woods and soon was joined up by a couple more old boys. They all went into that cabin and we listened at one of the opened windows. Well, it was a Klan meeting. They was talking about hanging a nigger. When we heard that, me and that boy hightailed it out of there. He went home and so did I. I told my Daddy, but we didn't know who they were going to lynch. Later we found out it was a feller from down in Mobile County that we didn't know. Somebody said he didn't get out of the way of a white woman fast enough."

He harrumphed, "Can you imagine that? Didn't get out of the way fast enough so they lynched him." He slapped his knee and mused, "If that don't beat all." He got to his feet with a grimace, gathering up the dynamite.

"Mama, me and Abel here are going down to the creek and wash up. There's some grub in my bag tied up on the back of that cycle out back. Would you make it up for us all, please?"

She nodded, not looking at them. "There's a part bar of soap on the shelf on the back porch."

"Yes'm," he mumbled. As they went out the back door, Cuddy cautioned, "Don't mind her. She's not used to white folks in her house. We'll be gone by morning."

"What do you mean we?"

Cuddy only smiled and led the way through the woods to a small brook. Upstream a bit was a pretty little pool. There were soap stains on some of the rocks, indicating its frequent use. To Abel it looked like heaven. The heat had been pressing down on him, and a good wash was a long time coming. He quickly stripped and immersed himself.

"Aren't you coming in, Cuddy?" he called.

"In a bit. I got something to do first. I'll be back in an hour or so. Relax, enjoy yourself."

Abel shrugged, figuring Cuddy was going visiting a friend or maybe an old girlfriend. The hour passed slowly and dreamily. Abel thoroughly scrubbed himself twice, his hair three times. He was drowsing, legs in the pool, back against a tree when Cuddy returned smiling. He quickly undressed and, keeping his freshly bandaged leg out of the water, scrubbed himself thoroughly. In a few minutes he was dry and ready to go back.

Abel idly noted that the motorcycle had been moved, Cuddy's bag removed and just his tied in place. Inside Mrs. Fowlette had laid out a sparse meal of chunks of pork, collard greens and grits. On the top of the stove, however, was an apple pie. Abel smacked his lips.

"So, where are you going, Mr. Abel Landis?" Mrs. Fowlette asked guardedly.

Abel repeated his story as he'd told Cuddy.

The old lady shook her head, "Too much death in this world. I'm damned tired of it."

Cuddy was taken aback. He'd never heard his mother swear. What was the world coming to?

Before he could reply, there was the roar of an engine outside. He cautioned Abel to stay out of sight and went to the door. An old pickup truck stood outside the house, two men in the cab and another in the bed. The one in the back held a shotgun on his hip. The driver pushed his hat back and spoke, "Heard you was back, Cuddy. Stayin' long?"

"Howdy, Chester. I'm just stayin' long enough to make some trouble, raise a little hell, you know?" He turned his head as Abel came out on the porch and stood next to him, thumbs hooked in his belt.

The driver's expression darkened. "You stayin' with this nigger?"

"Just for the night," answered Abel, letting his Florida accent thicken a bit. "What's it to ya?"

"I guess you ain't from around heah." The man in the truck bed spit a glob of tobacco juice in the dust, regarding the two men from under prominent brows.

"No, I ain't," answered Abel and kept quiet, wondering if he and Cuddy could duck fast enough if the man in the pickup bed drew down on them.

"Say, Chester, was you one of them cowards who strung up my Daddy and my Uncle Mo?" Cuddy was grinning all the time, leaning against a support post, hands in pockets.

The men stiffened and looked at them silently. Finally the third man, a fat, florid fellow in a stained white shirt leaned across the driver and hollered, "You an' your white friend better be out of here tonight, nigger. Or else." The menace hung in the air.

"Hell, Lester, you couldn't get your fat ass out of that truck to make me leave. Who you gonna get to help you, that dumb son of yours?"

The driver and the passenger argued for a minute, looked at them again and drove away.

Cuddy looked down, smiled and shook his head. He went back inside whistling. "Mama, let's have a big ol' piece of that pie now, all right?"

"Son, are you crazy? It won't be safe for any of us to live here again." She stood wringing her hands.

Cuddy went over and put his arm around her frail shoulders. "Don't fret, Mama, I've got everything taken care of." They polished off a great piece of pie each and even had seconds. Cuddy quietly asked Abel to make sure the motorcycle was ready to go at first light, gassed up and his gear packed. Abel nodded, wondering if he'd have that long. Cuddy wouldn't answer any questions from either Abel or his mother. He just sat there grinning. As the sun set, Mrs. Fowlette lit an oil lamp and placed it on the table. Cuddy got out a deck of cards and he and Abel played hand after hand of draw poker. Finally, around ten PM, Cuddy got up and stretched, hands reaching for the ceiling.

"Mama, you go on to bed. Me and Abel are going to take a little walk." He leaned down and kissed her on the forehead. She looked up apprehensively.

"Be careful, son. Please don't go into town."

"No, Mama, don't worry, we'll be back in a couple of hours. And don't worry about those men. They never come around until after midnight and we'll be back before then." He reached for his shirt and a box of matches and made for the door. Abel just stood there. Cuddy turned. "You coming?"

Abel shrugged. "Sure." He slipped on his own shirt. As they stepped out the back door, Abel quietly asked, "Do you have a gun?"

"Naw." Cuddy smirked in the dark. "You're just along

for the ride. Follow me closely." He walked quickly and surely into the woods, Abel fast on his heels. It was almost pitch black, with just a little starlight. If the moon was up somewhere, it sure wasn't up in southern Alabama. Abel wondered how the hell Cuddy found his way through the woods, so surely, so swiftly. Abel did his best to keep behind him. In about fifteen minutes they came to a clearing. Cuddy stopped at the fringe, behind a large old live oak tree. Abel could make out a small cabin in the glen, a light showing through a cracked window. An old T-Model pickup was pulled up outside and they could hear shouting coming from the inside. Cuddy dropped to his knees and was about to crawl out into the clearing when Abel grabbed the back of his shirt.

"Where the hell are you going?"

"Take it easy. I was just going to see how many of them were here." He started crawling again. Abel followed until they were up against the sidewall of the rough-hewn building, under the window. Slowly they raised themselves up to the sill and peeked inside. There were only four men sitting at a table playing cards, a bottle of whiskey between them. Cuddy sat back down. "There's only four. We gotta wait," he whispered.

"Wait for what?" Abel whispered back.

Just then a pair of headlights shone through the trees. A big sedan pulled in next to the pickup truck. Five men got out, stretched and went inside. Abel glanced at Cuddy and could just see his teeth gleaming in the moonlight. They waited a few more minutes, then looked in the window again. Now all the men were wearing white robes and standing in a rank, one of them forward and facing the rest. He was wearing purple robes, though faded and patched as they all were. Cuddy pulled Abel down and whispered urgently, "They're all here. Let's get back in the woods." With that, he gave Abel a shove toward the big tree, just barely distinguishable in the faint glow from the window. Abel dropped to his hands and knees and scurried forward. When he looked back, Cuddy was nowhere to be seen. He debated a moment whether to go back. He saw a brief flare, then Cuddy was behind him urging him to get behind the tree. They fell to their bellies and Cuddy pushed Abel's head down into the soft forest mulch. Abel tried to shake off the firm hand and had nearly succeeded when a thunderous explosion showered debris down on their heads.

"Come on, man," Cuddy ordered, yanking on Abel's arm. The devastation was pretty near total. The cabin was just a pile of smoldering boards, one corner burning hotly. Cuddy ran to the scene and started poking through the bodies and clothing. Abel subconsciously counted seven bodies or parts of bodies. The other two might have been blown to bits or were out in the forest. Cuddy looted the corpses, putting coins and a few bills in his pockets. It only took a few minutes and then they were gone, Abel once again running through the woods close behind Cuddy. He heard Cuddy chuckling to himself, coins jingling in his pockets. In what seemed like only a couple of minutes, they emerged from the woods and were in the back yard to Mrs. Fowlette's cabin, breathing hard. Abel stood gulping air, bent over, hands on his knees. He glanced back at the dark woods but could see nothing of the recent devastation. The woods were either thicker than he remembered or the fire had gone out already.

Cuddy slouched down on the porch, resting his head against an upright log.

"Jesus, Cuddy, what the hell did you do?"

"Something I should have done a long time ago. Something I should have done instead of run away." He sighed and rubbed his face between his hands.

"But that was murder. You just murdered nine men back there." Abel angrily gestured toward the woods. He sat down next to the thin black man.

"Man, you don't know nothing. Those assholes, those Klanners murdered my Daddy and my Uncle Mo and God knows how many other innocent people." He chuckled, "I was just a duly appointed judge, jury and executioner."

"Who appointed you?"

"Why, Abel, their ghosts. The ghosts of every nigger lynched, burned or shot in the southern part of Alabama."

"But that makes you no better than them." Abel was by turns scared, angry and confused.

"Where'd you get that bullshit, man? You ain't thinking straight." He turned to Abel and gripped his arm. "Let me try to explain it to you, white boy. A man kills another man, they catch him, put him in the pokey, right?"

Abel nodded, silent now gazing into Cuddy's intense dark eyes.

"Then they have a trial, the jury finds him guilty and the judge sentences him to be die. In a while the state pen guys hang him, or electrocute him or shoot him, right?" Cuddy was intently trying to explain to Abel, and perhaps to himself, too.

Abel nodded again.

"Okay, then the jury, the judge and the state guys are all guilty of murder because it wasn't a fair fight, it wasn't self defense or it wasn't wartime." He held up a hand before Abel could speak. "I know what you're going to say, 'That's different', they're operating within the framework of the law. Well, since their law don't apply to niggers, then we have our own law. They were guilty as hell and all I did was carry out the execution order, and," he reached into his pockets and brought forth a handful of money and laid it on the porch. One twenty-dollar gold piece gleamed there, a dozen or so silver cartwheels, some smaller change and a few crumpled bills. "I got paid for it, too!" His teeth gleamed whitely again. He quickly counted out the money.

He pushed a small pile of change over toward Abel. "You take that. The rest goes to my Mama for bus fare to Philadelphia."

"I don't want any dead man's money," Abel pushed the pile back to join the rest. "Give it all to your Mama." He hesitated, "What are you going to do? You can't really stay here."

"Why not? Who's going to run me off? Mama's landlord?" He let out a macabre laugh. "He was the one in the purple robe. The sheriff? He was on the left end." He laughed out loud this time. "No, man, I ain't going no place. After I put Mama on the bus, I'm going to rest, do a little fishing and just wait." He sighed again and almost whispered, "Besides, man, I ain't got more'n a week or two left to me. I can feel it inside."

Abel shifted uncomfortably. He said half-heartedly, "You're welcome to come on with me down to Clearwater in Florida."

"What for? You think a white doctor in Florida is any better than a white doctor in Alabama? None of 'em going to treat a nigger – and besides, I'm too far gone, Abel Landis. Why don't you go on inside and get some shuteye. You'd best be gone in the morning." He withdrew into himself, head resting on crossed arms propped on his knees.

Abel slipped quietly inside, washed his face and lay down on the wood floor, a light blanket pulled up to his chin and looked at the black ceiling. Sleep didn't come easy, and when it did, his dreams were spooky, dark and threatening.

The sunlight threaded its way through the small window and sneaked across the floor, caressing the side of his face. He awoke with a start, wondering if the past evening's activities were part of the dreams, but he knew they weren't. He felt as if he hadn't slept in weeks.

As he scrambled to his feet, Mrs. Fowlette said, "Good morning, Mr. Landis. I made some cornbread." She bustled about the small kitchen, putting a cast-iron frypan on the table with some cracked bowls and two knives.

"Cuddy, son," she called out the door. "Come get somethin' to eat."

Cuddy stumbled in, looking as if he hadn't slept too well either.

After Abel ate and washed, he loaded up the cycle and with a quick handshake, left that evil town.

Chapter 10

Tom's Hearing: Present Day

Tom was roused out of his sleep the next morning by the guard. "Let's go, Novak. Bail hearing time." He slid open the cell door and took Tom by the arm. He was a little taller than Tom but not as broad. Few people were. When they stopped at the street side door the guard said, "I've got to cuff you. Turn around, please." Tom complied and hopped easily into the dusty Ford van. The door slammed, and they were on their way to the courthouse, only two blocks away. Tom would gladly have walked, but the city fathers deemed it too dangerous to let criminals walk two whole blocks.

His lawyer, Sy, met him at the steel rear door. He frowned and leaned in close. "Don't say anything, just stand there with your head hanging and let me do the talking, okay?" Tom nodded. Since he was the only prisoner this morning, the bailiff let his lawyer walk up the three flights of stairs with him.

"I've talked to the people at the bar and all the stories are the same, of course, except for the Brotherhood boys. Whew, slow down, will you? I'm not as young as I used to be," Sy chided the guard. He leaned on the steel handrail for a couple of seconds trying to catch his breath.

Sy Goldberg was a fat man in his late sixties. He had taken to wearing pale blue suits with loud, florid ties, often with palm trees on them. Tom figured he either washed his suits in the sink at home or had a closet full of pale blue pre-wrinkled suits. His briefcase was always bulging with papers sticking out the sides and top, but the courtroom officials liked and respected him, even the judges. He never failed to appear on time, always had his motions in order, and never, but never, refused a judge's request for a court-ordered representation. He'd represented politicians, judges, derelicts, other lawyers and even policemen, as well as dope dealers and murderers. He was a lawyer's lawyer, had a small office over one of the town's better delis and always took on a law student or two each summer, usually at the request of a former professor or judge. If he didn't stop meeting his clients in the deli, he would probably weigh fifty pounds less. Tom liked the old man and often was asked to fly him somewhere when Tom was delivering a plane or chopper.

The newly remodeled courtroom was only partly full, this being a quiet day. A couple of reporters lounged in the front row behind the railing, and the usual regulars slouched in the remaining seats, enjoying the air-conditioned comfort of the cool, high-ceilinged room. Ceiling fans lazily stirred the cool air as Tom sat down at the defendant's table. Dave and Chris sat behind him, Sy next to him. At the prosecutor's table, three well-dressed lawyers sat with the two heavily bandaged security guards. Tom shook his head and chuckled. He whispered to Sy, "Jesus, all I've got is a couple of skinned knuckles. What the hell did they say I hit 'em with?"

Sy was about to answer when the bailiff called the court to order. They rose for Judge D.J. Marietta, a man so black and big they had had to order a specially built chair for him. He was enormous with a shaved head and a thin moustache, with hands the size of catcher's mitts sticking out of the voluminous black robe. The gavel looked like a tack hammer in his hand.

"What have we got this morning, Mr. Goldberg?"

Still standing, Sy stood and greeted the judge as the bailiff slid the charge sheet under his nose.

"Your Honor, my client, Mr. Novak, is accused of viciously attaching these two young men in Harrington's Grill & Bar yesterday afternoon."

"Yeah, I can see that." He glanced up at Tom who smiled, and nodded at him; then at the two invalids and their lawyers. "You fellas with the Brotherhood?" he asked.

One of the lawyers stood up, a slim, immaculately dressed patrician-looking man in his early fifties. "Yes, your honor. Our clients have sworn that Mr. Novak did attack them without provocation and injure them so severely that they must spend several months in rehabilitation therapy and, indeed, may never recover from their grievous injuries."

The judge looked from one group to the other and shook his head. "Did you do that, Mr. Novak?" He pointed the gavel handle at the two guards.

Sy still stood and answered, "Your honor, my client stipulates that he did indeed engage in fisticuffs with the two gentlemen in question, but their injuries were minor and they walked away."

"I didn't ask you, Sy. Please sit. Mr. Novak, how old are you?"

Tom answered without rising, "Fifty- eight, your honor."

"How old are those two boys there, Mr. Lucas?" he asked the patrician lawyer.

"I don't see…" Lucas started.

The judge tapped the gavel just once. "Mr. Lucas, you see, here in my court, when I ask you a question, all, and I mean all, I want you to do is answer it. You understand?"

"Yes, your honor." He consulted briefly with the two men who squirmed uncomfortably. "Twenty-three and twenty-five, your honor."

"Do you have a list of their injuries?" The lawyer handed a fistful of pages to the bailiff who then gave them to the judge. The judge studied them for a few minutes, half glasses perched on the end of his broad nose. He looked up under his brows. "What'd you hit 'em with, Novak, a truck?"

Sy poked him, "No, sir, just my hands."

Leaning in, Sy muttered, "Keep it short and simple and make eye contact with the judge." Tom nodded slightly.

"They're asking for a million in bail, Mr. Goldberg. You know that?"

Both Sy and Tom were taken aback. Sy jumped to his feet, "A million for a bar fight, your honor? Isn't that just a tad steep?"

"Yes it is, but considering the condition of the two men, I have to consider it." He consulted his papers and asked the lawyer for the two men, "Mr. Lucas, I do find the bail request high, do you have supporting information I don't?"

"Yes, your honor." He handed another sheet to the bailiff. "Mr. Novak's work history indicates that he spends some time out of the country, and," he paused for dramatic effect, "he was in possession of a pistol at the time of his arrest, a violation of the state and local codes pertaining to weapons in bars and restaurants."

"That right, Mr. Novak?" The judge was frowning now.

"Your honor, Mr. Novak was acting as a security guard for the owner of the restaurant, a," here Sy consulted a paper in the open folder on the table before him, "Mr. Arthur Hadad. He was at the restaurant in order to escort Mr. Hadad to the bank for his usual deposit." He handed a paper to the bailiff. "This is a sworn statement from Mr. Hadad, your honor."

"Mr. Lucas?" asked the judge.

"We'll strike that from our charge sheet, your honor."

Sy spoke again, "Your Honor? I would also like you to see a security tape from the restaurant in question. It actually shows these two men attacking another patron and Mr. Novak coming to his aid." He held up a video tape cartridge.

"Is that right?" The judge leaned back in his enormous chair, eliciting a protesting shriek from the springs. "Well, we don't have a player here. Mr. Lucas, Mr. Goldman, you have any objections to viewing this tape in my chambers?"

Neither man voiced any objections and followed the judge out of the courtroom. Tom leaned back in his chair and clasped his hands behind his head, a smile on his face.

Dave leaned in over the rail. "You better get out of town for a while. Anybody who messes with the Brotherhood usually ends up with the shitty end of the stick." He indicated the two scowling guards. One was drawing a finger across his throat. Tom discreetly flipped him the bird.

Before either man could leap to his feet, the judge came back followed by the two lawyers.

He sat heavily and indicated Tom and the two guards with a flick of the handle of his gavel. "On your feet." He pointed to Tom, "You stop beating up kiddies, you hear?" Tom nodded.

"And you two," he paused. "The video tape clearly shows you in the wrong. I ought to file charges against you myself. In fact, if Mr. Tofflemeyer or Mr. Novak or even Mr. or Mrs. Hadad wants to charge you, I will entertain them most heartily. He slammed the gavel down hard, "This hearing is dismissed!" As an aside, he said to Mr. Lucas, "I don't want to see these two assholes in my courtroom again, you hear?"

"Is that it?" Tom asked rising to his feet.

"Yep," smiled Sy, patting Tom on the back. "You owe me dinner and a ride to Miami next time you're going, okay?"

"Deal!" said Tom sticking his mitt out and shaking hands with the fat lawyer. "Thanks, Sy."

CHAPTER 11

The Beach: Present Day

Abel arrived in Clearwater after three days riding in sunny, nearly cloudless days. The weather was warm and, though the roads were primitive, he was able to ride the one main road from Tallahassee, the state capital, nearly to Tampa; diverging at the top of Tampa Bay for the coastal community of Clearwater. The last was pleasant riding past miles of citrus groves, the economic staple of Florida's West Coast. Occasional stops for rest and gasoline brought workers crowding around his motorcycle. They all gave him oranges or grapefruit to quench his thirst and he pinched a few bottoms of the buxom Mexican wenches, much to the surprise of their brothers or fathers.

Before anyone could protest, Abel was off with a wave

and a cloud of dust. He rode across the new causeway to Clearwater Beach, formerly known as Tate's Island, marveling at the size of the town behind him. Why, there must be more than ten thousand people in Clearwater now, he thought. He came to the end of the causeway and noted the tremendous amount of development on the north end of the skinny island. A huge pink hotel poked above the palms and the old Joyland Pavilion and dance hall had been replaced by a newer wooden building sporting freshly painted clapboards and a large sign, 'Everingham's Pavilion'.

As he turned the corner and headed along the dirt road toward the south end, he spotted an old shiny railroad car tucked amidst a large grove of mixed trees. He detoured, pulled in front and stopped. When he was a kid, a Mister Laplant had moved the shiny car to its resting place as a sort of men's club and hangout for himself and his rich friends. It rested on a hundred acres acquired by Mr. Laplant on the south beach and had grown quite a reputation. Abel remembered riding a bicycle past in the evenings and hearing loud music and laughing, both men's and women's, coming from the brightly lit interior. He pushed open the door and strode into the dim interior. A barely distinguishable form leaned over the bar, head resting on a glass, a derby hat pushed back on his head. Quiet snores came from the sleeping man.

Abel touched him on the shoulder lightly. Eliciting no response, he shoved harder. "Huh, what?" groaned the form. As Abel's eyes adjusted to the gloom, he noted that the man was of medium height, had longish hair and a dark, unshaven face. His sleeves were rolled up to his flabby biceps and red suspenders hung loosely from his shoulders. He wiped a hand across his bleary face and tried focusing on Abel's face. After a few long minutes, he asked, "What d'ya want?" He squinted and put his face near Abel's, trying to recognize him.

"How about a cold beer?" asked Abel, settling himself on a rickety stool.

The bartender reached into a Coke cooler, brought forth a long-necked bottle and popped the cap. "That'll be a nickel."

Abel tossed the coin on the counter and watched it disappear in the hairy hand. "What happened to Laplant and his gang?" he asked off handedly.

The bartender swiped a rag ineffectually across the wood in front of him and growled, "Gone. A few years ago. It's mine now." He squinted again, "Who wants to know?"

Abel reached a hand across the bar, "Abel Landis." They shook tentatively. "And you are?"

"Fett, Alfred. Folks just call me Scruffy now."

Scratching his chin, Abel asked, "You go to Clearwater High?"

"Yeah, one year, then I hadda quit."

"I think we were in school at the same time." Abel cleared his throat and took a long swig from the cool bottle. "Though I don't remember anybody calling you Scruffy then."

"Yeah, well, times change." He stood a little straighter. "My Ma got sick with the flu and I stood home to take care of her." He scratched under one arm and said, "Were you Archie Landis' kid?"

"Yeah. We lived down at the end of Laura Street. My Ma ran a boarding house and my Pa fished for the big hotel down on Fort Harrison and was a pretty fair carpenter." He swigged again. "It still there?"

"Sure is. Don't seem like hard times bothers them rich folks. They got two boat clubs, now and they even had boat races last year in the bay." He puffed his chest out and added, "Sold a lotta beer them three days!"

Abel eased into his questioning, "You know a guy name of Bob Brightwater?"

Fett's eyes grew narrow, "Yeah, lives out on the point." He gestured toward the south end of the narrow island. "Leastways, he used to. Got himself drowned couple of months ago."

"That right?" Abel finished his beer and let the empty bottle slide through his hand until it thunked on the bar. He slowly spun it around in the wet circles. "His wife doesn't think so." He hesitated, "What do you think?"

Scruffy shuffled back from the bar, a puzzled look coupled with fear on his face. "I don't get paid to think. What's it to ya anyways?"

"Martha, his wife's, my sister." He let it hang there between them like a challenge or an invitation.

Finally, after thinking it over or moving the ponderous rocks in his head, a thought floated to the top of Scruffy's brain. "I don't think Bob Brightwater was fool enough to go swimmin' where they found his clothes." This torturous statement took him as much by surprise as if someone else had said it.

Abel didn't want to push it, so he just muttered his

thanks and put another nickel on the bar and strode out. Interesting. Why was Scruffy scared? Of him?

As Abel started the worn Harley, he gazed out at the startling blue water of the Gulf of Mexico. He'd swum in it, fished it and just plain stared at it from the small beaches. He felt good and ready for whatever waited for him. He gunned the throttle and spun out of the shell-covered parking lot in front of the old railroad car saloon and headed south for the point. There were still only a couple of shacks on this south end of the beach, then nothing but scrub until you got near the water again.

He slowed and putted up to the small neat wood house on the point of land, which looked out into the pass and the gulf. The silence when he shut off the cycle was complete. A few gulls soared overhead in the blue sky, their occasional cries the only sound in the sweet salty summer air. The house had white clapboards with deep green trim. Abel noted the porch was in good repair, with two wicker rockers tucked against the wall under a small window. A stovepipe, slightly askew, stuck through the tin roof as if tipping its hat to him. He rubbed his unshaven face and swung a leg off the cooling machine. He patted the teardrop tank and whispered a soft thank you.

The house was silent until a small boy ran around the corner of the house, pursued by a slightly taller black boy. They were both laughing but stopped dead when they saw Abel. Neither said a word for a long minute, then the white boy slowly walked up to the motorcycle and touched it. "Wow, a Harley-Davidson motorcycle! I seen pictures of them in magazines but I never seen a real one." He looked up at Abel, "Can I have a ride, Mister?"

"Maybe, sport." Abel figured he was about ten or eleven. "Do you live here?"

"Yes sir, me and my mom." He looked up at Abel from under a tattered straw hat. "Who are you?"

Abel liked that, forthright, to the point. "Are you the one they call BB?"

"Yes sir. And this here's my friend Captain." The almost identically dressed black boy bobbed his head shyly, hanging back.

Abel nodded back with a smile and said to BB, "I guess that would make me your Uncle Abel." He stuck out his hand.

BB grasped it awkwardly like children do and said, "Howdy. We thought you weren't coming. Mama sent you a telegram more'n a month or two ago."

"So where is your Ma, boy?"

"She's inside lying down. She does that a lot lately." He turned and ran up the porch and slammed into the house, "Ma, Ma, Uncle Abel's here! And he's got a motorcycle!"

In a few minutes a slim woman who had once been pretty came out onto the porch and stood with her hands on her hips, a wan smile on her face. He blonde hair had been pulled back, and her dark tan had started to fade. She wore a faded blue housedress printed with small flowers. She was barefoot. "Hello, Abel," she said simply and in a moment she was in his arms sobbing.

He held her and stroked her hair and murmured sounds of comfort until she had cried herself out. The boys looked uncomfortable so Abel motioned them away. They stood looking at each other for a minute and then darted away behind the house.

After a while, Abel moved the two of them to the porch. She dabbed at her eyes with a small scrap of handkerchief. "Oh, Abel, I didn't think I had any more tears left." They sank into the two rockers. Abel pulled his around to face hers.

"Sorry it took so long to get here, Sis. The roads between here and Wyoming aren't too good or too straight. I started as soon as I got the telegram." He looked at his sister, slouching in her chair, barely moving. Martha looked thin and washed out despite the tanned face and arms.

"How are you holding up?"

"How do you think? Somebody killed my husband, we've got almost no money left, nobody will tell us anything." She bitterly exploded, "And that police chief, that son-of-a-bitch came out here and just about accused me of forcing Bob to kill himself or whatever. Then," she paused to take a deep breath, "then, he tried to get close to me!" She hugged herself. "I don't know what to do, I just don't know what to do, Abel." She looked up beseechingly at her baby brother.

Abel stood up and reached into his jeans and pulled out some change, then took a wad of bills he had in his wallet out. "Here, I'll just keep a couple of dollars and some change. The rest is for you and BB, okay?"

"Oh, Abel," she groaned, "I didn't ask you to come back to take care of us. I just want to find out what really happened to Bob."

"Hey, it's no big deal. I'll be staying with you and eating here and I'll need some laundry done and all, and besides, we're family, right?"

Martha took the money and looked at him gratefully. "Thanks, Abel," she whispered quietly and stood up. "Come on inside and we'll get you settled. Do you have to do anything to that…thing?" she motioned toward the motorcycle.

"No, Mart, it's a cycle, not a horse." They giggled together.

At dinner that night, Abel asked BB what he did for excitement around here. BB fidgeted a little and said, "Well, me an' Captain sometimes put out some crab traps and sometimes we go out on his Daddy's boat and fish and sometimes we just walk up the beach and back." He swallowed what was in his mouth and when Abel asked about school, he just giggled, "It's summer, Uncle Abel. There ain't no school."

"Isn't any," corrected Martha.

"So what do they teach you in school these days?" Abel was actually interested since he hadn't finished high school.

With a serious frown on his freckled face, BB set his fork down and turned to Abel, "Let's see, last year we had arithmetic, United States history, English – that's mostly reading and writing stories, um, art, and social studies."

"What do you mean, social studies?" asked Abel.

"Well, we learned about how our government works, or at least how Mom says it's supposed to work."

Martha smiled, proud of her son. "I want him to learn about the weak areas – and politicians, too."

Abel nodded in agreement. He, more than either of them, knew about corrupt politicians. "So tell me about your friend, Captain." Abel knew that the more he knew, the more he knew.

"He's two years older'n me and lives up the road and back off it a ways on the bay side. He's got a Mama named Lucy, a Daddy named Jack, a sister named Sukie and a big brother named Travis." He ticked the names off on his fingers.

"What's their last name?"

"Oh, they're the Toffelmeyers."

After BB had gone to bed, Abel and Martha sat out on the porch, quietly rocking and watching the moonlight on the wavelets. Martha had fixed them each a jelly glass of sweet tea. It was pleasantly warm, the salt breeze barely ruffling the curtains behind them. An occasional gull or brown pelican flew across the moon, gliding on silent silvery wings.

"So Sis, this is gonna be hard, but I want you to tell me about the last few days before Bob died. Was there anything unusual or different about him, any letters, work from the office, visitors, anything?" Abel avoided his sister's look and the faint tremble of her lower lip.

"What do you mean?"

"Well, where they found his clothes, or said they did, Bob had never swum there. Ever. Why would he stop on the way home and take a dip out here on the island so close to home? And he didn't even have a swim suit, just his shorts on, and his auto was no where near. It was still in town. How did he get there?"

Abel thought for a minute, picturing the affable Bob Brightwater, at least as much as he remembered. "Do you have his clothes? His belongings?"

"Just what they gave me. They said they didn't find a shirt or tie." She snorted. "Like he went in with his shirt and tie on."

"Who's this 'they' you keep referring to?"

She thought for a minute, "Well, the first person I heard from was a policeman named Brodsky. He's the one that drove out and told me that a couple of fishermen had found Bob floating in the bay. The police searched the shoreline and found a pile of clothes on shore in a grove of mangroves. His wallet identified Bob." She broke down and sobbed, face in her hands. Abel scooted his rocker over next to her and awkwardly rubbed her shoulders. Martha was a willowy woman with soft reddish blonde hair, a broad face with a high forehead and wide-spaced blue eyes. You couldn't say she was pretty, but her mouth had a way of turning up at the corners when she smiled and the corners of her eyes crinkled. When she smiled, it was as if the sun came out. Abel remembered when they used to play in their backyard on a set of swings he and his Pop had built. She used to laugh, a high screaming laugh that made the gulls look down as they flew over. His heart ached for her, but he didn't think there was much he could do for her and his nephew BB.

To get her talking again, he asked, "So who was the other 'they' you mentioned?"

"Well, a Mr. Gibbons came out. He was Bob's boss and the town's attorney. Oh, and the Chief of Police, a feller named McBride. I didn't get his first name, and ….."

Abel interrupted her, "McBride? What's he look like?" He knew it was a long shot and probably wasn't the same McBride, but with a sinking heart, he had to ask.

She shrugged, "Tall, long hair, wears a long black coat and two pearl handled revolvers. A moustache, I think. He came with that mean-faced one, Brodsky, the second time."

"Second time?"

"Yes, the first time he just came out to express his condolences. The second time he sort of invited himself in and asked an awful lot of questions about Bob's work." She clasped her hands in her lap and looked at them. "Bob didn't talk about his work much. Said it was boring and he didn't want to talk about work at home." She sighed and dabbed at her eyes with a scrap of a handkerchief.

The moon sat on the water like a huge saucer, a silver pathway leading right to their doorway. Abel felt he could just step out and walk right up it. Maybe he should, because it sure sounded like the same McBride he'd known in Texas and if it was, he knew he might open his mouth at the wrong time and end up in the jail, or worse. He thought he'd better get the lay of the land better before he started asking too many questions. He'd ask some basic questions like where Bob worked, hours, pay, colleagues, stuff like that.

CHAPTER 12

Fishing for Answers: 1938

That night he slept far better than he'd slept in the past month, clean sheets pulled up to his neck, head settled into a goose down pillow.

The next morning he walked down the road with BB to visit with his friend's family, the Toffelmeyers. The morning was warm with a wisp of fog floating in from the gulf, the palms swaying in the soft breeze. Small shore birds scattered out of their way. BB went on about how he and Captain sometimes caught birds under old fruit crates. They'd lie behind a sand hill and bait the trap with small pieces of fish or shrimp. When a bird would walk under the propped-up box, they'd yank a string and pull the prop out. He never explained what they did with the trapped birds. Abel was deep in thought, looking around at the clumps of grassy sand, the graveled road and the mangrove stands half in the water of the bay.

The island that was Clearwater Beach was approximately ten miles long and barely a quarter mile wide, a sandy barrier between the gulf and the bay. At the north end it sometimes joined to a sandy islet another couple of miles long, depending on hurricanes and storms. A cut often opened or filled in, allowing passage of shallow draft fishing boats. About halfway down the east side, a causeway had been built to connect it to the mainland. The north end of the island was being currently developed and a huge hotel had been built, the Mandalay, and a number of new houses around it were in various stages of construction, adding to the twenty or so that were already there.

At the junction of the causeway, just on the northwest corner, a large dance hall and restaurant, Everingham's Pavilion was the current occupant, though Abel remembered other dance halls there. The old places had burned or been torn down over the years. He fondly remembered dancing with schoolgirls at the one they called Joyland. When he'd left home, they'd just started the causeway, replacing the rickety old wooden bridge, the two-mile-long and one-car-wide contraption that occasionally allowed courageous motorists access to the island. There were so many boats at the foot of Clearwater Bay that not many people undertook the dangerous trip on the bridge, but to Abel, it had been a real kick tearing along at top speed in his Dad's old Buick touring car, the side rails whizzing by.

They turned off the dusty road and onto a narrow path through the dunes until they reached a small clapboard and tin shack on low stilts near the water's edge. A sturdy dock led out into the water and a wooden fishing boat was tied to the pilings. The boat was painted white with red trim, was well maintained and about thirty feet long. The broad, low transom was painted with a bright red feather and the name Featherlite in rolling script inscribed on a polished wooden plaque screwed to it.

"Hey, Captain, you home?" BB called through cupped hands. He and Abel stood before the front porch. In a few seconds, the door flew open and Captain raced out. Just before he jumped off the porch, he stopped short, eyeing Abel.

Abel grinned and said, "Howdy, Captain," and gave him a little wave.

"Howdy back, suh."

"Is your Daddy home, son?" Abel wanted to meet the family. You never knew people until met them face-to-face and might need an ally or know who your enemies were.

"Yassuh. I'll get him." He turned and reluctantly went back inside, letting the screen door slam behind him.

He returned holding hands with a large, powerfully built black man wearing neatly patched tan pants and a well-washed white shirt without a collar. He was barefoot, and his pants were held up with a wide leather military style belt. The wooly black hair was just starting to gray at the temples, though his powerful build belied his age, which could have been between thirty-five and fifty-five.

"Something I can do for you, mister?" He asked in a deep melodious voice, holding Captain back and behind one of his thick legs with a gnarled hand.

Abel grinned and held out his hand, striding forward, “How do, Mr. Toffelmeyer? I’m Abel Landis, Martha’s brother.” Abel looked up at the broad black face. His hand was suddenly engulfed in the big mitt.

“’Day, Mista Landis.” The voice was lower, mistrustful, the accent thicker. “I’m Jack and this here’s my wife, Lucy.” He indicated an equally large woman standing just behind the screen door.

Abel squinted, shading his eyes with his hand. “Ma’am!” He gave a little feeble wave. “Mr. Toffelmeyer, can I talk to you for a bit, please?”

Jack Toffelmeyer thought for a minute, still appraising Abel. “We’re goin’ fishing. You’re welcome to come along, Mista Landis.” He turned on his heel and walked around the corner of the house, still towing Captain by the hand. “Come along, BB,” he called. They all walked around the side of the house and through a small garden built off the ground in about eight foot squares. There were tomatoes, squash, some large leafy plants Abel couldn’t identify and green beans on a trellis frame.

Abel clumped down the dock and hopped over the rail. Jack handed over BB and Captain. He then handed Abel a pail and just muttered, “Bait.” As he swung aboard, the boat tilting crazily for a minute before bobbing upright. In a minute the engine started and as Abel and Captain threw off the dock lines, Jack pulled away slowly. Fifteen minutes later, they were through the pass, tossing a wave to Martha who was hanging clothes out back of her house amid chickens pecking around the yard. They headed north along the coast for a while, Abel taking in the landmarks, the big pink hotel, the water tower, finally the small strip of sand that stuck near the north end of Clearwater Beach. Abel noted the pass was open, or at least not entirely closed in. The next storm would either fill it in or wash it open, whichever way the tide was running during the storm.

The sun was warm and the boat ran on steadily, only a low throbbing from the engine to break the quiet. Abel slipped his shirt over his head and laid it on the aft deck next to the bait box. The boys sat before him, and he regaled them with stories about his travels, his ride from Wyoming, the oil fields in the west and his many adventures. All this was accompanied by him acting the parts of the various characters, voice changes, wild arm gestures and facial grimaces. At turns he fell to the deck clutching his chest, walked with a piece of old oar to simulate a crutch or a gun and yanked himself up by the collar. At one point he caught Jack looking at him, a half smile on his face.

Finally the engine slowed and, with a final chug and wheeze, fell silent. They were about five miles out into the Gulf of Mexico off the town of Dunedin, just north of Clearwater. Abel looked over the side and could see clear to the bottom, starfish littering the sand. Jack rummaged in a box built into the side of the boat and came up with two heavy rods and two hand lines. The hand lines went to BB and Captain. He handed the shorter of the two rods to Abel. The old brass and wooden reels were polished and well oiled, and each held many yards of pale green line with triple hooks on the ends attached to a piece of shiny metal on which a pair of eyes had been painted. Jack offered the bait bucket to Abel who quickly removed three shrimp, baiting his hook and those of the boys.

"Here, Mr. Landis," Jack offered an old straw hat to Abel and unfolded two handmade wooden chairs which he placed so they could rest their feet on the low transom.

"Much obliged, Mr. Toffelmeyer," Abel replied. If this guy wanted to be formal, he would match him.

After a long minute's hesitation he replied, "It's Jack."

Abel looked at him startled, then nodded, "Abel." They fished in silence for a few minutes, then Abel asked, "You known Martha and Bob long?"

Jack considered this question carefully, "Well, we been living on the island for quite a while. When Mr. Bob and his Daddy started building his house, I came over and helped him and I guess that's how the boys got being friends." He looked at the two boys, heads together and giggling.

"So, Bob, he was a good man?" Abel asked innocently, flicking his line, letting it pay out and drift in the current.

"Yeah, I think so. If you want to know if he beat his wife or kid, or drank a lot or got into fights, I'd have to say I didn't think so." He turned and placed a huge hand on his knee and leaned toward Abel. "What you want to know for?"

"Look, Jack, Martha sent me a telegram and asked me to come and find out how Bob died and why. I'm not trying to make waves for you or your family. At this point, I'm just trying to put together a picture of what he was like, his friends, if he had any enemies, you know, that kind of information. Do you think he drowned?" He looked away out at the bright light sparkling off the wavelet tops. "You got anything to drink here?"

Jack stood and stretched. In a minute he returned with two bottles of beer and a bottle of root beer. "Here, you two share this bottle. Later you'll get another – if you catch me some fish." He looked sternly at the two boys and they tried to keep straight faces, but dissolved into giggles again.

He sat heavily and took up his rod, reeling the line in slowly. "Well, since you asked me, I'd have to say no, he didn't drown. The man swam like a fish, and the day they found him, the bay was as calm as glass. But if you want to know if I know what happened to him, I'd have to say no, I don't. To be honest, Mr. Abel, I figure that's white folks' business. It ain't got nothing to do with me. My lady and I'll help Martha and little BB here all we can, but I can't stick my nose into the whys lessen I get it cut off. Y'all know what I mean?" He seemed anxious to explain this to Abel.

Abel nodded, understanding fully. He didn't like it and, having been down and out at times, felt he understood somewhat the plight of the Negro in Florida. To him it felt as if he walked around with a sign around his neck that said 'Poor and Dumb' all the time, then that's how people, all people, would look at him. And no matter what he did or how much money he made, he'd always have that sign. You can hide a lot but you can't hide your color.

The rest of the day, they talked about the town government, the police, and the changes that had been made since Abel had left to go off to war and Mr. Laplant's rail car bar. On this, Jack waxed eloquent, laughing often.

"Mr. Laplant, he'd throw parties out there for his high

falutin' friends, and some of them was ladies, too. He hired that good-for-nothing Fett to run the place for him. Pretty soon, Scruffy was invitin' all his worthless friends out to drink Mr. Laplant's beer and throw darts and all. At first, Mr. Laplant's friends didn't mind rubbin' elbows with them bums, but that couldn't last long. One night, the way I heard it, Mr. Laplant's missus and some lady friends of hers came out and busted the place wide open. Gave her old man an ultimatum, home or git out." He laughed a deep, merry laugh, slapping his knee in enjoyment. "Next day, he sold the bar to Scruffy for a buck. Way I heard, though, Scruffy don't actually own it, just leases it. Mr. Laplant owns the land on the south end and the bar and most of the houses and all, but he's okay, for a white man, no disrespect intended, Abel."

"None taken, Jack." Abel processed this information, keeping it for future consideration. "Do you know anybody at City Hall where Bob worked?"

"Nope, don't want to neither. I pays my rent to Mr. Laplant's man end of each month and I guess he takes care of the taxes." He thought for a minute. "My niece, Clara, is one of the cleaning women there, but that's all I know 'bout that place."

"How about the cops?"

Jack shuddered and shook his great black head. "I used to think old Brady, the last chief, was a bad one, but this man McBride is one mean son-of-a-bitch."

"How do you mean? Where did he come from?"

Jack looked at the boys leaning over the rail, pulling in

a fish. "He's been here maybe seven or eight years. Dresses like a goddamn picture show cowboy. Long hair, long black coat, two pistols on his belt, mustache, you know?" He paused as if sifting wheat from chaff. "They say he killed a feller out in Oklahoma and came east. I heard he was in town for a funeral and when he heard that Chief Brady was retiring, applied for the job. A case of being in the right place at the right time. He's been getting rid of longtime cops with friends of his since he came here. They're basically a mean bunch there now. Even some white folks is scared of him. I don't think they could get rid of him if they wanted to. He's pretty chummy with the mayor and the lawyer Gibson or something like that."

"Where's he live?"

"Don't know, don't want to."

The rest of the day, they chatted about fishing, life out west, tall stories and more fishing. When they headed back, they had three nice big dorado, a mackerel and a mess of yellowtail snappers. Jack said that he sold his catch to the hotels on the beach and in town. If he could get into the big Fort Harrison Hotel, the chef, Oscar, paid the most, but most times, he couldn't get into town unless he walked. Didn't have a car and only recently the town had prohibited horses so he'd sold their old nag. Abel offered to take one of the dorado in on his motorcycle and Jack offered to split the take with him. They even talked about rigging up a little trailer with a box full of ice on the back for hauling the catch in every couple of days. Abel said he'd consider it, though he didn't know how long he'd be around.

When they returned, Martha was gone. Abel wondered

where.

"She's probably at north end, Uncle Abel. She sells eggs to the ladies there," BB informed him nonchalantly. They went out back to the small wharf and cleaned the pair of yellowtail that Jack had given them.

While they were eating dinner, Abel questioned Martha about her income and living situation. She was uneasy at first, then when she realized that he was trying to help and not pry, she opened up to him. She kept about fifty hens and a couple of roosters and sold eggs to the families at the north end of the beach. She occasionally baked bread for them and supposed she could take in washing and ironing. When Bob and his father bought their land from Mr. Harrington and built the small house, they'd been allowed to run electricity from the pole at the old dining car. Bob and his dad and brothers had hand dug the holes and floated the poles across the bay behind a rowboat. The local utility service ran the cable and in 1928, after Bob and Martha had been married, she proudly threw the switch and they had electric lights.

"Of course, we don't use them all that much now what with summer here and it doesn't get dark until near bed-time."

"I'm just trying to think of ways for you to make more of a living, Sis. I think we'll have to get some more hens and you'd better start baking more bread. What about the hotel on the north end?"

"Oh, the Mandalay? Why, I know Mrs. Kelly in the kitchen there. I suppose I could talk to her about buying some bread from me and maybe some eggs." She trailed off uncertainly.

"No, I wasn't thinking of more than bread. What about fancy pastries?" Abel was pacing in that bowlegged walk of his, waving his arms while BB and Martha sat spellbound. "You work the same as baking bread but you get a lot more for your stuff. Hmmm, let's see, what would be a good pastry to start with..?" He scratched his head, sat down and immediately jumped up. "I've got it! Cinnamon buns, then you can branch out to more exotic pastries. Why some of those Frenchies made the most wonderful sweets I've ever eaten. I…"

Martha jumped up, "Abel, stop. I can't do that." She hung her head and he put his hands on her shoulders.

"Why, why not, Mart?"

"Abel, dear, I, I don't know how. All Mama showed me was bread. Remember, we never had sweets unless it was store bought when we were kids?" She slumped back into her chair, forearm over her eyes.

Abel leaned over her and pulled her arm down, "That's okay, Sis, I know how! When I was married, my wife and I had a boarding house, and she showed me how to make sweets. I always had a sweet tooth for 'em but never figured I'd have to show somebody." He squeezed in between BB and Martha on the small sofa, putting his arms around both of them. "It'll be the BB, M and A bakery!"

"You were married?" asked Martha.

"Yeah, Uncle Abel, where is she? What was her name? Where did you live?"

"Hold on now, sprout. If you and your Mama want to hear about the most beautiful woman I ever laid eyes on in

East Texas, why it was Ellen Riley." Abel went on to describe his former wife and how he'd met her while painting a mural on a barn for her daddy. How they'd married, moved to his house in town and opened it as a boarding house. He said that she'd died, but didn't say how. He sat staring out the window at the star sparkled night, remembering and trying not to. Finally he roused himself, "So, anyway, Ellen taught me to bake some, and now I'll teach you two, all right?"

They nodded, smiling. "Maybe tomorrow we can go to town and get some baking stuff, huh, Uncle Abel?" BB smiled an angelic grin. "I'll probably have to go with you on your motorcycle, huh? You know, to help carry all that stuff."

Abel looked at Martha, and BB implored her, "Please, Mama, please?"

"Well, we'll see. If anything happens to him, I'd skin you alive." She shook a finger in his face. "Now, BB, you get washed up and turn in. I've got a feeling tomorrow will be a very busy day."

Gunfight on Clearwater Beach

Chapter 13

Captain's Next Installment: Present Day

Tom took a long gulp of his beer and gave a loud belch. Chris had been leaning on the bar and giving him an update on the gunfight story the old black lawyer had been telling them. "So that was how Abel finally got to Clearwater and met Mr. Toffelmeyer's father."

"That's it? What about the gunfight? And what happened to the black guy, Cuddy." Chris shrugged. "Jesus, it's not right, leaving us hanging like that. So do we have to make up the rest or what?"

Chris grinned impishly, "Nope, he said he'd be at Harrington's tomorrow morning for breakfast and we could hear the rest of it then. Ha, ha!"

"Since when do Artie and Brooke serve breakfast?"

"They're making a special exception tomorrow so we

can hear the story." She wiped the rag across the polished mahogany in front of Tom and refilled his glass.

"Oh, great, and what's that going to cost?"

She grinned, wrung the rag out and threw it at him, "Nothing, you cheap bastard, it's on the house for us special people."

Tom deftly caught the rag and flicked it back at her. "Good. What time?"

"Eight-ish," she replied. "Can you make it?"

"Yeah, but I've got a chopper delivery in the afternoon to Miami. It's a Broward County sheriff's piece of crap." He ran his hand through his bristly hair. "I'll probably have to stay overnight. But, hey, the cops are paying for it." He grinned. Tom always liked 'expense account' flights.

"What kind of bird?" asked Dave coming up behind him and playfully punching him on the shoulder.

"A fucking Gazelle." Tom shook his head. "How the sheriff's department got ahold of one of those pieces of shit, I don't know."

"So why didn't they send their own man over to get it?"

"Not checked out on it yet. I'm supposed to check him out. I told them they should have sent him over to ride back with me, but for some reason they decided not to. I'll take him up, do a couple of loops and drop him back on the ground all checked out! Oh yeah, Sy's coming along for the ride." He gave a loud laugh. Dave and Chris just shook their heads. Tom was the consummate aviator. He'd flown everything from Stearman biplanes to Lears and most military jets to just about all makes of helicopters. Dave was well-versed, but when it came to jumping in any kind of aircraft, Tom wouldn't hesitate to fly it, or at least attempt to fly it. He yearned to fly an SR-71 Blackbird, the fastest aircraft in the world, but they'd been mothballed, at least officially.

Tom sipped the last of his beer, burped again and said; "I'll see you in the morning." He tipped his Stetson cowboy hat to Chris and walked out.

The next morning, Dave and Chris let themselves into the kitchen of Harrington's through the rear door. Serge, the day cook, was busy chopping vegetables and flipping them into a large stainless steel pot.

"Hey, Dave, Chris, how ya doin'?"

"Finer than frog fur, Serge. You?" Dave stopped for a minute and sampled a piece of carrot while Chris went into the bar.

"Pretty good, man. Say, have you still got that old wooden car?" Serge asked.

"Yep, out in the parking lot, why?" Dave always had lots of inquiries about his 1947 Mercury Woodie Station Wagon. He, Tom and several of his friends had lovingly restored it, souped up the engine and added air conditioning. It was a beauty in metallic green and highly polished maple and teakwood.

"You ready to sell it to me yet?" Serge grinned.

"Serge, buddy," Dave said, arm across the man's T-shirt clad shoulders, "you couldn't afford it. Frankly, if I had to buy it now, I couldn't afford it!"

He grinned as Serge's face fell. "I'll tell you what, if I hear about another one that needs work, I'll let you know, okay? And I'll help you do it."

"Aw, thanks, man." He grinned back at Dave. "Okay if I take a look at yours again when I'm done here?"

"Sure, why not?"

Dave entered the bar and joined the group at the large corner booth. Shelly was on one knee at the end, her short skirt revealing her fine legs. Dave playfully slapped her on the bottom, "Out of my way, shortcakes."

She jumped to her feet, face in a frown until she saw who it was, then turned and gave him a friendly hug. "Hey, big guy, what're you having to eat?"

Dave eased into the booth next to Chris, gave the Captain a nod and said, "Ham and cheese omelet, toasted bagel and a cup of tea." He turned back, "Howdy, Captain. Did I miss anything?" He shook the old man's hand.

"No suh. Haven't started yet. Just finishing my coffee."

Dave looked at his watch, "Well, it's after eight, let's get started." He looked around, "Where's Tom?"

Chris looked also and said, "He's not here yet. But he had a date with the nurse practitioner last night, Bobbie?"

"Yes, Bobbie," Brooke chimed in. "So he'll probably be late. You know Tom, he's never on time, especially when he's with a woman."

Chris raised an eyebrow at Brooke who tilted her chin up and at least had the decency to blush. Her husband, Artie, missed all this.

"So, Mon Capitain, where were we? Abel was helping out his sister and her kid or something like that?" Dave realized by now that he had to let the Captain tell his story in his own time and at his own pace.

"Yes, that's right, David, Abel taught Martha and BB how to make fancy pastries and soon she had to buy another oven to keep the folks on the north end of the beach and the Mandalay Hotel supplied. Over the next month, Martha started supplying all sorts of goods to those north beachers. My daddy would sail over to the foot of Gulf-to-Bay and they would go shopping together. You see, even in those days a lot of the folks living on the north beach were retirees, so Martha found a ready market for her goods. But I'm getting ahead of myself."

"Yeah, so, that's it?" Dave asked? "What happened to the gunfight?"

"I'm getting to it, David, jest hold your horses." He sipped his tea and cleared his throat, "As I was about to say," he looked sharply at Dave, "before I was so rudely interrupted, while Martha and BB were busy building up the business, Abel was, let's just say, snooping?" He chuckled.

CHAPTER 14

Martha's Future: 1938

Abel rode into town one morning on the Harley, trying to keep the exhaust quiet. He stopped at a Sinclair gasoline station to put a quarter's worth in the tank and asked the boy pumping if there was a motorcycle dealer in town. The young lad scratched his head and answered, "I don't think so, mister. There used to be, but old man Farrell closed up four or five years ago. You might try his house, though, he don't live far. Jist go down two blocks and turn right, that's south. Go another coupla blocks and y'all 'll see a green house with'n white trim. He's probably out back in his garage. He's got a ol' Hudson he's been workin' on fer years." He paused to scratch his ass and pick his nose, then said, "That'll be twenty seven cents. Hit ran a little over."

Abel counted out the change and gunned the freshly

washed cycle down the street. He and BB had risen early and washed the dusty bike. He then gave BB a ride to the north end of the beach, around the drive of the Mandalay Hotel and back down, waving to Scruffy as he shuffled around the steps of the old diner, ineffectually pushing a broom around. He'd dropped in for a beer now and then and pumped Scruffy for info on the town fathers, grandfathers and uncles.

Scruffy knew a lot of their secrets, and after he'd got over his initial suspicions, opened up, often sitting at one of the small tables with Abel or engaging in a friendly game of darts or cards. On Friday and Saturday nights, a few more of the local men dropped in. They were mostly small shop-keepers or civil servants who worked in town and lived on the north beach. Most had been affected pretty severely by the depression. They just called it 'hard times' and went on as best they could. Scruffy kept the radio on, playing the baseball games during the day and sweet music at night; sometimes twiddling with the dial until they could hear 'The Green Hornet' from Tampa or 'The Shadow' from a small station in St. Petersburg.

Abel and several other men sat and listened raptly to the Cincinnati Reds games as Johnny Vandermeer pitched back-to-back no hitters; and one evening even caught the broad-cast of Orson Wells' 'War of the Worlds'. Abel thought it was a corker as some of the men actually thought the United States was being invaded by Martians!

He pulled up in front of a green and white house and heard hammering and cursing from the rear. With a blip of the throttle, Abel made a U-turn and rumbled up the drive-way to a swaybacked framed garage nestled under a pair of tall oak trees. An old Essex touring car was up on four tree sections and a pair of overall clad legs jutted out from under the passenger side. Another clang was heard, followed by a curse and then a large crescent wrench came flying out, just clipping Abel in the shin.

"Shit and damn," a voice called out, followed by "Ow, Ow, Ow!"

"Ow, Ow, Ow is right!" Abel yelled hopping around on one leg holding his shin.

A thin man slid out from under the car, a dirty rag wrapped around his hand. He wore overalls, a scuffed and torn pair of work boots, and a grayish sleeveless T-shirt. His face was thin and unshaven. His bright nose showed a history of drink. The once thick brown hair was oil matted, graying and thinning. He looked up from the ground, "Who the hell are you?"

When Abel stopped hopping around, he muttered, "Abel, Abel Landis. You Farrell?"

"Yeah. Who'd you say you were agin?"

"Abel Landis."

"You kin to Archie? Lived over on Golden or near?"

"Yeah, I'm his son." Abel was walking the pain off now, turning small circles in the dirt driveway.

"Archie ain't around no more. I think he's dead."

"Yep, I heard." Abel stuck his hand out. "Howdy, Mr. Farrell."

Farrell stuck a grimy hand out, but then quickly wiped it on the bloody rag, "Shit, just call me Ray. 'Scuse the dirt 'n blood. Sorry 'bout the wrench. That goddamn front end's gonna be the death of me yet." He gestured at the right front wheel, then spit in the dirt next to it.

"You ever have trouble with the timing chain?" Abel asked innocently.

"Oh, you know about that problem, eh? Fer some reason, when the driver let off the gas and turns left, the timing chain on these old Essex's sometimes come off. I guess I ain't gonna sell you this car then, right?"

Abel laughed, "No, I'm not in the market for a car right now. I'm just trying to find some parts for my cycle and the feller up at the Sinclair station said you were the man to see. At least you used to be."

"You ain't far wrong, young Mr. Landis. Ran a cycle shop in town here since before the war. Opened in '12 and just closed 'er up in '32. Twenty years. Did 'em all, the Harley-Davidsons, Injuns, Popes, Henderson's; even worked on a coupla them British cycles, Beezers an' Nortons." He was looking at Abel's motorcycle, walking around it as he absently wiped his hands on the rag. "That there's a JD model Harley." He pointed at the front brake. "That front brake makes it a real late '27 or a '28." He shook his head. "Too bad it ain't one of them twin cammers. Lawd, they was fast. But I like the new knucklehead what come out a coupla years ago. Anyway, what parts you lookin' for?"

He went inside the garage and Abel followed him. It was completely filled with motorcycles in various stages of disassembly, parts hanging from the rafters, boxes and barrels filled to overflowing with barely recognizable greasy parts. One whole wall had gaskets hanging on nails. Another had three long planks with jars full of nuts, bolts, screws, washers, and many other small parts.

"I just need an oil filter, an air filter and a couple of quarts of a good thick oil. I also need a tail light bulb," Abel replied.

"Be jist a minute," Ray called from somewhere in the gloom. In a minute, an oil filter came flying out at Abel, who fumbled it, then caught it. Ray emerged with the air filter around his wrist and two quart fruit jars filled with oil.

"Here ya go, Abel. You wanna change 'em here? Won't charge ya nothin' if'n you'll help me free up this kingpin." He indicated the crippled Essex.

"Sure, be glad to oblige." Abel removed his long coat and laid it across the seat of the cycle.

Ray brought out some tools and a shallow pan and in a few short minutes, they had the new filters on, the oil changed and even pulled and cleaned the spark plugs. "Well, thanks, Ray. Now let's tackle that Essex. What seems to be the problem?"

"Passenger's side wheel won't turn. Kingpin's froze up."

"Okay, let's drop the tie rod and maybe with you and me pushing and shoving, we can free 'er up." Abel rolled up his sleeves as Ray crawled back underneath the front of the big car.

A nut dropped and then Abel heard the clank of the tie rod hitting the ground. Ray got out a large brass oilcan and doused the spindle and kingpin area. "I squirted it with some kerosene. Okay, young feller, let's put our backs inter it. I'll push on the front of it an' you put yer foot up here on the bearing and pull fer all yer worth."

"Gotcha. Ready? One, two, three!" Abel gave a grunt and pulled with all his strength. Ray dug his heels in and leaned his back on the wheel. With a loud squeal it started to move. "Harder, harder!" Ray shouted.

Abel thought the muscles on his back would pop, but the wheel was moving. It turned all the way to the left. They changed places, and repeated the procedure after Ray gave it another couple of squirts. It turned easier this time. Three more times, they tugged and pushed and each time the squealing grew less and the wheel turned easier. Finally Ray could move it himself.

"Hot damn, that ought t'do 'er, son. I'll keep workin' on 'er, but she's free now." They were both streaming sweat and gasping for breath. "Cain't tell ya how much I 'preciate the help. I owe you one." Ray grinned a nearly toothless grin. "You just sit yourself down and I'll get us a coupla glasses of lemonade." He returned in a minute and he and Abel sat side by side on an old car seat in the shade sipping the cool drink.

"Allus feels good when somethin' goes like you 'spect." They clinked glasses.

"So you knew my old man?" asked Abel.

"Yep, he was," here Ray paused, searching for the right words. "He was a feller of strong opinions, he was." He frowned. "The good Lord took him in one o'them typhoid sicknesses a while back, I believe." He studied his lemonade and Abel waited for him to continue, but he said nothing more.

"My sister wrote me. It was back in '33 or '34. Ma went

in '28 and I guess if the fever didn't take him, the drink would have."

"Your sister still around here?" Ray asked changing the subject.

"Yes, that's why I'm here. She was married to that fellow Bob Brightwater. He worked at city hall. They found him drowned in the Bay. My sister doesn't think it was an accident."

"Oh? Why's that?" Ray was turned sideways on the seat, looking at Abel.

"Well," Abel began, "she says he was on his way home to go swimming with his son and one of his friends. She said he never swims from the spot they found his clothes. Nobody does. His car wasn't there either." He paused and looked at Ray. "She wants me to see if I can find out anything. Got any ideas?"

"Well," he scratched his jaw, leaving a dirty smear, "you kin check with the coppers, see what's on the report. Gotta have a report, don't they?"

"Yeah, well, that's part of the problem. See, I think this chief they've got, McBride? Well, I think I've had a run in with him a few years back in Texas, so I'd kinda like to stay away from him."

"You're probably right to stay away. That feller's a snake, that one. An' he's bin bringin' his own fellers in from out west ever since he got the chief's job."

"How many coppers are on the job now?"

"Let's see," Ray stopped for a swig and a scratch. "There's the chief hisself, there's Brodsky, Wilson, Mendez the Mexican, Kaminsky, and Huffman the Kraut. Oh, and I almost forgot Chick Warner. He's the on'y local lad still in there. And they got an old nigger watches the cells and cleans up."

"That it?" asked Abel jotting the names on a piece of paper with a pencil stub.

Ray scratched one ear. "Well, they got a gal what does the office work. Think her name is Ada something. Never met her. Seen her at the Arcade once. A real looker!" Ray had a dreamy look in his eyes as he described the 'looker' that worked at the police station. "If y'all wanna know more, go stop in to the Dutch Kitchen an' ast Johnny Livingston. I swear that kid knows everybody and everything that's goin' on in this here town. Y'all kin tell 'im I sent ya. He's a nephew or some such."

"Tell me more about the coppers. I gotta know who I'm gonna be dealing with."

Ray proceeded to tell Abel what he knew; descriptions, as much history as he could remember, how long they'd been on the force and where they lived when not on duty. Brodsky was the only 'plainclothes' copper, but they all had worn civilian clothes at various times. McBride always wore the long black coat and the Stetson and the pearl handled revolvers, though he had a strict uniform code for the others. He finished with a warning, "Jest be glad you ain't no young nigger girl. We've had a coupla them disappear in the last year or so. A white girl, too, though they say she was jist a whore."

Abel thanked him and asked if he could drop around again. He liked Ray's lemonade. Ray just laughed and said sure.

The Harley started on the first kick, Abel nodded at the old man and slowly drove down the weed-covered driveway. He headed back into town looking for the Arcade, which he found on the corner of Cleveland and Garden. This was just about the center of town and had changed little since Abel had left. There were some different signs and some of the buildings had newer facades. Since the fires in the early days, the town had mandated the downtown buildings be built of brick and stone. The streets were hardpacked gravel and oiled but the main streets downtown were cement, scored into squares. One side street leading to the railroad station was still cobblestoned, he noted out of the corner of his eye. As he pulled to the curb on Cleveland Street, a thirtyish fellow came running out the side door. He was dressed all in white with a paper fore and aft hat perched on his narrow head. He wore black-framed spectacles on a longish nose and had a prominent Adam's apple. He whipped a small notepad out of his back pocket and yanked a pencil from behind his ear.

"Howdy, what can I get ya?" He talked fast and bobbed his head as if listening to some inner rhythm.

"Just a cola, please. You must be Johnny Livingston?"

"Yep, that's me. Be right back." And he was gone in a flash. Abel turned off the cycle, listening to the pop and crack of the cooling metal. The sun was warm on his face so he backed the cycle along the curb until it was in the shadow of the awning on the tall building. Just as fast, Johnny appeared beside him. "That'll be a nickel, pal."

"Sure thing," Abel replied, reaching into his pocket and bringing out a handful of change. He handed two nickels to Johnny. "One for the Coke and one for you."

"Say, thanks Mister!" He smiled a toothy grin. "Don't get many tips any more what with hard times and all."

Abel smiled back at him and introduced himself. "I'm a friend of Ray Farrell. You know him?"

"Oh, I sure do. He's my uncle on my Ma's side." Johnny looked at him quizzically, "Do I know you? I don't recall seeing you around before."

"Naw, I'm new in town. I'm Martha Brightwater's brother." He looked at Johnny innocently. "Do you know Martha and Bob?"

Johnny swallowed hard, his adam's apple bobbing, "Sure, I know Martha. Knew Bob, too. Real nice fella." Johnny had stopped his bobbing and was looking intently at Abel. "Too bad about him drowning." He looked around furtively and said in almost a whisper, "What a shame right after being picked up by a copper." He glanced around again, "Look, bub, I can't talk here. Where you staying?"

"I'm staying with Martha and her kid. I don't want to meet there. Do you know the old dining car on the beach?"

"Yeah, Scruffy's place. Okay, about eight o'clock." With that he turned to a polished Pierce Arrow just pulling into the curb.

Abel finished his Coke, crumpled the paper cup and crammed it in his pocket. Again the cycle started on the first kick. He pulled out into the sparse traffic, drove past the bank, the courthouse and a large house with a sign in the window saying 'Rooms to Let'. A man was coming down the front steps, head bowed, lighting a thin cigar. He wore a black Stetson pulled low and for a second he looked up and his eyes met Abel's; then Abel was past, speeding down the street. McBride, Abel was sure of it. He looked the same as Abel remembered, thin dark moustache, long coat, only this time he had a badge pinned to his coat. "But did he recognize me?" wondered Abel?

He leaned around the corner and sped down the street until he came to a large grocery store. He bought baking supplies until his saddlebags would hold no more. He'd have to either borrow a car or get Jack Toffelmeyer to bring the boat over to the dock at the foot of Cleveland Street.

As soon as he arrived at home, he had Martha and BB mixing ingredients and baking. "See, you roll the dough out after you pound it down, sprinkle the cinnamon and brown sugar all over it and then roll it up like a big thick snake." He wiggled his eyebrows at BB, who giggled back. Abel wore one of Martha's aprons and was nearly covered with flour. "Now you cut the pieces off with a big knife about an inch thick. If you want, before you roll the snake up, you can put some nuts or raisins on his belly. 'Course, you get more for the raisin or nut ones." He expertly laid out the slices on two cookie sheets.

"After, we'll dribble some sugary stuff over them and then we're done!"

"Uncle Abel, what do we do with the end ones that ain't as pretty?"

Abel leaned down and pulled the boy's head close, giving him a conspiratorial wink, "Why, me lad," he paused for effect, "we eats 'em!" Both BB and Martha broke into gales of laughter.

The first batch was ready in a short time. Abel taught Martha how to make the confectioner's sugar frosting, which they then drizzled over the cooling buns. They stood back and admired their handiwork. The kitchen table was softly lit with two oil lamps. The cinnamon buns were piled high on two plates, and a smaller one held the 'ugly' ones. He took one and bowing low, offered it to Martha. She curtsied low and regally bowed her head. BB followed suit and also bowed at the waist.

"Can we try 'em Mom? Please?"

"Well, you should wait until after dinner, but since this is a special occasion, why not?" In a few minutes, the small plate was cleaned. Abel leaned back and loudly burped.

Martha looked at him sharply. He profusely apologized and offered, "You know, in China, it's considered polite to burp after a meal. Shows you enjoyed it." He sat back with a smug smile on his face.

BB was about to copy him but a stern look from his mother caused him to put a hand over his mouth tightly.

"Next time you two are in China, you can burp all you want!" retorted Martha, cleaning the table and covering the two large platters with waxed paper. "Tomorrow, I'll ride up to the hotel and see if I can sell them." She turned to Abel, who was shrugging into a clean shirt. "How much do you think I should ask, Abel?"

"Probably ten or fifteen cents apiece without the raisins or nuts and another nickel for the filled ones." He started toward the door.

"Where are you going, young man?" Martha had her hands on her hips.

Abel paused and looked over his shoulder considering his answer, "Look, Mart, you're my sister, not my mother. I'm free, white and over twenty-one. I'll be up at the bar, you know, Scruffy's place." He turned and walked out before she could reply. BB just stood watching the sharp exchange.

Abel shut the cycle down and slid off the saddle. Two cars sat in the parking lot, a T-model flivver and a big Cadillac or Packard, he couldn't tell which in the dimming twilight.

The lamps inside were bright, however, and Abel strode through the door banging it back against the wall. Scruffy was leaning on the bar and swiping ineffectually at the gleaming bar top with a damp rag. There were three men hunched over their drinks at a small table and a skinny guy at the bar nursing a glass of beer. The skinny guy was Johnny Livingston. Abel strode over to him and clapped a friendly hand on his shoulder.

"Glad you could make it, Johnny." He turned to the barkeep, "A beer for me and another for my friend here."

Johnny looked around nervously, Adam's apple bobbing. "Look, Abel, I can only stay a few minutes. I just wanted to tell you that on the day before they found Bob's body, I saw Arnie Brodsky put him in a car and drive away. And it didn't look like Bob was all that thrilled to be along for the ride." He swigged at his beer, hand shaking, spilling a little on his pants. He didn't seem to notice.

"Did you see where they went?" Scruffy leaned closer to hear better. They both looked up at him. "What do you want, Scruf?"

"Nothin'. I might be able to help you is all. You never know," he mumbled, running the rag back and forth. He scratched at his crotch.

Abel looked up at him hard. "How the fuck are you going to help me?"

He looked down and shrugged, "I dunno. For instance, see them guys at the table there?" He indicated the three men at the table.

"Yeah, I see 'em."

"Well, the fat guy with his back to us is Gibbons, the town's attorney. He was Bob's boss." He leaned closer. "The big guy on his right is Teague, the mayor."

"How do you know the attorney was Bob's boss?" Abel asked, eyes narrowed.

"Heck, everybody knew," replied Johnny. "It's a small town."

"Yeah, Bob came in here onct in a while, you know."

"Yeah? Did Martha know?" Abel sat back so he could see the three men in the bar's back mirror better.

Scruffy shrugged, "Wasn't none of my business."

Abel considered this and dismissed it. "Who's the third guy?"

Scruffy shrugged again, "Don't know. Never seen him before. You know him, Johnny?"

Johnny craned his neck, "Nope, I don't know him but I think I've seen him in town sometime ago." He considered, "I've gotta go. I'll nose around, see if I can come up with anything." He looked at Abel for permission, "If I find out anything, I'll let Scruffy here know and leave word, okay?"

Scruffy nodded enthusiastically and whispered, "You can count on me, Abel. I don't like them townies. No offense, Johnny."

"None taken, Scruf." He slid off the stool and disappeared out the door. In a minute they heard the flivver start up and then the sound faded.

Abel leaned close to Scruffy, "How well do you know Johnny, Fett?"

"Aw, Johnny's a square shooter, Abel. "'J'ou see that little scar under his eye?"

"Yeah, what's that about?"

"Chief didn't think he brung out his order fast enough one day an' give him a backhander. That there ring he wears cut up Johnny's face. Tried to get Johnny fired, too, but Kane, the owner o'the Dutch Kitchen wouldn't do it."

Abel considered the information. "How come they don't get rid of him if nobody likes him?" Abel looked over his shoulder again at the threesome at the small table.

Scruffy brought him another beer. "'Cause they're scared of him. I think the mayor an' maybe the lawyer got something going on with him, too. They all been in here a coupla times." He poured himself a shot from a bottle under the counter. "There was a movement to get rid of him a year or two after he come here, but you know, it bein' hard times an' all, folks's got jobs sure wants t'hold onta 'em. I think he's got somethin' on most folks what count in this here town, too."

"Hmm, is that right? I think it's time I introduced myself to the lawyer."

He slid off the stool, leaving his beer on the bar and sauntered over to the group.

Edging around next to the lawyer, he offered his hand, "'Scuse me, are you Mr. Gibbons? My name is Abel Landis, Bob Brightwater's brother-in-law." He kept a stupid grin plastered on his face.

The lawyer shifted his bulk in his chair and, after removing a cigar from his mouth and placing it in a large glass ashtray, extended his hand. "Yessir, Mr. Landis, I'm Avery Gibbons." They shook firmly, testing each other. He looked out at Abel from under bushy white brows, appraising him all the time shaking his hand. "Sorry about your brother in law, Mr. Landis, he was a good man."

"Can I ask you a couple of questions, Mr. Gibbons?" Before he went on, he introduced himself to the other men. The mayor smiled cherubically, his pug nose almost wiggling below close-set eyes.

"Please to meet ya, Mista Landis. Ah knew Bob and he was a fine man, a fine man." The mayor sounded like he was in the middle of a campaign, vigorously shaking Abel's hand.

They declined to introduce the third man who sat hunched, face hidden beneath a large snap-brim hat. He was slimmer than either of the others, coat a little shabbier, and what Abel could see of his face was pocked and pasty. He was also in need of a shave. He sat with hands clasped on the table, a small gold band on one pinky.

The attorney spoke, "I'm afraid I'm a little busy right

now, Mr. Landis, but if you want to stop by my office tomorrow in City Hall, I'll be glad to tell you everything I can about our Bob's unfortunate death. Just call my secretary and make an appointment, y'hear?" Abel felt like he was dismissed. He stood for a minute, then shrugged and went back to the bar, finished his beer and left.

The next morning, he discussed his findings with Martha, gaining her impressions of the men from the bar. She knew Johnny, of course, everybody knew Johnny. The mayor she knew from his campaigns and having seen him at City Hall when she'd attended functions with Bob. She also knew the attorney, Gibbons, and didn't like him. She felt that there was something creepy or slimy, as she put it, about him. He seemed to be always touching her; holding her hand a moment too long. She'd finally asked Bob if she could stay home, rather than attend the occasional dinner or opening, pleading a headache or 'women's problems'. Bob understood and didn't press her. He hadn't wanted to create a poor impression with his immediate boss, and the hard times had limited the necessary functions either would have had to attend.

Martha had good news to report of her baking and sales efforts. She'd ridden her bike to the Mandalay Hotel and met with Mrs. Kelly, the head cook. Mrs. Kelly had loved the cinnamon buns and ordered several dozen each week as well as other pastries if she would bring samples. Though occupancy at the hotel was down, there was still a core group of regulars who demanded good food and service. Mrs. Kelly had been forced to lay off staff and had searched for outside people to continue to supply the hotel's' needs. In a flurry, she told Abel and BB about the hotel's need to find someone to wash and iron sheets.

"You know, I could do that, too," she offered. "It would make us some more money."

Abel shook his head, "Nope, don't do it."

"But why? I'm strong, I can do the work. And besides, we have a washing machine," she indicated the wringer model in the corner under a cover, "and I have a steam iron Bob bought me just last year."

"Nope, I'll tell you why. You stick to baking. It'll get bigger than you can imagine. If you want, get what's her name, Jack's wife, to do the sheets, pay her half or two-thirds. I'll bet they can use the money. You handle the hotel people. They'll pay more to a white woman." Abel was pacing furiously around the small, neat kitchen. "You stick to food and try to find some other people to buy your baked goods. We've got to look at this in the long term." He was thinking furiously, poking a finger in the air, running his other hand through his hair, sometimes scrubbing at his skull, trying to force the ideas out.

"Look, Sis, some day the hard times are going to be over and people will have money to spend. All those houses they started on the north beach are going to be full and this here south beach is going to be full, too. We've got to be ready for it. The way I see it, you've got to get enough money together for a little store or bakery somewhere here on the beach. Folks won't want to drive all the way into town just for some eggs or bread or milk and stuff. You're already selling eggs and some bread and now pastries. We got to expand on that and soon. You understand?"

"Oh, Abel, I don't know, that's more'n I can even dream about. I'm not sure I can do all that, what with taking care of BB and all," she demurred, hanging her head and twisting her fingers in her lap.

"Sure we can, Mom!" interjected BB. "I can help. Look how easy it was making the cinnamon buns!" He looked from his mother to Abel.

"He's right, Mart. Soon it's only going to be the two of you."

"Why, what do you mean, Abel? Where are you going?" She was clearly distraught at the thought of him leaving.

"Aw, heck, Mart. In a few months, I've got to go. I'm just here to help you find out what happened to Bob. I've got a job to go back to. I'm a cowboy!" He stuck his thumbs in his belt and pranced around the kitchen.

Though they pleaded with him, he remained adamant. Over the next few days, he showed them how to make coffee cakes, flaky pastries with fillings, and doughnuts. This was the extent of his knowledge, so she was on her own after that. He bought her a cookbook on making pastry and more supplies in town. She contacted Lucy Toffelmeyer, and they reached an agreement to do the sheets and pillowcases for the hotel at Martha's. This would give the ladies time to talk and swap recipes.

Meanwhile, Abel continued his snooping.

CHAPTER 15

Tom in Hospital: Present Day

The old man was just about to tell them about Abel's first meeting with the town's lawyer when two suits pushed through the front door at Harrington's. They located the group at the large table and came swaggering toward them. The taller of the two spoke. "Who's Manley?"

Dave nodded. "Yes, that's me. What's up?"

He flipped his coat back and showed them the gold shield on his belt then took a small notepad from his back pocket and flipped a page. "You live at a place called Chesney's?"

"Yeah, my wife owns it. Why?"

The cop consulted another page, "You know a Thomas Novak?"

Dave was getting tired of answering now. “You know I do or you wouldn’t be asking. What’s this all about?” Chris put her hand on his arm.

“This the same Thomas Novak was released from custody yesterday?”

Dave just looked at the taller cop, waiting for his question to be answered. The policeman looked down at Dave from under a heavy brow ridge, eyebrows raised.

Dave just sat. Finally the policeman said, “Mr. Novak’s in the hospital. We found a card in his wallet with your name on it. We went out to your place and the guy in the kitchen sent us here. Guy named Potts.”

“Which hospital?” Dave asked, carefully, controlled.

“Laplant. He was admitted last night about midnight.” He flipped the notebook closed and stuffed it back in his pocket. The other cop stood with his arms by his sides, a bit behind and to the right.

“What happened?” All eyes in the booth were on the tall cop and Dave. Chris was holding her breath.

“Doc says he was beat up pretty bad. Probably more than one guy. Uh, he was brought in with a woman. You know a woman named Barbara Young?” The second cop had his notebook out and shouldered up beside his taller colleague.

“Oh, my gosh,” exclaimed Chris. “Is she okay?”

The shorter cop looked at her and shook his head, “No, Ma’am, she’s been beaten up. Raped, too.” He paused, face ashen. “Were you her friend, Ma’am?”

“I just met her but I liked her. She was Tom’s girlfriend," Chris responded, face drawn. She clutched Dave's arm impulsively. "Come on, we'd better get to the hospital." She pushed him out of the booth and stood up.

Dave turned a stricken face to the policeman, "Any idea who did it?"

"Did Tom say who did it?" Chris asked anxiously.

"I'm sorry, Mr. Manley, Mrs. Manley. He was unconscious and he's still in a coma. Do you have any idea who might want to do this?" The cop flipped his pad open again and snared a pen out of his shirt pocket.

"Yeah, try a coupla assholes from the Brotherhood. He had a run in with them a couple of days ago. They pressed charges but the judge threw them out."

The taller cop shook his head, "We talked to them. They're heavily alibied and then they lawyered out. Can't touch 'em." He gave a sidelong glance at his partner. "You know what they're like in this town, Mr. Manley. We'll never get anything on them we can use."

"Any clues? Forensics?"

The tall cop shrugged, "Whoever did it was wearing gloves. The only blood we found at the scene was your buddy's," he paused, "and the lady's."

His eyes narrowed suspiciously, "Where were you last night, Mr. Manley?"

"Fuck you!" Dave growled and, clutching Chris' arm, strode out of the restaurant.

They arrived at the hospital, which was only a few blocks away in a hurry, the tires squealing. They jumped out and ran for the entrance. The receptionist directed them to the nurses' station on the intensive care floor. Dave got the name of Tom's doctor and waited impatiently while he was paged. In a few minutes a young Indian doctor walked wearily up to them.

He led them into the small waiting room and sat down, exhausted. "Mr. and Mrs. Manley? I'm Doctor Patel. What can I do for you?"

"Tom Novak, tell me about him," Dave growled.

He looked from one to the other, "Are you next of kin?"

No," Dave replied. "He doesn't have any. His folks are dead and he doesn't have any brothers or sisters that I know of. I'm his best friend. Well, my wife, Chris and I."

The doctor nodded. He leaned forward, forearms on his knees. "I'll give you the simple version. If you want more details, ask, all right?

Both Dave and Chris nodded.

"He's in a coma. He was beaten badly. Worse than anybody I've ever seen." He shook his head, not wanting to meet Dave's fierce gaze. He went on, "He's got four broken ribs, a lot of bruising around the abdomen and kidneys, possible internal bleeding, damage to his kidneys and possibly a ruptured spleen. We're running some tests right now. His right leg is broken just above the ankle. I think he was hit with a club or bar. His fingers on one hand are broken. Looks like somebody jumped or stepped on it. But the worst is his head." He paused, eyes narrowing in disgust. "You sure you want me to go on?"

Dave nodded but Chris just sat there wide-eyed, nostrils contracted and whitened.

"Okay," the doctor sighed. "He was hit from behind.

Hard. Suffered a subdural hematoma. When he fell forward, he suffered a second and a brain contusion. We've drained them and I've given him medication to decrease the swelling and put him on a respirator. As I said, he's in a coma, and it's probably for the best. Gives him time to heal. We'll probably keep him under for some time until we're sure we've got the swelling under control." He wiped a hand across his eyes. "We'll do the best we can but, of course, there are no guarantees."

Chris wiped at her eyes, "You mean he could die?"

"I'm afraid so, Ma'am. I put his chances at 50/50, optimistically. But he looks to be in good shape and pretty tough, judging from the x-rays and his scars."

"What about Bobbi, his girlfriend?" asked Chris anxiously.

The young doctor shrugged, "She's got lots of bruises, a broken wrist and a clump of her hair was ripped out." He paused again and said bluntly, "She was raped. Probably gang-raped. Jesus, I wish I didn't have to tell you this."

Dave gripped his smock in a big hand and pulled him close, speaking softly, "Tell it all. Get it out once. I won't ask you again."

Chris gripped his iron hard forearm tightly and whispered softly, "David, let him go. I'm sure this is just as hard on him as us."

The doctor sat back astonished when Dave released him. "Please, Mr. Manley. I'm sorry. My sister was gang-raped a few years ago and, and it wasn't pleasant. I was on duty when they brought her in." He looked haunted, then his face flushed with resentment. "A few nights later they brought in one of her attackers. He'd been stabbed in the abdomen and I had to save the bastard's life!" He was pounding his small fist on his knee. He paused a minute to collect himself and get his breathing under control. "Miss Young had massive bruising to her vulva and tearing of the vaginal walls. She can't see. Do you know if she was blind?"

They both shook their heads no. "She was a nurse practitioner." Chris' voice was strained.

"Then it is probably hysterical blindness."

"Is it permanent?" Chris asked.

The doc shook his head, "No, it may pass in a few days. It must have been horrible what she had to watch. My sister was the same way."

"Can we see her?" asked Chris.

"I don't think you ought to for a couple of days. We're keeping her sedated also."

Dave stood, pulling Chris up with him. "Thanks, Doc." He held out his hand. The doctor placed his slim hand in his and gripped it firmly. "If he needs anything, if there's some test you think he needs, don't worry about insurance. Do it and let me know. I'll cover it." Dave handed the doctor a business card.

"Sure, Mr., Mrs. Manley. Leave a number at the nurses' station also where I can reach you. If anything changes, I'll notify you." And he turned on his heel and strode away, shoulders slumped.

Dave and Chris walked to the great windows of the intensive care unit and looked in. If they didn't know it was Tom, they wouldn't have recognized him with all the monitors and tubes going into him. The area reeked of hospital smell. The lighting was dim and the nurses seemed to glide on silent shoes. They watched the green blip of the monitor rise and drop, rise and drop.

Dave's heart hammered and he stood, digging his nails into his palms. He mouthed a silent promise to both Tom and Bobbi to get the people who did this.

CHAPTER 16

The Hunt: 1938

The next day Abel rode into town and parked in the dusty lot behind City Hall. He dressed in his best clothes and wore a white shirt and tie of Bob's at Martha's insistence. The building wasn't much to look at compared to the recently refurbished county court house. It was poured cement construction with broad steps leading up to the double sets of wide doors. Large windows looked over the square, grass starting to yellow in the warm sun. A pair of slowly moving Negroes pushed two lawn mowers over the grass in the center of the square, walking side by side and talking quietly. One wore a broad brimmed straw hat and had a thistle straw sticking out of his mouth. The other had a tattered felt hat and a chew of tobacco in his cheek. They both wore faded blue overalls with no shirts.

It was only nine o'clock and already uncomfortably warm. There was a large spreading tree in the small patch of lawn just outside of the city hall. Abel knew that it was known as the 'hanging tree', where runaway slaves and criminals had been put to death in the past. A poor legacy in a poor town, he mused. At least not as poor a town as the one he'd dropped Cuddy in. He wondered if the fellow was still alive.

He shrugged out of his coat and draped it over his arm, pushing through the shining doors. A hurrying young woman directed him to the stairs and up to the second floor where Avery Gibbons, the town's lawyer, had his office.

He announced himself to the secretary, who quickly walked into an oak-framed office. In a minute she was back and told him to wait a few minutes. He sat in a straight- back chair and smiled at her. She shyly smiled back, so he winked at her and asked if she knew who he was. She shook her head.

"I'm Abel Landis. I'm Bob Brightwater's brother-in-law." He waited for a reaction, which wasn't long in coming.

She half rose from her desk, "Oh, Mr. Landis, I'm so sorry about Bob. He was such a fine man. We all are just broken up by what happened." Her face was twisted in anguish. She waved a hand aimlessly.

"Thank you, Miss?" Abel slid forward on his chair.

"Knightington, Ann-Marie, Mr. Landis. Please call me Ann-Marie."

"And you can call me Abel, Ann-Marie." He grinned a boyish grin and tried to plaster his hair down.

Her eyes sparkled with tears, and he asked her if she

knew Bob well. She replied, "I worked every day with him for more than five years. I even went out to his house and had dinner with him and Martha and Junior, my boyfriend, a couple of times."

"That right?" Abel grinned at her, "Martha a good cook?"

"Oh, yes, sir. We had lobster tails. It was the season, you know."

Just then the door to Gibbons' office opened and the large man came out, offering his hand to Abel. Abel stood and they shook hands as they walked back into the law office. Abel winked over his shoulder at the dark-haired secretary.

Abel and the attorney sat. Abel waited while Gibbons lit his cigar. The office was fairly large, paneled in a dark wood. A ceiling fan turned lazily, and the air smelled of the ten or so cigars that had been consumed that day and all the countless others that had given their lives to the fat lawyer.

Abel shifted in his straight-backed wooden chair centered before the large oak desk.

"What can I do for you, Mr. Landis, is it?"

Abel considered the lawyer slouching in his padded swivel chair, keeping silent in the hopes of causing the lawyer to loose some of his composure. He didn't. Gibbons just sat and puffed, eyeing Abel through the acrid smoke.

Abel finally cleared his throat and said, "My sister thinks her husband was killed. She thinks the police didn't investigate because they had something to do with it or had something to hide." He sat back and crossed his legs letting that sink in. The smoke kept rising, forming a white or gray cloud under the fan, only to be broken up and thrown around the room.

The lawyer shifted his bulk and leaned forward, hands clasped on the desk in front of him. He peered earnestly at Abel from under bushy white brows. "The police did a thorough investigation and came up with suicide or an accident." The chair squeaked as though contradicting Gibbons.

"My sister says that nothing happened. Nobody came to see her with a report, except that lame-brain chief of police of yours, and that was to question her and then try to, um, get close to her." Abel narrowed his eyes, brow furrowing.

The lawyer removed the fat cigar and blew smoke at Abel, "Can't blame him. She's a handsome woman."

Abel pursed his lips and struggled to keep his temper. "Was there an autopsy?"

"Yes, sort of. Doc Hayward checked the usual stuff." He reached into a desk drawer and pulled out a file folder. He flipped over a couple of pieces of paper and handed a paper to Abel. "You do know how to read, don't you?"

Abel smirked, "Well, I'm a product of the local school system. 'Course that don't mean much any more." He ran his eyes down the single sheet of paper, noting the date, time, condition of the body, tissue destruction put down to fish bites, bruises and abrasions, scars and birthmarks. "It says here that he had a large bruise on the back of his neck. Doc say how it got there?"

Gibbons shrugged, "Maybe he floated into a rock or pier. Don't mean anything. See where it says that they found lots of water in his lungs?"

Abel nodded, finding this near the bottom of the page.

"He inhaled water. Can't breathe that stuff. He drowned, Mr. Landis. That's it. Case closed." He drew the sheet out of Abel's hand and put it back in the folder, flipping the cover closed.

Abel nodded thoughtfully, wondering why the lawyer had the file at hand right in his desk. He examined the conversation but came up empty. The answers were short but to the point, conclusions were logical. But something nagged at Abel. "What was he working on recently? I mean before he was killed?" asked Abel innocently.

The lawyer puffed on the stub of the cigar and looked at the ceiling, his face creased in a thoughtful frown. "Nothing unusual I can think of. Budget, or what passes for one these days; water and sewer contracts; pay slips; hell" he stuck his face out toward Abel, "I don't know, the usual. Ask Ann-Marie. She knows more than I do. I'm only the town's lawyer. Bob was the accountant. He counted things." He shook his shaggy head, "Gonna be damn hard to replace him." He struggled to his feet and stuck his hand out over the desk. Obviously the conversation was over. "Now if you'll excuse me, Mr. Landis, I've got work to do."

As Abel opened the door, he looked back and said, "If you can think of anything, Mr. Gibbons, please let me or Martha know, okay?"

Gibbons nodded absently, not bothering to look up. Abel quietly closed the door.

Ann-Marie was ready with a bright smile, half out of her seat. "If there's anything I can help you with, Mr. Landis, please let me know." She handed over a small piece of paper, which Abel stuffed into a pocket.

"Thank you, Miss Ann-Marie. I just might do that." He smiled a deliberately goofy grin, hitched his pants and straightened up, standing a little taller. Well, it looked like Miss Ann-Marie Knightington just might be a good girl to get to know! "Can you tell me where I can find this Doctor Hayward, the guy who did the autopsy on my brother-in-law?"

She smiled and said, "Sure, he's at the Laplant Hospital in the Pathology Department. It's on Druid Street, just off Fort Harrison." She waved her hand vaguely toward the south.

"Great!" He grinned, "And thanks. I hope to see you again, Miss Ann-Marie."

She blushed and smiled back, "I hope so too, Mr. Abel Landis," she said in a small voice.

Inside his office, Gibbons pulled his phone close to him and lifted the receiver. Puffing furiously on the fat cigar, he dialed the police headquarters.

"McBride," was all he said when a young woman answered the phone.

After only a couple of seconds, the Chief answered. He listened intently for a couple of minutes, nodded and hung up.

Abel was determined to find out all he could in as little time as possible. As he walked out of the city building, he rounded the corner, and there was a policeman writing a ticket, one foot propped up on the front fender of the cycle. "Hey, what the hell are you doing?" he shouted.

The cop eyed him from behind a pair of sunglasses, cap tipped back on his head. He kept writing.

"I asked you what you were doing."

"What the hell's it look like, sonny? I'm giving you a ticket." He pointed in the general direction of a sign that warned that cars parked more than ninety minutes were subject to violation and then it gave an ordinance number.

"But I've only been inside for no more'n thirty minutes," Abel complained, hands planted on his narrow hips.

"Ain't what I heard." The cop tore the ticket off his pad and folded it in half, then half again, thrust it into Abel's shirt pocket. He stood glaring back at Abel.

Abel smiled and said, "So that's how it's going to be, huh? Say, what's your name, pal."

The cop jerked a thumb at the patch sewn to his shirt. It read 'Rob't. Wilson'.

"Wilson, huh? Say, where you from, Bob? Out west someplace?"

"Yeah," the cop replied hesitatingly. "I last worked in Tulsa. That's in Oklahoma."

Abel nodded slowly and stuck out his hand. He gripped the cop's hand and pulled him close. "Be careful you don't get wrapped up in something you don't want to, Bob. This is between me and McBride and a couple of other fellers."

The cop pulled his hand away quickly. "I don't know nothin' about that. I'm only doing what I was told, I mean, just doin' my job, is all." He gestured at the ticket. "You got ten days to pay that. It's a dollar, is all." With that he turned and strode away to a couple year old sedan with the city logo on the door and drove off.

Abel shook his head and stuffed the ticket in his back pocket before climbing on his cycle and driving away, being careful to observe every stoplight and speed sign. In a few minutes after passing the ornate front of the Ft. Harrison Hotel, a Chevrolet dealer and a couple of junk shops he found the hospital.

He was directed to the basement in the rear where the morgue was located. Dr. Hayward was in his disordered glass-walled office. He was a small man, about Abel's height with sandy hair parted in the middle, thick glasses on the end of his prominent nose. His white lab coat had smears of what looked like blood on it where he'd wiped his hands. A couple of pencils peeked out of a pocket on the left breast.

Abel knocked twice on the door and the doctor raised his head quickly like a chicken, all jerky motions. He motioned for Abel to enter, same jerky motions. He didn't get up but paused to put a pencil down and leaned back in his chair, pulling a pack of cigarettes from a desk drawer. As Abel sat in a facing chair, the doctor offered him one, shaking the pack at him. Abel waved the proffered pack away, saying, "Sorry, gave 'em up a couple of years ago, but thanks anyway."

They sat looking at each other for almost a minute, Finally Abel leaned forward and said, "Tell me about the autopsy you performed on Bob Brightwater."

The doctor frowned, reached into a desk drawer and pulled out a frayed file folder. "Sure, but who are you, sir?"

"I'm his brother-in-law and don't shove that report at

me. I've already seen it in Gibbons' office. Tell me what's not in there."

The frown didn't leave his face and he looked around uneasily. "You know," he answered nervously, puffing on his cigarette until the tip glowed furiously, "this is only supposed to be for the police and next of kin."

Abel glared at him, "Well, just consider me the fucking next of kin, all right?"

Dr. Hayward gulped and started telling Abel what was on the report, elaborating on some details.

"And?" urged Abel.

The doctor gulped again and looked over Abel's shoulder to make sure the door was closed. He went on, "Two things struck me as odd, Mr....?"

"Just tell me, dammit."

"Okay, okay, take it easy. The first was the bruise on the back of his neck. Looked like impressions, bruises. We call 'em pitting edema, from fingers. Strong fingers." He was sweating now and his cigarette was almost burned down to his knuckles. "And the second thing was that most of the water in his lungs was fresh water." This last he barely whispered, eyes cast down.

Abel frowned and snatched the report off the desk. He flipped open the folder and rapidly scanned the sheet. "Why isn't that on the report?"

The doctor scratched his head nervously and muttered, "I was told to leave that part out. That it didn't matter."

"Didn't matter? Didn't fucking matter? Who told you that?" Abel was on his feet leaning across the desk, his face inches from the doctor's. He smelled the sour odor of tobacco, sweat and something else, fear. It was a sour smell, a smell like something had died in the doctor's mouth. Maybe it had. Maybe it was truth.

The doctor leaned as far back in his chair as he could, head against the shelves behind him and again mumbled, "The police chief. He was here with one of his men, Brodsky, I think was his name."

"Shit," spat out Abel. "Tell me more about the bruises on his neck."

"They weren't post-mortem," he answered hurriedly.

Abel frowned. "Does that mean that he had them before he died? They weren't from banging against rocks or something after he drowned?"

"No," the doctor mumbled again. Before Abel could comment, he said, "I was told to keep that out of the report, too."

Abel paced the small office. Finally he stopped and pointed a finger at the doctor, "Don't say anything about this to anyone, ya hear? And if I find out you called the coppers after I leave, you better hope to hell they kill me, 'cause if they don't, I'll sure as hell come back and do you in. You understand?"

The doctor nodded vigorously and said in a sick voice, "I understand." Then even sicker, hands shaking, he said in a low voice, "Oh, how did I get into this mess? I'm just a pathologist. I don't want any trouble." He had his face in his hands now, on the verge of tears.

Abel said in his meanest voice, "You just keep your mouth shut and you'll be okay."

CHAPTER 17

Follow the Money: 1938

In a short time he was back on the island. He stopped at the old dining car for a quick beer, though it was still early in the day. Scruffy sat on a tall stool mopping the dry bar absently, looking down at a cheap magazine propped up against a glass. He was munching a cinnamon bun, which sat partly eaten on a square of newspaper by his right hand.

"Oh, hullo, Abel. Kin I get you somethin'?"

Abel looked at the bun, then at Scruffy. "Well, I was going to wet my whistle with a beer, but I think I'll just have a sarsaparilla, Scruff. By the way, where'd you get the bun?"

"The bun? What bun?" he looked around bewildered.

Abel indicated the partially eaten pastry on the bar, "That one, yeah, where'd you get it?"

"Oh, that one. Well, Martha Brightwater stopped by to

see if I wanted to buy any for my customers." He guffawed. "I tole her I usually din't have many customers so she gave me one to try." He munched another bite. "It's pretty good! She brung me this magazine, too."

"'Course it's good. I showed her how to make 'em," Abel said proudly. But he was disturbed that she'd come into the bar without him. "When was she in?"

Scruffy considered this question carefully. He looked around absently for the clock that wasn't there. Then looked at the shafts of sunlight that patterned the floor. Finally he looked at Abel and answered, "Some time ago." And that was that. He hunched over the magazine again.

Abel prodded him again, "The sarsaparilla, please?"

After he finished his drink and elicited no more information from Scruffy Fett, Abel rode on slowly back to Martha's home. The bay was blue and sparkling in the high sunlight. Near the pass a pod of dolphins played, jumping nearly near clear of the water. A large turtle floated nearby and a brown pelican dove majestically into the water, scooping up a fish, which flopped half out of his large beak. What a beautiful place, Abel thought. In not too many more years, this place would probably be overrun with too damn many people.

Martha was busy rolling out dough on the floured white pine table when he breezed in. He recounted his meeting with Avery Gibbons and the doctor while wolfing down a sandwich. Then he started, "Mart, how come you stopped at the bar down the road? That place might be dangerous."

She gave a short laugh, "Dangerous? Who? Alfred Fett?" She laughed again and wiped her face, leaving a white smudge on her cheek. "Why, Alfred and I went to school together. He's harmless. Well, at least to me." She looked up at Abel from under her brows. "Beside, I promised I'd drop off a couple of more magazines to him later today or tomorrow."

"Magazines?" Abel exclaimed. "What the hell does Scruffy need with magazines? He can barely read."

Martha frowned at him, "Oh, now Abel, don't you go making poor jokes at Alfred's expense. He's had a very sad life. His parents died when he was fairly young. Then a drunken automobile driver killed his sister. He was such a bright boy in school, too."

She wiped her hands on the apron and dug a hand into a cloth bag of dark brown sugar, sprinkling it on the soft dough. Abel followed up with a heavy dusting of cinnamon then scooped up butter with a wooden spoon. Using a knife, he dropped small pats onto the waiting dough. Martha expertly rolled up the mixture and quickly cut the dough into one-inch slices, as Abel had taught her, placing them on the waiting greased flat pans. An hourglass indicated it was time to remove one load from the oven and another to go in. She exchanged the trays and the room quickly filled with the aroma of fresh baked pastry.

Abel leaned back in a chair and just inhaled deeply. "You know, Sis, if we could figure out how to bottle that smell, we'd be worth millions!" He grinned broadly, sniffing again. "Say, where is BB today?"

"Oh, he and Captain are fishing on the bay side with Sukie, you know, Captain's sister?"

"Okay," Abel said absently. He was trying to figure out his next step. He'd talked to Bob Brightwater's boss, the lawyer, Avery Gibbons, and the pathologist, Dr. Hayward. He sighed and figured the logical next stop was the police station. He hated to beard McBride in his own domain, but the parking ticket gave him at least some legitimacy and reason for going there.

And he still needed to figure out if and why Bob had been killed. It was usually money, he thought. Find out and follow the money.

CHAPTER 18

Declaration of War: Present Day

Back at Chesney's, Chris and Dave held a war council with their friends and neighbors. Chris and Dave sat at one end of the large oval table. Beside Dave sat Rusty and then his wife, Anna. They lived on a big old restored WWII era PT boat tied up at the end of the T-dock. Across from them sat Vinny and Joan. Vinny was an ex-plumber and Korean War veteran. They lived on a beautiful 42' Gulfstar sailboat in slip #3. Charlie Potts, the cook, sat in, his ample belly spilling over his tightly tied apron, and a rolled sailor hat perched on the back of his round head. Emile LeDuc was next. He lived with a continually changing coterie of women on an old Krogen trawler in slip #2. Emile was the resident computer whiz.

Dave addressed them, "Well, I guess by now you all know what happened to Tom and his girl." They nodded grimly. "I have to do something. I cannot let this pass without response." This last was a simple declaration. Dave's fists were clenched tightly on the table. Chris gently put a hand on one of his.

"I'm afraid I have to agree with David," she said quietly. "We've spoken to the police but they can't do anything." She sighed deeply, "You know this will go down into their books as "unidentified assailants".

"What have you got in mind, Dave?" Rusty asked, leaning forward, his meaty forearms resting on the dark table. His wife, Anna, tipped her curly red head forward, intently.

"Yeah, Dave, you wanna go whack these guys or what?" Vinny was from South Brooklyn and grew up surrounded by mob guys.

His wife, Joan, slapped him on the arm, "Oh, don't be a dope. Dave isn't going to go whacking anybody." She looked fiercely at Dave. "You're not, are you?"

Dave hemmed and hawed, "Well, not exactly, Joanie. But we might make them wish they were dead." He scratched his head, then his thin beard. They all knew a plan was forthcoming. "The way I see it, we've got a twofold job." He ticked them off on his fingers, "First, we need to identify all the perps. Second, we need to make them disappear." He looked expectantly around the table.

Vinny asked, "We gonna torture them?" He looked a little sick.

Joan smacked him on his skinny arm again, "No, you dumb Guinea, we ain't gonna torture them, are we, Dave?"

Dave smiled a crooked smile, "Well, yes, in a manner of speaking, we are."

He grinned at their shocked expressions. Then he leaned forward and wiggled his eyebrows, "Then they're going to disappear – for good." He used his best pirate voice. It only took a half-hour to disclose the outline of his plan. Charlie Potts and Rusty whooped with glee. The women were disappointed at the small role for them in this plan. Dave placated them. "Your roles are crucial to this plan, and you'll be out of harm's way." Before they could protest, he held up a hand, "If anything goes wrong, if the Brotherhood figures out it's us, we'll be in deep doggy doo for a long time to come. They'll come at us with every lawyer at their disposal. We could all lose everything." He looked around. "Anybody want out, now's the time to speak up." Silence filled the air. One by one, heads shook.

The next evening, in a borrowed cube van with carefully painted Brotherhood logos on large magnetic signs stuck on the doors, Chris pulled into a parking lot behind a Brotherhood dormitory, formerly a pleasant motel on the outskirts of Clearwater. Dave and Rusty wore Brotherhood uniform jumpers and had flesh colored silk facemasks rolled up on their heads. Long minutes later Chris quietly called back, "Here they are. Only two. Nobody else around. They're the two who fought with Tom at the bar."

Dave and Rusty quickly exited the rear door and strode across the parking lot, pulling the masks down over their faces. Dave pulled a small .38 revolver out of his pocket and held it against his trouser leg. They came up behind the two laughing security guards.

Dave stuck the gun in the taller guard's ribs and whispered, "Don't make a fuss. Just turn and walk to the white van." Rusty did the same, stabbing into the shorter guard's rib with his blunt finger.

The guards stopped in their tracks and began to raise their arms. "Put your fucking hands down and move it." Dave jabbed the gun harder. As the guards hesitated, Dave said quietly, "Don't even think about it. Just think about not dying in the next five minutes."

The air went out of the two guards, they turned and walked back toward the van, Dave and Rusty right behind them, crowding them. When they reached the rear of the van, Dave urged them up and in. Then Rusty and Dave climbed in behind them and lowered the door. Dave quickly used two large cable ties to secure both guard's wrists behind them. Then using a second pair, he secured their feet together. Rusty nodded at Dave. Chris was driving around the city and finally up the main north/south highway. In a few minutes she slowed and Rusty jumped out the front door. She watched him jump in a car in which Vinny was driving and speed away. Phase one was complete and phase two was in progress. It would take about an hour to set it up. Her job was to just drive around.

In the rear, Dave started questioning the two immobile guards. First he took his facemask off. "Look at me, you two pieces of shit!" he barked.

Their heads snapped around and glared at him. "Fuck you!" the tall guard spat.

Dave held the gun nonchalantly in his right hand. "The

reason I took this mask off is because I want you to see me. I want you to recognize me. Do you know why?"

The shorter, younger guard started to cry. "You're one of the guys from the bar. Oh, Jesus, we are so fucked."

"That's right. He knows." Dave indicated the crying guard to the taller one. It suddenly dawned on the taller guard and he gulped, his Adam's apple bobbing.

"But before we do the deed, I need some information. This is called the easy way or the hard way time." He leaned forward, forearms on knees, "This isn't the movies or TV. This is for real. You will tell me or you will die, understand?"

"Why should we tell you anything? You're just going to kill us anyway." The taller guard glared defiantly at Dave.

"Because I need information. I need it in a hurry, and there's a slim chance I might let you live." Dave emphasized slim.

"What do you want to know?" the shorter guard blubbered.

The tall guard looked at him scornfully, "Shut up, Dennis. Pussy-boy," he muttered.

Dave shook his head sorrowfully, "Now that's the kind of attitude that'll get you killed fast." He held the gun up to the head of the tall guard who winced. "Look, kid, if I blow your partner's brains out all over this van, will you tell me what I want to know?"

The short guard nodded rapidly.

"Good, because I only need one of you, understand?" Dave asked.

Chris pulled the van into the huge parking garage at the nearby airport and went round and around until they were on the rooftop parking. It was evening and nearly deserted. She backed the van in until the rear hit the guard railing with a jar. She checked her watch. They had just over an hour. She reached back and knocked twice on the separating wall. The burly Anna climbed into the rear of the large van shoving a diminutive figure before her. The figure was clad in the green uniform of the Brotherhood's high-ranking administrative staff. All her decorations were correct down to the ornamental sword in its sheath. Her head was covered by a black facemask and her hands were tied behind her in a similar manner to the two guards. Anna tore the facemask off.

Dave grinned at the guards. Anna stood to one side of the rear door. She wore a white jumpsuit and a white facemask, white boots and white gloves. She had a large automatic pistol tucked in a white holster at her side. "Now boys, either you tell me what I want to know or we'll throw you out the back and down, down you'll go.

"You don't have the guts," sneered the tall guard.

"I'll tell you. I'll tell you. Anything," the shorter guard cried. He was breathing rapidly now, looking from one to the other, Dave to Anna. "He did it!" he cried pointing at the tall guard. "Not me, I didn't do anything."

"Good, good. That's my boy. Now who was with you two the other night when you beat up my friend Tom Novak and his girlfriend?" Dave smiled beatifically at the two.

The shorter guard groaned, "It wasn't me. They didn't let me go with them. Said I was too young." He started crying again. "Don't kill me. Please don't kill me," he pleaded.

"Except for Andy here, I don't know any of the other guys. All I know was there were five altogether. Please don't kill me."

"Shut up," Dave said harshly. He turned his full attention to the tall guard. "Now, Andy, is it? Who are the other guys?"

"Fuck you, I don't know shit. You ain't goin' to toss me over. You ain't got the balls." He spat at Dave. Anna kicked him in the side eliciting a loud grunt.

Dave sighed in resignation, "Andy, my boy, you're right. I don't. That's why we brought Huey." He looked regretfully at the defiant guard. Dave leaned across the guard and knocked twice on the side of the van. Chris started it and pulled forward a couple of feet. Anna reached down and yanked the rear door up. A shuffling was heard outside and a huge shadow blotted out the twilight. A large gloved hand gripped the side of the van doorframe and a figure swung into view. Huey was huge, easily seven and a half feet tall and bulky. He had white gauze wrapped around his face and some yellowish goo leaked through in several places. Huey growled deep in his throat and placed a huge foot on the rear bumper. The van squatted under his weight.

Dave casually pointed the barrel of his gun at the now white-faced guards struggling on the floor. The uniformed woman opened her mouth to scream but no sound came out, just gasps. Huey bobbed his head and reached into the van. Even Dave backed away. The woman kicked out with her foot and Huey reached down and dragged her out the back.

"No, Huey, not that one," Dave shouted in a panic.

"This first," Huey replied in a deep hoarse voice, grabbing the woman by an armpit and easily swung her back over the rail and dropped her. Without looking back, he reached for the tall guard's leg and began to pull him back also. The guard was yelling and gasping for breath. His pants blossomed a widening urine stain as the huge gloved hands pulled first one leg then the other. The shorter guard was strangely calm as Dave looked at him. Passed out from fear.

"Don't, don't, please," the tall guard implored. "I'll tell you everything. I'll tell you anything you want! Oh, God, please don't let him kill me."

Dave rose and grabbed one of Huey's bulky arms, "Wait, wait, Huey. I need some information from him." He straddled the guard and shoved back at Huey.

Huey looked up from his work. "Not kill?" He hesitated, waiting for a sign from Dave.

Dave turned to the two guards. "I want the names of the other assholes who beat up my friends, then I might be able to hold Huey off, but not for long. Understand?"

"Yes, yes, yes, anything you want." While he gave Dave the names of the other guards in on the rampage and the name of the official in the Brotherhood who'd ordered it, Dave just stared into the guard's eyes. Oh, this time he was telling the truth! Dave kept one hand on Huey's huge overall-clad front, trying to hold the enormous man back. Huey kept opening and closing his hands and grunting deep in his chest.

Chris thumped on the wall twice when the tall guard was finished. Dave turned to Huey and pushed him back against the railing. "Huey, stay, please." Then he turned to the two guards and demanded, "If, and I say if, I let you go, here is what you will do. You will get on planes for your hometowns." He pushed his face right up against the taller guard's face. "You will leave Florida and never come back. You will not call the Brotherhood. You will not call any of your friends there. We have a contact inside and will know if you do." He pushed the gun up under the guard's chin. "If I ever hear your names again, Huey here," and he gestured over his shoulder at the grunting giant, "will visit you and your families, and you won't have me to stop him. Do you fucking understand?"

Both men nodded rapidly, looking over Dave's shoulder all the time. Dave removed four one hundred dollar bills from his pocket and stuffed them into the tall guard's shirt pocket. He then pulled a pair of wire cutters from his rear pocket and clipped the cable ties from the men's wrists. In a flash they were out the back and edging past Huey who made a half-hearted lunge for them. They ran fast across the dark parking lot and almost fell into a waiting elevator. When Dave saw that the door was closed, he knocked on the side of the van twice. Chris came into the back from the front seat, Joanie came around the back of the van rubbing her arm.

"Ya didn't have to grab me so hard, ya big lunkhead!" she slapped Huey's huge arm. "Here, let me help ya get out of that rig." She began unbuttoning the plaid shirt and slid the overall straps off Huey's huge shoulders. When the shirt was open and the large denims were in a pile on the ground, Huey stood tall. Vinny unwrapped his feet from Rusty's back and jumped down with some help from Joan. She helped him slip off the football shoulder pads and unwrap the gauze from his face.

Anna just leaned against the rear wall and laughed, a hand covering her mouth. “You guys were great! I almost wet my pants looking at you. When Rusty grabbed Joanie and dropped her over the rail, I thought that big guard would have a heart attack.”

“Yeah, the net one floor below was just the ticket. Good thing they didn’t look over the rail on their way out!” Joan chuckled.

Dave drawled, “Well, I don’t think we’ll hear from those two guys again. If we’d asked them to run home, they would have!”

“You’d better not take out any more of them until Tom gets better,” said Chris.

“Why not?” asked Joanie.

Chris stopped and chose her words carefully, “I think for Tom to stay Tom, he needs to do some of this himself. For him to believe in himself, he has to heal, then find some of those who beat him. I don’t quite know how to put this, but he has to make things right in his own mind.”

“You’re really saying that he has to seek his own revenge and not depend on us, right?” said Dave.

“Something like that, but I think that we’ll have to be there to help him.”

“Well, you know that I’ll have to back him up,” answered Dave, looking around at the others.

Rusty and Vinny nodded, understanding exactly what Dave was saying.

"Why can't we just do these guys for him?" asked Anna. "Then he'll have nothing to worry about when he gets better."

Dave just shook his head, "Nope, we can get all the intelligence for him, assist him, but he has to do this himself."

"But suppose he dies? Or doesn't get better?"

Dave smiled, "Oh, well, then it will be up to us. Remember, we'll be doing this for Bobbie too."

CHAPTER 19

Bringing in the Press: 1938

The next day, Abel rode out across the causeway, the morning sun in his eyes. The day was already warm and was going to be a scorcher. Maybe the afternoon would bring some breeze or even a shower off the water. Tonight might even be a good time for a swim with the boys. He passed a police car with its light blinking by the side of the road, a fat cop giving a ticket to a slender girl, one foot propped on the running board of a snappy looking couple year old blue Ford Cabriolet. She glanced at Abel as he went by and gave a small limp wave that the cop couldn't see. He nodded and recognized the girl as Anne-Marie. He wondered at the ticket. Didn't Gibbons have enough pull in this burg to get his secretary some immunity?

He decided to go see the newspaper editor before he went to the police station. Usually the editors knew everything that was happening in a small town. When he filled up the cycle at the same Sinclair station, the same red-headed kid pumped and took his money.

"Say, kid, I was wondering where I might find the newspaper office." He took the kid's rag and wiped a little spilled gas off the tank.

The young fellow pointed down the street at the arcade building. "It's in there, mister. Editor's name is Mr. Perkins. Why, ya wanna sell this here cycle?"

Abel looked up at the young lad, "Naw, not just yet. Need it to get around. Why? You interested?"

"Mebbe," he replied tucking the rag back in his rear pocket. "What's yer name?"

Abel stuck out his hand, "Name's Abel Landis. And yours?"

"Billy Herbert, Mister Landis. Pleased ta meetcha."

"You got wheels now?" Abel asked casually.

"Naw, just a push-bike. Like t' get me a Harley-Davidson motorcycle some day. I got me some money saved up. Keep me in mind, will ya?" With that he turned and walked back to the office.

Abel sat and watched him for a long minute. Something told him there was a tad more to Mr. Billy Herbert than met the eye. He started the cycle and eased off down the street to the arcade. He parked behind an old T-Model touring car and turned a wheel into the curb.

Johnny Livingston came out to serve a couple in a two-tone green Chevrolet and gave Abel a wave and a howdy. Abel waved back and entered the hallway between the small shops. At the end he spotted the newspaper office. The sign painted on the glass read "Clearwater Courier". He glanced around and saw an office with a sign for the editor, Arthur M. Perkins. Perkins was hunched over his desk, his thinning hair falling over his forehead. He had a pair of garters on his sleeves to keep the lower parts tight and out of the inked pages he was marking. When Abel knocked, Perkins motioned but didn't look up.

Abel slid in quietly and eased the door shut. He stood before the desk, his leather hat and goggles in his hands. He waited patiently.

Finally, with a flourish of his pencil, Perkins glanced up and said, "If you've got news, give it to the kid out front. If you've got money, give it to Molly, the lady in the corner office. If you want a job, we ain't hiring. Now, just what do you want?"

Abel was used to newspaper people. Very few of them were overly courteous. He'd done some drawings for some a few years ago. He smiled, "Mr. Perkins, I need some information. I hope you'll be able to help me."

Perkins looked up and leaned back in his chair, lighting a cigarette. "Why should I, Mr…?"

Abel pondered this for a minute, mouth pursed, then said, "Mind if I sit down?"

Perkins gestured toward a beat up straight-backed chair facing the desk.

Abel put his helmet and goggles on the corner of the desk and leaned forward, "I'm Bob Brightwater's brother-in-law, Abel Landis. His wife, my sister Martha, asked me to look into his, shall we say, unfortunate demise. I thought maybe you could kinda fill me in on some of the characters involved, the circumstances surrounding his death, and what was reported in your paper."

Perkins considered this, blowing smoke at the ceiling. Then he leaned forward and pointed his cigarette at Abel's chest. "You going to make some trouble in this town, boy?"

Abel grinned and said, "I certainly hope so, sir."

Perkins grinned back and said, "What exactly do you know and what do you want to know?"

"First off," Abel started, "did you know Bob?"

He snorted, "Course I knew him. Everybody downtown here knew Bob. Good man. Good family man. Good accountant for the town, too." He paused, lighting another cigarette off the tip of the butt. "He was here the day before he died. Came in asking about the water and sewer contract out to the beach. I told him stuff he already knew or should have known. Johnny Livingston says that Arnie Brodsky grabbed him after he left here. That's the last anybody saw him. The Chief says he talked to him and then let him go. Next thing anyone knows, he's found floating in the bay."

Abel said, "I talked to Doc Hayward yesterday. He said that Bob's lungs were full of water."

"Yeah, I got to look at a copy of the autopsy report too. Didn't say much." He leaned back again.

"What it didn't say," Abel went on, "was that most of the water was fresh water."

"Hmm, that's interesting. Doc didn't say nothing about

that when I talked to him."

Abel grinned again, "I maybe kind of encouraged him to spill his guts; I mean, be a little more forthright about his autopsy."

Perkins eyebrows lifted. "You don't say? What else did he say?"

Abel shook his head, "Mr. Perkins, before I go on, I want you to do me a favor. I want all this to be off the record until I give you the okay to print it"

"Aw come on, kid, I'm running a newspaper here. I'm trying to make a living." He made a dismissive gesture at Abel.

"Nope, that or nothing, Mr. P. I'll give you all I've got. You tell me all that your snooping comes up with and I'll tell you what I find out. In the end, you can print it all. That's the deal."

Perkins leaned across the cluttered desk and asked, "And what happens if you're right and Bob was killed? What happens if whoever did him in kills you too?"

Abel shrugged and said, "Then you can print it all, and keep digging on your own."

"Oh, thanks, and then they can lay me out alongside you." He thought for a long minute, then said, "Okay, Landis, but if things get hot, you better start checking in with me pretty often. If I'm not here, leave anything you've got with Bernie out there at the counter. He's a bright kid." He stopped and gave a fake smile and a little wave to Bernie, a scrawny kid with spiky hair and a prominent Adam's apple who was looking their way.

Abel looked over his shoulder and said, "He doesn't

look too bright."

"Yeah, that's his forte. Everybody thinks he's dumb, so they talk a lot when he's around." He sighed, "When are people going to learn?" He shook his head wearily, "All right, so who do you want to know about?"

For the next half-hour, Abel grilled Perkins about the Mayor, Police Chief, Gibbons, the coppers, some of the people he'd met and the office staff. He found out that the Mayor was married, had three kids, one of whom died last year at age eleven or twelve. That McBride was universally disliked and gave out very little police information. That Ann-Marie and Ada, who was the police secretary, were first cousins. That the coppers were all brought in by McBride and were probably not former policemen. That two young girls had disappeared in the last year-and-a-half. That they were Negroes, but the word put out by the police was that the girls were whores who ran away from home. This was thought to be a wild guess, as the girls were only twelve and thirteen, the same age as Sally Mae, the lawyer's daughter who died. The police had no explanation for her death. In fact, remarked Perkins, there seemed to be little investigation of the disappearances or death.

Abel frowned and said, "Doesn't it seem just a little strange to you, Mr. Perkins, that there are so many disappearances of young girls in so short a time?"

"I thought so, too, but we are in some hard times and the kids may have just run away from home to find something better." It even sounded weak to him.

Abel scratched his chin. "Maybe the Negro girls? And

as young as they were? I don't know, Mr. Perkins. Sounds fishy." After a minute of silence he asked, "Did you do any digging? Did any of them have a boyfriend or not get along with their parents or friends out of town where they could have hopped a ride or a bus? Did they have any money of their own?"

Perkins held up a slim hand, "Whoa, easy, boy. I asked around a little, more for background for the story in the paper. Put young Bernie there on it for a couple of days.

"He said he couldn't find out much." He leaned back, packed a slim pipe and flicked a wooden match on the underside of the center desk drawer in a practiced motion.

Abel slid to the front of his chair, "Well, we're kinda getting off the subject, that being Bob's getting himself killed. Anything suspicious you can think of? Money problems somewhere in this town?"

Perkins shook his head again, "Nope. Nothing that wasn't caused by the depression. Everybody's broke these days. Good thing the feds are coughing up dough to put the water and sewers to the Beach. It'll give jobs to some local folks who can sure use them."

"Did Bob say anything about the city wasting money on those projects?"

Perkins eyed him warily. "Well, maybe, but it sure doesn't have anything to do with him now, does it?" He knew that they were getting way off the track, but Arthur Perkins had been longing for someone to discuss this problem with. They had tossed it around at the office but had dropped it a couple of months ago. It still rankled him and he was glad for Abel's, an outsider's, view. He thought that maybe with a fresh look at all the available facts, speculations and rumors, he might be able to make some sense of it. The police didn't seem to care one way or the other. Maybe this Abel guy could shed some new light on the disappearances. He considered and said, "I'll tell you what, Landis. How's about you do some pokin' around, you know, see what you can dredge up. I'll do the same and we'll get together and compare notes."

Now it was Abel's turn to consider. He was new in town, hardly knew anyone, trusted no one except maybe Martha and BB, which sure wouldn't be much help. He figured Perkins saw him as expendable but that couldn't be helped. Perkins could be a valuable ally and resource and he thought, what did he have to lose? He reached a hand across the desk and said, "Okay, Mr. Perkins. I'll see what I can come up with, but understand that my main objective is to find out if Bob was murdered and if so, who did it."

Perkins nodded and took his hand and gave it a squeeze. "Anything else I can do for you right now, kid?"

Abel thought for a minute and grinned, "Just one other thing. My sister got left without a plugged nickel. I've been….."

Perkins held up a hand and said gruffly, "Don't look to me for a handout, Landis. These days, if I was to give every poor, deserving soul a handout, I'd be broke in a week."

"No, that's not what I want. See, Martha's been baking up some mighty sweet pastries for the hotel out on the north end of the beach. I thought that maybe you could give her a couple inches of advertising once in a while, you know, to kinda help her along." He sat back and waited.

Perkins shrugged and said, "Why not? But you'll have to keep me supplied too."

Abel laughed, taking in the skinny editor, "Sure, I'll bring you a bag of whatever she's baking whenever I come into town, how's that?" The deal was struck and Abel got to his feet.

As he was leaving, Perkins shouted after him, "Be careful around that McBride. I hear he's a mean one."

Abel already knew that, but his next stop was the police station. He had to confront McBride sometime or another. Might as well get it over with. Besides, he had to pay his dollar fine.

Chapter 20

The Plan: Present Day

A week later the hospital called Dave and Chris. They were told that Tom had regained consciousness. They immediately left for the hospital to see him and his lady friend, Bobbie. They were still in the ICU and Tom had barely woken. Dave pulled up a chair alongside the bed and put his face close to Tom's. "You in there, old buddy?"

Tom lay on his back, tubes and monitors and bags and bandages all doing what they were supposed to be doing, Dave guessed. Tom's head was swathed in gauze bandages. His left hand was strapped to a board and also wrapped. His right leg was in a cast and raised by a pulley at the end of the bed.

Dave couldn't see the wrapped ribs, nor any more bandages. The flesh around Tom's eyes was a weird shade of purple and yellow, what he could see of it. Tom opened the eye on Dave's side and blinked twice. He wriggled the fingers of his good hand that lay on top of the sheet. It, too, was discolored and the skin on the knuckles had bandages wrapped loosely. Dave slipped his hand into Tom's and bit down hard on his lips to keep from crying out in rage. His friend was badly hurt and would take a long time to heal. A long, long time. But Dave knew he would one day be 100% again and God help the remaining four assailants.

Pulling his chair closer, Dave put his lips to Tom's ear and told him what they had done. Tom listened without moving. Dave couldn't tell whether he heard him or not. Finally when he was done, Tom squeezed his hand once.

Tom's lips moved slightly. Dave put his ear close. "Bobbie?" Tom whispered.

Dave looked at Chris. Tears were rolling down her face, though she didn't make any noise. He leaned in again and repeated what the doctor had told him.

All Tom said was okay. He squeezed Dave's hand again and Dave put his ear close to his lips again. "Tall guy, about thirty-five, black hair, mustache. Other guys called him Mac. Leader." Dave looked him in the eyes, what he could see.

"We'll take care of the others and save him for you, okay?"

Tom squeezed Dave's hand one last time and seemed to fall asleep almost instantly. The machines continued their chirping and burping.

Dave rose and clasped Chris to him in a fierce hug. She started crying harder and seemed to shrink in his arms, quivering. He stroked her hair and didn't let himself do the same.

He wanted to. Lord how he wanted to just break down, but he couldn't. He had a list of names he had to take care of. They let themselves out of the room as a nurse came in to check on her patient. Dave stopped her and said, "Whatever he needs, just give it to him." He stuck a folded hundred-dollar bill into her hand. She looked and nodded.

After checking in on Bobbie, who was still unconscious, they left and silently drove back to the marina in Sunset Pointe, each lost in their own thoughts. Dave had never seen Tom like this and it left him feeling shaken. Tom always seemed invincible to him. Even in 'Nam, Tom had always seemed to be the survivor, the jokester. Sure, he'd been wounded before, just not seriously. Dave remembered one-time Tom had crash landed a small transport plane and they'd had to cut the cockpit to pieces to extract him and his dead co-pilot. He'd been joking with the rescue crew. They'd taken him to a field hospital with lots of bruises and lacerations, but three days later, he'd been hobbling around, and a week after that was flying again. "One lousy SAM missile isn't going to ruin my whole day!" he'd declared.

By the time they returned home, Chris was cried out. She felt foolish and exhausted; angry and sad. She wanted to do something, something bad. She turned to Dave in the seat and put a hand on his arm after he'd turned the motor off. The silence was only broken by the waves slapping against the pilings and the ticking of the cooling engine. "What are we going to do, David? My God, he looked so helpless. Usually he's the one to bail us out." She sniffled, "Now we have to help him. Him and Bobbie. Christ, I don't even know her and I feel like they did to me what they did to her." She slumped back against the cool leather seat, resting her head against the headrest.

Dave sat back, too. "I don't know, babe. I feel like killing the whole damn bunch. We're going to have to get past this anger part and do some real planning. I don't know how I'm going to ever not be angry with these guys but we've got to decide what to do rationally. Remember, we're still up against a huge, rich organization. By now, they'll know what happened, but may not yet know who did it. But they will soon. The real security at the Brotherhood isn't the guys in the tunics. They won't want one bit of this to get out or the public will crucify them."

"So what do you think will happen?"

"I don't know for sure but my guess is that they'll probably get these bastards out of town as soon as they find out. The guards probably aren't in any hurry for their higher-ups to find out what they did but I guess we'll have to get the other four guys before they leave town."

"But Tom wants us to leave the leader for him," Chris said.

"I know, and we will, but we can't let the other three just walk. I've got the beginnings of a plan. Let's go inside and talk to the gang." Dave swung open the door of his Ford Station Wagon and strode to the rear door of Chesney's, followed by Chris.

Chapter 21

McBride: 1938

Abel carefully parked in a free zone and shut the old cycle down. He looked at the police station on the backside of the courthouse. It was red brick with white painted doors. You had to walk up several steps to get in, and Abel took his time. It was with a sense of foreboding that he went inside. The first person he saw was a young woman at a long counter-desk off to his left. She was in her mid twenties, had curly brown hair and a high-necked blouse with puffy sleeves. She would have been pretty except she had a hooked nose and a red birthmark on the side of her face and neck. She looked up as Abel entered, and he smiled at her. There was no nameplate on her desk but a paper sign above it said Pay Fines Here.

He pulled the folded piece of paper from his shirt pocket and handed it to her. She glanced at it and without looking up, said in a deep voice, "Illegal parking? That will be one dollar, please, sir."

Abel shook his head and said with a grin, "I want to see the chief about this."

Behind her, leaning on another desk, was a uniformed policeman. He eased to his feet and slowly came over. He was chewing on the stub of a cigar. It stuck out of his fat cheek. His uniform was clean and dark blue, the tie carefully knotted and his badge polished to a high shine, as were his shoes and belt buckle. He was intimidating in a fat cop way, Abel thought. Why did they always have to be fat? Was that to show that they lived by feeding at the public trough? Abel hated fat cops. They seemed to always be the worst ones. This one, with his pig eyes, bristly yellow hair and thick fingers embodied everything Abel detested in a cop.

His name tag said Huffman. He snatched the paper out of the young girl's hand, looked at it and said, "Says here you owe the city a dollar, bub. Pay it and get out or go to court." He dropped the ticket back on the desk next to the girl.

Abel stood up a little straighter. "I'd still like to see the Chief," he said quietly, not backing down. The girl looked scared and eased her chair away from the pair.

"Oh yeah? What for? You got a beef with the ticket?" Huffman leaned across the counter, resting his considerable weight on his fists. His ears reddened and a slight twitch began in his right eye.

Abel also leaned forward and growled, "Listen, Huffman, I got no beef with you. I want to see the chief about a personal matter. Just tell him Abel Landis is here. He'll see me."

Huffman eyed him warily for a minute, then heaved himself up. He seemed about to say something else when the girl got to her feet and said, "Just a minute, Mister, I'll tell him," and she scurried away through an archway in the rear of the room. Huffman and Abel stood eyeing each other.

"You know, you aren't very friendly to your taxpayers, are you?" Abel asked innocently.

Huffman leaned over the counter again and said, "I ain't in the friendly business, Bub." He eyed Abel's worn clothes and said, "You don't look like much of a taxpayer to me anyhow."

Before Abel could reply, he saw the girl approach. She said quietly, "It's okay, Officer Huffman. Chief McBride said for me to bring him back to his office."

Abel opened a low gate in the railing that separated the waiting area from the working area and followed the girl's back. She had on a pleated dark blue skirt and low, scuffed black shoes. She was tall and slim and wore no jewelry of any kind. Abel moved up beside her, and she whispered out of the corner of her mouth, "Ann-Marie called me and said you might be coming over. My name is Ada, Ada Griver. If I can help you, Ann-Marie can get in touch with me. I don't have a phone at home. Don't call me here. The chief sometimes listens in on calls." As she left him at the door to the chief's office she put a slim, pale hand on his arm and whispered again, "Be careful."

Abel didn't bother knocking, just opened the oaken and

glass door and strode in, letting the door close behind him. McBride sat at a large dark wood desk, smoking a cheroot. His black western hat was on a hat rack behind him, partly covering a pair of six shooters with white bone handles in polished leather holsters. On either side were flag poles, one with a stars and stripes and the other the state flag. The office was large and neat. A map of the city and outlying area was on one wall, and a big window looked out on the busy city street. In one corner was a low pine trestle-style table with three wicker chairs surrounding it and in another was a higher table with magazines and books in neat piles. Abel pulled a wooden chair up opposite McBride and sat.

McBride looked just the same to Abel though he hadn't seen him in ten years or so. McBride still dressed in a long black coat, white shirt with a string tie and, he guessed, western boots. McBride was about ten years Abel's senior, had a narrow face, a thin mustache and a broken veined nose. His lips were thin and colorless with a slight overbite. Black, slicked back hair covered the bony scalp and the dark eyes pierced Abel like a pair of arrows. Inside Abel gulped but didn't let it show. This was a dangerous man.

He said, "So Landis, long time, eh?" A small smile played around the corners of his mouth.

"Yep. Unfortunately not long enough, McBride."

McBride smiled showing a mouthful of yellow teeth, "It's Chief McBride now, sonny. Try to show a little respect."

Not after what you've done to me, Abel thought. He just sat there a long minute staring at the chief and said, "Nope. I just tried and can't seem to find any. Sorry." He sighed and sat down on the edge of the hard wooden chair. Abel leaned forward resting his forearms on the desk. "Look McBride, we've had our differences in the past but all I'm here for is to try to find out what happened to my sister's husband, Bob Brightwater."

McBride stopped trying to smile and narrowed his eyes, "Brightwater drowned," he said harshly. "That's it. End of the story." He cut the air with a slash of his hand.

Abel nodded tiredly, "Yeah, yeah, I know, but there are some, shall we say, inconsistencies in the official report. As soon as I get them cleared up, I'll be out of here." He thought for a minute and said, "I'd like to talk to a copper named Arnie Brodsky, if you don't mind."

"Look, Landis, my boys are really busy and don't have time for this kind of bullshit. Your brother-in-law's dead. Get over it." He stood, towering over Abel.

Abel kind of figured the interview was finished, but he wanted to give it one last good try. "So you have no explanation why Bob had fresh water in his lungs or hand-shaped bruises on his neck?" This last was a reach, but he wanted to see if he could get some kind of reaction out of the Chief. He thought he saw a flash of something in the Chief's eyes but it was quickly replaced by that same deadly glare.

McBride waited a beat, then called, "Karl? You out there?"

The floor squeaked in protest as Huffman came around the corner and flung open the door. "Yeah, Chief, you wanted me?" His hand was itchy and was reaching for the gun on his wide hip. When he saw the Chief and Abel just standing there, he relaxed a little but kept his hand hovering above the gun butt.

"Yeah, Karl, would you mind showing Mr. Landis to the door?" He sat back down at his desk and ignored them, feigning pressing paperwork.

Huffman took Abel roughly in a viselike grip and nearly dragged him out of the office and down the short hall. "Asshole, doesn't pay to piss off the Chief," he muttered.

"Gimme that dollar and you can go."

They stopped at the counter and Abel gave the girl a dollar bill and winked at her as he did so, not letting the hulking cop see him. She stifled a startled smile and quickly scribbled a receipt. Abel thanked her and Karl led him to the door, roughly shoving him through and out onto the portico.

Interesting, thought Abel. Maybe this girl, Ada, could get him some information when he needed it. He pulled out the crumpled piece of paper that Ann-Marie had given him with her phone number and, with a stub of pencil, added Ada's name to it. Not having much more to do in town, Abel headed back to the beach. The new causeway sure was a lot more comfortable riding than the old days when you had to either take a boat or ride the old wooden one-laner.

Next to the causeway, a crew was surveying the grassy area for the water and sewer system. As Abel got near the Beach, he saw a roped-off area that he figured had to be for a pumping station. He hoped there would be two. Wouldn't pay to have one station pumping both fresh water and sewage.

The wind whipped through his long hair, and the salt smell was in his nostrils. It was another beautiful day in

Clearwater, Florida. He swung a wide left in front of the Palm Pavilion and dropped onto the dirt and gravel road that went south, unlike the macadam road that went north to the newer houses and the big pink Mandalay Hotel.

Abel reckoned that there were about six hotels in the city now, and maybe he could get contracts for the pastries for another one or two. It would mean a lot more work for him and Martha, but with the hard times and all, there had to be lots of people looking for work. Maybe they could rent some space at Scruffy's or even in town.

CHAPTER 22

Mayor Teague's Daughter

Abel slowed the cycle and turned into the old railroad car. There were two other cars in the dusty lot, a bedraggled A-Model Ford sedan and a shiny Cadillac convertible, red with a tan top. He slowly walked around the beautiful car, admiring his reflection in the glossy paint and the huge chrome covers on the side-mounted spares. When he entered, it took a minute for his eyes to grow accustomed to the dim lighting. He could make out Scruffy behind the long wood bar, ineffectually swiping at an imagined spot with a damp rag. He was leaning over and talking to a man in a light-colored summer-weight suit. The man was about sixty, medium build, dark hair shot with gray. His thick neck was tanned, and his shoulders were broad, stretching the suit jacket tight. He had his boot heels hooked on the crossbar of the high stool and was gesturing with a finger pointed at Scruffy's face, obviously angry about something.

Abel walked over and slid onto a stool to his right. He listened.

Scruffy was nodding and saying, "Yup, right, uh huh, right, sir." He looked trapped and glanced pleadingly at Abel.

Abel nodded slightly and said loudly, "Hey, barkeep, how about a beer?"

Scruffy held up a hand and muttered, "Just a minute, Mr. Teague," and scurried away to get Abel's brew.

The man looked over his shoulder at Abel, bleary-eyed, obviously well past the beer standing before him, "And just who might you be, young man? I don't believe we've met." He reached out a large, slim hand and said, "I'm Llewellen Teague, mayor of this fair city." He waved his other arm expansively, "However, my friends just call me Lew, and we're all friends here, aren't we?"

Abel took the proffered hand and gave it a squeeze, "Abel Landis, Mr. Teague. I think we met once before, here." He looked critically at the mayor, looked at the dark eyes, the dark circles under his eyes and the broken veins in the nose of this lifelong drinker. Inwardly he recoiled slightly. Oh, well, he smelled better than those rascals back in Wyoming, Ike and Amos Carper.

"Allow me to express my condolences on the death of your niece. I just heard about it today."

Teague gave a start and a look of, perhaps, fear that showed in his eyes for a second or two before he regained his composure. "What? Oh, thank you, thank you, young feller." He took another long pull on his beer and belched.

Abel took a chance and asked, "What did she die from, sir?"

Teague turned on his stool full to Abel now and said, "Well, now, we don't know exactly. Might have been pneumonia or diphtheria. She was a sickly child, you know." He leaned slowly toward Abel and said in a low voice, "There was nothing they could do for her. Lovely child, absolutely lovely." This last was said in a dreamy voice while his eyes fluttered upward, away from Abel's gaze.

"Really, sir? I heard she had the influenza?" This was stated as a sort of question.

He seemed to turn this over in his mind as if hearing it for the first time and wondering if it could be true. "Influenza? Influenza? Well, maybe that too. I don't know, son. I'm not a doctor." He signaled Scruffy for another beer. Scruffy was at the other end of the bar talking to a fellow in overalls and a limp straw hat. He looked up, taking his time before returning with the mayor's beer.

Scruffy said, "Don't you think you've had enough, Mr. Mayor?" He glanced at the dirty window. "It's getting' dark and you've got a ways to drive that purty car o'yours afore you get home."

"What's that you say, my good man?" He waved his hand negligently. "Any time Lew Teague can't drive his own car home after a few beers…" He drifted off, forgetting what he was going to say, and slumped on the bar, snoring softly.

Abel and Scruffy just looked at each other. "Now what

do we do, Scruff?"

Scruffy shrugged. "Sometimes we just stretch him out on the floor and throw a blanket over him 'till he sleeps it off."

The last patron waved and slipped out the door. The place was now empty except for the three of them. Abel thought for a minute and said, "Can you drive a motorbike, Scruff?"

"Aw, no, I ain't never driven one o'them, Abel. I'd be too skeered."

"Well, then, how about his car? If you can drive it home, I'll follow you with the cycle and bring you back."

"Aw, I don't know. I ain't never drove a fancy car like that 'un." He stuck a thumb towards the door.

"But you can drive a car, can't you?" Abel asked.

Scruffy thought for a long minute as if searching his mind for an elusive answer. "Well, yeah, if it ain't too different from a Ford or Chevrolet or Plymouth."

Abel grinned, "Nah, it's the same as a Chevy. You'll see. Here, give me a hand with him." Abel threw one of the mayor's arms over his shoulder and lifted him into a semi-standing position. Scruffy came out from behind the bar and took the other. Together they managed to drag him out the door and stuff him into the passenger seat. The car smelled of leather and expensive cologne. Scruffy got into the driver's seat and, after fishing the keys out of Teague's jacket pocket, started the sleek car. The big 12-cylinder motor roared to life, half scaring Scruffy. Abel slammed the door and asked, "Do you know where he lives?"

Scruffy nodded and shouted, “Yeah, jist follow me. Ain’t too far.” Slowly he backed the big car out of the lot and onto the dirt road. Abel cranked up the cycle and followed at a distance. There wasn’t too much traffic on the causeway and Abel could follow easily. They drove east on Cleveland Street for about a mile, then had to detour around the gladiolus farm on the outskirts of town. Teague lived south on Belcher Road in a big house on the west side. There were several large houses nearby along a road lined with huge elm trees. Between the elms were queen palms and in front of two of the houses were tall flowering hedges, their white blossoms glowing in the moonlight.

Scruffy pulled into a long driveway and stopped under a portico that extended from the side of the house. There were lights on in the front windows and when the car stopped, a yellow light lit up the yard. The door to the house opened as Scruffy unlatched his door and a small woman dressed in a long dark dress stepped out. She stopped momentarily, hand to her mouth as she saw a roughly dressed, dirty and unkempt man alight from her husband’s shiny car.

Abel pulled in behind the Cadillac and turned off the cycle. When he approached the woman, she backed up to the small porch. “Sorry if we frightened you, ma’am. We didn’t feel it was, uh, safe for your husband to drive home alone.”

She stepped forward and peered into the car, its interior dimly lit by the glowing dashboard lights and the weak foot light. Teague was just waking up. “Oh, hello, Patricia.” He blearily looked over her shoulder and then said, “And hello to you too, Sarah.”

Abel looked back at the door and saw a young girl

about ten years old looking through the open door. She had blonde hair pulled back into a pony tail, a blue and white checkered nightdress and was barefoot.

Teague raised an arm shakily and said, “C’mere and give yer old dad a hand getting’ into the house, honey.”

The girl shrunk back almost out of sight, but Abel was shocked to see the look of hatred on so young a face. It was the firm clenching of her jaw and the narrowing of her eyes that struck Abel. Her hands fisted, and the knuckles turned white. She was silent and didn’t move.

Mrs. Teague grabbed her shoulder and pulled her outside. “Go do as your father says, Sarah,” and shoved her rather roughly toward the drunken Teague.

“Come on, baby, you can help me get undressed and into bed too.” He was smiling beatifically. The girl drew back and looked wildly around and whimpered, “Please, no, Mama.”

She seemed terrified to Abel, so he stepped forward and said, “Here Scruff, give me a hand with him. He may be too heavy for the little girl.” He opened the passenger door and pulled Teague’s arm out and up over his shoulder. With a wrench, Abel jerked him to his feet. Teague tried to shrug off the help but Abel held him in a strong grip. Scruffy ran to help and together they walked him to the door. Mrs. Teague backed up, hands held out in front her. Abel couldn’t tell whether she was offering to help or pushing them away. When they got to the door, Scruffy shouldered it all the way open. Mrs. Teague was in Abel’s path, so he turned sideways and relinquished his support, which Mrs. Teague assumed.

"Why don't you two take him up and get him into the sack. I'll lock up the car and give the keys to little Sarah here." Abel smiled at the kid, leaned into the car, pulled the keys out and closed the doors. Then he sat on the running board to wait for Scruffy and Mrs. Teague to return. "How are you doing, Sarah?" he asked pleasantly.

She glared at him. "Why did you have to bring him back?" she snapped.

Abel frowned, "What do you mean? He's your father, isn't he?"

She snorted, "So what? He's a bad man. I wish he was dead, dead and buried."

"Aw, kid, he can't be that bad. He's just drunk, that's all." Abel was watching the child's face carefully. He had a sudden inspiration, recalling his conversation with Perkins, the newspaper editor. "Why is he a bad man?" he asked quietly, not wanting to frighten her.

"He killded my cousin," she hissed, and looked around furtively.

"Naw, kid, I heard she died of the influenza or something like that, didn't she?"

"No!" She stamped her bare foot, "I saw him. He hurted her with a pillow on her face when she was sleeping over. She kicked and hit him, but he just pushed and pushed until she stopped." She looked around again, wanting to get it all out before her mother returned with Scruffy. She took a deep breath and went on, "Esther was buck-naked too. I saw it. I told my Mama but she didn't believe me and slapped my face right here," she turned her face and pointed to her cheek.

Abel took her chin in his hand and turned her face to the light. He couldn't see anything but nodded and said, "Ayep, it looks pretty bad, but you're a brave kid, right?"

She nodded firmly and said almost in a whisper, "I don't want to help him get undressed. He hurts me when I do and I don't want a pillow on my face too." Her eyes were large and round.

Just as she was about to go on, the door opened and Scruffy and Mrs. Teague came out into the cool evening. Mrs. Teague's arms were folded over her thin chest, and a shawl over her bony shoulders. She looked from Abel to Sarah and said, "Go into the house, Sarah and go back to bed." Then she turned to Abel, smiled a thin-lipped smile and said, "I don't know what tall tales that child's been telling you, sir, but you shouldn't believe anything she says. She makes up a lot of stories. You know how children that age are."

Abel answered, "Yes, ma'am. By the way, my name is Abel Landis. My sister's husband was Bob Brightwater."

She put a hand out and touched his arm, "Oh, I'm sorry for your loss, Mr. Landis."

"And I yours, Ma'am," Abel returned. He handed her the keys to the car and said, "Well, we'd best be off. Come on, Scruff." He turned and said over his shoulder, "'Night, ma'am."

She nodded and replied, "Thank you again for bringing Mr. Teague home, gentlemen." She continued standing under the feeble light as Abel and Scruffy got onto the cycle. Behind her Abel could barely make out the pale face of the small girl in the partially opened door.

CHAPTER 23

The Second Man: Present Day

Dave and Chris sat at a large round table at Chesney's with Anna and Rusty, Vinny and Joan and Charlie Potts, the cook. They all had either beer or iced tea, and a beaded pitcher of sweet tea sat on the bright yellow tablecloth. As Dave was sipping his beer, the door opened and Brooke came in, her handbag slung over her shoulder. She was followed a minute later by Emile, their boat dweller and computer whiz. Emile helped everyone and ran a small business solving computer glitches and banishing viruses. He was in his late twenties, slim, dark haired and wearing thin gold-framed glasses perched on his narrow nose. His usual dress was a pair of cutoff jeans and a Sloppy Joe's T-shirt, but today he had on a neat pair of khaki slacks and a nicely pressed pink short sleeved dress shirt. However, he still wore a pair of leather sandals on not quite clean feet.

Brooke, on the other hand, had on a flouncy peasant skirt and a Donna Karan T-shirt sans bra. Dave nodded appreciatively and muttered, "Thank you." Chris elbowed him in the ribs and he grunted.

When everyone was settled, Dave called the meeting to order. "You all know why we're here." He placed a small stack of cards on the table. "These are the names of the five guys who beat up Tom and Bobbie. They are all members of the Brotherhood. The top guy," he pointed to the cards, "is the one who ordered it, Mac Mayer. The other four are all in their security group." He paused while Chris dealt each one a card. The second card was Andy Holzer, the tall one from the airport. The next one was Alex Gruber. The fourth one was Carter Donovan. The fifth one was Mike Russell. "So now we have to decide what we're going to do about them."

Anna looked around, "Don't forget, they gang raped Tom's friend, Bobbie, too."

"That's right," said Chris. "We already figure that they'll have ironclad alibis and will probably be out of town, probably the country, by the time Tom and Bobbie are able to testify against them."

Nods all around the table. Dave said, "I've already spoken to Sy Goldberg, the lawyer, and he told me that it was a waste of dough to sue them. The city too, for not doing anything. He said the Brotherhood's lawyers would twist it all around and make the Brotherhood look like victims and Tom a bigoted, loose cannon who attacked some guys who were just hanging out, and yada, yada, yada, like that." He sat back frustrated.

Joanie piped up, "So what do we do? We can't just let 'em get away with it. We've gotta do something, right?" She smacked her husband hard on the arm. "Tell 'em, Vin."

Vinny just looked around, waiting for someone else to take the lead. Dave said, "Well, there's only three things we can do." He ticked them off on his fingers, "We can kill them. We can beat the shit out of them, or we can hit them in their pocketbook."

Brooke protested, "Who, these four guys? Or the Brotherhood?"

Dave looked at her quizzically, "What do you mean?"

Brooke looked back defiantly and said, "Who can you hit financially, these four guys or the Brotherhood? You know these guys won't have anything. They did sign a contract for life with the Brotherhood. We can't let them get away with this." She pounded the table, rattling glasses.

Dave looked around the table at each of them and said, "You all seem reluctant to say what you are all thinking. That we should kill these guys." He looked slowly around again, making eye contact with each person. Some nodded tightly, like Rusty and Charlie Potts. Anna and Joanie dropped their eyes and wouldn't speak. Vinny looked at Dave and Rusty.

"Well, what else can we do?" He raised his palms. "These guys are scum. If we don't do something drastic, they'll figure it was okay." They all looked at Vinny.

"Hey don't look at me, I think they oughta be croaked but I don't wanna do it." Joanie looked at her husband and gave him a light tap, nodding.

Emile cleared his throat, "Well, if you want to hurt

them financially, I guess I can handle that. By them, I mean the Brotherhood. I can hack into their bank accounts, their investments or even their overseas investment stashes. I can funnel off enough for Tom and Bobbie to take care of their bills and some, of course, for punitive damages," he grinned. "And a few bucks for us, you know, for expenses."

Again there were nods. Dave said, "We'll leave that to you, Emile. Just make sure you don't get caught."

"No problem. I'll set up a numbered account in a bank in Grand Cayman and one in Lichtenstein. I'll run it through them, then back here into our joint operations account a little at a time and in a few months, voila, we'll be rolling in dough. I know Tom has an account in a bank in Saigon, excuse me, Ho Chi Min City. When he's okay, we'll send his there. Bobbie can decide about hers later."

"That all right with everybody?" Dave asked. Nods all around.

Rusty growled, "We still haven't decided about those guys. I've got a suggestion." They looked at him tentatively. "We could farm this job out to somebody like the mob or Klan or even J.B."

Anna shuddered, "Jesus, do we really want to get J.B. involved in this?" J.B was an old friend, if that was the right word for what he was, of Dave and Tom's from Vietnam. The Army Rangers had trained him as a killing machine right out of high school. As soon as the Special Forces were formed, there was J.B. He was a wild-looking guy, rugged and compact like a pit bull. He had crazy eyes like Jack Nicholson in the movie 'The Shining', only all the time. He had absolutely no conscience, and Dave and Tom had wondered over beers how the military could have even thought of letting him back in civilian society. Though they remained on polite terms with him, they avoided J.B. whenever they could. He was one scary dude. All that they'd heard was that he did "contract" work.

Dave agreed, "J.B. is an absolute last resort. Christ, do we want these guys returned to their families cut up in cardboard boxes?" A chorus of no's greeted this question.

Again Rusty commanded the table's attention, "I, uh, think that anyone who doesn't want to be making decisions about this part of the operation ought to excuse themselves. It might get messy, and some of you don't have the stomach for it." He raised his eyebrows while leaning on his massive forearms.

Brooke and Emile were the first to leave. Anna looked at Rusty and said, "I trust you'll do what's right, dear." And she left.

Joanie nodded and pushed back also. That left Charlie Potts, a retired army cook, Rusty, Vinny, Dave and Chris. Chris said, "I feel like them," she gestured toward the departing wives, "but someone had better stay and keep you guys from getting out of hand." She sent a small smile at Dave.

CHAPTER 24

The Gun: 1938

Abel arrived home late that night. He shut off the motorbike a ways up the street and let it coast into the yard. The night was warm, but with a cool breeze blowing off the Gulf. The stars were shining in all their brilliance and the moon sat over the water, large and silver. A pelican swooped low overhead, and in a few seconds he heard a splash. Another fish gone. He shivered at the thought that he might just be one of those fish soon.

McBride had told him nothing that he didn't already know. Perkins was helpful but seemed fixated on the disappearances of the girls from town. Tomorrow he'd relate his conversation with little Sarah Teague to both Martha and Perkins. He was no closer to finding out the truth about Bob's death than he was a couple of days ago. He heaved a sigh, went into the dark house and was soon asleep.

The next day was overcast with the wind and rain squalls whipping in off the Gulf. It was a good day to stay home and help Martha. Outside the wind lashed sand off the dunes and against the house. Captain and his mother, Lucy, came at nine to help Martha and Abel make pastries. Today was a day for pies, something Martha had introduced to the hotel kitchen the week before. They had ordered two dozen assorted fruit pies so Abel and Lucy Toffelmeyer set to work making the crusts while the boys peeled apples.

Martha rinsed the pie tins and dried them. Then she sorted through several quarts of blueberries and blackberries, which had been delivered to Scruffy's the day before. Martha had woken early and ridden her push bicycle to the old bar, returning with them strapped to the carrier behind the seat. Abel vowed to build her a 3-wheel bicycle with a box out back for carrying her goods. The push bike was too awkward and couldn't hold enough. In fact, if she could handle the Harley-Davidson, he thought he could fix it up as a 3-wheel carrier. They discussed this as they worked.

Abel started humming a tune, that was popular then on the radio, and soon Lucy chimed in. Then the boys sang along in their high-pitched voices and finally Martha. The kitchen was warm from the stove, five people hard at work and the Florida summer. It was nice, Abel thought. It was nice being part of a family, something he missed since he and his wife, Ellen, had parted company. They'd always talked about a family, but somehow it had never happened. Abel was now coming up on thirty-eight years of age. Was it too late for him? He thought about Ann-Marie and Ada.

They seemed like nice girls. Maybe he should ask one of them out.

While he worked, he talked in a low voice so the boys wouldn't hear about the story the little girl had told him last night. Martha and Lucy expressed surprise and shock. Lucy picked up a sharp knife and, looking fiercely at Abel, said, "Any man, white or black, lays a hand on my kids will get this knife in his belly."

Martha asked, "Do you really think he was, well you know, with his niece? I can't believe a man would do that, do you?" She looked at the two other adults with a troubled look.

Abel shrugged, "Well, I wouldn't, but you know, there are lots of strange and crazy people out there." All he knew about the mayor was that he was a drunk, though, so far as he could tell, not a mean one.

Lucy looked from one to the other. Were all white people as naïve as these two? She stood up straight and said, "I'm gonna tell you a story, but y'all can't tell anyone else. Promise?"

They both nodded uncertainly. Lucy went on, "A couple of years ago down in Dogtown, what some white folks call niggertown, a man was caught by his brother doin' it to his little girl." She was silent for a minute, looking down at the flour-dusted tabletop. She took a deep breath and choked back a sob.

Martha put a hand to her arm to help settle her. Lucy got control of herself. "Abel, you wasn't here then, but there was a lynchin'. The Klan got blamed, and folks was all up in arms about it. Well, it weren't no Klan lynchin'. That man's brother an' a bunch of his friends done it one night. Nobody wanted to say that niggers hung a nigger so they blamed the Klan, but we all knew. That no-good bastard was diddlin' his own sweet daughter, and he got what he deserved." She stopped and took a huge breath and let it out slowly, leaning on the table. "So, yeah, I kin believe it. White folks ain't no different from us." She looked from one to the other, her eyes large and white in her dark, dark skin.

"But he didn't kill her, did he?" asked Martha tentatively.

Lucy shook her head, "No, but supposin' the little girl threatened to tell somebody? Think he mighta left her be? Supposin' that's what happened to the mayor's li'l niece? If she was threatenin' to tell somebody, maybe a friend's mama or a teacher, what then?" She snorted, "We talkin' about the mayor of the whole city here." A sudden thought struck her, "If the older girl is now dead and buried, he's gonna need somebody to take her place, and that leaves only one, the li'l girl who talked to you." This last she said while pointing the sharp knife at Abel.

Abel had to agree. He said, "You know what else bothers me?"

"No, what?" asked Lucy while Martha just looked on dumbstruck at the turn in the conversation. A few minutes ago they were happy and singing along with each other. Now a chill seemed to invade the room.

"I think the mother knows and isn't doing anything."

"Ah, my Gawd, you may be right. That poor li'l girl, she don't have nobody to turn to." She leaned on her stiffened arms and the tears came trickling down her face, dropping one by one on the floured tabletop. Lucy's shoulders shook and Martha went and held her, crying also. Abel could just stand and watch, feeling all tightened up inside. Now he was wondering if the mayor's appetite for little girls had something to do with the disappearance of the little black girls.

When the ladies finally stopped and wiped their wet faces on their aprons, Abel asked Lucy, "Do you know where your husband is today?"

She turned and said, "I expect he's at home. Not a fit day to go fishin'. He's probably mending a pole or net. Why?"

Abel frowned and chose his words carefully, "I just want to talk to him a bit. Won't take long." He took a yellow slicker from the row of pegs beside the door and slipped into it. The slicker had a hood, which he pulled over his head and left before he had to explain any more to the ladies and children.

Cutting through the scrub brush and palmettos was a well-worn path which led to Toffelmeyer's place. Jack was sitting on the back porch smoking a corncob pipe while he carefully mended a small bait net; his large body overflowing the chair, which was tilted back against the wall. His bare feet were propped up on an old wooden toolbox, and he was quietly humming a gospel tune. Abel made a scuffling noise as he came around the corner of the house. "Howdy Jack," he said, smiling.

Jack looked up, gave a nod and pointed his chin at another chair. "How do, yourself, Mr. Abel. What's got you out in this weather?"

Abel sat for a minute, then leaned forward, elbows on his knees and asked, "Jack, do you know where I can get a gun?"

Jack stopped what he was doing and cautiously asked, "What you want a gun for, Abel?"

Abel proceeded to tell him about his adventure the night before and his talk with McBride, the police chief.

"I'll ask again, Abel, what do you want a gun for? Who you planning to kill?"

Abel shook his head and said, "No, sir, I'm not planning to kill any of them, but I've got a feeling I'm turning over some stones that some people would rather I didn't, and I just want to be, uh, prepared in case."

Jack pondered and said, "Son, I don't want any part of this deal of yours. I don't want anythin' to come back on me or my family. We been livin' here peaceable for a long time." He paused, then went on, eyes boring into Abel, "You come here from Gawd-knows-where and stir up a whole load of shit. Well, when it all hits the fan, you'll be hightailin' it back to where you came from and be leavin' us holdin' the bag."

"Yeah, you're probably right, Jack. I can't deny it, but Martha and Bob were your friends, and Martha asked me to come and help her find out what happened to Bob and I aim to do that. If that doesn't set right with you, well, I'm real sorry, but I gotta do what I gotta do." Abel had put some steel in his voice and half rose to his feet.

"Now hold on there, Abel. I didn't say I didn't want to

help. I'm just tryin' to figure out how to, let's say, keep my distance."

"Don't you worry, Jack. There ain't no way I'm about to tie anything I do to you or your family. Or to Martha, for that matter. I've just got a feeling that all this crap is tied together somehow. Knowing McBride as I do, I expect that he's at the bottom of it all. I don't know how yet at this point, but I aim to find out and the reason I want a gun is because I know he likes to use those big ol' Colts he's got hanging on his belt and I just want to be prepared."

Jack considered and asked, "Do you know how to use a pistol, Abel?"

"I was in the war. I was only a dispatch rider, but we all had to be trained in rifles and us riders were given pistols 'cause we woulda had trouble wieldin' a long gun. So my answer is, yes, I know how to handle 'em. I don't like 'em, but I can shoot one if I have to."

"Well," Jack said, "I sure hope you don't have to, young fella. Lemme think on it an' I'll let you know." He heaved himself out of his chair, putting the net carefully aside and went into the house. In a couple of minutes he was back with two glasses of lemonade. "I was down in Cuba with Teddy Roosevelt, you know."

"So how'd you get into that little scrap?"

Jack sat back down with a sigh. This was evidently a story he was reluctant to tell, but war stories between old soldiers were somehow okay. "I was workin' for a man in a small sawmill east of Tampa at the time, and this man read in the paper about what the Cubans had done to that there

Navy ship in the Havana harbor and got real mad for some reason so, since the mill wasn't doin' so good at the time, he decided to go fight. There was lots of rumors goin' round at the time about there bein' lots of gold an' stuff just for the takin'." He laughed and shook his head, "Boy, was we dumb back then."

"Well, since I was a kid and was soon to be out'n a job, I ast could I go too. So we went and signed up near the docks in Tampa. The next day they took us out to an island in the bay where they was trainin' troops. We was there for maybe a month, marchin' an' firin' rifles and feedin' and waterin' horses."

"Course, I was assigned to cookin,' but I didn't like it so I ast if I could look after the stock. The Captain allowed as how that was okay with him, so I groomed an' took care of the animals. A while after that they loaded us all on ships and we set sail for Cuba. Lots of the boys got sick 'cause the ride down was a little rough, but I never did. I kinda liked bein' out on the water. I guess that's why I'm a fisherman now." He laughed a deep belly laugh now, and Abel joined him.

He continued, "There was already some ships ahead of us that'd come down from the Keys, I guess, and they'd secured the beach. We got in as close as we could, then lowered some boats and took the boys ashore. It was tough getting the horses in the boats so I had 'em lower a couple of 'em into the water an' I swum them to shore. The little Colonel was mighty impressed with that and he tole me so. That's when I met him the first time. See, the Colonel didn't think nothin' of complimentin' a man, black or white, when he done good. I liked that about him."

"So you went up San Juan hill with them?" asked Abel.

Jack nodded, "Oh, yeah, only San Juan hill was only one of them hills. The Cubans had a big ol' fort at the top that they was defendin'. Our boys set up our big guns at the bottom of the hill in some trees and proceeded to shell hell out of that fort. When the Colonel ordered the charge, he tole them gunners to keep it up 'til just before we got to the top. That's what they did and just as we got there, a big ol' hole was blown outta that wall and our boys jist stormed right in." He sighed and wiped a hand across his face.

"Lots of our boys got shot up pretty bad, but we did right proud. The Colonel wouldn't let our boys shoot or stab them Cubans that surrendered neither."

Abel asked, "So what did you do with 'em?"

Jack shrugged, "Near as I could tell, we disarmed them and got their officers' word that they wouldn't pull anythin' funny an' they jist kinda kept to theirselves. We fed 'em and let 'em get their tents and duds and bed down in a big clearing at the bottom of the hills. Later I heard they got on their ships and went back to Spain. They wasn't real Cubans anyway."

He sighed again and reached into a tub filled with cold water and chunks of ice and pulled out two bottles of beer, handing one to Abel.

"Here, I think I need another drink now. All this talkin's makin' me thirsty." He looked around and said, leaning toward Abel, "'Course, I'd like somethin' a mite stronger, but Lucy don't allow nothin' stronger 'round the house here."

"Thanks, Jack. I don't suppose Martha wouldn't smile at me keeping whiskey around either." He popped the top with an old wrench and clinked bottles with Jack Toffelmeyer.

After taking a long swig, Jack stood and went into the house. He returned a few minutes later with a rag wrapped around a long pistol. He sat with the pistol in his lap, then showed it to Abel. It was loaded. "I'll hold onto it until you think you need it, okay Abel?"

Chapter 25

The Second Guard: Present Day

Dave and Rusty strolled outside and down onto the dock. Dave had his hands jammed into his pockets, his shoulders hunched. The day was warm but not unseasonably hot. A nice breeze came in off the Gulf, fluttering the sail covers and the palms back at the buildings. Small waves slapped the barnacle-crusted pilings. Dave watched seabirds glide low over the waves searching for prey. "Rus, you know what we've got to do."

"Yeah, I know. Well, we've done it before and these guys really deserve it. I've been thinking on this since it happened and trying to figure out how the cops could handle it with a satisfactory outcome, and I really can't. I think the police chief runs a little scared of the Brotherhood and that'll put a crimp in the investigation." He shook his grayed head, running his meaty hand through his hair.

"Yeah, you're right there, buddy. If the cops don't get on the Brotherhood hard, it'll all go away. The only thing that bothers me is them coming back at us if we act." Dave leaned against a bollard, scratching his back.

Rusty paced ponderously up and down a short section of dock, "So what do you think we ought to do?"

"Well, if we walk away, it just mean Tom's going to take care of it in a few months or a year and you know we'll be helping him then." He thought a few seconds, then said, "We also won't be able to live with ourselves."

"Yeah, I know what you mean."

"So, if we can figure out which one used the brass knucks, we can do two of the others and make it look like he did them. Maybe the Brotherhood will take care of their own." Dave sat on a dock box and Rusty settled in beside him.

"I guess we're past the deciding stage and are now into planning?" Rusty slid his cap back and scratched his head.

Reluctantly Dave agreed. "Yeah, you know I could probably do this myself if you want out."

Rusty shook his head, "Nah, I just look at it like a war, and these are the bad guys. We gotta do it and knowing what they did, it won't bother me. Just don't tell Anna."

"Oh, shit, don't you think I want to keep the ladies out of it? I think Vinny too." Dave felt at times like the camp daddy. Who needed protecting? Who could be counted on for some help? Who could be counted on and would still be able to sleep at night? They had been involved in adventures, or misadventures, several times since they all lived together at the dock and worked in the restaurant and bar.

Rusty had been a PT boat cap during the war and had done his share of killing. If he could convince himself this was war, he'd be fine. Dave would learn to live with this thing. He still wondered if they should call in J.B. The problem with J.B. is that he actually liked what he called "wet work" and might not want to stop with the three.

The next thing would be to figure out which one used the brass knuckles. He'd go to see Tom again.

Next day he and Rusty took the old station wagon into Clearwater to the hospital. Tom and Bobbie were still in intensive care but Tom was awake when they stopped before the glass separating his room and the nurses' station. He moved his head slightly and winked. A small smile came to his lips as they entered, pulling up chairs.

"Hey, asshole, are you giving the nurses a hard time?" Dave asked jokingly.

Tom lay with his head still swaddled in bandages, leg in a cast and stretched out and up on a pulley with weights. He had two pillows under his head, but otherwise the bed was flat.

"Do you want me to crank the bed up?" asked Dave solicitously.

"No," Tom shook his head slightly. "Can't. Ribs."

"Okay," Dave said. "Look, we've got a couple of questions to ask you. We've got the names of the guys who did this to you. I need you to tell me who used the brass knucks." He smiled a tight-lipped smile. "We've got something special planned for him."

Tom thought for a minute, reliving the experience yet not wanting to. He motioned Dave closer. "Where'd the doc say I was hit with the knucks?" he whispered.

Dave was trying to remember the conversation with the young doctor. "I think that was the guy that hit you in the back of the head and maybe in the ribs."

Again Tom shook his head, "The head, yeah, but not the ribs. They kicked me there. Musta had steel toe boots."

"So?"

"Tall guy, maybe three inches more than me, dark hair, I think. Had a tattoo on his right hand, eagle, I think." He stopped, breathing hard and said, "Look for a bandage on that hand. I bit him pretty hard."

Rusty smiled delightedly, "No kidding? You bit him?"

Tom continued to grin, "You bet. Thought I was gonna take his thumb off. So did he!" He thought again and continued, voice getting weaker, "Big guy was leader, stayed back until I was down. Had a moustache. Two guys grabbed Bobbie and the other two big guys nailed me." Tom laid his head back, exhausted now, but he motioned Dave closer. "Save the moustache guy for me."

Dave nodded and gripped Tom's hand, "We've been thinking of bringing J.B. in. What do you think?"

Tom shook his head slightly, "No, just you guys. He's crazy." In a couple of seconds he was asleep.

Dave looked up at Rusty, who was standing next to him. Rusty shrugged. "I guess it's up to us."

Dave nodded and gave Tom's hand a good squeeze. He thought he detected a return squeeze, but it may have been just a reflex.

When they were outside again, Dave breathed deep. The sky was cloudless, a washed-out blue. The day was warm but not uncomfortably so. They drove back to the compound in silence with the windows open, not needing the air conditioning yet. Dave was planning his moves, psyching himself up for the task ahead. He didn't like killing.

He tried to get his mind around the fact that he and Rusty were going to take the lives of two young men in the next week or so. Young men who had families, friends, maybe girlfriends or wives. But it was something that had to be done. These young men had stepped over a line. On one side were the law and decency and courtesy, the ability to get along in a civilized society. On the other was lawlessness and corruption. The Brotherhood had corrupted these men, who were old enough and smart enough to say no – but they hadn't. They knew what they were doing. They knew there might be consequences. That didn't deter them. When you're young and strong and in the prime of your life, you think you are invincible. Well, he and Rusty would fix that. If they just gave them a good beating like they had done to Tom and Bobbie, they'd be looking over their shoulders for the rest of their lives.

He remembered a scene from 'Saving Private Ryan' when Tom Hanks' character wanted to kill a captured German prisoner but was talked out of it by another soldier. Later in a battle, the German had led his platoon or division against them and killed a number of his men. No, that wasn't going to happen to Dave's friends. His father had always told him, never leave your enemies alive. They'll always come back and bite you on the ass.

They could turn the job over to J.B., but that was an easy way out. That just involved money. No, this was personal. He and Tom were friends, friends forged by war and something deeper. A man doesn't have many friends whom he would lay down his life for or would expect his friend to do the same. Tom and he had that kind of friendship. He thought he and Rusty had that too and he felt fortunate in that respect to have two close friends like them.

After parking in the large graveled lot behind Chesney's, he turned to Rusty and said, "We'll have to find out where these two guys hang out. They way I see it is we'll have to grab them up quietly, take them to one of their own places, do the job and get out without being seen. If we handle it right, the Brotherhood will think that one of their own guys did it. If they check on Tom, they'll realize it couldn't have been him."

"Yeah, we might get away with it if they don't check and find out that Tom has friends here," Rusty mused. "You know, their security is pretty good. If they even get a hint of us, we are screwed. We'll be in a shooting war or at the very least a legal one for a long time."

Dave smiled, "Well, we'll just have to be real careful, have ironclad alibis and be very good at what we do." They moved out of the car and onto a picnic table under a large queen palm tree. "We're going to need some help with logistics. Let's get the girls on this part."

"Won't that be kinda dangerous?" asked Rusty, a thick hand brushing at a persistent fly.

"I don't think they'll mind. We'll just keep it vague. I think the first thing we need to find out is where they hang out. I think I remember Vinny saying he knew a carpenter or plumber or some tradesman who did a lot of work for them. Maybe he can have a drink with him and find out where they go. We also need a warehouse or storage unit or some other kind of deserted building where we can do them without being discovered. I think our best bet will be to make it look like they killed each other." He heaved himself up and stretched. "Let's get this started."

Chapter 26

Dead Girls: 1938

The day was unseasonably warm along the Gulf. The water was calm and the sun beat down heavily. Abel kissed Martha goodbye and jumped on the motorcycle, firing it to life. As he headed toward the new causeway, he saw Scruffy outside the old railway car sweeping the long, narrow porch. This struck Abel as somewhat out of character for the fellow, so he had to stop. It was also very unusual to find him up at this hour.

As he putted to a stop in the graveled lot, he said, "Say Scruff, are you feeling all right?" He shut off the engine and cocked a leg over the tank.

Scruffy looked up from his sweeping and smiled shyly. Abel was taken aback. He was cleaner somehow, a little neater. Abel frowned.

"There's something about you, Scruff. I can't quite put

my finger on it..” Abel studied his friend. His hair was shorter, his beard was trimmed and his skin actually looked clean. What the hell was going on?

“Can’t a feller get a little cleaned up, Abel?” He stood leaning on his broom staring back at the seated rider.

“Yeah, you can, but what I can’t figure out is why.” This was perplexing. “Are you cleaning up the bar too?”

Again Scruffy replied, “Yeah, just doin’ some sweepin’ an’ scrubbin’.”

Abel scratched his head, “But why? It ain’t like your regular customers don’t like it the way it is.” He frowned and tried puzzling it out. Maybe it wasn’t because of the regular customers. He scowled, “Has Martha been up here again?”

Scruffy looked down at the freshly swept porch and mumbled, “Yeah.” He shuffled his feet and slowly twisted the broom in his hands. “She thought the place could use a little cleaning. Me too, I guess.”

“Ah, Jesus, what a busybody,” he thought to himself. Out loud he said, “Don’t let her tell you how to run things, Scruff. She’s just sore she doesn’t have a man to boss around.” He waved his hand dismissively. Before he jump-started the cycle, he asked, “Do you need anything in town? I’m picking up some nuts and raisins for Martha.”

“Naw,” Scruffy replied. “I got a beer delivery comin’ later. He’s bringing some more flour and sugar for Martha.” He looked down at his shoes again. “She said she was gonna come an’ get it an’ bring me a coupla Bob’s old shirts.” He looked up quickly, “That okay by you, Abel?”

Abel shook his head, "Don't make no matter to me what you and her do. I ain't staying around here forever anyway. I got a life out west, you know. I got a good job to get back to." He jumped up and down on the old cycle until it started. With a quick glance over his shoulder, he roared away. The ride into town was uneventful. The breeze felt good cooling his sweat soaked shirt. Hmmph, he thought. Giving good shirts to Scruffy. He could use a couple of shirts himself, couldn't he? Wasn't he the one who showed her how to bake the stuff she was selling to the hotel? Wasn't it him who was lining up another hotel for her to sell to? Scruffy was just a broken-down barkeep.

He pulled up outside the Arcade and waved to Johnny Livingston. The energetic youngster quickly walked over and shook Abel's hand.

"Howdy, Abel. What's doing?"

"Just going in to see Perkins, going to put a little ad in for Martha. Maybe we can get some more business for the bake goods." He thought for a minute, then asked, "Say Johnny, do you know anything about what Bob was working on up there at the courthouse?"

Johnny scratched his head and said, "Not really, just the same stuff everybody knows – the water and sewage out to the beach. Maybe the project to build the new post office. I mean, that was his job, wasn't it?" He shrugged.

Abel asked, "Anybody else I could talk to about that?"

He shrugged again, "Well, Avery Gibbons is the county lawyer. And Lew Teague is the mayor. They'd know about it. Probably their secretaries. Probably Alice Bennett."

"Alice Bennett? Who's she?"

"County Clerk"

Abel nodded, "Thanks, Johnny." He pulled the key out of the small dashboard. "Keep an eye on the cycle for me, will you?"

"Sure thing, Abel." Johnny grinned.

The arcade was busy this morning. Abel managed to wend his way through the crowd to the newspaper office at the end. He found Arthur Perkins talking to a large round man in a white linen suit. He hung back but Perkins waved him forward. "Abel Landis, this here's Otis Kane. He owns this building and a couple more in town."

Abel appraised the man, shaking the proffered hand. Kane's hand was soft in Abel's firm grip. He looked down and saw that the man's nails were manicured with a shiny coating on them. Abel looked up into the round face, with red jowls framing a small, pursed mouth. "Pleased to meet you, Mr. Landis," he said in a surprisingly high voice. It was almost like a woman's voice. He wore a white slouch hat low and cocked to one side.

"Likewise," replied Abel.

"Are you in town for long, Mr. Landis, or just visiting?" he inquired blandly.

Abel carefully measured his words, "Well, that depends on a few things, Mr. Kane. Once my business is cleared up, I guess I'll be heading back out to Wyoming where I've been working these past few years."

Kane appraised him and said, "Well, that's too bad, sir. The town could use some good strapping fellows like yourself. We're growing like a weed here, you know." He smiled with his small mouth and stuck a thumb in the pocket of his waistcoat. “Clearwater’s going to be the gem of the Florida Gulf Coast soon.”

Abel smiled back and said, “I don’t doubt that for one minute, sir.”

Kane stood, smiling at both Abel and Perkins, “Well, gentlemen, I must be on about my business.” He touched the brim of his hat, “Arthur. Mr. Landis.” The stout man turned and waddled back out the door and down the center of the arcade, nodding and smiling, occasionally stopping to shake a hand.

Arthur raised the folding leaf on the counter and motioned Abel inside. “Come on in, Abel.” He led the way into his office and settled behind his desk. Abel took a chair before the cluttered desk. When he was settled, Perkins asked, “Got something for me, son?”

Abel related all that had happened and what had been said the previous evening. Perkins frowned and took his time lighting his pipe. He eyed Abel across the desk and blew out a cloud of acrid smoke. “You know what that might mean, don’t you?”

Abel nodded. “Yeah. Two things. If he killed his niece probably after doing you-know-what with her, the daughter is probably next on the agenda. And if his niece is dead at the same time a couple of other kids have disappeared, he might have something to do with them, too.”

Perkins nodded slowly, sadly, puffing on his pipe. “If this gets out, all hell is going to break loose.” He puffed some more, “’Course, we need something more than the word of a ten-year-old kid.” He mused, “Wonder why the coroner didn't pick up on the sex stuff."

Abel shrugged, "After the flu epidemic back in the late teens and early twenties, it's not uncommon to see kids die, and who thinks to look at the girl's privates at that age?"

Perkins nodded again. "Yeah, I guess you're right. Damn, I hate for a man to get away with something like that."

"So do I, Mr. Perkins, but this is kinda sidetracking me from finding out what happened to my brother-in-law." Abel slumped in his chair, chin on his chest.

"Yeah, sorry about that, kid. Maybe if you talk to one of the secretaries in Bob's office you might be able to get a handle on what he was working on. Maybe that's what happened. He mighta found out something he wasn't supposed to. You know, there's a lot of federal money comin' into this town." He frowned and said, "Just the water and sewer lines running out to the north end of the Beach is making a lotta loot for somebody." He rocked forward and pointed his finger at Abel, "And the new post office, now that's federal dollars for sure. I wouldn't be surprised if the main contractors aren't above putting a few dollars in the pockets of the men who awarded the contracts." He just leaned there puffing on his pipe.

As Abel started to leave, he said, "I half believe that Mr. Lew Teague is a bad man. I just need more to go on, son."

Abel sighed, "I'll see what I can do, Mr. Perkins."

Abel left the older man sitting there, his head wreathed in blue pipe smoke. At the end of the arcade was a wooden phone booth. Abel looked up the number for the city attorney's office and slipped a nickel into the slot and dialed.

The voice on the other end was girlish and professional, "City attorney's office. How may I help you?"

Abel lowered his voice, "Uh, yes, is this Miss Ann-Marie Knightington? I'm calling from Mr. Abel Landis's office."

On the other end Abel heard a stifled giggle, then, making her voice equally deep, she replied, "Yes, I believe she might be at her desk. Is this Mr. Landis or his, uh, secretary?" She giggled again.

Abel smiled into the phone. "Hi, Ann-Marie. Yeah, this is Abel. Can you talk?"

"Sure," she said. "The old man is out of the office right now. What can I do for you?"

He didn't quite know how to put his request without getting her in trouble. "Uh, can you tell me what Bob was working on last? That might give me an idea if he stumbled across something he wasn't supposed to or maybe saw or heard something."

"Sure," she answered, "He had the contracts out on his desk for the federal grant about the water and sewer lines out to the North Beach. He was...." She paused and said in a much lower and softer voice. "I've gotta go. His Nibs just got in. Call me at home after six. Maybe we can get together." She left it like that. There was mischief in that voice.

CHAPTER 27

The Kid: Present Day

Dave and Rusty were sitting in a couple of deck chairs on the stern of Rusty's big PT boat, lines bobbing gently in the placid gulf. They had their shirts off and draped over the backs of the chairs and beaded bottles of beer sat in cup holders attached to the chair arms. They heard quick footsteps approaching from the dock. The boat gave a gentle rock and soon Vinny was pulling a chair up beside them. He reached into the cooler before he sat and uncorked a brew for himself. He sat with a sigh, patting his small round stomach.

"Well, Vin, what have you got for us?" Dave asked without opening his sun-glassed eyes.

Vinny burped and said, "Well, I had a drink with Oscar, that guy I told you about who works for the Brotherhood. He's a plumber there and once called me in to help with a problem. Anyway," he leaned toward the two friends, "all I was able to get from him was where they worked and where they live." He pulled a scrap of paper from his pocket and read, "The tall one, Mayer? He lives in the spiritual HQ on the third floor. Oscar says he's fuckin' some broad works in the gift shop. He, himself, works outta the security office over on Dade Avenue, behind the old Chevy dealership. Says he works the midnight to eight shift usually at the HQ." He looked expectantly at Dave, then Rusty who just nodded, absorbing the data.

"What about the other one, what's his name? Gruber? Grubber?" asked Rusty.

Vinny consulted his notes again, "Gruber, Hans. Sounds like a Kraut, doesn't it?" When he got no response, he went on, "He lives in the old Oceanside Motel over on King Street. Bottom floor, room 107. Oscar thinks he's a queer. Says he bunks with a couple of other guys and are always stopping up a toilet. One day he goes in and finds some queer video sex tapes piled under the coffee table." He looked again at them, then sat back swigging his beer.

"How old are these guys, Vin?" asked Dave.

Vinny sighed. "Mayer is about 34, maybe 35, but the other guy, the Kraut, is a kid, only about 21, 22. The good news is that Mayer is old enough to know better, but the bad news is the kid is a mean little bastard. Oscar says that even the guys who work with him hate his guts. He thinks the boss, the one named Mayer, is friends with the kid and some of the other rougher guys. This Mayer is some kind of big shot in the Brotherhood."

Rusty said, "We know , but what department does he

work in?"

Vinny shrugged, "Oscar says he doesn't know and he doesn't want to. Something spooky about him. When I pressed him, Oscar shook his head and left."

"How about the fourth guy? Tom says he's big." Dave rolled the cool beer bottle on his forehead.

"Yeah," mused Vinny, "him. Oscar says his name is Mike Russell. Says he used to be a football player back home in Indiana. Got a big mouth. Thinks he's tough."

"Do you think Oscar'll remember you asking about these guys later?"

Vinny shrugged again, "Dunno. He likes me, but might remember if something happens to these guys."

Dave sat up, "Well, we needed the intel and you got it. If we have to visit Oscar later and remind him to keep his mouth shut, we will."

Vinny gulped and mopped his head with a dark blue bandana.

"Why don't you go get something to eat, Vin? Rusty and I have some more talking to do."

Vinny looked from one to the other. "Hey, you're not cutting me out, are you?" He complained.

Dave flipped his shades up to his forehead, "Vin, you're logistics. I don't want you involved any deeper unless we really need you. Rusty and I will handle the, um, physical end. The less you know, the better, understand?"

Reluctantly Vinny bobbed his head and departed.

"You were pretty rough on the little guy," Rusty said, swallowing the last of his beer.

"Well, it was necessary. He's not cut out for wet work. Me? I don't give a damn after what they did. Those guys, young or old, crossed the line. They took themselves outside the law. We know that the law isn't going to do anything about this, so we have to." And Dave was adamant. "Let's go tonight. We'll see about the kid first. If I remember, there's a café across the street from that motel or one of the two or three near it."

That night, Dave parked his truck in the lot beside the Bo Peep Café. He noted that the place stayed open until midnight. They were there about 9:00 PM. The lot in front of the former motel was well-lit and said a small sign said 'Brotherhood Dormitory #6'.

They ate slowly and sat sipping coffee, not doing much talking, keeping their eyes on the dorm. About 10:30 a black Chevy Suburban pulled up in the lot and five men clad in the black and blue security uniforms got out and went into two different rooms. The kid, Gruber, was one of them. He loosened his tie and yanked it over his head. On his hip were the accoutrements of the job: short sword, nightstick, taser, and radio. As one of the others opened the door, Gruber unbuckled the heavy web belt and slung it over his shoulder. Only two of them entered that room. The door closed.

Dave scoped out the motel. The back of the wing facing them backed onto the bay. There was a walkway between each of the three wings and what looked like a narrow deck over the water. Narrow alleys separated the three wings. Two doors down from Gruber's room was a soda machine, brightly lit.

"Keep your eyes open, Rusty. I'll be back," Dave said,

sliding out of the booth and pulling a dark ball cap over his short hair. He had on dark jeans and a dark-patterned shirt. If you dressed all in black, it looked a little obvious. Beneath his loose shirt, he carried a 9mm Taurus automatic pistol that he'd bought a couple of years ago at a flea market up in Crystal River. It was a cheap, nickel-plated little gun usually known as a Saturday night special. He walked back to the white pickup and pulled a pair of thin leather driving gloves out of the door pocket, along with a black silk balaclava with a facemask. He jammed them into his pocket, sauntered across the street and walked the sidewalk until he was past the end of the dorm building.

He had a wrist rocket slingshot in another pocket along with a supply of 3/8" ball bearings. He slipped into the shadows and drew on the gloves. With his second shot he doused the streetlight. It just went out with a very faint ping and the broken glass floated down quietly. The back of the dorm was now shrouded in darkness. Dave slipped onto the narrow deck that hung over the gulf. Staying low so he'd be beneath the windows, he was soon in the narrow alley between the dorms. The alley was illuminated by a naked bulb overhead. Dave waited a minute before unscrewing the bulb a turn. It went out. The only illumination was now from the side of the soda machine. Dave settled down to wait.

In no more than five or six minutes, a figure came out in shorts and Dave heard money drop into the machine. Dave eased forward. When he got to the corner, he saw that it was the other guy from the kid's room. Good. He pulled the mask down and stepped out pointing the gun. "Pssst!" he hissed.

When the young fellow turned, Dave clocked him on the side of the head with the gun butt and caught him as he fell. Very quietly, Dave dragged him back into the alley and laid him down. He waited by the corner.

In a minute, Gruber came out in his shorts also. “Hey, asshole, where’s my drink?”

Dave stepped out and leveled the gun at the boy’s right eye. He spun the boy and shoved him back toward the room. “Don’t give me any trouble, kid.” Dave shoved him through the door and closed it behind him. He surveyed the room. It was about 15’ x 20’ with two sets of bunk beds and a row of four dressers. It was littered with uniforms, pizza boxes, and action figures. A large TV sat on a low table covered with old food, dirty plates, video tapes and crumpled napkins. “Sit down, kid, I need some information.”

“What did you do with Gary?” he asked sneering, his close-set eyes narrowing. He was just wearing a pair of threadbare boxer shorts and worn rubber flip-flops. He sat down on a grubby couch arranged before the TV.

Jesus, Dave thought, why did he have to be so young? He’d had to kill young people when he was in Vietnam, but that was war and they were trying to kill him.

“Gary’s just sleeping in the alley. He’ll be out for a while.” Dave swept the crap off one side of the TV table and sat, keeping the gun trained on the kid. He had to work fast. No telling when the third one would return or when Gary might wake up. “Where does Donovan work?”

“Don’t know who you’re talking about,” the kid answered stubbornly.

Dave shook his head and picked up an empty 20-ounce

soda bottle. In a flash he held it over the end of the pistol and shot the boy in the knee. The pop was loud, but not so any-one would hear.

The kid's eyes went wide. Then he screamed, clutching his bloody knee. Absently Dave thought, if I let him live, he'll walk with a permanent limp. Dave reached over and flipped on the TV, turning it up. He got to his feet and back-handed the boy across the face, knocking him back. "Kid, I only ask once. Where does Donovan work?"

The kid gasped, trying to catch his breath. He muttered something under his breath. He indicated a dirty towel lying on the couch next to him and then nodded at his knee.

Dave waved an assent with the gun. The kid reached for the towel and his hand snaked under it. He pulled a small black pistol out, but before he could aim it, Dave shot him in the chest twice. A double tap, bang-bang. The kid flew back, the gun slipping out of his hand. Dave put the gun back in his lap and went to the door. It was quiet outside. The shots hadn't been heard over the loud television. Quickly he slipped into the alley and gathered the other one, Gary, under the arms. He was still out. Dave looked around again and carried him back into the room.

He sat Gary down on the floor against the TV table and put his Taurus in the kid's hand, after wiping it carefully. He put the other pistol in the dead boy's hand. If he knew the Brotherhood, maybe they wouldn't even report the death. Lucca Brazzi sleeps with the fishes, he thought. They'd probably end up in the bay. Meanwhile the Brotherhood would be looking closely at Tom. Hah, still in ICU.

With a last look around, he picked up the blown-out plastic bottle. Probably shouldn't leave that. He stuck it in his pocket and with a quick look, ducked out, pulling his facemask off. Rusty silently pulled up to the curb and Dave got in. In a few minutes, they were heading north on Alternate 19. When they got to the Sunset Pointe turnoff, Dave breathed a long sigh. As they went over the high hump of the bridge, he balled the gloves up and tossed them over the side and into the dark water. Later he'd ditch the shirt, jeans and anything else he'd been wearing in a Goodwill dumpster.

"Everything okay?" asked Rusty quietly.

"Yeah, it's done. Little bastard pulled a gun on me." He slumped down into the seat, cocking a knee against the dash. "That's one."

As they drove away, Rusty slapped Dave on the leg, "Actually, that's two. Two more and then save the last guy for Tom."

Chapter 28

The Girls: 1938

Abel called Ann-Marie from the phone at Scruffy's that evening. She agreed to meet him, though she had no car. He asked if there was an ice cream parlor that was open in the evening but wasn't in the Arcade. She said she'd heard of one on the Bay Boulevard down near Belcher Rd. It was only about a half mile from her house so she said she'd meet him there. Though he offered to pick her up with his motorcycle, she demurred, saying that she didn't think it would be proper and that her daddy would have a fit.

When Abel arrived, he noted that the place was called The Grill and Chill. At least he hoped it was the right place. He crossed the opposing traffic lane and puttered into the gravel lot. The sun had gone down. A string of lights hung from the side of the place to a pole near the street, illuminating the lot and the side of the building. On the blank wall was painted a large mural of a parking lot filled with cars, carhop girls on roller skates and even a hot rod. With professional curiosity, Abel looked for a name. In the lower corner, barely recognizable, was the name Franny. He frowned. Franny sounded like a girl's name. Interesting. He'd have to look her up and maybe swap stories. He looked again. Pretty good, he thought noting the colors and attention to detail.

Through a large glass window he saw Ann-Marie sitting sipping a malt opposite another girl. He recognized the other girl as the one from the police office, Ada. He thought he remembered someone telling him that Ann-Marie and Ada were cousins. He removed his leather riding hat and goggles and tucked them beneath a twist of rope across the rear of the seat. Brushing himself off, he entered by the front door.

The place was about half full of teenagers and younger kids. Since it was summer, he expected this. The parking lot held seven or eight cars and a slew of push bikes. His was the only motorcycle. Ann-Marie looked his way and smiled shyly, motioning him to join them. He slid into the seat when she made room for him.

"Hey, Ann-Marie and hi, Ada, isn't it?" He grinned broadly at the ladies. They were older than the school kids but not by much. Abel could probably have passed for either of their fathers.

"Hi, Mister Landis," said Ann-Marie quietly. Ada echoed her, looking down at her soda.

"Say, what are you lovely ladies drinking? I think I'll get something and how about a refill?" Abel was just about ready to get up when a young girl wearing an apron came up to the table.

"Whatcha havin', bub?"

"Um, that looks good," he said, pointing to a tall glass on the next table. "What is it?"

Without looking, she sighed, "That's an ice cream soda. Vanilla ice cream, chocolate soda. We call 'em a Black and White." She made a note on her pad and looked up. "You guys havin' another one?"

Ann-Marie looked at Ada and lowered her eyes.

Abel caught the look, "'Course they're havin' another." He smiled again at the two girls. "You two get whatever you want. It's on me!"

Ann-Marie smiled, nodded at the waitress and said, "Yeah, Judy. Thanks."

Abel rubbed his hands together and said, "Well, I'm glad to get the two of you girls together." He looked from one to the other. Ann-Marie looked at him boldly, but Ada just glanced up and then down at the table again.

"Ada?" Abel asked. "What can you tell me about the coppers and especially the chief?" He sat expectantly, leaning forward and toying with a straw.

She mumbled something, hands in her lap, chin on her chest.

"What was that?"

She spoke a little louder this time, "I'm not supposed to talk about it." She looked into his eyes, then quickly back down. "They told me."

Before Abel could speak, Ann-Marie said, "Oh, Mr. Landis, the chief and that goon of his, Arne Brodsky, told Ada that she shouldn't talk about the department to anybody, ever." She leaned forward and, grasping Ada's hand on the table, whispered, "She's told me some of the sounds that go on down there. Some are terrible!" Her serious face clouded. "Some I just couldn't believe!"

Abel asked gently, "Like what?"

"Beatings," mumbled Ada. "Down in the dungeon, they call it." She looked up and seemed a little braver. "The cell block is behind the chief's office but underneath the cellblock is the dungeon. It's in the basement. I've heard some awful screams come out of there. Of course, I've never seen what goes on, but sometimes I've heard." She hung her head again, seemed on the verge of tears. Her ice cream soda sat untouched.

Abel reached across the table and took her other hand. She flinched but didn't pull away. "Ada, do you know what happened to Bob Brightwater?"

She shook her head.

He pushed on. "Were you working on the day he disappeared?"

She nodded, scarcely moving her curls.

"Did you see or hear anything?"

Ann-Marie prodded her with an elbow and said in a low voice, "Tell him. Tell him what you told me. Please, A."

"I can't. I can't."

Abel tried a new tack. "Look if I guess, will you nod yes or no? That way you wouldn't be telling, okay?"

She nodded.

Abel organized his thoughts. Then he said, "Did McBride have anything to do with it?"

Ada nodded, still not looking up but he could tell she

was listening carefully.

"Who else? This Brodsky character?"

Again the slight nod.

"Any others?"

A side-to-side headshake.

"So just McBride and Brodsky, right?"

Nod.

"Was Bob Brightwater murdered by those two?" He dreaded the answer but had to ask.

Nothing.

Shit, thought Abel, how am I going to find out the details? "Did they do it at the police station? In the dungeon?"

Again she refused to nod.

Abel eased his grip on her hand and just patted it. "Almost done, honey." He thought and asked, "They drowned him?"

She just started crying.

"Why did they do it?"

Ada looked up at him. Her brown eyes were full of tears and fear. She frowned at the question. It was not a yes or no she could answer with a head movement.

She took a deep breath and let it out with a hick, "Contracts. They were stealing money from the contracts from Washington to put water and sewer pipes to the Beach. I heard Chief McBride and the county attorney, Mr. Gibbons, talking about it. Mr. Gibbons said that Mr. Brightwater found out what they were doing." She hiccupped again and sighed, "I didn't know who to tell. Who is there to tell? He's the police chief and Mr. Gibbons is a lawyer, and they both meet often with the mayor." She looked at him imploringly, "Who could I tell?" She sounded lost and plaintive. She looked from Abel to Ann-Marie, her best friend. "If either of you tell, they'll kill me, too." She put her head in her hands and sobbed, "Oh God, what have I done?"

Ann-Marie put an arm around her and squeezed her shoulder, "Don't you worry, honey, we won't say a thing." Then she frowned, "But what are we going to do now, Mr. Landis? What can we do?"

He smiled at the two young women, "First of all, you have to start calling me Abel. We're in this together. Ada," he said looking her right in the eye, "If anything leaks out from any of us, all of our gooses are cooked."

Ann-Marie giggled, "You mean geese. Geese are cooked."

Now Ada giggled behind a hand. "Gooses, geese…"

That seemed to lighten the mood a little and the girls started sucking on their straws. Abel watched the levels go down in the tall, vase-like glasses. He drank some of his too. He leaned forward and tapped a finger on the table, "When's the next election for police chief, Ada?"

She shook her head. "The chief is appointed by the town council. The chief has been trying to get that changed like some of the other towns, but I guess the council members like the, I dunno, the power?"

Abel snorted, "More likely, either they've got something on the chief or he's got something on them."

"What would the council do if something happened to the chief?"

Both girls shrugged, "Appoint a new chief, I guess,"

said Ann-Marie. Ada nodded.

"Would it be from the ranks? From the other officers?"

Ada shook her head, "I don't think so. I don't think the others are, you know, as smart as Chief McBride. They're just policemen, men that the Chief hired."

"Is Gibbons on the council?"

Ann-Marie shook her head, "Oh, no. He can't be. The charter states that they have to be independent of any other government office. Right now, Mr. Teague is the mayor. We don't have a vice-mayor, though it's in the charter that we can. After Mr. Rollings died two years ago, they sort of didn't bother replacing him. There are only five commissioners right now." She ticked them off on her fingers, "There's Mr. Banks, the jeweler; Mr. Putnam who owns the gladiolus farm; Mr. Laplant who owns the hospital; Mr. Springstead president of the big bank on Cleveland Street.; and Commander Fortescue, he owns the big hotel off Fort Harrison."

He turned to Ann-Marie, "Do you know any of these guys?"

"Sure, they come into Mr. Gibbons' office now and then. All except Mr. Laplant. When Mr. Gibbons wants to see him, he goes to Mr. Laplant."

Abel grinned. He knew about Mr. Laplant from Scruffy. "Who votes how?"

Ann-Marie frowned and twisted her mouth, "Let's see, Mr. Putnam is currently the chairman. Most of the time he and Mr. Banks do whatever Mr. Springstead wants. Commander Fortescue doesn't seem to care as long as they leave the hotel alone. When Mr. Laplant attends a meeting, which isn't that often, they all do what Mr. Laplant wants." She thought for a minute, and then said, "He's a pretty nifty guy, Mr. Laplant. He usually wants what's best for the town and even the county. He's the one who got the money from the federal government for the new post office and the piping to the Beach. He finds money for Cdr. Fortescue's hotel and even makes them take in people who don't have any money, which is often these days." She was talking more and more, and Abel thought this was good.

He interrupted, "I think I may have to see Mr. Laplant. How do I do this? I mean, where does he live?"

"Oh, Abel, I don't know. Mr. Laplant is a very busy man. He doesn't come into town very often." She thought for a minute, "I think he mostly stays at his hospital or in his railroad car."

Abel frowned and played with his glass, "Then who would be able to get to him easily and that he might believe?"

Ann-Marie asked, "Believe about what? Right now you don't have anything to tell him. Let me go into work and when Mr. Gibbons is away from his desk and out of the office, I'll look around for, for something we can use, but I don't know if Mr. Laplant can do anything. Jeepers, not if the city attorney, the mayor and the police chief are all in on it, Abel." She looked down and shook her head.

Ada patted her hand, "Don't worry, honey. If anybody can do anything, Abel here can. After all, he rode all the way from Wyoming just to come here to find out how Mr. Brightwater died, didn't he?"

Ann-Marie nodded. “I sure hope so. Maybe you just need to get some names off those contracts. Then Abel can go talk to them and find out what they’re getting paid and stuff. But if these fellows are stealing money from the contracts, who told the chief to kill Mr. Brightwater?” She leaned across the table and whispered, “Do you think it was one of them?”

Abel frowned, “No, but I know the police chief had a hand in it. Probably your Mr. Avery Gibbons, too. The mayor?” He shrugged, “I don’t know. Maybe, maybe not, but I sure intend to find out and get them what’s coming to them.” He looked both girls right in the eyes, “Look at this as a war. You two are sergeants and I’m a captain. We’re in intelligence gathering. When we have enough to go on, we take the information to the general, that’s Mr. Laplant, and the information officer, that’s Mr. Perkins, the editor of the paper.”

Chapter 29

The Lawyers: Present Day

Dave, Rusty and Chris were sitting at the bar in Chesney's. Dave was feeling down but consoled himself that there was one less guy to deal with; for Tom to deal with. He hadn't planned on killing the stupid kid, but it seems that even good plans have a way of backfiring. He sipped his beer. It was the middle of the afternoon and the place was empty. The lunch crowd was gone, and the evening drinkers and diners weren't due for another couple of hours.

The door opened and two figures cut off the sunlight streaming through the doorway. Their shadows reached across the floor and slowly crept up the barstools and onto the bar, like a virus creeping across the land.

"Which one of you is Tom Novak?" the one on the right asked. He was tall and wide, wearing an expensive dark suit, striped shirt, and a Hermes silk tie. His partner was similarly dressed but was almost cadaverously thin. He had a shaved head, and an enormous wristwatch, which he kept looking at.

Dave and Rusty swiveled around on their stools almost in unison. Chris was slower. Charlie Potts eased out of the kitchen and stood behind the bar close to the .45 Dave kept there for emergencies.

"He isn't here," said Chris, leaning back, elbows on the bar. "Last we heard, he was still in the hospital." She caught a warning look from Dave.

"Say, who are you guys, anyway?" Rusty asked.

The beefy one slowly pulled a card out of his breast pocket and handed it over. Dave read it. Samuel Holmes, Attorney at Law. "This is my associate, Donald Bailey," he gestured with his right hand. The thin one nodded curtly.

"I'm surprised you couldn't find a partner named Watson," joked Dave.

"And you're here because?" asked Chris.

"We, ah, have been retained by the Brotherhood. It seems that one of our, ah, security guards was, um, found deceased last night."

"Yeah? So? What's that got to do with us?" Dave was now standing in front of the lawyer.

Holmes smiled benignly, "Well, we..., I mean the Brotherhood, during the course of their investigation, determined that two of the men involved in the, um, altercation with Mr. Novak have, ah, disappeared, and now another has found himself, um, deceased. We, I mean the Brotherhood, find this, ah, rather unusually coincidental." He glanced at his partner.

"We were sent to find out who, ah, perpetrated this heinous act. Naturally, Mr. Novak's name came up, and in checking with the, um, police, this address came up. We thought we'd have a little, uh, chat with him." He smiled again, though it never reached his eyes.

Dave stood with his hands on his hips, his body taunt, "Well, thanks to your little tin soldiers, Tom Novak and his friend, Barbara Young, are in comas in the hospital. So I think Mr. Novak has a pretty good alibi, don't you?" He was near spitting at the two men.

"Now take it easy Mr. …?"

"Manley, Dave Manley."

Chris stood next to her husband and pointed a finger at the two lawyers, "Those men beat and raped Ms. Young. Mr. Novak was trying to defend her, but it took five, five of your clients to beat them. I hope when he gets out of the hospital, he'll go after those guys and beat them up!" She was spitting fire now and Dave tried to calm her. She shook his hand off and went on. "If you men get too deeply involved in this, you'd better watch your backs too!"

Samuel Holmes started and took a step back. He narrowed his eyes and asked, "Are you threatening me, Madam?"

Chris smiled and crossed her arms across her chest, "Oh no, not me, Mr. Holmes. My job is to just help Thomas Novak get well." She sneered, "Then, well, what happens, happens."

Rusty stood and pointed to the door. "I think it's time for you two to leave." His bulk was imposing and he stood alongside Dave and Chris.

The two lawyers stepped back. Holmes narrowed his eyes and said, “You people will be hearing from us.”

He nodded to his partner and spun on his heel. The two strode to the door, briefcases banging against their legs. Bailey scowled at the group over his shoulder and slammed the door.

Chris collapsed into her chair and gave a big sigh, “Well, that was, um, interesting!?”

Dave grinned, “We sure gave it to those guys, huh?” He was trying to figure out if they actually knew anything, enough to have the police look into the previous night’s affair.

Rusty sighed, “I guess we better have some damn good alibis when we take care of the next one, fellas!”

Chapter 30

The First Hit: 1938

Abel rode his cycle to see his friend Ray Farrell, the retired motorcycle mechanic. As he pulled into the sloping driveway and killed the motor, Ray came out from under the hood of the old Hudson he'd been working on forever. The motor was popping and coughing and Farrell was scowling.

"Oh, it's you, Abel." He wiped his hands on a rag. "What's up, kid? Cycle not working right?" He slung the rag over his shoulder and stood, hands on hips.

Abel chuckled, "Running better than that Hudson, Ray. What's the problem? Sounds like the timing is off." Abel walked beside Farrell to the open hood of the car.

Ray reached in and tried wiggling the distributor. "See? The bugger's frozen. Rusted. Can't move it."

"I see," said Abel, rubbing his chin. "Have you got any

vinegar?" He eyed the man from the corner of his eye.

"Vinegar? What the hell for, kid? You hungry or something?"

Abel smiled, "No, but during the war, I used to see the mechanics use it to loosen stuck nuts and bolts." He shrugged, "It's worth a try, yes?"

Farrell looked at Abel for a long minute, then said, "You didn't come all the way here just to help me with a stuck distributor, did you?"

Abel stood and put a hand on Farrel's shoulder. "Ray, I guess you know why I'm in town here. I might need your help. Could you come out to the railroad car bar on the south end of Clearwater Beach tomorrow night?"

Farrell frowned, "Why? What's going on, kid? You in trouble?"

Abel thought for a minute, "Not sure, Ray. I may need your help, or at least your advice. I'm trying to get a few people together to decide where to go with the information I've collected so far." He stepped away and said, "I can use your help."

As Abel sat on his cycle and put his leather helmet on, Farrell nodded and said, "I'll be there, Abel. Are you askin' anybody else around here?"

"Yeah. Johnny Livingston. You know him?"

Farrell laughed, "Know him? He's kin on my wife's side somewhere. I taught the little bugger to ride!"

Abel stopped when he was reaching for his ignition key. He was stunned. "You have a wife?"

Ray's mouth turned down, "Had. She died in the flu epidemic a few years after the war."

Abel nodded, "Sorry to hear that, Ray." And then he kicked the old cycle into life and rode away with a brief wave.

Next on his agenda was Perkins, the newspaper editor. Abel turned down Main Street and idly looked in the rear view mirror. There was a big sedan coming up rapidly behind him. Abel casually waved his arm for the sedan to pass him, but it didn't swerve. Abel could see a large man in the driver's seat with a scowl on his face. It dawned on him that the car was not trying to drive around him. Looking around wildly, he saw a narrow opening between two parked cars and swung the front wheel between and gunned it onto the sidewalk just as the sedan clipped the rear wheel of the Harley. The cycle bounced off the rear of a Nash coupe and Abel was thrown over the handlebars, landing on the sidewalk. He heard people screaming. Then he blacked out.

As he came to, he felt something cool on his forehead. His vision started to clear, and he looked up at a woman who was wiping his face with a handkerchief wet with cool water. Over her shoulder he saw Johnny Livingston nervously dancing from foot to foot.

His mouth was moving, and Abel faintly heard him shouting, "Abel, Abel, are you all right?" Johnny asked the woman, "Is he going to be okay?"

The woman, an older woman with brown hair graying at the roots, answered, "He'll be fine. I'm a nurse. Just give him some room." She turned to Abel and asked, "How many fingers am I holding up?"

Abel looked at her hand and replied, "Twenty-seven."

She frowned and started taking his pulse.

He chuckled, "Naw, I'm just kidding you. Two, and I'm okey-dokey now." He pushed himself upright and felt the egg on his forehead. "Wow! A big one, huh? It'll make for a good story!"

Johnny helped him to his feet. Abel swayed a little and blinked rapidly. "Thanks, lady. You too, Johnny. I don't suppose you got a look at the driver, did you?"

The woman smiled at him and patted him on the arm. "You'd better stay off that cycle for a day or two, young man."

He smiled back and nodded, "Thanks, I will."

Johnny pulled him aside and said in a low voice, "Didn't recognize the car, but it sure looked like Brodsky was driving." He looked around to make sure nobody was listening and said, "Didn't look like an accident, Abel. Better watch yourself."

Abel nodded and whispered back, "Can you come out to Scruff's place about seven tonight? I got your Uncle Ray and a couple of others coming. I need some advice on where to go with this here thing."

Johnny nodded rapidly, "Yeah, sure, sure, Abel. I'll be there. I'll talk to my Uncle Ray, see if he needs a ride." With that, he helped Abel retrieve his cycle.

The rear wheel wobbled a little but a good kick seemed to straighten it. The fender rubbed on the tire but Abel and Johnny were able to pry it off. "Good enough, Johnny. You better get back to work. I'll see you later."

"Yeah, sure, sure, Abel," Johnny said over his shoulder

as he rapidly strode to a car idling along the curb outside the Arcade. After parking his cycle safely, Abel strode into the Arcane and back to the newspaper office. He leaned over the counter and waved a hand at Perkins, the editor. Arthur Perkins was on the phone but saw the wave. He gestured for Abel to come in.

Abel sat and waited, listening in on the phone call, but seeming bored and uninterested. Perkins was talking to one of the contractors for the water and sewer lines. He seemed exasperated and finally said, “Yeah, yeah, all right, Joe, if I hear anything, I’ll give you a call.” He dropped the heavy handset onto its cradle and pulled a pencil from behind his ear.

“So, what have you got for me, kid?” He squinted over his reading glasses and remarked, “Say, that’s quite a bump on your noggin. What trouble have you got yourself into now?”

“I’ll let you know when I have some more info. What’s up? I’m busy.”

Abel pondered for a minute, then said, “I’m getting a little nervous about this investigation we’re both doing. I’ve called a meeting of those folks I’ve met. We’ll be at Scruffy Fett’s on the South Beach tonight. I’d like you to come, you know, in case something happens to me, you’ll know what I’ve uncovered.”

Perkins chewed on a thumbnail, then nodded. “Sure, what time?”

Abel stood and replied, “About 7. See you then, sir.”

Next, Abel climbed back on his cycle and thought his next stop had to be the Toffelmeyer’s place. He needed to talk with Jack. As he drove across the causeway, he kept looking into his rear view mirror and over his shoulder, expecting to see Brodsky barreling down on him. But he was alone on this drive.

Scruffy was outside sweeping again as Abel rode by. They waved a hand at each other. Abel rode the cycle right down to the Toffelmeyer's place. As he shut the loud engine down he saw Jack sitting on the porch sewing a fish net. He was wearing his customary overalls and was barefoot.

Abel tucked his leather helmet onto his handlebar and approached the porch. "Jack, you remember that gun you showed me?"

"Yeah?"

"If you've still got it, I think I need it now. That fat cop Brodsky tried to run me down today."

"You gonna shoot him, young feller?"

"Naw, but I just want to have it if I get cornered, you know?"

"Well," Jack said, "I sure hope you don't have to use it, Abel." He heaved himself out of his chair, putting the net carefully aside and went into the house. In a couple of minutes he was back with that big hog leg of a pistol. As Jack unwrapped it from a rag, Abel saw it was clean and had a long barrel. It gleamed dully in the overcast light. It was an 1898 Colt Model called the Peacemaker. "Here, boy, I got this in my war, Cuba, just before the century turn. I was with Colonel Teddy's boys." He pointed to the grip. It was a dark wood with entwined R's and beneath was a TR 1898.

Abel put out a hand and Jack handed it to him, grip

forward. They just nodded at each other. It fit comfortably in one of his saddlebags. Abel said, "A few of us are meeting at Scruffy's tonight. Will you come? I could use your advice."

Jack scrubbed his chin, "I don't know. They usually don't like us folks in a place like that."

"Ah, yeah, Jack. Sorry, I forget about that. Had a friend who was one of you guys. Rode with me a long way coming here. He got to go home to his mama in Alabama."

Chapter 31

Money: Present Day

The whole gang was on its way to see Tom and Bobbie in the hospital in Clearwater. Dave had installed the third row seat in the old Ford Station Wagon so the three couples would fit. They pulled into the parking lot of the imposing building complex.

Vinny and Joan were trying to clamber over the middle row seat. "Jesus, Vin, slow down, will ya? Give us a chance to get out." Anna scowled, "We can fold the seat down, you know." As she did. Joan slid out first follower by Vinny.

"Do you know how cramped it is back there? Huh? My legs'r killing me." Vinny danced from leg to leg.

Joan grabbed his arm, "Come on, honey. Let's go see Tom."

Anna walked next to her, "And don't forget Bobbie, his

friend."

Rusty held the door for the others. The lobby wasn't crowded. Down the hallway and to the left was the Emergency Room. They could hear talk and some shouting from there. An older woman sat at a large desk. She looked at them over half-framed glasses.

"Can I help you ladies? And gentlemen?" She said this last with just a hint of distain, a bit of a sniff in her voice. After all, they were a motley-looking crew. Dave and Chris wore shorts and T-shirts, Joan wore faded Capri pants and a tank top, Rusty had on jeans and a short sleeve shirt and Vinny wore baggy cut-off jean shorts and a green golf shirt.

"Yeah, hi Ma'am, me and my friends are here to see Tom Novak." Dave said. "Is he still in ICU? And Bobbie, uh." He turned to Chris, "What's her last name?"

Chris sighed, "Young. Barbara Young."

The woman scanned her computer. "Let's see, Mr. Novak has been moved to an isolation room. That would be 244 on the second floor in the rear. Ms. Young is still in ICU." She looked up at the ladies. "Who are you going to see first?"

Chris said, "That will be Thomas Novak." She turned and strode toward the bank of elevators. While they waited, they noted a plaque on the wall which read, 'Dedicated to Dr. Henry Laplante'. Chris wondered who he had been.

They crowded in and spilled out on the second floor. "Jeesh, we could have taken the stairs," muttered Vinny.

At the nurses station, Dave asked for directions to Room 244. Without looking up, an oriental nurse pointed down a side hall. When they reached the room, Dave held them back. "Let's do this just a couple at a time, huh?"

"Good idea," agreed Rusty, pushing by Vinny and Joan. He had Anna by the arm, and they went into the room. The rest stayed in the hallway. Vinny and Joan pressed their ears to the door.

"What do you hear?" asked Dave leaning over their shoulders.

"Shhh," whispered Joan waving a hand at them. "Ah, they're just talkin', how'r ya feeling, stuff like that."

In a few minutes, they came out and before Dave could make a move, Vinny and Joan slipped behind Rusty and Anna. They were also gone only a short while, but laughter followed them from the room.

"What did you say?" asked Chris.

Vinny waved a palm at them, "Nuthin', just some good cheer." They crossed the hall and sat on a low, padded backless bench next to Rusty and Anna.

Dave looked at Chris, and they went into the hospital room where his best friend lay swaddled in bandages. He looked at the freshly shaven face and the clean sheets. An IV drip still hung beside the bed and his leg was still elevated on a pile of pillows.

"Hey," said Dave and reached out a hand. Tom bumped fists with him and grinned. Chris slipped into the bedside chair and kissed Tom on the cheek. As a tear trickled down her cheek, Tom wiped it with a corner of the top sheet.

"Come on, why the tears? I'm getting better. Is Dave beating you again?" He looked at Dave and winked.

Chris chuckled, "No, you idiot, these are tears of joy.

I'm so glad you are on the mend. How long before you get out of here?"

Tom shrugged. A small frown of pain crossed his face, "I don't know. Doc says my leg and my ribs've got to heal more before he'll let me go. Another week, maybe two. Says I'll be okay, can walk, talk, fly, shoot if I have to." He glanced at Dave's frowning face. "So what do I need to know?"

Dave pulled a chair close and sat near his head. "Any mikes in here?"

Tom shook his head, "Not as far as I know. No reason, really."

Dave nodded but kept his voice low, "The first guy is gone. We scared the shit outta him and sent him home. The next guy, the shorter one," Dave looked at Chris who was leaning in close so as not to miss a word. "Well, Rusty and I had a little problem with him. The sucker pulled a gun on me so I had to shoot him. We made it look like an argument between friends, but I think the Brotherhood goons have their doubts."

He continued, "A couple of lawyers from the Brotherhood showed up asking a bunch of questions. We still have to figure a way to get rid of the next two. They'll be on their toes."

Tom considered and said, "Just pop 'em and don't leave anything to link you to them? A good alibi and the cops can't do anything."

Dave looked down and muttered, "I really don't want to kill these guys if I can help it. You got any other ideas?"

The three of them thought for a minute and Chris suddenly perked up and said, "What's the Brotherhood love more than anything?" She looked from one to the other. "Think!"

Tom said, "Power?"

Chris rolled her eyes, "Yes, yes, of course, but what else?"

Dave and Tom smiled at the same time, "Money!" they chorused.

"Yes," Chris agreed, "now listen to my plan." For the next ten minutes she, Dave and Tom formulated the plan. It was crude to start, then they added bits, changed a little here and there and finally left Tom with a smile on his face.

The last thing Dave told him was, "We'll leave the last guy for you. We'll just keep track of him as best we can, okay?"

Tom gave him an exhausted thumbs up after they promised to look in on Bobbie. He immediately fell back on the bed and was asleep almost before his head hit the pillow.

Chapter 32

The First Meeting: 1938

Abel stopped at home, or at least where he was living with Martha and BB. As he strode up to the porch, BB came out the door and hugged him. "Thanks so much, Uncle Abel for helping Mom and me."

"What brought this on, kiddo?"

Martha came out dusting her hands off with a thin dish towel. "We just appreciate all you are doing, little brother."

Abel scuffed a shoe on the porch floor and gave the two of them a quick hug. "Aw, it ain't nothin', Sis." As he drew back, clearly embarrassed, he asked, "Say, Mart, what ever happened to Bob's car? He did have a car, didn't he?"

She smiled, "Oh yes, it was a 1929 Ford Model A coupe. I used to ride next to Bob and BB, and sometimes Captain rode in the rumble seat. When the chief of police came to see me, he said that they took the car to find out if there were any clues in it."

Abel frowned, "And they never gave it back to you?"

Martha sniffed, "Oh, it doesn't matter. I don't know how to drive anyway." She opened the door and waved the two boys in, "Come on, dinner is just about ready. I made us a chicken and vegetable pie."

"Good, Mart, but it will have to be quick. I'm having a meeting at Scruffy's place tonight." He sat and stuffed a clean, neatly folded napkin under his chin.

BB started, wide-eyed. "A big meeting, Uncle Abel? So

who all's gonna be there?"

"Yes, brother, who is going to be there, and what is this all about?" Martha stood before the stove with her hands on her hips, frowning.

Shoveling the stew into his mouth and munching a crust of bread, Abel mumbled, "Just some of the people I've met here, Jack Toffelmeyer, maybe; Perkins, the newspaper editor and a few others." He swallowed, took a drink of milk and went on, "We're trying to find out why your husband was killed and talk about a few other things that have been going around in this town."

Martha went back to stirring the pot before spooning portions for BB and herself. "And if you do? Will that bring my Bob back? Will that get you killed also? And the Toffelmeyers?" Her spoon was now smacking against the side of the pot. BB looked from his mother to his uncle and back.

Abel stood and touched his sister on the shoulder and said softly, "I'll be back in a while, Mart. Why don't you get some sleep? Go to bed early." He turned and said, "You, too, BB." He tousled the boy's hair.

"Be careful, Uncle Abel," he said in a low voice.

Abel grabbed his leather helmet and strode out the door. In a minute, they heard the cycle start, the engine race, then fade into the darkness surrounding the small house.

Chapter 33

Computer Attack: Present Day

On the drive back, Chris shared the plan with the others. Even Joan and Vinny were on-board. “You know, we need that inside friend of yours, Vin, the plumber. Do you think we can get him on our side?”

Vinny scrubbed the back of his neck with his hand, “Jeepers, Chrissy, you know these people, they’re fanatics. I was lucky getting’ the info I did.” He grimaced, “I think if I push him, he might tell the upper bosses. Then that puts a target on us, all of us.”

“Yeah, you’re right,” agreed Dave, “but do you think you can have one more meeting with him, just to drop a little hint?”

“I can probably do that. I’ll tell him I’m looking for some work with the Brotherhood, looking to make some cash.”

The rest of the ride was in silence, each one reviewing the plan, trying to find holes in it.

When they arrived at Chesney's, the men went to the garage/workshop and the women went into the bar. Charlie Potts was scrubbing the kitchen prep tables. Ringo was mopping the floor, humming a quiet tune to himself, his ever present long coat almost sweeping the floor behind him. Every once in a while he dunked the mop in the rolling bucket, squeezed it out and resumed mopping.

Chris walked over to him and patted him on the shoulder. "Nice work, Ringo. We're all very proud of you."

He grinned a toothless grin and softly said, "Thank you, Missy Christine," and kept on mopping.

Joan and Anna sat at the bar while Chris went behind and drew them each their favorite drink, a draft beer for Anna and a glass of white wine for Joan. She poured a cherry Coke for herself.

Chris called, "Charlie, is Emile around?" She looked around and into the TV corner. Emile wasn't there.

Charlie yelled, "I dunno, maybe on his boat or on the dock."

Ringo gestured out the rear door with his mop. Chris understood and walked out back. Emile was sunning himself in a chaise on the back deck. Chris walked up and squatted next to him. "Emile, oh, Emile," she sang.

He sat up with a start, "Oh, it's you, Chrissy. I was having the most marvelous dream, and then you came." He smiled a warm, sleepy smile. "Thank you for the perfect ending."

She stood and held out a hand, "Come on, Romeo, I have a little job for you." Together they walked back inside. The whole gang was waiting in the TV area. "Sit," she said and pushed him into a comfortable chair.

Dave leaned forward and told Emile their plan. When finished, he asked, "Well? What do you think? Can you do it?"

He pursed his lips, calculating, "How much?"

Chris shrugged, "Couple of million each? Think that ought to do it?"

"Sure," Emile replied, "might take a while to set it all up. I'll need a couple of clean laptops, used ones, and you guys are going to have to figure out how to get them into their rooms. The offshore accounts won't be a problem, but I'm not used to leaving a trail."

"No problem getting the laptops. If we get them, can you set them up? You know, clean them out and put in all the stuff we'll need?" Chris asked.

Emile drew himself upright in his seat, "Do you know a hacker better than me, my dear?" He brushed back his long auburn hair and tugged his T-shirt down, tucking it into his khaki shorts. He walked to his computer terminal in the corner and lit up the three screens.

Turning, he said, "I'm going to need these guy's names, locations, preferably any nicknames they might have. What I'd really like is fingerprints and pictures of them. How complicated do you want me to make this?" Emile swiveled around in the high-back office chair he kept there.

Chris frowned, "What do you mean?" This was getting more complicated than she'd imagined.

"Well, if these guys are smart, I have to make it more complicated. If they aren't, I don't have to work so hard!" he laughed. "If these guys are just low-level security guards, maybe not too swift? Maybe I'll make it a little sloppy?" Then he pointed at Chris, "And, if you want someone to uncover it, how smart will they have to be? And, lastly, if the big shots do uncover this, what happens to those two guys?"

Now it was Dave's turn to step in. "That, my friend, is not your business. They, or we," he gestured at his crew, "will take care of that."

Emile considered this. It troubled him. He knew that it would probably result in the demise of the two men.

While he was pondering his role, Dave showed him an early picture of Tom in the ICU. He brushed his phone to a picture of Bobbi, Tom's lady friend. She was in a coma, face battered and bruised. "You do know what these guys did to them? Whatever they get isn't enough."

Emile nodded. "I'll do it. Get me the info I need."

Dave and Chris decided that since Chris was young and beautiful, they would use her as bait to try to get access to the two men. One of the girls from their favorite restaurant, Shelly, agreed to go with her. All they had were two names: Mike Russell and Carter Donovan. They were both security for the Brotherhood. The only place they could start was a snack bar owned and run by members of the Brotherhood.

Dave would drop them off there, a place called The Dagger off Gulf-To-Bay Blvd. when the rest of the plan was in place.

The next day was a Sunday. Rusty and Anna and Joanie

and Vince set out for a flea market about two hours north of Clearwater, up near Crystal River. Their job was to buy two laptop computers with the specifications Emile had written down. It didn't take them long to locate a vendor who had several laptops for sale.

The vendor, a man and his wife, almost twins, dressed alike in khaki slacks, tan shirts and red sweaters, looked at the specs in Vinny's hand. The wife snorted, "Don't you want something a little more modern than that? Those specs are about four to five years old."

Anna smiled and said, "No, they're for my grandkids. I don't want them to have anything too up-to-date. They're just learning." She hoped she wouldn't have to field too many more questions like this. She barely knew how to use computers herself.

The man nodded and said, "Come back in about twenty minutes. I'll load the software and games you want." He picked up two computers, different brands but with about the same scuff marks.

Rusty asked, "'Bout how much. For the kids, you know."

The man looked at them shrewdly, then glanced at his wife.

"About $100 each, be okay?" she asked. She was rubbing her thumbs and fingers together unconsciously.

"How about $80 each?" countered Vinny.

They settled on $90 each. As they walked away, Joan saw them smile at each other. "Well, fellas, we've got $10 each to blow. How about some of those big cinnamon buns we saw in that little bakery?"

An hour later they were on their way home, the two laptops tucked beside Vinny and Joan in the back seat of Rusty's ten year old Oldsmobile.

That evening after the crowd had left and they'd all helped clean up, they held another meeting in Emile's computer corner.

Dave asked the slim hacker, "So what have you come up with?"

Emile lit up the screens and pointed to one. "These are the three guys we're after. The first," he pointed, "Is their fearless leader, Mackenzie Roland Mayer. 6' 2" tall, 220 lbs., Black hair, dark eyes, thin moustache. Thirty-six years old, born in Minneapolis, Minnesota." He printed the sheet out. "I hacked into their personnel files. His file says he was busted a few years ago for mail fraud. Didn't say why."

"Okay, what about the other two?" asked Chris, leaning over his shoulder.

Emile took a deep breath of whatever perfume she was wearing. Lilac, he decided. "Carter Donovan and Michael Russell." He brought each of their pictures up on a separate screen. "Russell is thirty-five, comes from Talbert, Louisiana, small town down in the bayou. He's ex-Army , six-one, 210 lbs., brown hair cut short, blue eyes. Russel's the guy with the eagle tattooed on his right hand. He's got a couple more tattoos on his arms and back." He scrolled down. "Got a record too. Tossed out of the Army three years ago for knocking his CO on his ass, stole a couple of cars when he was a kid and was a bouncer in a New Orleans bar before the Army."

He printed his picture out also, and gave it to Chris. "I think this is the guy you told me about who hit Tom with the brass knucks."

"And the other guy?" asked Dave, pointing at the screen.

"Yeah, Donovan. He's 26, 5'10", 190 lbs., blonde hair, blue eyes, comes from Portland, Maine. Used to be a drag racer until he got hurt in a crash. Limps but not much. He and a sister are in the Brotherhood. Their father was one too, but left or was forced out at some point."

Rusty asked, "Education?"

Emile shrugged, "Russell quit school at sixteen. Couldn't find anything else. Donovan went to community college for a couple of years in Maine but I couldn't find out for what." He turned to Dave and Chris, "I can try hacking into the college records and see what I can come up with, if you like?"

"Probably not necessary. What about the computers?" Dave pointed.

"I think Donovan likes playing computer games. He's got a Facebook page and talks about it a lot. Russell, I don't know. Couldn't find anything about him online. Only thing I found is that the two of them like the ladies and drink together at that Brotherhood owned bar downtown, the Dagger."

Chris took the two pictures with the names beneath and folded them. "I'll have to talk with Shelly. See which one she wants." She grinned, wrinkling her nose.

Emile went on, "I'll load up the computers with games, Facebook accounts, some links to their hometowns and a couple of contacts with friends from their hometowns. I can get them from Donovan's high school yearbook. I'll dig up a couple of names from Russell's past, too."

"And the money?" asked Rusty, taking a long swallow from his beer.

Emile frowned, "I'll start dating small withdrawals from a couple of Brotherhood accounts a year or so ago, then increase the amounts up to recently. I'll make it odd numbers but total it out around a mil and a half for both. I thought if I make the last couple of amounts the same, it will look like they are doing this together. That okay?"

Dave sat back rubbing his chin, "That looks good. Are you going to have a deposit for them someplace?"

"Yes, I've been doing some checking. The Brotherhood has a training center in Panama. I'll set up accounts for both of them there, then put some talk between them on the computers about getting transferred there in the next few months. I won't make any of it encrypted, so if their bosses hack into the accounts, they'll get caught pretty easily."

He sat back in his chair and rocked for a few seconds, hitting a pencil against the desktop.

"Something else?" asked Chris.

"Yeah, I figure that if Mayer goes on the run, that's where he'll go. Their place is pretty big down there. Probably pay out a lot of bribes to the government to turn their heads."

"Like Jonestown in Guyana. Just don't drink the Kool Aid." Rusty snorted.

"How long will this take?" asked Dave.

"I'll have the computers done tomorrow and the money things by the end of the week. I don't want their people to find out what they've been doing for a week or two. After that, I don't want to know nuttin'!" Emile grinned and stood up. "Once this is over, I'm taking a little vacation and I don't mean to Panama."

"What about our expense money?" Chris had her notebook out and was writing.

Emile still smiled and stretched his back. "Oh, don't worry about that. I'll arrange for it. I'm taking ten percent, if you don't mind." And he walked out onto the back deck and down to his boat.

Chapter 34

Plan of Operation: 1938

Abel pulled up outside the old railway car and was satisfied that there were three other cars parked haphazardly in front. One, he noted, was the old Essex, so Ray Farrell must be there. He hoped that he'd brought Johnny Livingstone with him. As he was trying to figure out who the two other cars belonged to, lights lit him up and a roadster with a ragged top pulled in next to him. Arthur Perkins stepped out, still wearing his visor and arm cuffs.

"Howdy, young feller, you waitin' for me?" He reached in and pulled a notepad off the passenger seat. "Come on, let's get this show on the road."

He strode to the front door and held it for Abel. As they came in, Scruffy leaned out and hung a sign on the door that said Closed. "Come on in, Abel and Mr. Perkins. The others are waitin'."

There were two tables pulled together. Ray Farrell was entertaining the two young ladies, Ada and Ann-Marie. The two girls waved limp hands at him. Beside Ray sat Johnny Livingston. The four had drinks in front of them, and a tin of cookies sat on the table. Scruffy was nervously walking back and forth. "Here, here, Abel, you sit here, an', an' Mr. Perkins, you sit here, sir." He indicated two chairs opposite the ladies, for Johnny and Ray.

"Howdy, Abel. Perkins." Ray reached a hand across the table and shook with Perkins. "All-righty now, what's this all about?"

Abel said, "Thanks for coming. Look, I didn't want to involve you folks, but I think somebody tried to run me down today. Whether it was because of what I'm trying to find out or something else," he glanced at Perkins who lifted an eyebrow, "I'm not sure. But I figured I'd better tell all of you what I've found out so far, you know, in case something happens."

Ray frowned and clenched a fist, "You know who tried to whack you, kid? You let me know, an' I'll take care of 'em."

"Easy, Ray. We don't know for sure, and we all need to figure out who killed my brother-in-law, Bob." He was about to go on when there was a soft tap at the door.

They all looked at each other and Abel nodded at Scruffy, "Go see who it is, please."

Scruffy quickly walked and leaned his head against it. "Who's there?" He asked in a low voice. They couldn't hear the reply, but Scruffy turned toward the group. In a loud whisper, he said, "Said his name is Jack Toff-something. Said he knows you, Abel."

"Yeah, yeah, I know him. Let him in. He's okay."

The big black man squeezed through the door and stood, cap in hand. He nodded at Abel and the others.

"Well, hell, don't just stand there, Jack, come over here and sit down." Abel moved his chair to make room and waved a hand at Scruffy. "Scruff, get my friend Jack a chair, will ya?"

Scruffy frowned as did Perkins and Ray Farrell. Ray said, "You want him to sit with us, Abel? Here, at our table?"

"Yeah, why not? He's my friend." He stood and introduced him to the others.

Jack held out a large, calloused hand. "Howdy, I'm Jack Toffelmeyer. I live kinda next to Martha Brightwater an' BB, her boy." Nobody reached out to shake his hand.

Abel looked from one to the other. "Oh, for Chrissake, are you all segregationers?" He spun his chair aside and pointed, "Sit down, Jack. We need you here."

Arthur Perkins asked, "Why do we need him? What can he do that we can't?"

Abel poked a finger at him. "Suppose we find out something we need to know in the colored community? Who better than a colored guy? And his family?" He held out a hand, indicating Jack.

Jack smiled at the group. The others nodded reluctantly. Finally Ada said, "All-righty, can we get on with this? My dad will want his car back soon."

Abel agreed and spent the next fifteen minutes explaining what he'd found out from the police report, the autopsy, the information from Ada Griver and Ann-Marie Knightington and the speculation of Arthur Perkins.

He wound up with, "So, we think that Bob might have been killed, not had an accident. He might have been killed because of something he learned at his office about the WPA money or maybe he learned something about the missing kids. That right, Mr. Perkins?"

Perkins shrugged, "Maybe, but we're going to need a lot more info if we're going to take it to, I dunno, the Marshall Service, Rangers?" He turned to Abel, "They don't have a statewide police force here."

Ray answered, "There ain't one yet, though they're talking about it up there in Tallahassee. See, they're afraid that it'll be too much like the Klanners an' they're afraid they'll start killing off the coloreds. Can't abide by that." He nodded to Jack Toffelmeyer who nodded back. Ray slouched in his seat and lit a hand-rolled cigarette with a wooden match he ignited on a ring he wore on his left hand.

Abel was pacing back and forth now, muttering to himself, counting on his fingers. Perkins was just about to say something when Abel paused and confronted the crew. "Okay, my friends, it looks like we have some more work to do." He pointed to Ann-Marie, "You, can you see if you can get some info on the WPA contracts? You know, just who was doing the work on the stuff going out to the Beach?"

Ann-Marie looked sideways at Ada, who nodded a little, lips compressed. She looked back at Abel and said, "I'll do my best. Do you need copies?" She gnawed at a lip.

"Aw, that would be great, but how're you going to do that?"

Ada said, "We've been using carbon paper for a few years. We both have some. I will retype some of the papers we have. The Chief or Attorney don't usually pay much attention to what we're doing, as long as we finish what they want on time. It should be easy to make copies." She looked at Ann-Marie again. "We usually bring our lunches so it shouldn't be impossible to get some papers out."

Ann-Marie chimed in, "I can always crumple them up and throw them in the trash cans. We have to empty our full cans out back in the large bins." She frowned, "I don't know what happens to them after that."

Jack raised a hand, "I think my cousin Hayward and a coupla guys pick up all the trash from the guv'mint buildings. I could, maybe, have him bring certain bags to his place where he could kinda hold 'em for us?" He sat, arms crossed.

Abel turned to the others, "See? I knew my buddy Jack here could pull his weight."

Perkins grudgingly nodded at the big black man. "I think those guys pick up the trash from the Arcade too."

"No offense, Mr. Perkins, but white folks don't much like handling trash, garbage and stuff like that. Some of them folks have built small houses with stuff white folks throw away."

Perkins nodded, "No offense taken, Mr. Toffelmeyer. I'm sure you're right, though since the hard times started, some white folks will take just about any job." He said this with a note of sadness in his voice. "I'm hoping that Mr. Roosevelt will be able to squeeze some more money out of Congress for us regular folks."

They all nodded. Ray smiled and said, "Any of you listen to that Woody Guthrie fellow on the radio?"

Johnny Livingston nodded rapidly, his Adam's apple bobbing, "I do. I think he's the cat's meow. That feller sure has a good feel for what's happening."

Ann-Marie tossed her hair and said, "I like jazz better." She snapped her fingers and hummed a few bars. Then she sang in a soft voice, "Marie, the dawn is breaking, Marie, you'll soon be waking…" She hummed a bit more, then flushed as the others grinned and clapped.

Abel was pacing again, "Can we get back to what we were talking about, please?"

He turned and leaned on the table. "You understand that we can't let the Chief or Attorney know what we are doing, yeah?" He looked from one to the other. "Especially Chief McBride. I know what a son-of-a-bitch he is." He looked at the two young women and winked, "Excuse my French, please."

Ann-Marie giggled, "It's not like we haven't heard swearing before, Mr. Landis. Or should we call you Commander?"

He laughed and said to them all, "Let's meet back here again in a couple of days. If they're trying to kill me now, we must be getting close. Ann-Marie, if you can get any information, give it to Johnny here at lunchtime, okay?"

They both nodded. "Got to keep this on the QT. You know what I mean?"

The two nodded again. Johnny got up, nervously swaying from side to side. "I, I got to go, Abel. Come on, Uncle Ray." He quickly walked to the door, looked over his shoulder and skipped outside.

Ray slowly got to his feet and clapped a hand on Abel's shoulder. "Give me a shout, kid. I'm here to help."

Abel nodded his thanks. "I hope I'll see you back here in a coupla days, Ray. I'll let Johnny know."

Ray said, "Count on me, Abel." And he left, followed by the two women. "You can count on us too," said Ada. "We all liked Mr. Brightwater."

Outside, two small faces were looking through the newly cleaned window near the back. BB turned to Captain and whispered, "What do you think they're talkin' about?"

Captain shrugged, "I dunno but early today I saw my daddy give your Uncle Abel a gun." He whispered this with a note of awe. "Do you think he's gonna kill somebody, BB?"

BB sucked in a breath, "A gun? I don't know, but you listen when your mama and daddy talk tonight and I'll make believe I'm asleep and listen to my mama and Uncle Abel talk, okay?"

BB nodded. "Tomorrow we'll compare what we heard, okay?"

"Okay." And they scampered back to their homes.

Abel and Jack said their goodbyes to Scruffy and went outside. Abel climbed on his cycle and said, "Hop on, Jack, I'll give you a ride home."

"Aw, thanks, Abel, but I'm afeared my big ass won't fit

on that there cycle. That's okay, I'll walk home." He started off just after the sun set.

"Hold on, Jack, its pretty level, I'll walk with you." He got off and started pushing the big cycle. Once he had it rolling, it wasn't too bad.

Jack put a hand on the rear of the seat and the two friends walked back easily to their homes on the south end of Clearwater Beach, talking quietly.

Unseen, a thin man was watching from behind a small stand of palm trees.

Chapter 35

Feminine Wiles: Present Day

Dave and Chris went to see Tom two days later. He was feeling better and they told him what was planned. He listened and nodded as Chris spoke. In his left hand was a soft rubber ball that he kept squeezing. The right was still wrapped up with splints. Dave gestured at it. "How long until they unwind the mitt? Looking better, no more discoloration."

"The doc says another week or ten days and then start exercising." He shrugged. "I'll be on my feet by then. They're going to put one of those braces on my leg." He turned his mostly unbandaged face to Chris. "What's my mug look like. Still handsome and boyish?"

"Well," she drew it out, "since you were never a pretty boy, you didn't have much to lose." She noted the stitches to his cheek and forehead, the two black and purple eyes and the straightened nose with the metal and tape on it.

His leg was now resting on a stack of pillows and was in a metal and plastic leg brace. He wiggled his toes. "See, still got feeling in my pinkies."

Dave and Chris laughed and stood. "I guess we'll go see Bobbie now. Have they told you how she's doing? Is she still in a coma?"

Tom frowned and grew somber. "She's gone. Her parents came and got her. A private ambulance took her to their place. Her old man gave me a ration of shit, then left. Told me to stay away."

"No shit?" Dave whistled. "He say where they live? Is it here in Florida?"

Tom shook his head, "We never got that close. I'd just started seeing her. Guess that's over, huh?" He sighed and laid back, head on two pillows.

Dave and Chris glanced at each other. Chris cleared her throat, "Look, we're going to get out of here. If you need anything, give us a call, okay?"

He remained silent. Dave touched her arm and motioned to the door with his head. She nodded. Silently, they left the room.

They drove back in silence. Chesney's had only a couple of mid-afternoon fishermen drinking at the bar and one couple in a booth. Rusty and Vince were in the TV corner with Emile. He was pointing to one of the computer monitors and explaining something to them.

Chris saw the two laptop computers sitting on a chair beside Emile. "Are we ready?" she asked.

Charlie Potts came out of the kitchen and handed her a plate with a sandwich on it. “Here, Chrissy, you’re going to need some nourishment. You’re going up against those two assholes from the Brotherhood.”

“Yes. Don’t much feel like it, but Shelly and I are going to do our part.” She went to the bar and pulled out her cell phone. She made a time to pick up Shelly and they discussed how to dress.

That evening, Dave and Rusty followed the girls to the downtown bar and grill, Daggers, that the Brotherhood security guards frequented. Chris drove Vince and Joan’s Toyota SUV. She picked up Shelly at Harrington’s, then drove the few blocks to the bar. They spent a few minutes looking at the pictures of the two men they were stalking, Donovan and Russell.

Shelly asked, “Which one do you want, Chrissy?” They each held a picture. She pointed at the one in Chris’s hand, “He’s kind of cute. I like big guys. Can I have him?” It was Mike Russell, tall with dark hair and a boyish face.

“Sure, leave me the kid, huh?” Chris replied. “Doesn’t matter.” They swapped and she held Carter Donovan’s photo. He looked average, nothing distinctive about him. Young, in decent shape, short blonde hair, no facial hair, but wide set eyes, a nose that had been broken at least once, and a square jaw. He didn’t look mean, she decided, just distant, blank. She snorted and said, “This ought to be fun. Let’s go.”

The Dagger was dimly lit, music played in the background. The bar was along the right hand wall and bent 90 degrees. Across from the bar were random tables and against the far wall were a row of high-back booths.

Chris couldn't identify the music or the singer. They looked around but didn't see the two men. It was still early. She leaned on the bar and the bartender wandered over, absently swiping the bar with a soft towel. "What can I get you ladies?" He took in the low cut tops, short skirts and heels.

"Could we get a couple of glasses of white wine and bring them over to that table, over there?" She pointed to one a little way in from where they were standing.

Shelly smiled at him and winked. "And some peanuts or pretzels too, please, kind sir?"

He smiled and nodded, "Sure, ladies. Anything else?" When they said no, he went back to the other end of the bar where two couples were seated. The men were in Brotherhood uniforms.

When they sat, Chris said, "Looks like we're in the right place." Over the next hour, they sipped their wine and even had another. They kept glancing at the door, evaluating everyone who came in. A little after nine, the two men they were looking for strolled in. They waved at the bartender and took a booth next to the two women.

Shelly took out her computer and the two started playing World of Warcraft. After a few minutes, they got into an argument. While they were pointing fingers at each other, the taller one of their neighbors got up and stood next to Shelly. "Easy, honey, take it easy. What's the problem? Is she beating you?"

"No, we're just trying to figure out how to get the gnomish city back from the troggs. This game is tough!"

Chris giggled, "Now how would you know what this is about?" She closed the laptop and took a sip of her wine.

"Naw, lady, you're talking to one of the world's greatest experts on the World of Warcraft here!" he pointed to himself, then at his tablemate. "My name is Mike and that no-good bum is Carter." Carter wiggled a two-finger salute and waved the two women toward their table.

"Ladies, won't you join us? The evening is yet young." He kicked a chair back and Chris slid in next to him while Russell pulled a chair back for Shelly. She batted her eyes at him as she sat, then fluffed her hair.

It was everything Chris could do to keep from rolling her eyes. They spent the next two hours joking and telling stories and asking their tablemates lots of questions. Eventually, the two men asked them to go back to their rooms for some instruction in World of Warcraft. The ladies had had several more glasses of wine, while the men stuck to beers. Shelly and Chris had eaten lots of bread before coming out for the evening hoping it would help counteract the wine.

The two men lived nearby in a former hotel now owned by the Brotherhood. The ladies followed them in their car, and the two parked in the lot beside the five-story building.

Shelly tucked her arm into Mike Russell's and Chris tolerated Carter putting his arm around her. The women each had their large purses containing their laptops. Upstairs, on the third floor, the men had rooms next to each other. Shelly and Chris huddled together and Chris whispered, "Remember, we're here to act drunk and accidentally leave the laptops, right?"

Shelly smiled dreamily and nodded. "Don't worry, I got it. I'll meet you at the car later." She hugged Chris then took Mike's arm again, following him into his room.

Carter urged Chris into his room. As soon as the door closed, he backed her against the wall and started groping her. She pushed him away and said, "Easy, big guy, let's play some vid games first. Isn't that why we came up here?"

He sighed and said, "Yeah, sure. Some computer games first. It'll be fun."

She patted him on the arm, "Come on, cowboy, we can play around later." During the next half hour they sat on the side of his bed, each with a laptop, relaxed, joking and trying to beat each other. Occasionally, Carter's hand strayed to her thigh. She would cover it with hers and squeeze it. He leaned over and kissed her neck. Chris felt it was time.

She stood and kissed his cheek. "Where's your bathroom, honey? I want to, um, get ready." She winked at him and followed his pointing finger.

He waited a minute after she closed the door, knocked and asked, "Are you all right, baby? Need a little help?"

She called, "Yeah, Carter, I, uh, just started my period. Shit. Have you got any paper towels or napkins or something? I kinda have a pretty heavy flow this month." She started running the water in the sink. "Give me a hand, will you?"

As he opened the door, she was standing in her underpants. The short skirt was on the floor and the front of her underwear and her legs were covered in blood. It was running down her legs. She smiled at him, "Aw, hell, you're not afraid of a little blood, are you?" She reached for him and said, “Come here, baby, let’s get it on.” She wiggled her hips and winked at him.

Carter stumbled backward, one hand clutching his belt. “Oh, god, no, no. Please, maybe it’s time you left. Yeah, yeah, honey, it’s been fun, great night. I’ll, uh, wait for you out here.” And he closed the door.

Chris giggled and dabbed at herself with some toilet paper. The small flat flask, now half empty of chicken’s blood, slipped back into her skirt pocket and she shimmied it back up. Chris would have to remember to thank Charlie Potts for the blood.

She staggered back into the room and slurred her words, “Oh, come on, baby, let’s have some fun.” She saw her laptop on the floor where she had set it, and, as she went to him, surreptitiously kicked it under the bed.

Carter jumped to his feet and grasped her arm, “Lemme help you out there, lady.”

She bent and picked up her bag and was soon out in the hall. He muttered after her, “Let’s get together sometime, huh?”

A minute with a damp rag from the bag wiping up the remaining blood, she hummed as she walked down the stairs and into the parking lot. As she waited for Shelly, she listened to music on the radio. ‘It’s a Beautiful Day’ by U2 was playing. Chris leaned her head back and hummed along with it.

It took fifteen minutes before Shelly came skipping over to the passenger side. She was disheveled, and her normally neat hair was mussed and tangled. She flopped back and sighed, "God, I needed that."

Chris looked at her, mouth agape, "You didn't." A pair of headlights flashed across their window as another car entered the lot.

It lit up Shelly's flushed face, and she replied with closed eyes, "I sure did, and it was really good." She turned to Chris with eyes still closed, "You?"

"Oh, hell no, but I sure freaked him out." She lifted her skirt and Shelly looked at her.

Shelly whooped, holding her hand over her mouth. They both dissolved in giggles, leaning against each other. Chris broke it up, saying, "Let's get out of here. I'm tired."

"And hungry," chimed in Shelly.

Chapter 36

Ann-Marie's Message: 1938

The next day, Abel told his sister what had been discussed. "Why wasn't I there?" she demanded. "I had every right, little brother!"

In a placating voice, Abel said, "Yes, yes, I know, but I want you to have some distance from all this nastiness. If anything happens, I don't want anything to fall on you or BB." He changed the subject quickly. "Do you or Jack or a friend know how to drive a car? Someone who can give you lessons?"

She thought for a minute, "Well, I suppose Alfred could teach me. I don't know about Jack Toffelmeyer, but it can't be too much different from driving a boat, can it?"

Jeepers, thought Abel, those are her choices? "Look, I'm going into town. I'll get your car and bring it back here.

Maybe Ray Farrell could teach you. Once business gets booming, you're going to need one to get around, pick up supplies and stuff." He swallowed the rest of his oatmeal and coffee and headed for the door. Over his shoulder, he shouted, "BB, can you and Captain be here when I get back? I'd like you boys to wash and clean up your dad's old car, OK?"

BB ran to the door and shouted to Abel, "Sure, Uncle Abel. We'll do a super job for you. For mom too!"

Abel smiled, waved, and was off on his cycle again for town. He stopped at the old dining car and yelled for Scruffy who was washing the windows, "Hey, Scruff, I need some help."

Scruffy walked slowly to Abel's idling cycle, a frown on his face, "Whacha need, Abel?" A wet cloth dripped down his arm.

"Hop on. We're going to get Bob's old car from town. I need you to drive it back here." He almost choked on the next part, "Then I'm going to need you to teach Martha how to drive." He squinted at Scruffy, "Think you can do that?"

Scruffy gave a shy smile and just bobbed his head. He made to climb on behind Abel, then remembered the rag. "Just a minute." He quickly walked back to the bar, tossed the rag into the bucket and locked the door. He then jogged back and jumped on the cycle, gripping Abel's shirt with a wet hand.

Abel just shook his head. It was the fastest he'd seen Scruffy move the whole time he'd been on the Beach. They roared off in a plume of dust, turned at the big dance-hall and onto the causeway.

A large steam shovel and several trucks were working

on the ditch beside the road. He supposed this was for the water and sewer lines out to the homes and the big hotels. Looking at the work site, he was surprised that there weren't more men digging and working. He'd seen WPA projects in other places and they had been designed to employ as many locals as possible.

He drove through the light traffic, waved to Johnny Livingston and turned for the police station. When he pulled into the curb and switched off the engine, Scruffy said, "I think I'll just wait here, if you don't mind, Abel. I don't like this place."

"Fine, fine. Just keep an eye on the cycle, will you?" He slid off and walked up the three steps to the large mahogany doors. Inside, one of the officers was sitting at the counter. It was the local boy, Chick Warner. He frowned as Abel strode up and placed both hands on the desk.

"What's your name, officer?" asked Abel. He wondered if this was one of McBride's handpicked recruits.

"Uh, Chick Warner, sir, and who might you be?"

"I'm Abel Landis, Bob Brightwater's brother-in-law. I came to pick up his car. I was told you guys had it. Bob's wife, Martha wants it." He was blunt, expecting a fight.

He smiled at Abel, "Hi, there. I heard you were in town." Chick stood and held out a hand, "I, uh, just want to say how sorry I am about Bob. I knew him. He was my friend."

This wasn't what Abel expected. Over the policeman's shoulder he saw Ada Griver, the secretary. She winked at Abel and nodded. He smiled back quickly.

Chick gestured him to a nearby window. He pointed to a dusty coupe sitting in a parking lot below. "I think that's it, Mr. Landis." He looked at Abel, "It is Mr. Landis, ain't it?"

"Yep, that's it, Officer. You got the keys?"

"Uh, I think they're in the chief's desk. He ain't here right now. Could you come back? I'm sure there's some papers that hafta be signed."

Before he could make up excuses, Ada shoved a couple of papers in the center of Chick's desk. "Here they are, Officer." She also handed him a fountain pen. "I know where the chief keeps the keys. I'll get them, if that's all right, Officer Warner, Mr. Landis."

Chick looked confused for a minute, then realized Abel was still leaning over the desk, said, "That will be fine, Miss Griver." He handed the pen to Abel and turned the papers toward him.

Abel quickly scrawled his name on the three sheets of paper, then dropped the pen. As Ada handed him the keys, he leaned across the desk and patted the policeman on the shoulder. "Thanks, Officer Warner. You say hi to the chief for me, will ya?" He winked back at Ada and quickly walked outside. After he reached the street, he ran around to the back, waving to Scruffy as he went. The two men reached the car and he tossed the keys to Scruffy. "You know how to drive this Ford, Scruff?"

He nodded and climbed in. After cranking it for a couple of long tries, the old four cylinder sputtered to life. "You got gas, Scruff?" Abel asked.

Scruffy peered down at the dash and nodded, "About half a tank."

"Let's go then. I'll meet you at your place." And as Scruffy pulled out, Abel ran around front and jumped on his cycle.

As he drove past the Arcade, Johnny flagged him down. He ran out and handed Abel a scrap of paper. "Ann-Marie dropped this off. Said to give it to you." He glanced around as Abel stuffed the paper in his pocket. He raised his chin and said in a low voice, "I saw that fat cop, Brodsky, and the McBride up around the corner a half hour or so ago. You be careful."

"Thanks, Johnny. I owe you."

Johnny waved a hand dismissively and scurried back inside. Abel roared down the hill and across the causeway. He glanced in his rear-view mirror a couple of times and didn't see the car that had run him off the road the other day.

At the bar, Scruffy kept the car idling. Abel waved him to follow and rode on down through the trees to Martha and BB's.

BB and Captain were sitting on the steps and leaped up as the two vehicles came into view. BB yelled, "We been waiting on you, Uncle Abel." He held up a rag and Captain held out a bucket.

Scruffy pulled in and shut the motor off. "Howdy, kids," he said quietly. "Is your mom home, BB?" He just stood, swaying from foot to foot.

BB turned and yelled, "Hey Mom, Mr. Fett is here with Uncle Abel!" He smiled at the grownups and said, "She'll be out in a minute. She's bakin', and Captain's mom is helpin' her."

Abel leaned on his cycle and said, “Why don’t you lads start washing that car of your dad’s, eh?”

The two ran around the side of the house and dipped the bucket into a wooden barrel that was set up to catch rainwater off the roof. Just then, Martha came out onto the porch, wiping her hands on a dishtowel. She held a small box in her hand. “I’ve got some Rinso Laundry Detergent. Will that work? It’s what Bob used to use.”

Abel grinned, “Not too much, boys, and swish it around with your hands before you use it, all right?”

They said, “Yas suh,” and “Okay, Uncle Abel.” In a flash, the two had formed a bubbly dome on the bucket and were busy washing the dust and grime off the old Ford.

Scruffy handed the detergent box back to Martha. “Here you are, Missus Brightwater.”

She smiled, “Oh, Alfred, I’ve told you to call me Martha.” She turned to Abel, “Why don’t you and Alfred come inside. I’ve just baked a batch of cinnamon rolls for the hotel, and I’ve got some of those left over ends.” She smiled again, batted her eyes at Scruffy and said, “I’ve got a good one for you, Alfred.”

Abel just rolled his eyes, then remembered the piece of paper in his pocket.

Chapter 37

Message Across: Present Day

The next morning Chris whispered to David as they lay in bed, "I didn't let him touch me, well, not much. We ditched the laptops under their beds, so we're good to go. What's next?"

Dave stretched, throwing an arm across her. "My dear, I always know to trust you to do what you feel you have to. We were outside and just a scream away. If you'd needed help, we'd have come arunnin'." He kissed her soundly and said, "Have I told you how beautiful you are and how lucky I am?"

She batted her eyes fetchingly and replied, "Not nearly often enough, dearie."

They showered, dressed and walked up the dock to

Chesney's back door. Ringo was already there sweeping the floor from last night's merriment. Chris put a hand on his arm and kissed his stubbled cheek, "Good morning, Ringo. You are doing a wonderful job."

"Thank you, Miss Christine." Ringo smiled at her and continued sweeping the floor.

Charlie Potts was in the kitchen. He leaned over the serving shelf and shouted, "Breakfast, Chrissy? Dave?" They nodded sleepily. "The usual?"

They nodded again, "Yeah, Charlie." They sat at their usual table and Charlie came out with their coffee. "Eggs and toast'll be out in a minute. How'd you make out last night?"

Dave nodded, sipping the black coffee. "Bring out the breakfast, Charlie, and we'll tell you all about it."

Rusty and Anna came in, trailed by Vince and Joan. They were arguing about the tides, of all things.

In a few minutes, they were all seated at the table. Emile wandered in, filled his large mug from the coffee urn and sat with them. "Everything in place?"

Chris just nodded, dreading the next step. "How are you going to do it, leaking their 'theft'?" She made quotation marks in the air with her fingers.

He rubbed his chin and shrugged, "Probably an anonymous phone call?"

Dave shook his head, "Got to be someone inside, not an outside contact. If they get a call from somebody they don't know, it'll trigger an alarm." He turned to Vince, "Any chance it could go through your plumber buddy?"

Vince looked frightened, "I guess I could, but how

would a plumber know that?" He let them know that he really didn't want to do it.

Dave said, "Easy, Vince, that's off the table." He turned to Rusty, "You got any ideas, Russ? Anna? Joan?"

Rusty frowned and took a gulp of his coffee. "Any way we can have a message come from that guy Mayer, to their bookkeepers or accountants? Or maybe the other way?"

Anna asked, "Is that guy Mayer the head of their security? Or, at least, the boss of those other guys? Emile?"

"Yes, they have three divisions, and Mayer is like a captain of one. And, yeah, the other four guys were under him." Emile smiled, "You want me to send a message from one to the other? That's no problem, their firewalls are shit."

Joan spoke up, "I think that's too pat. You know, too, um, easy. If they interview Mayer and he says he don't know what they're talking about, they might believe him. Maybe have it come from somebody at the bar who, I dunno, overheard these two guys talking? Somethin' like that?"

Dave and Chris shook their heads slowly, mulling it over. "Maybe from one of the other guys in their gang?" Dave said, "One who goes drinking in the Dagger too?"

"How are we going to know that?" Chris asked, and then said firmly, "I'm not going in there again!"

Dave agreed, "We can't show our faces in there. And it's on too public a street for us to run surveillance." He threw up his hands and sighed, "Emile, we're just going to have to take a chance. Pick out a guy and send an email memo or cell phone text to Mayer." He looked around, "Are we all agreed?"

One by one, they nodded, said yes, or uh-huh. Emile stood and went into the computer corner. All eyes were on him. In a few minutes he raised a hand with one crooked finger, looked at them and when they nodded, punched down on the send key. It was done. Now it was out of their hands.

Emile came back and flopped down in his seat. "I just signed it with the initials of one of the newer guys. Hey, he can always deny it, and they'll never know. I'll monitor Mayer's emails and phone over the next couple of days and let you know what happens."

Charlie Potts stood and said, "Everybody want breakfast?" When they nodded, Chris and Joan stood and followed Charlie into the kitchen.

Chapter 38

Abel pulled the scrap of paper out of his pocket. It had three names on it: Kellinger Welding and Fabrication, McMullen Sand and Gravel and Hoffmann Haulage.

"Scruff, teach Martha how to drive, will ya? I got some business in town." Outside, Abel jumped on his cycle and roared off. He figured Ray Farrell would have a phone book and know where each of the businesses were located. There wasn't much traffic on the Causeway today. Abel left his leather helmet off and felt the wind in his hair. He held the throttle with his hand, raised his other hand and both legs and whooped! Damn, he loved riding this cycle!

In a few minutes he rode into Ray's dirt driveway and stopped. Ray heard the noise and came to the edge of the garage door, a long piece of water pipe in his hand. "Everything all right, Abel?"

Abel nodded while Ray put the pipe down and lit a cigarette. “Yeah, I just need some information and addresses.” He shoved the list into Ray’s hand. “Do you know any of these outfits?”

Ray walked over to an old car bench seat that was on the floor just inside the garage door and sat, staring at the paper. “Let’s see, Kellinger Welding. Yeah, that’d be Gerry Kellinger. His place is over on Court Street, by the railroad tracks. I knew his older brother Felix. Poor guy died of the influenza a couple of years ago.” He looked up and blew out a puff of smoke. “You can tell ‘im you know me, fer what it’s worth.”

He looked down at the paper again. “McMullen Gravel would be Elsie McMullen. Tough old broad. Good luck with her. Used to be a good size outfit before this here depression came in. Her old man, Oscar, was a good guy, hired lots of locals.” He thought for a minute. “Her outfit is outta town, north up by Dunedin. Can’t remember the road name. Just go up that way and ask. Everybody knows her.”

Abel raised his eyebrows, “And now?”

Ray Farrell shrugged, “Not much construction work going on now.”

“What about the water and sewer lines out to the beach?” Abel sat down next to Ray and looked at the sheet.

Ray looked at the younger man and snorted, shaking his head, “You drive the Causeway, don’t you?”

“Yeah, why?”

Ray replied, “The purpose of the WPA is to employ locals. How many guys do you see digging and working out there? Three or four? There should be fifty guys working.

There's a big shovel. That ain't right."

Abel asked, "What about the last one, Hoffmann Haulage Where are they located?"

Ray shrugged again, "Never heard of them. And I been here all my life. They might be outta Tampa or St. Pete, but they sure ain't local." He handed the paper back to Abel, who pulled a short pencil out of his shirt pocket and scribbled down the directions on the back.

"Thanks, Ray. I'll get back to you. I'm gonna go see these folks. Say, have you got a chunk of rebar I can borrow?"

"Yep, hold on." Ray fished around in the garage and emerged with a piece of ½" rebar about 15" long. He handed it to Able. "You figgerin' on whackin' somebody with it, kid?"

Abel grinned, "Never know." After tucking it into his boot, he hoisted himself to his feet and walked back to his cycle.

Later that evening he rumbled back across the causeway. As he turned left in front of the dance hall, a pair of headlights illuminated the cycle and followed closely behind. Abel noted them immediately and started to speed up. Before he got to Scruffy's, another car pulled out across the road and blocked him. A man got out of each car. Abel stopped and slipped the length of rebar out of his right boot, keeping it close to his leg.

He sighed. It had been a long time since he'd had to deal with violence. He didn't see the hulking Brodsky. One was a Mexican, for sure. That must be Mendez, though neither of the men were wearing uniforms. He had never met the other man. At a guess he asked, "You Kaminsky?"

The man frowned in the evening twilight. "How'd you know? Did you tell him, Mendez?"

Abel smiled, "So, two coppers, no uniforms. Let me guess, this isn't official? Any chance I can talk my way outta this?" He started moving slowly toward Kaminsky, but not taking his eye off Mendez.

"Don't think so, bub. Chief said to rough you up. Kinda let you know he ain't too happy with you lookin' inta somethin' that ain't none of yer bizzness." Kaminsky was starting to bounce on his toes as Mendez moved in from behind.

"Yeah, like he just roughed up Bob Brightwater. That you guys too?" Abel was just turning a little sideways now. Both men were bigger than he was, but a little sloppy, out of shape.

"No, not us. That musta been Brodsky."

Mendez shouted, "Shut up, Will!"

Abel thought quickly, "So, Brodsky killed Bob Brightwater, huh? And you two think you're going to do the same to me? And you are cops, too. Let me ask you something? What would you do if you were me?"

Mendez stopped and scratched his head, "Whaddya mean, man? Hey, we got our orders."

Abel turned so he was facing Mendez. "I know that McBride told you what to do. But do you know what he did to me? Did he tell you that he killed my wife back in Texas?" Abel snorted, "No, he never told you that, did he?" He turned his head back and forth, looking at both men. "Look, I've got no beef with you guys, just McBride, but if you're determined to beat me up, bring it on." Abel crouched low.

Mendez came in first and swung at Abel, who ducked, feeling the breeze as the hand flew over his head. He straightened and hit Mendez on the side of his head with the hunk of rebar as hard as he could.

Mendez collapsed in a heap. Kaminsky looked at them in shock. "Jesus, the chief said this'd be a piece o'cake." He exhaled a big breath, "Sorry, kid, I got my orders." He pulled a hand out of his pocket. A brass knuckle was on his fingers. He raised his hands in a boxer's stance and danced in front of Abel.

Abel stood his ground, backing up a couple of steps to keep the unconscious Mendez and the advancing Kaminsky in sight. He hefted the steel in his hand, waving it back and forth. Kaminsky feinted a left hand jab, then swung the brass knuckled hand at Abel's head. Abel ducked again but Kaminsky drove the hand down, catching Abel behind his ear and on the shoulder.

Abel swung the bar up between Kaminsky's legs. He gave a cry and clutched his crotch. Before he could recover, Abel switched the bar in his hand and whacked Kaminski on the left knee. The cop went down on his right knee.

Abel muttered, "Sorry," and clouted him on the back of the head. Kaminsky went down, out cold. With a grunt, Abel sat on Kaminsky's back, rubbing his own head and shoulder. He removed the brass knuckle from Kaminsky's hand and stuffed it in his pocket.

After a few minutes, he hauled himself to his feet. First he checked Kaminsky's pulse. Slow and steady. Then he knelt down and felt Mendez's neck. Thready, but there. Next he went to each vehicle and removed the keys. These also went into the pocket with the knuckles. Last, he went back to each of the men and rolled them onto their backs.

As he was preparing to leave, he felt a drip onto his neck. Reaching up, he swiped a hand and found blood. Kaminsky had broken the skin. That would cost them, decided Abel. He rummaged each of their wallets and grabbed all the bills he could find.

He remembered what his former sergeant had told him when he was in the army. "Don't leave your enemies alive. They'll just come back at you." But these cops weren't his enemies, McBride was. Abel would have to watch his back from now on.

He climbed on his cycle and, after a couple of jumps, it roared to life. Though his shoulder ached, he felt pretty good. He just hoped that they wouldn't come after him officially.

He decided to bypass Scruffy's place and go on home. Home, he thought. He didn't think he'd say that word again. In a couple of minutes, he pulled up in front of the small house. Martha was dozing on the porch in a wicker rocker, her mending on her lap. BB was sitting on the porch, back against a post, reading a thick book. He looked up as Abel shut off the cycle.

Abel swung his leg over the leather saddle and staggered a little. BB ran to him and put his arm over his shoulder. "Mom, Mom, wake up. Uncle Abel's hurt!" Blood dripped on BB's hand.

Martha jumped out of her chair, a pair of BB's coveralls

dropping to the floor. "What? What's the matter? What happened?" She pulled Abel up onto the porch and under the bare light bulb hanging down. She pulled his head back and scrutinized the cut.

"That looks pretty deep, Abel. Should we stitch it up?"

Abel jerked back away from her, "No, no, I hate that. Just get some adhesive tape and pull it together. Cut 'em in little pieces and space 'em apart. It lets the cut breathe. Heals faster."

Martha waved a hand at BB, who ran inside. He came back with a partially dampened rag, a small bottle of Mercurochrome and a roll of adhesive tape. "Here, Mom." He handed the rag to Martha who was standing beside the now seated Abel.

She wiped at the cut, then tore off a strip of rag and dabbed the cut dry. After dribbling the Mercurochrome into the cut, she tore short strips off the roll and pulled the edges together. He winced and gritted his teeth, "Enough, enough!" he growled, standing.

"So what happened, Abel?" Martha stood with hands on her hips.

He related what happened between him and the two cops. She sat, clearly frightened. Then he told her what he'd discovered in his travels that day about the contractors.

Now she was curious. "And you think Mr. Gibbons is stealing the WPA money?"

He shrugged, "Not only him, but I think Chief McBride, is in cahoots with him."

"Well, how can you be sure?"

BB swung his eyes from one to the other, listening to every word. "Do you think my dad was in cahoots too, Uncle Abel?"

Abel roughed his hair, "No, BB. I think they killed him because he found out what they were up to."

"Abel!" Martha was shocked at his revealing the truth. "Are you sure?" When she recovered she asked, "So, what's next?"

Abel frowned and thought, "Well, we'll see tomorrow. I think it's time for me to go visit this Mr. Laplante."

Chapter 39

The Difficult Patient: Present Day

On Saturday, Chris and Dave drove to the hospital in Clearwater. They ran into Tom's physician, Dr. Patel, in the lobby. Dave confronted him, "Doc, our friend Tom Novak, how's he doing?"

The diminutive doctor smiled and glanced at the electronic tablet in his hand. "Ah, yes, uh-huh," he coughed. "Your friend, Thomas, is, mmm, how shall I put this, a royal pain in the ass!" He glanced around quickly to see if anyone was listening.

Chris and Dave grinned. "Oh, we know that, for sure!" Chris laughed behind her hand. She gestured toward the cafeteria, "Can we buy you a coffee or lunch, Dr. Patel?"

He cocked his head and nodded, "Tea would be fine,

thank you."

They sat with their drinks. The cafeteria was nearly empty, only two tables with some nurses at this time of the day.

Chris leaned over the table, "Why, doctor, what happened?"

"Your friend, Mr. Novak, wants to go home, wherever that is. I don't believe he is ready. He tears the tubes out of his arms, he tries to get up and stand on his still-healing leg." He looked around and nearly whispered, "He tries to squeeze that rubber ball with his hand that is still taped to a splint!" He gulped his tea, then pointed a finger at the two, "He, he is becoming rude to the nurses. That I will not tolerate!" He tapped the table with his finger.

Dave looked at Chris and smirked, "That's Tom." He turned to Dr. Patel, "If we keep him comfortable and quiet, can he leave? Really?"

"Would he really be in danger, Doctor?" Chris asked. She knew Tom, and if he felt he was ready to go, perhaps the change would do him good.

"Well," Dr. Patel answered, looking at the chart on the tablet, "I suppose if you kept him in bed and on a diet I will prescribe, I would discharge him into your care." He wiped a hand across his face. It was obvious he'd been awake for many hours.

Dave reached a hand across the table and patted the doctor's hand, "We'll talk to him and arrange to pick him up tomorrow, okay?"

The good doctor nodded reluctantly. "I will give him one final check and leave you a diet and suggestions for physical therapy progression." He stood and, as they joined him, said, "Thank you so much for your continued support and for finally taking him out of here." He shyly smiled and shook each of their hands. They watched him walk to one of the tables where three nurses sat. He spoke to them and they jerked their heads up and grinned.

As Dave and Chris walked by, one whispered, "Thank you."

The next day, they arrived just before noon in a borrowed station wagon. All the rear seats were folded down and a thick foam rubber pad with a sheet over it was in the back. Vince was with them. All the gang wanted to come, but the car could only hold three plus Tom.

After checking with Dr. Patel, a nurse wheeled Tom out in a wheelchair, his leg on a board. "Hey, guys, thanks for coming. Are we going back to Chesney's?" His face was still bandaged, which covered the 35 stitches on his cheeks and forehead. He grunted and clutched his ribs as the nurse stopped the chair.

Vince hustled around Tom, pulling the blanket off his legs, wrapping it up and handing it to the nurse. "Come on, Tommy, lemme help you into the wagon." He slid a skinny arm around Tom's back and tried to haul him up. Vince weighed about 145 lbs. and, even though Tom was down to 200 lbs., nothing happened.

Dave and Chris hurried to help. Dave swung the wheelchair off the curb while Chris opened the tailgate and liftgate. Between the three of them, they managed to get him onto the tailgate and finally inside on the foam mattress. By now, Tom was freely sweating and muttering to himself.

As Dave drove back to Sunset Pointe, he called over his shoulder, "How you doing, buddy?"

Tom gasped as the wagon lurched, "Do you have to hit every bump? You're killing me!"

Dave grinned at Chris, "Wait, I just missed one. I'll go around and try again." Chris giggled and Dave chuckled.

"Asshole," Tom muttered.

As they pulled into the parking lot, Joanie, Anna and Rusty were standing on the porch. They had a brand-new powered wheelchair standing between them. Dave backed up to the porch, and lots of hands helped Tom into the padded chair.

Rusty slapped him on the back and said, "Welcome home, Tommy." Tom winced at the blow.

Vinny admonished the big guy, "Take it easy, Russ. He's in pain." He leaned down and shouted just inches from Tom's face. "You look better, Tom. You feeling better?"

Tom drew back, "I'm hurt, stupid, not deaf!" Joanie slapped Vince on the arm and drew him away.

Charlie Potts threw open the door and with a wide grin shouted, "I cooked your favorite dinner, Tommy, a T-bone steak, baked potato and Italian bread with lots of butter!" He looked down at Tom and said, "We're gonna put some of that weight back on you, pal."

After they ate, Chris showed Tom where they'd made the storeroom behind the bar into a bedroom. "You'll have to wheel yourself to the bathroom."

Tom looked up at her, "Are you going to give me sponge baths, Chris?" He had a mischievous twinkle in his eyes.

"Ah, my dear, dear friend, Dave, Rusty and Vinny have a special procedure set up just for that." She patted him on the cheek. "You'll see tomorrow morning. Get some rest. If you want to come out and join the crowd tonight, just text me or Charlie. We'll have Ringo wheel you out."

This became the norm over the next few weeks. Mornings, Chris made Tom and Dave breakfast. Before they opened for the lunch crowd, Tom was rolled out onto the rear porch naked in a standard wheelchair. Dave, Rusty and Vince hosed him down and gave him a bucket of soapy water with a sponge. Every once in a while, the three women stood off to the side and made snide comments.

Then it was out to the garage, where Dave and the gang had purchased or borrowed several exercise machines. Tom worked his body religiously daily. Each day he seemed to get better. He regained weight and his muscles got thicker and more defined. On a wall in front of the upper body machine, they had posted a picture of Maxwell Mayer, the last of his attackers and the leader of that gang.

By week four, Tom had abandoned the powered wheelchair and was putting in an hour on the treadmill and bench pressing one-hundred and fifty pounds six times; then seven and finally ten times. On Tom's fifth week there, Dave took him to a local gun range. They shot Tom's .380 chambered Walther PPK, Dave's .45, a 9mm Glock and a Ruger GP100 in .357 Magnum caliber lent by Al, the manager of the gun range.

Tom offered, "I like the Ruger but I'll never get two accurate shots off with the .357. Jumps too much. Your .45 is a bit overkill and your hand is a little bigger so that's out." He hefted the Glock in his good left hand and his Walther in the newly healed right hand. The bandages and straps had come off a week earlier. "I'll take these two."

The next week, Tom put out feelers for aircraft deliveries. He needed to make some money.

One night, as they were all gathered around the dinner table at Chesney's, Emile said, "I've been monitoring our two friends' emails and Facebook posts. The posts stopped three days ago. I hacked into their personnel records and they aren't there anymore." He looked at Dave and Rusty, "I guess the Brotherhood takes care of their own."

Dave nodded, "Good, then we don't have to. What about the dough?"

Emile pulled a scrap of paper out of his pocket. "They recovered the money from those two but," he smiled, "so far they haven't a clue as to the last $995,000 that went missing at the same time. I've run it through a half dozen shell corps in different countries. It should be here tomorrow, and I'll shut the back door. I'll take my hundred and you guys can split up the rest, okay?"

They nodded and Chris said, "Thank you, Emile. Are you all right?"

He nodded, "Yeah, yeah, I'm just glad it's over. I need some time off." He stood and informed them, "The Bahamas is calling me. I'm taking off tomorrow. I'll be back."

He cocked a finger at Dave, "Don't rent my slip."

They talked for ten minutes about how to divide up the money. Even Tom was to get a share.

In a week Tom got a helicopter delivery from Florida to Northern Alabama. When he got back, a Lear 45XR jet was waiting for him for delivery to Atlanta. They promised more when this was finished.

There was a text message waiting for him from Key West when he returned. It was from Emile. All it said was: Mayer's in Panama.

Tom asked to be put in touch with a broker who needed a plane delivered to Panama. He got a DC3 to Vera Cruz, then, when he'd almost given up, a broker in Miami called and said he needed a pilot to fly a Gulfstream G450 to Tocumen Airport, near Colon, Panama. The job was worth $5,000 but he'd need a co-pilot. The plane was worth $15 million.

Tom agreed, signed the emailed papers and called down to Dave. Tom was now living in the comfortable apartment above the bar that Chris and Dave sometimes used. "Hey buddy, I got us a trip. I'll need a co-pilot. You up for it? It's worth a grand."

Dave already knew Tom's games with money, "Sure – for two grand, I'll right seat for you."

Tom was pulling on a T-shirt and coming down the stairs. "Hah, screw you, I'd have given you twenty-five hundred!"

Dave laughed, "I'll eat five hundred bucks worth of steaks on your tab. Where we going?" He was used to flying second seat with Tom on some of his wild ventures. Dave was the planner, Tom was the spur-of-the-moment action cowboy.

Quietly Tom said, "Panama. Airport called Tocumen." Chris looked at Dave.

He sighed and said slowly, "Well, we all knew this day was coming. When do we leave?" He was scribbling notes on a napkin.

Tom drank from his tall glass of orange juice and said, "We should get out before the weekend. We've got to pick up the plane in Savannah." He did some calculations in his head. "I guess we can refuel in Cancun or someplace."

"Jesus," muttered Dave, "have you ever flown a 450 before? It's probably got a range of four or five thousand miles. Anyway, who is crazy enough to let you have a ten or fifteen million dollar airplane, even for a day?" He was shaking his head in disbelief.

Tom shrugged, "I dunno, Wally at UDSA Brokers in Orlando called and said he heard I was looking for a ride to Panama. Guy in Panama bought the plane from some lawyer in Georgia. I'm just a cab driver. What do I care?" He turned to the others, "Anybody want to fly down to Panama with us?"

Chris slowly shook her head no and stared at each of the others. Vinny had a big smile on his face and was about to jump on board when he caught Chris' look. "Maybe some other time, big guy. Me and Joanie got some stuff to do on the boat, right, hon?"

Dave said, "It's a straight shot. We should only be gone a couple of days." Charlie Potts brought out a large plate with sub sandwiches.

Chapter 40

The Commissioners: 1938

Abel needed somebody to introduce him to Mr. Laplante, He rode the old cycle to the railroad car and went in to talk to Scruffy.

Inside, Scruffy was nowhere to be seen. "Hey, Scruff!" he yelled. Abel climbed up onto the bar and looked over the top. Nope, not on the floor.

He heard a noise from outside. Scruffy came in carrying a bucket in one hand and a mop in the other. "Did you call me, Abel?" His trousers were neat and pressed, his shirt was clean and buttoned properly. Abel looked down and noted that even Scruffy's shoes were shined.

He pointed at the shoes, "What the hell is going on, Scruff?"

"Um, I'm gonna start teaching Martha to drive her car. I, uh, thought I ought to clean it first." He set the bucket down and leaned the mop against the bar.

A mop, thought Abel? Oh, well, that's Scruffy. "Look, I was attacked last night by a couple of McBride's cops. I think I'm getting close to finding out what's been going on here. Can you put me in contact with Mr. Laplante?"

"Uh, I guess so. Why?"

"Before those bastards kill me, I ought to lay it all out for him. Then let him deal with it." Abel was sweating a little now, fidgeting on the bar stool.

"I guess I could call him for you," said Scruffy.

"Do you need a ride into town to make that call?" asked Abel.

Scruffy just shook his head and reached under the counter. He pulled out a dial telephone and placed it facing Abel.

Abel looked from the phone to Scruffy and back several times. His eyes narrowed and he stood on the stool crossbar. "You had this here all the time and never told me?" He pounded his fist on the bar and yelled, "I drove into town every time I needed to see someone, and I could have called them from here? Why didn't you tell me?"

Scruffy stepped back stunned, "Um, you never asked me, Abel. 'Sides, Mr. Laplante don't like me usin' it 'cept for emergencies."

Abel sat, deflated, "And me almost getting killed ain't an emergency?" He sighed, remembering who he was dealing with. With his head in his palm, he waved a hand at Scruffy, "Call him and set up a meet with him and me, will you? Please?"

"Okay. Give me a minute, will ya?" He picked up the phone and dialed one number and waited. "Yes, hi Diane, this is Alfred Fett. Could you connect me with Mr. Laplante, please?"

Abel perked his head up. Scruffy was speaking in a normal, cultured voice. Before his eyes, the fellow had changed, improved somehow. "Yes, hello, Mr. Laplante, this is Alfred. I'm at your restaurant on Clearwater Beach. There is a young man here who has been investigating the death of Bob Brightwater and the probable theft of the WPA funds being used to install water and sewage lines to the Beach. He'd like to meet with you and tell you what he's learned."

He listened for a long minute, nodded twice, then said, "Yes, sir, I understand. I'll tell him." He hung up, then said to Abel, "Uh, he said he'd see you tonight at the hospital in town. Uh, eight o'clock. He wants to get the other members of the council there." He looked up at Abel. "Kin I go now? I told Martha I'd be at her place soon. Fer a drivin' lesson." He slipped back into his, what? Abel didn't know what to call it, his uneducated mode?

"Yeah, sure, Scruff. Or do I have to call you Alfred now, or Mr. Fett?"

Scruffy ducked his head and gave him a small smile, "No, Scruffy is fine, Abel.

Abel took a ride into town, stopped at the Sinclair station and tanked up. It cost him 50 cents. He gave the kid, who carefully filled the tank without spilling a drop, a dime tip. "Thanks, kid."

"Thank you, sir," he replied.

Abel then went by the Arcade. As usual, Johnny Livingston was out chatting, this time with the driver of a 1937 Ford Roadster. The top was down, and Johnny had one foot on the running board. As he got closer, he heard Bob Wills singing "Right or Wrong." Obviously this fellow liked his country music. Abel gave him the thumbs up at the sound.

As Abel pulled up next to the slick red roadster, Johnny grinned and said, "Abel, this here is my friend, Andy Leven." He turned and put a hand on Abel's arm, "Andy, this here is my buddy, Abel Landis."

Abel reached out and shook Andy's hand. "Howdy. Nice to meet you, Andy." He turned to Johnny, "Um, can I talk with you for a minute?"

Andy waved a hand and said, "I've got to get going anyway. Nice meeting you too, Abel." He drove off down the street, turning the radio up as he went. Roy Acuff was singing as he faded around the corner.

"So, what's up Abel?"

Abel thumbed the cycle off and leaned close to Johnny. "I'm meeting with the Clearwater Commissioners tonight at eight. I ought to be done in a coupla hours." He told Johnny what had happened the previous night. "I'd like to get everybody together tomorrow night out on the beach at Scruffy's. Think you can alert everybody? Ray and Perkins and the girls? I'll get Jack Toffelmeyer. Things are getting hot, and I may have to get my ass out of town while I still can."

"Okey-dokey, Abel. Count on me." Johnny looked both ways, then hot-footed it back into the Arcade, holding his paper hat on his head.

Abel looked over his shoulder. Cleveland Street was

busy, cars going back and forth, crossing Missouri Avenue, most even paying attention to the stoplight. He saw a copper, foot up on a tire across the street, writing up a parking ticket. There was no sign on the telephone pole prohibiting parking there. He figured it was just McBride and his goons drumming up money. Most of the money probably never made it to the city coffers.

Abel went back across the Causeway. He had time to kill until eight, so he went back to Martha's to organize his thoughts and write down some notes. BB and Captain were throwing a ball outside. Abel pulled up and parked the cycle. Captain tossed the ball to him. Abel caught it one handed and tossed it to BB. For the next fifteen minutes he played with the boys, narrating a made-up game between the New York Yankees and the Cincinnati Reds. He finished with, "Baby Doll Jacobson goes back, back and he's up against the wall. He snares it, and the crowd goes wild!"

This drew cheers from BB and Captain. They flopped down on the porch exhausted. "So what's happening with the guys in cahoots, Uncle Abel?"

Abel proceeded to tell them some of what he'd learned, how he might have to leave town soon. "Oh, no, Uncle Abel. But Mom needs you. Me too," pleaded BB.

"Yassuh, Mister Landis, we all need you around heah," chimed in Captain.

He placed a hand on each of their heads and said, "Thanks, lads, but right now I need some grub and a nap. I'm off to see the big shots at eight." He wagged a finger at them, "Don't you fellers let me sleep past seven, now, hear?"

They both nodded and followed him into the small kitchen. He rummaged around in the refrigerator and found some food for the three of them. He noticed that there was a large tray of cinnamon buns on the stove top, covered with waxed paper. After they gulped down the food, he handed them each one of the buns.

Abel burped and patted his stomach. The boys were just about to follow his example when they heard Martha mount the porch. They covered their mouths and giggled.

They heard Martha say, "Thank you so much, Alfred. Same time tomorrow?"

"Ah, no. I have things to do tomorrow evening, Ma'am. Maybe Tuesday?"

She replied, "Yes, yes, that will be fine. I'll see you then. Oh, and here is two dollars for gas, Alfred."

When she came in, the boys greeted her and slipped out onto the porch.

Abel spoke to her for a few minutes about his upcoming meeting, then went into the spare room and lay down on the bed.

At seven o'clock BB came in and shoved Abel's arm. "Wake up, Uncle Abel, wake up." He pinched his arm and quickly stepped back as Abel flailed at him.

"Okay, okay, I'm up." He swung his legs over the side of the bed, rubbing his face and knuckling his eyes. He looked up at BB's big, round eyes. "Get me something to drink, will ya, kiddo?"

"Yessir," he mumbled and ran out of the room. Abel stood, stretched and pulled his suspenders over his shoulders. He finished dressing as BB handed him a glass of sweet lemonade. "Thanks, BB." He gulped it down and grabbed his leather helmet.

Before he left, he squatted down in front of his nephew and took him by his slim shoulders. He said, "If anything happens to me, kid, I left a few bucks under that there mattress. Make sure your mom gets it, ya hear?"

BB just nodded, his eyes even larger.

Abel breezed past Martha, who was sitting on the porch darning sox. "I'll be back in a while, Mart. Don't wait up."

Before she could comment, he straddled the cycle and cranked it to life. He waved a hand and roared off. There was a small light on in the dining car but no sign of Scruffy. It was twilight and a cooling breeze blew in from the Gulf. Many cars were leaving the Beach for the mainland. The few restaurants on the Beach were emptying and the tourists were going home. Abel envisioned the day when there would be traffic both ways, hotels and restaurants and private homes on both ends of the Clearwater Beach island.

He supposed that would displace Martha and even the Toffelmeyers; but hopefully, the baking business would make her rich enough to build a bigger house. He knew he wouldn't be there to see it, but maybe he'd come for a visit.

Abel noticed a car pulling out from the parking lot of the dance hall at the turn for the causeway. He gunned the cycle and roared across, the thin strip of land off to his right and the setting sun sparkling on the waves. He easily outran the following car, not knowing if it was a copper or just a civilian on his way home.

Once across, he headed south on Fort Harrison toward

the sprawling hospital and the conference room. As he pulled into the doctors' parking area, a man in uniform waved to him. Abel putted over and let the cycle idle. "Are you Mr. Landis?" he asked.

"Yessir. Can you show me to the board room? I'm supposed to meet Mr. Laplant and some other guys."

"Yes, Mr. Landis. I was told to show you there. The gentlemen are already waiting." He pointed to a small row of autos and told Abel to park next to them.

Abel left his leather jacket and helmet on the cycle and walked next to the security guard. "What's this Laplant like? Do you know him?" Abel wanted to gather as much information as he could before the meeting.

The guard nodded and smiled, "Oh, Mr. Laplant is one of the good guys. He likes people, likes jokes, but takes his position on the commission seriously. See, Clearwater is growing and there's lots of tourists coming. He wants to make 'em welcome and give 'em lots to do, to make 'em want to stay, know what I mean?" The tall guard took off his hat and wiped his crewcutted head with a kerchief. Absently, he said, "A mite warm tonight, hm?"

They had entered the largest building and were walking up a stairway to a mezzanine that was lined with doors. At a large mahogany door with two narrow windows, the guard stopped, knocked twice and opened the door. He stepped back and motioned Abel to enter, then closed the door behind him.

Abel stood and looked at the large table and the five men evaluating him. Abel was wearing his best trousers, one of Bob's dress shirts but no necktie. Two of the men wore suits, one was in a golf outfit, another was in green medical scrubs and the last was in comfortable casual clothes.

"Gentlemen, I am Abel Landis, Bob Brightwater's brother-in-law. My sister, Martha asked me to come to Clearwater to find out why Bob was murdered."

One of the men started to say something, but Abel held his palm out. "Please let me finish, then I'll answer any questions you may have." The man, the one in casual clothes, nodded. Abel pegged him as Putnam, the farmer. The suits had to be Fortescue, who owned the hotel; and Springstead, the banker. That left Banks, the jeweler, in the golf clothes and Laplant, in scrubs, who owned the hospital they were presently meeting in.

Abel continued, slowly walking back and forth, his hands and arms waving, pointing, gesturing along with the tale he was telling. "So, after doing some investigating, I found that a) Bob would never swim where he was found, b) the water found in his lungs was fresh water, c) he had hand shaped bruises on the back of his neck, and d) he found out that the police chief and the town's attorney were stealing money from the WPA, maybe the Mayor Teague, too." He saw the men looking at each other, frowning.

"Let me continue, gentlemen. I must be getting close to the truth because twice," held up two fingers, "twice, policemen from this town have tried to kill me." He stopped pacing and turned to the man in the medical scrubs, "Mr. Laplant, I presume?"

"Actually, Dr. Laplant, though I don't practice anymore. Just observe."

"Okay, Dr. Laplant." He looked up at the other men who were now leaning forward. "So, here's what else I found out. The contracts for the sewage and water lines are supposed to employ lots of locals. Any of you drive out to the Beach lately?" He pointed a finger at each man. "You, Mr. Putnam? How about you, Mr. Banks, Mr. Fortescue, Mr. Springstead?" They all shook their heads. "I thought not. Well, I drive the causeway every day. Last time I counted, there were four men working on the pipeline. Four." He held up four fingers this time.

"Ah, but there was a steam shovel and a grader. McMullen Sand and Gravel? Nothing. Kellinger Welding? Nope. And that other one on the contract? That Hoffman Haulage? They probably consist of the four guys actually doing the work and coughing up dough to the police chief and Avery Gibbons."

Banks, the jeweler, asked, "What about Llewellyn Teague?"

"Ah, the good Mr. Teague. Well, you might want to ask his daughter what happened to her cousin. I believe that the fine Mr. Teague was using her, um, in a sexual way, and when she threatened to expose him, he smothered her. Blamed it on influenza or pneumonia or something else. No autopsy was done on this little twelve year old girl."

The men looked shocked, not wanting to believe him. Abel paced back and forth. Putnam and Banks lit cigarettes, nervously puffing.

Dr. Laplant frowned and said, "How do we know that any of what you say is true, Mr. Landis?"

Abel ran a hand through his hair and answered, "Sir,

gentlemen, would I be here if there was another group I could go to? Florida has no statewide police agency, though they're mumbling about forming one. Maybe the Federal Bureau of Investigation? I'm sure that you'd like Mr. J. Edgar Hoover to come sailing down here with a bunch of agents to take over our town?"

Springstead, the banker, harrumphed and said, "No, no, of course not, but we'll have to investigate, form a committee, decide what to do after."

"But that will take quite a while. Suppose they cover up all that they're stealing?" Putnam, the farmer, injected.

The arguments went on, each man taking a different tack. Springstead wanted to drag it out. Putnam wanted to get the water and sewer to the Beach done as quickly as possible. He valued his workers less than the others. Banks, waited to see what Dr. Laplant wanted to do, while Fortescue, who owned the large hotel, hated the police chief, and was all for getting rid of him right away.

Dr. Laplant raised a hand after ten minutes of the back and forth. "Gentlemen, gentlemen, quiet please. I believe this young man. I knew his father and even met his brother-in-law once or twice. A fine, very detail-oriented young man." He turned to Abel, who was now leaning against the wall in the rear of the room, and waved him forward.

"Mr. Landis, we want to thank you for the information you have provided us. We," his arm encompassed the members of his commission, "will continue to discuss this and come to a decision."

The other men, said, "Thank you." And it was obvious

to Abel that he was being dismissed.

He nodded and touched a finger to his brow. “Well, gents, thanks for giving me a chance to unload all that I learned. I’m glad to hand it over to you fellas in case the coppers succeed next time they try to kill me. I hope you realize that McBride, that fat bastard Avery Gibbons and your mayor have to go; and as soon as possible.” He spun on his heel and let himself out the door. Behind him the men went back to arguing.

The same security guard was waiting outside the door. “How’d you do, Mr. Landis?” The two walked slowly side by side down the corridor.

Abel shrugged, “I guess we’ll find out soon enough.” He stopped and touched the man on the arm, “Say, what’s your name?”

They faced each other, and the man smiled, “It’s Robert Rainey. Folks call me Bob.” He stuck out a hand and he and Abel shook.

“How long have you been a, whachamacallit, security guard, Bob?” Abel was working on a plan.

Bob rubbed his jaw, “Oh, ‘bout eight, nine years. I was a sergeant in the Army before this.” They talked about the military and Europe for a short time.

Abel was leading up to the next question, “Bob, ever think of doing something else besides this?” They were outside in the cool night air now. The men walked to Abel’s cycle.

“Like what?”

Abel drew in a deep breath. He knew Bob lived nearby, probably had lots of friends and was used to commanding men. “How about Police Chief of Clearwater?”

Bob laughed, “Naw, they already got a chief. I hear he’s a real SOB too. I wouldn’t work for him.”

Abel sat on the cycle and said, “Suppose he was fired. Think you could handle it?”

Bob considered for a moment, removed his cap and scratched his head. In a long drawn out, “Well, if Mr. Laplant asked me to, I guess I could handle it.”

Abel patted him on the shoulder and started the cycle. He held out a hand to Bob and pulled him close, “You might want to mention that to Mr. Laplant.” And he took off for the Beach again.

Chapter 41

The Setup: Present Day

Two days later, Tom got a short delivery, a Cessna 210 from Clearwater to Savannah. They said their goodbyes and Chris drove them to the airport in the reliable old Mercury station wagon.

Chris kissed Dave and whispered, “Try to keep him and yourself alive.”

“Don’t worry. I found the engineering drawings for their base down there. Emile got them for me before he left. If we need to get in, I’ll get us in and out.” He kissed her again and said, “See you in a couple of days, babe.”

“Love you.” Chris watched them climb into the little plane and roll out onto the runway. Five minutes later they were airborne. She watched the plane pull a near vertical climb, then Tom rolled it over the airport and wagged the wings at her. The last thing she saw was the aircraft disappearing behind a cloud.

Less than an hour later, they put down at Savannah Hilton Head Airport. This was convenient as the Gulfstream was here. Tom taxied over to the private side and pulled up before a large hanger with three planes sitting outside. Through the rollaway doors they could see two more inside with crews working on them. After powering down, they climbed out and were approached by a man in a brown leather jacket with a large clipboard. “Hey, who are you guys? What are you doing here? This is private, ya know?”

Dave stepped in front of Tom and held a hand up. “Take it easy, man. We’re delivering this plane and supposed to pick up a Gulfstream.” He turned to Tom, who shoved a handful of papers into Dave’s hand.

The guy grabbed them and thumbed through them. “Oh, you’re the guys, huh?” His tone was a little calmer now. “The 450 is over in that hanger, all fueled and ready. What are we supposed to do with this thing?” He pointed first at a hanger two down to the right and then back at the Cessna.

Dave and Tom both shrugged. Tom pulled another paper from his jacket pocket and glanced at it. “I got it from a guy named Wally at UDSA in Orlando. He said bring it here, and we did. If you’ve got any more questions, call him.” He thrust the paper at the guy. “His number’s on that paper. Give him a kiss for me, will ya?”

He and Dave turned and started walking toward the other hanger, leaving the guy with the crumpled papers in his hand. “Nice reception,” said Tom.

Dave snickered, "We've had worse. Remember that time in Taiwan with that DC6?"

"Oh, hell, yeah. I thought they were going to shoot us!" They both laughed, remembering landing a military airplane with the numbers painted out on a Taiwan military base with no permission.

There were two guards in front of the small door beside the hanger doors. They were both armed with semi-automatic rifles and were in military style clothing, though without any collar or sleeve tabs. "Private," muttered Tom.

They walked up to the guards and Tom brought out his pilot's license and a copy of the sales bill. "Howdy, fellas. Me and my buddy here," he poked a thumb at Dave, "are supposed to fly this aircrate outta here for some lawyer. I heard he sold it."

The guard spoke into a microphone, part of an earbud, hanging on his right side. He read info off Tom's card and, with a nod at the other guard, they both stepped back.

Dave and Tom went through the door and gazed at the somewhat larger plane inside. There was a technician wiping down the handrails on the steps. He was short and stocky with a full beard and was wearing blue plastic gloves and a tan flight suit with the name Andy on a patch on his right breast.

He stepped back and bowed to the two. "She's ready to go, gentlemen." He patted the rail, "I'm gonna miss the old girl. Mr. Arnold, my boss, was, um, pretty generous to us who took care of her."

"She sure is pretty," said Dave. "Why's he selling her?" He was walking around checking out the engines and landing gear. Tom was already up the steps and scoping out the cockpit.

Andy raised his hands, "Knowing Mr. Arnold or one of the other partners, they want one with more seats or faster or longer range. Who knows?" He grinned, "At least they haven't fired me." He turned and pointed at the wings. "I topped it off. You've got about twenty-nine thousand in the tanks, the rubber is new, the avionics are all up to date and working." He led Dave up the steps, "Wait until you get a load of the interior."

Dave stopped, his mouth hanging open. He counted eight soft, comfortable brown leather reclining seats with folding tables. He had just passed through a galley with a large refrigerator and handcrafted wooden storage cabinets. Andy pointed, "I put some cold drinks in the fridge for you guys." He pulled open a drawer and said, "There's some sandwiches and chips in here for you, too." He held out a hand and shook Dave's, "You fellas have a safe trip. I'll get the doors for ya."

He hopped down the steps and Dave pulled them up and inside. Their bags were placed on one of the seats. He slipped into the cockpit and sat in the co-pilot's seat. "Nice guy."

In front of them, the doors started opening. Tom was staring at his cell phone and carefully flipping switches. As the doors opened, Andy jumped on a low-tow vehicle and started pulling them outside. Dave was busy on the radio talking to the tower. Outside, Tom fired first one, then the other of the Rolls Royce engines. Andy drove off to the side and gave them a thumbs up. In ten minutes, all gauges were where they were supposed to be, the flaps were smooth and both fuel tanks read full. The brakes tested and all the avionics fired up.

Dave pressed a button and spoke to Tom on his radio, "Tower says we're okay for runway 64L." He pointed out the window. Looks like it's over there."

They were behind a Southwest jet, then a Delta, then them. Ten minutes later, they were airborne. Tom was enchanted. "Oh, buddy-boy, this is some awesome bird!" He ran it up to twenty-eight thousand feet and banked it out over the Atlantic. They would cut across southern Florida, then the Gulf and south to Panama.

Dave calculated their airtime would be about three hours. "Andy left us some drinks and sandwiches in the galley. You ready?"

"Sure, Pally, let me figure out this autopilot and we can sit back and eat." He was still awestruck, "Damn, I would love to own this bird!"

After they had sandwiches and beers, Dave took over while Tom explored the passenger compartment. He was back in ten minutes. "Oh boy, oh boy, ain't this the cat's ass?" He slapped Dave on the shoulder, "I'll bet we could sell this baby and get an easy ten mil!"

Dave laughed, "And where would we hide to spend it?"

Three hours later, Dave got the call from Panama Air Control. "Your heading is 250 degrees and you will land on runway 3 at Tocumen Airport. There will be a car to follow and customs would be will be waiting. Have passports ready."

Dave said to Tom, "You heard all that? Guns secured?"

"Yep, got it. The rods are in a false bottom in a coffee tin in the bottom of my bag. There are two tins. We'll let the customs guys take one. I've got a Kevlar under my sport coat in the garment bag."

Things went as planned, and the customs officers took the top tin. Dave and Tom went into the terminal, where they were met by agents of Señor Rodriguez, the purchaser.

"Señor Novak, I presume?" An elegantly dressed man with straight black hair, a thin moustache and a briefcase in his hand introduced himself. "I am Pedro Antonio, Señor Rodriguez' lawyer. I wish to thank you for safely delivering this beautiful airplane. I know that you have been paid by the broker, but Señor Rodriguez would like you to have a small token of his appreciation." He handed Tom an envelope.

Tom stood at attention and gave the man a military salute. "My thanks to Señor Rodriguez, Señor Antonio."

"Is there anything else I can do for you, Senor Novak?"

Tom scratched his head and said, "Well, my friend and I would like to get a ride to Panama City. If you could direct us to a taxi or a bus, we'd be much obliged."

Pedro grinned, "That will not be a problem. I will have a car take you to a fine hotel in the city." He nodded to the envelope still in Tom's hand, "You will be easily able to afford it." He laughed and walked with them to the front of the terminal, where he bid them good day.

A Lincoln Town Car arrived in a few minutes, and the driver opened the passenger window, "Hey! Are you the two Yanks going to PC?"

They nodded, and the driver yelled, "Hop in. It's about an hour's ride. Boss said to take you to a good hotel. My cousin Artie, uh, Arturo, has a nice, exclusive joint out by the beach. It's called the Sand Castle. How's that sound?" He gunned the Lincoln out the gate and onto a modern highway.

Dave and Tom relaxed in the rear. Tom pried open the envelope and looked inside. There were quite a few US $100 bills. Dave peeked over his shoulder and grinned.

Tom flipped through them, divided them roughly in half and handed Dave his share. "You sure?" asked Dave.

Tom leaned close, "It's only money. Now we go hunting." He pulled a picture of the man from the Brotherhood who was the leader. "Emile gave me this before he left."

Dave leaned forward, "Excuse me, man, but what's your name?"

"Lopez, Ricardo Lopez, Ricky to my friends. You know, like Jennifer Lopez!" He laughed, "Unfortunately, no relation."

Tom now leaned forward, "Hey Ricky, you know an organization called the Brotherhood?"

Ricky grew quiet, "Yeah, a bunch of bad dudes. I'd stay away from them if I was you." He glanced in the rearview mirror. "My cousin, Jesus, sometimes drives for them. Lousy tippers. Why, you looking for somebody?"

Dave nodded at the eyes looking back at him in the mirror, "Yeah, a guy in their security squad."

They pulled into Panama City. After several turns, Ricky drove them down a narrow road to a wide thoroughfare. Two blocks later, he pulled up onto a semi-circular drive and under a portico. “Here you are, gents. Tell cousin Artie, oh wait, here its Arturo, that Ricardo sent you!” He laughed then gasped when Tom handed him one of the bills from the envelope. “Oh man, thanks, dude!”

Tom leaned in the driver’s window and asked, “Say, Ricky, how’d you learn to speak such good English?”

Ricky snorted, “I was brought up in Brooklyn. Drove a cab there for a while.” He smacked the steering wheel. “My grandma is getting’ old so my Ma asked me to come back and keep an eye on her. Mr. Antonio gave me a job that lets me go home at night. Oh, and that Brotherhood joint you’re lookin’ for? It’s about two or three blocks right up the road.”

Tom smacked the roof of the car. “Thanks, man. Stay cool.”

Dave said through the passenger window, “Hey, kid, you got a phone number? We might need a ride again.”

Ricky handed him a card. “Anytime, guys, anytime.” With a cock of a finger to his forehead, Ricky drove back up the playa.

After they checked in, they showered and napped. Dave woke around dusk and kicked Tom’s foot. “Come on, let’s get something to eat. I’m starving.”

They dressed and each took a weapon. They stuck them in their belts in back where their flowing Guayabera shirts covered them well.

Though the hotel offered meals out on the patio overlooking the water, the men strolled south along the beach sidewalk. Soon the small seaside hotels and bars trickled out, and a tall gray wall started at one corner. They crossed the street and walked past a multi-story marble-faced building with tall curved-top doors. A large brass plaque set into the stone announced The Brotherhood of God.

Diagonally opposite the entrance sat a small café with outdoor tables. "This is as good a place as any, buddy-boy," said Tom. After positioning the chairs so that they could see the entrance to the Brotherhood building, they sat.

A waiter soon approached and asked for their drink order. He handed them each a small plastic-coated menu. Tom ordered Cerveza Gallo and Dave a cup of tea with lemon. The waiter looked at him funny, shrugged and went back inside.

When he returned, they ordered fried fish dinners. Tom took Mayer's picture out of his shirt pocket and showed it to Dave. They both studied it and memorized the features. As it was getting dark, streetlights and lights outside the Brotherhood came on. There were comings and goings from the Brotherhood building. Frequently, uniformed members came into the café for drinks or to pick up food. Dave switched to Panamanian Iced Tea.

"Wow, this tea is delicious. You ought to try some and no more beer. It'll throw your aim off." Dave sat back and belched. "How long are we going to stay here anyway?"

"As long as it takes," replied Tom. He took his sunglasses off and hooked one side into his shirt neck. They stayed until ten that evening, then made their way back to the hotel.

The next morning they ate in the hotel cafe. Ricky came in just as they were finishing. "Hey, guys, I thought about this Brotherhood shit you asked me about. I found out something you might want to know."

Tom and Dave looked at each other. Tom asked, "So what is it, Rick?" he put his fork down and stared at the youth, blank-faced, hard-eyed.

"Take it easy, man, I'm with you guys." He leaned across the table and spread out a small piece of paper, smoothing it with one hand. "This here is us," he pointed, "and this here is Playa de Agua Clara."

Dave looked, "So?"

Ricky pointed again and said, "This here is a training ground for their security guys and, um, girls too." He tapped it. "They have a barracks there, a small restaurant and bar. I don't know if civilians are allowed, but my cousin Miguel says that he's seen townspeople there during the day sometimes." He shrugged, "Any of this any help?"

Tom nodded and waved to the waiter, "Give this kid whatever he wants, Amigo."

The waiter and Ricky spoke rapidly in Spanish. While Tom and Dave leisurely ate, Ricky filled them in on all that he knew about the Brotherhood in Panama. It was the usual, the Brotherhood pays off the police, the wealthy families support them and the locals really don't like them.

When they were finished eating, Ricky offered to take them to the Playa. "You guys better get some beach clothes and blanket and stuff. You gotta look the part, ya know?"

"We'll be out front in ten minutes. Bring the car around, Rick." Dave signed the check and they went up to their room. They were down in a short time, got in the car and Ricky sped off toward the Playa of the Brotherhood.

It was only twenty minutes away. The parking lot was dirt guarded by a chain on two stakes. They sat and studied the layout. To the right was a small building with several outside tables and chairs. Behind it was a long, low military-style building. Tom pointed, "That must be the barracks. I wonder if Mayer is there."

"Mayer?" asked Ricky, "Is that who you're looking for?" He sat back with his arms crossed. "I picked him up at the airport once with my cousin Luis. I didn't like him. I think he's a mean bastard. Just a feeling."

Dave turned and showed Ricky the photo, "This him?"

He looked at it briefly, "Yep, that's him all right." Ricky gathered up his and Dave's bag and said, "Let's go down on the beach. Looks like a good day for a swim."

The three walked almost to the water before spreading the blanket. Tom put down a box of food, and Dave plopped down with the towels. Ricky walked shin-deep into the water, kicking his feet.

Dave lay back with his head on his bag. He'd peeled down to his swimsuit and a T-shirt. "Ah, this is the life, huh?" He pulled his hat low over his eyes. Tom was sitting with his arms folded on his knees. Ricky came back, kicking his toes in the sand. All Dave could see was Tom's back and Ricky's legs when a pair of green-clad legs stepped into view.

"You guys are going to have to move. We've got a squad going to do some training here in a few minutes."

Dave pushed his hat up a bit and looked at the guy who stood with his hands on his hips, wearing a khaki green t-shirt and work boots. He was very fit and stood about six feet tall with a close military-style crewcut. Dave sighed, a tough guy. He pushed himself up and slapped Tom on the shoulder, "Come on, guys, let's move over to the side, okay?" He looked up at the guard and smiled.

"No, you better scram. We're gonna need the whole beach. You guys don't belong here anyway. This is our beach."

Dave kept smiling, "By our, I assume you mean the Brotherhood?" His grip on Tom's shoulder tightened. Ricky had subtly moved behind Dave and Tom.

The guard now assumed a threatening pose, fists balled by his sides. "You boys aren't gonna give me any trouble now, are you? A whole bunch of my associates will be here in the next few minutes."

Tom asked, also smiling, "I don't suppose one of them would be a guy named Mayer, would it?" Dave could tell the smile never reached his eyes.

The guard frowned, "Maybe. So?"

Tom stepped closer, almost nose to nose. "You tell him an old friend of his will be here tonight. I'd like to talk to him." He tapped the guard's chest with a stiff finger. "Around midnight ought to do it."

He took his time gathering up his clothes and the blanket. The three of them slowly walked back to Ricky's car. As they settled in, a group of five men jogged out from behind the small snack shack. The one who told them to leave, pointed them out to another. As the second man, who they assumed was Mayer, started toward them, Tom told Ricky to leave.

"I don't think he was close enough to recognize us," said Tom. They headed back toward the hotel, but Tom pointed, "Rick, let's go back to that little place across from the Bro-hood HQ, okay?"

Ricky nodded, "Sure, man." He gunned the big Lincoln Town Car. "You guys hungry?"

Dave smiled, "I can eat." He sat in front while Tom lounged in the rear seat.

They parked behind the cafe so the car wouldn't be seen, then took a table under a canopy on the front patio.

They discussed their strategy for that night. "I think you guys need a little siesta before tonight." Ricky was right. They watched as three of the green-clad men from the Playa drove up, quickly mounted the steps and ran inside.

Tom chuckled, "Looks like we lit a little fire under them. I hope he doesn't decide to rabbit on us." He took a large bite of his burrito.

"I don't think so," agreed Dave. "I think we've got him interested and a little scared. Can't show that to his men, can he?"

Ricky looked from one to the other. "Mr. Tom, what did this guy do to you?"

Between Tom and Dave, they told him the highlights, leaving out many of the details. Ricky nodded, expressed outrage, gasped in the right spots and, in the end, showed sympathy for Tom, even patting him on the shoulder.

They finished, paid the waiter and drove slowly back to the hotel. "We'll see you around ten, Ricky. That okay for you?" asked Dave, leaning in the window.

"I'll be here, Mr. Dave." They bumped fists.

Chapter 42

Justice: 1938

The next day, Abel was up early and went to the Toffelmeyer's place. Jack was cleaning a fishing reel. He sat in a padded chair and had pieces of the reel spread out on a small orange crate between his knees. He looked up as Abel walked to the foot of the steps. "Morning, Abel. I'd offer you coffee, but I ain't got none. Got chickory an' some tea if you want."

"Thanks, Jack, I'm good. Just had some grits and tea. I'm gonna try to get the gang together this eve to tell 'em what me and Mr. Laplant and the others talked about last night."

"Ain't got nothin' to do with me, Abel." He started reassembling the reel. It looked tiny in his huge hands.

"Yeah, I know, but I think you oughta be there just to

listen. I'd consider it a favor, and a favor to Martha and BB." Abel stood with his hands on his hips, almost challenging his friend.

Jack looked up from under his bushy eyebrows and nodded. "What time?"

Abel shrugged, "'Bout six, six-thirty?"

Jack nodded and kept working.

Abel turned and stalked back to Martha's. He fired up his cycle and headed to Scruffy's. Outside, he parked the cycle and sat for a minute, trying to figure his next move.

Scruffy opened the door and motioned him inside.

"Abel, there was a copper here a little while ago looking for you. I tol' him I didn't know where you were but you sometimes stop in fer a beer in the evenings. That okay?"

"Yeah, yeah, sure, Scruff. Which cop was it?"

He furrowed his brow, trying to recall. "I think it was Chick Warner. I kinda knew him, but we never knew each other too much. Know what I mean?"

"Yeah, sure. Look, can you call Ray and Perkins and maybe Johnny and ask them to tell the girls and get 'em all out here tonight about six or so? I'll get some food together for all of us. I think I'm gonna have to move on after tonight. It's getting a little too hot for me around here." He looked beseechingly at his friend.

Scruffy nodded while pulling the telephone out from under the bar. Abel left while Scruffy was talking to Arthur Perkins.

He drove down the road to the big Pavilion and, after removing his boots and socks, walked down the beach and sat on a concrete bench under one of the shelters,

He reflected on his long drive on the old cycle, teaching Martha and BB to bake sweets and the new friends he'd made. He sure liked the gals, and he thought they kind of liked him. Could he live here? He guessed he could, but there would be endless trouble from the coppers. He dozed on the bench until a chatty couple from New York sat near him and woke him with their blabbering. He looked at them and asked, "Say, would you folks have the time?"

In a high-pitched voice, the woman gazed at his unkempt appearance and sniffed, "It is nearly two o'clock, young man. Don't you have to get to your job?" She and her husband snickered.

Abel smiled and sat up straight. "Ah, no Ma'am, I promised my stockbroker I'd call this afternoon." He strolled away and left them with their mouths hanging open. He didn't even know what a stockbroker did. Slowly, he drove back to Martha's house.

She was practicing her driving in Bob's old car. The car came to a jerky stop, nearly running over Abel's foot.

"Oops, sorry, brother. I'm still learning. Alfred has been teaching me. He says that I am getting better! Watch me!" And she was off again down the road toward Scruffy's, a fast turnabout and she roared back. The old car came to a skidding stop in a cloud of dust.

"Oh, I never knew driving was so keen!" Martha skipped out of the auto and up onto the porch. "Come, my two strong men, I'll make us a meal fit for a pair of kings!"

BB was sitting in a corner reading. He tossed the book onto his chair and ran into the kitchen.

"Say, sport, what's that you're reading?" asked Abel. He picked up the book and waved it at BB.

"It's a new book by a lady named Margaret Mitchell called 'Gone With The Wind'. It's about a bunch of people in the War Between the States. I got it out of the library a couple of weeks ago. It's a best seller, you know, Uncle Abel."

Martha shook her head as she grilled some fish fillets and snapped some beans into a small pot of boiling water. "I think it's too grown up for him, but he wants to read it. The librarian says there isn't anything too racy in it, so I let him." She chuckled, "We talk about it sometimes, and he describes what's happening with Miss Scarlet O'Hara and Mr. Rhett Butler."

In a few minutes they were eating. Abel looked up at Martha and saw his sister looking younger somehow, fresher. Her hair was brushed back and held away from her eyes by a pair of clips. Her frock was freshly washed and even her slip-on shoes were clean. He was uneasily happy that she was moving on from Bob's death.

"So, Mart, how is the baking coming? Selling more buns and stuff?"

Before she could answer, BB broke in, "Somebody must be buying them. We're makin' more and more of 'em every day."

"Shush," she admonished her son, "Abel and I have to talk business now." She smiled sweetly at her brother. "I think we can get more business from some of the hotels and even the cafeteria at the hospital, only I need a bigger oven, more storage space and, well, even help."

BB put his fork down and said in a high voice, “I can help more, Mom, an’ I’ll bet Captain’ll help too.”

She touched his head and said, “Thanks, sweetie, but what will I do when you and Captain go back to school?” She turned back to Abel, “Alfred has offered to go into town to fetch supplies for me and let me use his storeroom. I’ll do all that myself when I can drive better.” She sat up straight and smiled proudly.

Abel glanced over his shoulder and looked out at the dimming day. The sun shone through the palm branches and sparkled off the small wavelets in the Gulf. It was coming to the end of another hot day on Clearwater Beach. Abel felt an oppressive sense of gloom.

“I’ve got to go.” He wiped his mouth on a napkin and threw it down next to his plate.

“Where are you going, Uncle Abel?” asked BB, his mouth full of food.

“Oh, just up to Scruffy’s place. I’m, uh, having a beer with some friends of mine tonight.” He stood and grabbed his leather helmet and gloves off the small table next to the door. He looked back at his sister and nephew and wondered if he’d see them again. He thought of the Tommy Dorsey favorite, “Alone.” Well, he sure felt alone.

The cycle sat in front of the porch, dirty, old and worn. It had served him well. Abel gave a sigh and slung a leg over the saddle. He pondered his life for a moment, then turned on the fuel valve, flipped the choke on, gave the pedal a couple of pumps, then flipped the ignition. With one big jump, the trusty cycle sprang to life. It rumbled between his legs. With one flick of his foot, he kicked the stand back and roared off for the short drive to Scruffy's place.

As he pulled up in front, he wondered if this place ever had a name. Was it Laplante's, or Fett's or something special like South Beach Paradise Bar and Grill? That one he liked, and entered the place with a smile on his face.

His crew was all there. They sat around a pair of tables pushed together. Ray Farrell was at the head, with Perkins on his left. The were both laughing at something Johnny Livingston had said. Ann-Marie and Ada sat together looking at some notes. Jack Toffelmeyer sat at the foot of the tables nursing a tall beer. He seemed to be more relaxed than last time.

Abel greeted them all and pulled up a chair. "All right, my fellow conspirators, here's where we are, and by now I think we all can agree that my brother-in-law, Bob Brightwater, was killed, probably by the sheriff and that big bastard, Brodsky. Probably because he found out that the three guys, Mayor Teague, Gibbons, the attorney, and McBride were stealing dough from the WPA." He looked from one to the other and each nodded.

Abel went on to tell them of his meeting with the town council. "Now, I don't know what they're gonna do, but they better make a decision soon. Those coppers have tried to kill me twice. They might succeed next time." He hung his head.

Scruffy brought him a beer, "Here, Abel, this'll make you feel better." He stood rocking on his feet, left, right, left, right, thumbs hooked in his belt.

They heard a car crunch to a halt outside and two doors slam. Abel said, "Are you expecting anyone else, Scruff?"

He just shook his head. The door burst open and Cecil McBride strode in, long black coat flapping, Arnie Brodsky and Felix Kaminsky behind him. The two men stood on either side of the door as McBride strolled over to the table.

"Well, well, what have we here? Abel Landis and his backstabbers." He pointed at Ada Griver and shouted, "You! You're fired, you bitch!" He swung his arm and pointed at Ann-Marie, "You too! I ought to arrest you for stealing private documents. Who the hell do you think you are?"

He now turned on Abel, pulling one of his pearl-handled revolvers and aimed it right at Abel's face. "You son-of-a-bitch, Landis. I had a sweet thing going here. I got a phone call from Laplant today. He said I was fired! Fired! Me!" He cocked his pistol back and was about to pull the trigger when Abel smiled.

"I didn't know you were such a coward, McBride. Or are you only into killing women and unarmed men?" He stood up slowly, keeping the gun in the center of his face. "Come on, coward, are you going to shoot an unarmed man?" He turned his head a small amount and yelled, "Hey, Brodsky, are you a coward too? What's the matter, don't have any fresh water to drown me in like you did to Bob Brightwater?"

Brodsky pulled a revolver from a holster on his belt and waved it at the others at the table. "Don't none of youse do nuthin' stupid."

Abel batted the pistol away from his face and McBride stepped back in surprise. Abel strode forward and stuck his face nose to nose with McBride. "Leave these others alone, you bastard. It's me you want, so I'll tell you what. Let's go outside while it's still light. It's time for you and me to finish this." He pointed at McBride's two pearl-handled revolvers, "You can try to pop me with those two pea-shooters of yours. Let's see how good a shot you are."

McBride grabbed Abel's shirt and dragged him toward the door. "You little greaseball, I'm gonna love filling you with daylight!" Brodsky opened the door and McBride shoved Abel down the steps. Abel stumbled and fell to his knees.

McBride pulled his pistol again and aimed it at Abel, who held up his hands. "Now just a minute, McBride, let me get my gun from my cycle. After all, if we're going to have a shootout, you got to at least gimme a fighting chance."

McBride stuck the gun back in his holster and pulled back his coat until both pistols were visible and easily available. He barked a short laugh, "What? You've got a heater in those saddlebags?"

Abel scrambled to his feet and strode to his cycle, hoping McBride wouldn't shoot him in the back. Behind him, the rest of his crew scrambled outside, as did Brodsky and Kaminsky.

Abel retrieved the old Colt Peacemaker of Jack's from his saddlebag. He turned, keeping the long revolver against his leg. He and McBride were about twenty-five feet apart and surrounded by the others. "You all better move back while Dead-Eye McBride and I commence this here gunfight at the O.K. Corral."

McBride snorted, "You better say goodbye to your friends, Landis. In a couple of minutes you're gonna be croaked."

Perkins stepped forward and waved his arms. "Now, hold on, you two. You sure you want to do this? Why don't you just walk away, Chief? If you're fired, you have no authority here anymore. I guess that means you and the other coppers too."

McBride looked at the newspaperman and shouted, "Stay outa this, Perkins. This is between me and the runt. I killed his dame and I shoulda killed him then. This's been a long time comin'. It's all gonna end tonight." He looked at Abel and grinned, "What's that iron you got, kid?"

Abel held it up and McBride laughed, "That old piece of crap? That an old Peacemaker?"

Abel grinned, "Yep. 1898. Why? You scared?" He stood with the gun by his leg, pointed down. "You ready, old man?"

Perkins said, "One last chance." He looked from man to man. Both men shook their heads. "Okay, on my mark!" He didn't see BB and Captain peering from the corner of the building.

Perkins took off his hat and said, "When my hat hits the ground!" He looked to make sure everybody was off to the sides, then threw the hat in the air so it would land between the two gunfighters. It seemed to take forever. The setting sun was still above the horizon. In Florida it didn't set until near nine PM, and it was still just shy of eight.

Just before the hat hit the dirt, Abel saw McBride pull his right hand pistol. Before he could level it, Abel dove to the side and thumbed the Colt's hammer back. As he hit the ground he shot over his arm. He thumbed the hammer back again and fired a second shot. He could feel the whiz of McBride's shots just over his head.

McBride spun and dropped to one knee, his hat flying off his head. He turned and looked at Abel in surprise. Abel shot once more, and McBride flew backwards, arms outstretched, his gun skidding across the open ground.

Abel dropped his gun and rose to his feet. The two girls ran to him and looked him all over. "Are you hit, Abel?" asked Ada. She felt his arms and looked at his shirt.

He covered her hand with his. "No, he missed me. I'm okay." Some of his friends came running toward him. As Perkins knelt over McBride, Brodsky drew his gun.

"I wouldn't do that, copper, or should I say, ex-copper." Ray Farrell aimed a short shotgun at the big man. "Jist put yer gat on the ground there and kick it over to me." He gestured to Kaminsky, "You too."

The men dropped their guns and stepped back. Johnny Livingston stopped running to Abel and ran back to help his Uncle Ray. He gathered the two pistols and ran behind Ray. "What do you want me to do with 'em, Ray?"

"Just toss 'em in my bag, Johnny-boy." He spoke to the two ex-policemen, "You boys get in that flivver you come in and amscray. You better go back where you come from, ya damn Okies. I'd say, yer done in this here town. Tell them other coppers who come with you they better git too. Things'r gonna be a mite different here now."

In a minute the sedan started and faded down the beach. Johnny touched Ray's arm, "What are we going to do with the Chief, Ray?"

Abel strode up and thanked Ray. They both stood over McBride's body. Johnny scooped up the two pearl-handled revolvers, ran over to Ray's bag and tossed them inside. He then slid Ray's shotgun in also.

Abel squatted and felt for pulse in McBride's neck. No pulse. "He's dead," Abel muttered.

"No shit," snorted Ray. "He's got three .45 caliber holes in 'im." He pointed, "Pretty good shootin', kid."

The two girls stood hugging each other, whimpering. Abel walked over to them and pulled their heads to him. "Look, don't worry what McBride said. You still have your jobs. I think it best you get outta here though." He kissed them both on their cheeks.

Ann-Marie asked, "Are you going to be all right, Abel?"

Abel scrubbed his head and looked at them from under lowered brow, "Yeah, but I better think about hitting the road. It isn't often that you can stay free after shootin' the Chief of Police." He turned and swept his arm, "'Specially with all these witnesses."

The two girls nodded and kissed him back, then swiftly walked to Ann-Marie's father's car. They waved and drove away.

Johnny came up to Abel and nervously said, "Uh, I guess me and Ray better get goin' too. Uh, we'll see you around, Abel." He avoided shaking Abel's hand, wiping his hands together.

Ray gripped the young man's shoulder. "Lemme give you some advice, kid. If I was you, I'd git the hell outta

Clearwater, and soon. The shit's gonna hit the fan and maybe Laplant'll call in the Feds." He turned, "Hey, Mr. Perkins, I figure you're gonna report this in the paper. Think you could not attach Abel's name to it? Maybe just call him a drifter?"

Arthur Perkins walked over, rubbing his jaw. "I think that I could maybe leave that part out. There ought to be lots to write about if Laplant's going to fire the mayor and Gibbons too. Jesus, this town is going to be turned on its head for a while!" He scratched the back of his neck, walked over to McBride's body and nudged it with his foot.

He turned again to Abel and Ray, "Look, why don't you guys beat feet. I'll make a couple of phone calls. I'll say I just arrived when the "drifter" shot the chief and didn't get a good look at his face before he took off. How's that sound?"

Back by the building, BB and Captain crept over to where Abel had fallen. Captain picked up the old revolver. The two sniffed the barrel and could smell the cordite stink of gunpowder. Jack sat on the steps, elbows on his knees, chin in his palm. Captain held the pistol out to him.

Jack shrank back and batted it away, "Git that thing away from me, boy. I don't want no gun what killed the Chief o' Police."

Scruffy stepped down and waved his hand, "Follow me, boy. We'll hide it away 'til somebody needs it." Inside, he flipped open the hidey hole on the wall and Captain stuck the gun in. Scruffy muttered, "That oughta be as good and safe a place as any."

From there, he heard a car start up, thinking it must be Ray and Johnny, and a minute later, Abel's cycle rumbled to life. That only left Perkins and McBride's corpse.

Scruffy wanted to go to bed, hide, disappear, but Perkins would probably need to use the phone. He got it out from under the counter and placed it on the bar.

He needed a drink. A shot of whiskey suited him just fine. He poured a second for himself, and then one for Perkins as he came inside. Perkins nodded wearily.

Chapter 43

The Shootout: Present Day

After a nice afternoon nap, Dave had Artie send up some simple food. It was around seven. Dave and Tom sat at the table, disassembled the weapons, cleaned them and then re-assembled them. "I guess we're as ready as we'll ever be," said Dave with a sigh. "You gonna kill him?"

Tom nodded, "I don't figure I can leave him alive. He'll only come after me."

"What if he kills you?"

Tom laughed, "Then I expect you to kill him for me!" He pressed the remote and they watched an American cop show with Spanish sub-titles. When it was over, Dave turned it off and they stood. Their bags were packed. Tom slipped into his sport coat, gun in his belt in front. They stopped at the front desk, shook hands with Artie and paid their bill, leaving a healthy tip.

"Ricardo giving you ride to the airport, gentlemen?"

They nodded and went outside. Ricky had the car idling at the curb. They slid in without saying a word. The clock on the dash read 10:02. Ricky drove up the road and slowed as he got close to the little beach. "Don't stop, just slow down." Dave opened the door and slipped out, closing the door as he quick-stepped onto the sand.

"Where's he going, Mr. Tom?" Ricky watched as Dave faded into the night.

"Oh, he'll pick a place and have my six, just in case. We've been doing that for each other for a long time now." They had saved each other several times since Vietnam and after. Tom had no family and Dave and Chris were closer than he'd have been with a brother. They were his family.

Tom turned the radio on as Ricky drove down the coast. He stopped at a scenic overlook, and they watched the full moon sit over the water. After a few minutes Ricky asked, "Mr. Tom? How are you and Mr. Dave going to get out of here tonight?"

Tom shrugged, "I guess we'll find something, some-way."

"Wait here, Mr. Tom. I'll be right back." Ricky slid out of his seat and quietly closed the door. Tom saw him flip out his cell phone.

In a few minutes he was back. Resuming his seat he grinned, "Señor Antonio says he may have a plane he needs flown to Miami. Are you interested, Mr. Tom?"

Tom smiled and patted the kid on the head, "I guess so,

sonny. I wish you could come with us. We could use you."

Ricky puffed out his chest, "Thank you, Mr. Tom. The plane will be waiting at the airport with full tanks."

Tom looked at the clock, "Let's go. I've got a man to see." They drove back to the playa. Ricky looked at Tom, who said, "Be back here at twelve thirty. If Dave and I aren't here, just go on home. Mr. Antonio will have to find somebody else to fly his plane."

He got out and bumped fists with Ricky. "See you later, pal."

Out on the beach stood a man. The full moon was still above the water, its silver pathway looking for all the world like a highway up to that great silver globe. Tom thought he could just walk right up to it.

He hitched his pants and strolled up to the guy. "You Mayer?"

The other man turned just enough that Tom could see his face clearly. He was a few inches taller than Tom, about 30, the usual crew cut, "Yeah, who are you? They said you were an old friend." Suddenly he started, recognizing Tom. Without saying a word, he pulled a pistol and shot Tom twice in the chest from about five yards.

Tom went flying backwards and fell on his back. He was gasping, clutching his chest. Mayer approached and looked down, hand shaking. "You! How did you find me?"

Tom could hardly speak, the shots having robbed him of breath. Mayer kneeled, the gun in his hand resting on the sand.

Tom tried catching his breath while worming his hand under his jacket. His thumb clicked the safety off. He mumbled something and Mayer leaned down to hear. Tom hit him on the side of his head with the pistol.

Mayer collapsed. Suddenly three other men came out from behind the building running toward Mayer and Tom, who was struggling to his feet. One hit him, another started lifting Mayer and the third pulled a gun and aimed it at Tom's head.

"Drop it," said Dave quietly, pressing his gun against the man's head. His hand was steady, and he kept it there as the man stood, the gun dropping from his hand. Tom gathered up the guns he saw.

The guy helping Mayer reached under his shirt and brought out a pistol and spun, aiming it at Dave. Dave shook his head and shot the young man on the left side of his chest. As he fell, Tom staggered upright. "Look, you guys, I've got no beef with you, just Mayer. So I suggest you stay out of this." He moved next to Dave. They kept the four men in their view.

Behind them a shotgun blast sounded. Tom and Dave spun around, guns trained in front. Another guard lay facedown on the sand. A shadowy figure emerged from behind a palm tree just off the street. He walked forward, the shotgun resting against his hip.

Dave squinted. It was Ricky. He raised the shotgun to his shoulder, "Look out behind you!" Everything seemed to slow down. While the boys were looking at Ricky, the guards had pulled guns from their backs and small holsters on their ankles.

Tom dove to the left and Dave to the right. They shot as

they fell. Two of the guards went down. Mayer yanked one in front of him. Another was in a shooter's crouch. Dave shot the guard in the shoulder, his gun hand flipping the gun over his shoulder.

Tom shot at Mayer, hitting the downed target guard in the chest. Mayer got off a shot,which whizzed past Tom's ear. Tom ducked and rolled. By the time he got to his feet, Mayer had run backward a dozen yards. He took a bead on Tom just as a dribble of blood ran in his eye. He swiped at it with one hand, and squeezed the trigger with the other. It was all the time Tom needed. He sucked in his gut and spun sideways, offering as small a target as possible. His arm came up and the two men shot at the same time.

Mayer went flying backwards, arms out to the sides. As he fell, Tom shot him again. "Take that, you bastard!" He shot again, missing. Running up to the body, he aimed down, intending to empty the clip into him.

Dave grabbed his arm and forced it down. "That's enough. We've got to get out of here." He looked around expecting more guards but none. Dave mentally counted five down, at least three for good and two more maybes.

As Tom drew deep breaths, Dave grabbed the guns, including theirs, and staged the scene. He dragged two of the bodies away and then shuffled on the tracks. "We have to make it look like they shot each other."

"Ricky," he called, "bring me that shotgun. Quick now." Ricky jogged forward handing it to Dave. "Which guy did you shoot?"

Ricky pointed behind him. He couldn't speak. He'd never killed anyone, even in Brooklyn. When they were done, Tom shoved Dave toward the road. He grabbed Ricky as he jogged past. "Come on, come on."

As they jumped into the car, Dave said to Ricky, "Thanks, kid. Now hold it together." Ricky peeled out and Dave patted his shoulder. "Take it easy, slow down. Last thing we need is to get stopped by the cops."

Ricky was taking deep, gulping breaths and muttering, "Oh shit, oh shit, I killed a guy. Oh shit."

Once they were out of town, Dave said, "Pull over, kid. I think you need a break." When Ricky did stop, Dave opened the passenger door, then came around and pulled the driver's door open. Ricky sat, hands clasped on the wheel, his head resting on his hands. "Come on, I need you to do one more thing. Catch your breath. Get your phone out."

Ricky frowned and yanked the phone out of his back pocket.

Tom called from the car, "What the hell is going on?" He was leaning over the back of the driver's seat.

Dave waved at him, then leaned into Ricky and whispered instructions to him. Ricky nodded a couple of times and then grinned. He walked a short way and dialed. They heard him yelling in Spanish, then hanging and putting phone back in his pocket. He was chuckling now. He motioned to Dave, then slipped back into the driver's seat.

"You sure?" asked Dave walking slowly backward to the passenger's side.

Ricky nodded jerkily, grinning. He started the big Lincoln and merged back onto the long road to Tocumen Airport.

Tom asked again, "What was the call about? Ricky? Dave?"

Dave spoke over his shoulder, "I had Ricky call the local cops and say that he'd heard some men arguing, and then gunshots on that beach. That ought to buy us some time."

When they got there, a sleek Learjet 60 was waiting. Tom shook the kid's hand and climbed aboard.

Dave stood looking at Ricky and placed a hand on his shoulder. "Thanks, Ricardo, you saved our lives. If you come back to the US, look us up." He dug into his pocket and came up with an envelope. It was thick with money. He handed it to the youngster. "For you. Buy yourself a couple of drinks."

"Is, is this what Senor Rodriguez gave you and Mr. Tom?" He opened the envelope and thumbed the contents, whistling. "You don't have to do this, Mr. Dave."

"It's just my share. My card with my phone and address is in there too. Come see us." He gave the kid a hug, slapping his back. With one last look, Dave sprinted up the steps and swung the door closed.

Tom started the engines, ran through the preflight and called the tower. A sleepy voice gave them permission to take off. The lights were illuminating only one runway. In a few minutes they were airborne. Tom set the autopilot and promptly fell asleep, setting a dash alarm for one and a half hours.

Dave took out his phone and started reading a book of science fiction.

Late the next day, they were back in Chesney's, seated at their usual table with their gang. Chris was sitting very close to Dave, clutching his arm. Over the next hour they took turns telling everyone their adventures.

Rusty asked, “Where did this little gun battle take place?” He was sipping a frosty mug of beer.

“I told you, on a beach outside of the city. Some Playa de Agua Clara something.”

Anna smiled and asked, “ Do you know what that means, Tom?”

Tom frowned, “What does what mean?”

Anna laughed heartily and whispered to Rusty, who also started laughing heartily.

“It means Beach of Clear Water! Clearwater Beach!”

Chapter 44

Payback: 1938

Abel rode back to Martha's. Behind him walked Jack and the two boys. The sun had just set but there was a glow in the sky. Martha sat on the porch, rocking, her face stiff. Abel approached the porch and put a foot on the bottom step.

"I heard shooting and wondered who would be coming to give me the bad news. Was it the Chief?"

Abel just nodded.

"I guess you'll be leaving soon?"

Again he nodded. "Mr. Perkins, the newspaper editor, said he'd take care of the body and the report. To who, I don't know."

They were quiet for a long minute. Abel broke the silence, "I think I'm going to have to hit the road, Mart. Are you and BB gonna be okay?"

She nodded stiffly, “We’ll do all right. Alfred said he’d help out, and I’m going to hire Lucy Toffelmeyer to help me bake. Alfred said he’d put another oven in and we’ll do more baking there.” She nodded again, not looking at him “We’ll be fine, Abel.”

Behind Abel, he heard feet scuffling. Jack held each boy’s hand in his huge fists, holding them back. “Let ‘em talk,” he rumbled to the boys.

Abel strode into the house and gathered his clothes and toiletries. He came out a couple of minutes later and stuffed his things in the saddlebags. He squatted before BB and held out his hand. They shook and Abel said, “You take care of your Mom. I’ll be in touch.”

He was unprepared as BB threw his arms around him, hugging him tightly. He whispered, “Thank you, Uncle Abel. Be careful riding. Where are you going?”

He shrugged, “Not sure, kid. Probably back where I came from.” He stood and held out a mitt, “Jack, thanks for everything.”

Jack nodded and shook hands. Captain just stood and watched, wide eyed.

Abel climbed back on the porch, kissed Martha on the forehead and squeezed her hand. She turned and hugged him briefly. “Take care, brother, and thank you, you know, for avenging Bob.”

Abel nodded, climbed on his cycle and sat, taking in the only family he had in the world, then rode away. It was full night now.

Back in Harrington's Bar and Grille, Captain sipped his water. "Well folks, now you've heard the story of the Gunfight on Clearwater Beach. If you'll excuse me, I'm tired and I'm going home." He tipped his hat to his listeners and walked out of Harrington's.

Epilogue

Martha and Alfred Fett eventually married during the war. The business took off as the soldiers and sailors swarmed into town. The business became The Great Southeast Baking Company. Martha and Alfred retired in 1965 and sold out to the National Biscuit Company for $11,500,000. They had no other children. When they sold out, they gave Lucy Toffelmeyer $1,000,000, an unheard-of amount for a black woman at that time.

BB or Robert Bartholomew Brightwater enlisted in the Army in 1946 when he was 19. He applied to air cadet training and was sent to Southeast Army Air Corps Training in Montgomery, Alabama. He became a pilot of the first P-80 jet fighters and was sent to Korea where he distinguished himself shooting down three Russian MIG fighters. When the Korean War ended, Major BB Brightwater resigned and went back to Clearwater. His mother convinced him to attend college at the newly opened University of South Florida in Tampa. He majored in civil engineering. His greatest achievement was assisting to design the Sunshine Skyway Bridge. He visited his Uncle Abel twice and learned to ride horses and motorcycles.

Arthur M. Perkins reported the news for the Clearwater Sun. One of the stories he wrote was about the gunfight on Clearwater Beach in 1938. Mr. Henry Laplant paid him $1,000 for his story, and helped him get a job with the St. Petersburg Times when they bought the Sun.

Jack Toffelmeyer taught the Navy cadets the local shoals and sandbars when the war started. He had two helpers and sold all the fish he could catch to the military. As the south end of Clearwater Beach was developed, the Toffelmeyer family were forced off and moved to Tarpon Springs. The Greeks there were a little more tolerant of blacks than Anglo-whites. They made enough money during the war to buy a comfortable house and send Captain (Octavio Jacob Toffelmeyer) to Florida A&M University for both his undergraduate degree and his law degree. He remained in the Clearwater area as a lawyer for his entire life.

Ada Griver, the secretary at the police department, kept her job, and when the town council appointed Robert Rainey as Police Chief of Clearwater, they started seeing each other. Two years later they married and worked together for many years. Robert hired and deputized five former soldiers he'd served with. Tone of the first things he did was to arrest the mayor and town attorney. The Clearwater Police turned the case over to the federal prosecutor.

Gibbons, the attorney, served six and a half years in a federal prison in Coleman, Florida. Lewellen Teague, the Mayor, was charged with murder and child molestation. His wife and daughter were prime witnesses. He was convicted in 1939 and shipped to Florida State Prison in Raiford where he was killed by a fellow inmate during his first year.

Abel Landis drove his motorcycle back to Lander, Wyoming. It took two months, and the weather was getting cold. He went back to work for the Hartmanns and continued his trips to town. The Hartmanns retired and moved into town, leaving the entire ranch to Abel. He ended up whisking April out of the whorehouse, marrying her. They had three children. He and Gerta remained friends. When the war broke out, business was brisk. Abel resumed his painting, and taught April and their children. His oldest son, Walter, became a medic and was killed in Vietnam. His daughter, Sydney, became a doctor, and his youngest son, Victor, went to Hollywood and acted in more than one hundred movies, usually as a cowboy. Abel kept in touch with his sister and her husband, at first by letter and later by monthly telephone calls, though they never visited. Abel was well into his 90's when he died.

Excerpts from

MISSING PIECES

Another
Dave and Chris Manley Mystery

"I'll tell you what, Dave" Brad began. "I have a custom built 1979 Lincoln Convertible. I'd like to have it at the CES show in Las Vegas next month. How about if I pay you and Chris to drive it out for me?"

"Throw in a couple of nights in Vegas and you've got a deal, Brad," Chris enthusiastically replied.

"Deal!" Brad enthused. "Let me get back to the office and make all the arrangements. I should be able to drop the car off next week. You have until the 26th to get it from Florida to Vegas." He smiled contentedly at them and asked for a phone. Chris motioned him to the bar.

As soon as he slipped out of the booth, Chris grasped Dave's hands in hers.

"Well, how about that, Buddy Boy. A vacation for the two of us! And all expenses paid."

A week later the email showed up.

"DON'T GO TO LAS VEGAS - OR ELSE"

There was no header or return address. That made it even more curious. It was dated and timed during the previous night.

Three days later, a driver appeared with a beautiful 1979 Lincoln Continental Convertible. The car sure was special, as Lincoln did not make a convertible during 1979, so it was a custom job, and a good one, too.

Dave slowly walked around the car admiring its lines and the glistening red pearlescent paint. The white nylon top was up and fit perfectly. Dave shook his head in admiration.

The driver handed the keys to Dave and said, "Mr. Manley? Here's Mr. Atkinson's car. As per his instructions, the can needs to be in Las Vegas on or before the 28th of this month." He pulled an envelope out of his pocket and handed it to Dave.

"Inside are further instructions. I assume they tell you where and to whom you are to deliver it. That is all I know." Dave received the envelope and tucked it in the waistband of his shorts.

"If there's nothing else," the driver concluded, "I'll be going." With that, he climbed into the passenger seat of the white compact that had followed him in and was gone.

"Well, that was short and sweet," remarked Vinny who had been silently watching thedelivery. "What's in the envelope, David?" He bounced up and down on his toes, eagerly looking at the envelope.

"Well, let's see." Dave slit open the white envelope. Inside were ten $100 bills and a card with an address in Las Vegas. Turning the card over, Dave saw that it also had a name, "Arthur," and a phone number. He peered into the open envelope but there was nothing else inside.

Next morning at precisely seven AM, Dave and Chris loaded their gear into the big car. Dave had risen earlier and had stashed a pistol under the front seat, up in the springs. This looked like a straight upfront delivery, but on a cross-country trip it never hurt to be prepared.

As Dave drove out between the big tree Chris snuggled against him and turned to a soft music station on the radio. The top was up as it was still chilly out, a wispy fog hanging over the little seaside community.

The powerful car surged as Dave pressed the accelerator, flashing through the housing development and approaching the interstate. As they drove inland, the fog thinned to patches and here and there the sun was breaking through. The music swirled around them, muted by the plush padding that cocooned the passengers.

Chris dozed and Dave swept up onto the interstate headed north. The tires hummed against the slick road and Dave played with the cruise control. Chris had slipped down until her head rested on his thigh. She looked like a little girl, her short hair falling in her eyes, a little smile on her face. Dave rested a hand on her shoulder over the thin T-shirt and though about the first time he'd seen her.

She was only twenty-one years old at the time and doing volunteer work at a local VA hospital. Dave had come in to see one of his old squad mates who'd lost both legs in an anti-personnel mine in Viet Nam over a dozen years before. As Dave came around a corner, he'd run square into her, knocking her down.

Despite a rocky start, after a few dates, she'd seemed less angry, and a few months later had moved onto his boat. A year later they were married.

Yep, Dave remembered it all like it was yesterday. He stroked the fine yellow hair spread on his leg. Chris gave a small smile in her sleep. The big Lincoln surged on down the highway, smooth and fluid, like a day under sail.

"What time is it?" Chris sat up knuckling her eyes. She was wearing a Harley-Davidson T-shirt that read Ride to Live, Live to Ride, and a pair of tight jeans. Shifting around, she tucked her legs beneath her and leaned over and gave

Dave a kiss on the cheek. Then she stretched and said, “Find a place. I have to pee.”

Up ahead, Dave saw a sign that said EATS. He looked inquiringly at her. Chris cocked an eyebrow and shrugged. “Fine with me. I’m hungry, too. How late are we going to drive?”

“Another couple of hours. There should be plenty of motels around Mobile. It’s only around three-thirty now.” Dave drove with his hand draped over the top of the wheel, the other over the back of the seat. He rode barefoot, his shoes tucked under the front of the seat.

“Yuk, Mobile.” Chris wrinkled her nose. “Tomorrow can we get off this crummy freeway and take some back roads? You know how much I hate the interstates.”

“Sure, Babe. We’ve got lots of time. I only wanted to get out of Florida. We’ve seen this road enough times. After Mobile, we’ll drop on down to Pascagoula and take 90 until we’re outside of New Orleans. I think we’ll skip the Big Easy this trip. I’m about New Orleans’d out, okay?” Dave glanced over at Chris. She had the road atlas out and was tracing a route across Louisiana and Texas.

As the exit approached, Dave flipped the turn signal on and snapped the wheel to the right. He heard a loud screech of brakes and tires burning on pavement. Glancing to his left, he noticed a dark sedan attempting to slow to make the turn. He only caught a glimpse of the passenger, a clean-face, dark sunglasses, dark snap-brim hat, long hair and a dark suit coat. The man quickly turned his face away. Dave had to watch the turn, as it was a tight spiral taking them under the interstate to the local restaurant.

"What the hell was that about?" Chris asked spinning in her seat and attempting to see out of the rear window.

"Who knows. Maybe the guy was dozing at the wheel. Did you see the passenger? He was wearing a hat." Dave shook his head as they came to the stop.

"Yeah, so." Chris replied. "Lots of guys wear hats."

"No, not a ball cap but a hat hat. Like what's his name in the Blues Brothers. In fact he looked like, you know, not Belushi, the other guy." Dave couldn't remember the name.

"Ackroyd. Dan Ackroyd. David, are you losing your memory in your old age?" She kneeled on the seat and looked deep into his eyes up close. Then she smiled an impish grin and kissed him on the earlobe. "Get me to a bathroom or a clump of bushes fast, big boy, or you'll be pumping out this car."

Dave swung the wheel and turned the big car into the dusty parking lot.

He parked it beside an old Chevy pickup. The hood was up and there was an elderly fellow peering into the dim, dust-covered interior.

As they got out of the Lincoln, Dave asked, "What's the problem, old timer?" He ambled over to where the man was standing. Chris hurried off to the ladies' room.

The man stood up and scratched his head with one weathered hand. "Don't rightly know." He spoke slowly and carefully with a slight drawl. "She ran okay comin' in but she won't start now. Battery seems okay, jist won't catch." He hitched up his overalls and scratched his head again.

"Why don't you let me have a look? Maybe two heads will be better than one." Dave leaned over the passenger's fender and felt the wires from the distributor. "Here, this seems to be it." He pulled the wire free on both ends and showed it to the old timer. "Hold on, I think I can fix it." He reached into his pocket and pulled out a well-used Swiss Army knife. With a little digging and some quick snips and cuts, Dave put the old end back on the wire. In a second it was on. "Try that, Pop."

The old man opened the driver's door and sat down heavily. The motor caught right away, giving out a belch of black smoke. Dave looked at him and he smiled a toothless grin of delight.

"Well, I swan. Thank you, young feller. I'm afeared I can't pay you 'till next week but if you'll write your name and address on this here paper, I'll be glad to send you some money."

"Nah, that's okay, Pop. You just help the next guy that comes along, okay?" Dave grinned at him and slammed the dented hood. With a wave, the old man backed the truck out of the lot and was off.

Dave waited for Chris to return from the lady's room, then went in and washed his hands. When he returned to the table, Chris had tall glasses of iced tea for both of them.

"Thanks, Babe." He said gulping the cool drink.

The rotund waitress approached with a big smile. "That was shore a nice thing y'all did heppin' ol' Mr. Preston out theah. We all saw it an' 'r much obliged to y'all." She leaned forward, her fat arms shaking, and a twinkle in her eye.

"Now what can I git y'all? I'll put it on Mr. Preston's bill. I know he'd want me t'." She smiled again.

"No, that's okay," Chris said. "He doesn't look like he can afford it and that's not why we helped him. Well, why Dave helped him, that is." She crossed her arms and leaned back in the booth.

The waitress leaned back and gave a loud laugh.

"Not afford it? Why, Missy, that man's about the richest feller in these here parts." She leaned back and laughed again, shaking her head and pulling her order pad and a pencil out of her apron pocket. "He owns this place and a whole lot more hereabouts. You jist order any ol' thing you want and don't you worry about it. Not afford it," she snorted.

Dave shrugged and ordered. So did Chris. The food wasn't fancy, but it also wasn't bad.

When they returned to the car, Chris asked, "Did you notice anyone around the car while we were inside?" She was standing on the far side of the car, looking down, her hands on her hips.

"Not particularly. Why, what's wrong?" Dave asked walking around the car.

"Look," she said pointing, "the hub caps are missing." Sure enough, the small center caps on the custom aluminum wheels were gone.

"Maybe it happened when that car almost ran us off the road?" It was said as a statement but asked as a question.

"No, I don't think so. See, they're screwed on with two screws each. It would be a real coincidence if they both fell off at the same time." Dave walked around to the driver's side. The two caps on his side were still in place, screws tight.

"Well, shit. Make a note and if we pass a good size junkyard, we'll stop and get a pair of replacements.

That night the car's canvas top disappeared from the frame.

* * * *

Chris was driving. "Are You Lonesome Tonight?" blasted from the speakers, swirled around them and then was lost in the flowing wind. The sun was warm on their faces and the day promised to be hot … hot and muggy. Still, if they got a good breeze off the Gulf, it would be bearable. The Lincoln noiselessly eased down the old highway, cotton dotting the bottomland, on either side of the road.

Dave mentally tried to piece the vandalism together. First the wheel hub covers disappeared, but that could have just been kids or they could have vibrated loose. Next was the top, but whoever cleanly sliced it off must not have wanted it because Chris found it later in the dumpster. So why the hell would somebody bother to take it? He was baffled. Yeah, it might have just been vandalism, like everything today. People didn't need a reason for some of the stupid thing they did. But still, this was plain weird.

They were starting to see signs for New Orleans now, the big intersection coming up where the road split off and the interstate carried on into the Big Easy. They would have to make a decision as to their route soon.

"Jump back on 10, Chris. We'll take it around the Lake and through the swamp. We can look for 190 or something after we get up around Baton Rouge." Dave was peering at the open road atlas.

"Okay, but after we get on, let's stop for breakfast. There ought to be a Stuckey's or a grit house soon." She chuckled at the look on Dave's face. He hated grits, couldn't even stand the sight of them.

"Yuck," he mumbled.

Chris eased the big Lincoln up and into the early morning flow of traffic. She set the speed control to seventy and relaxed, letting the air flow through her short hair. The sun felt fine on her face and shoulders. Dave dozed in his seat, head back against the door.

She glanced in the mirror and was startled to see a dark sedan looming right behind her. Suddenly there was a terrific crash as the sedan slammed into their rear bumper. The Lincoln swayed wildly from side to side as she fought for control.

Dave came suddenly awake. "What the hell was that?" he yelled at no one. Chris was still fighting for control as the sedan hit them again. Crash! Dave spun in his seat and looked over the rear deck at the car behind them.

Though its windshield was tinted, Dave could make out the driver and passenger.

"It's them," he yelled. "The Blues Brothers!" He quickly described the two men in the sedan who were attempting to hit them again. "Nail it, Babe!" he yelled at Chris.

With a surge, the Lincoln flowed forward, turning the guardrails into a blur. The sedan was momentarily left behind. Dave was kneeling on the seat now and shaking his fist at the following car. He shouted at the top of his lungs, but his words were carried away by the wind. Chris only heard noise and focused all her attention on the road ahead. The speedometer crept up toward the hundred mark. Suddenly the black sedan was beside them and the passenger's window was coming down. Dave saw the barrel of a gun.

"Stop, Stop!" he screamed. He was suddenly hurled at the windshield as Chris stood on the brakes with both feet. Because he had been kneeling on the seat, he hit the top of the windshield with his right side and flipped over onto the hood. At the last second, he managed to hook a hand through one of the top clamps and held on with a death grip. The Lincoln stood on its nose, tires locked up and smoking. Their speed came down fast. Ahead, they could see the sedan speed away. Horns were starting to honk behind Chris as she attempted to pull over to the breakdown lane, anxiously grabbing at Dave's hand and trying at the same time maintain control. The Lincoln spewed up clouds of dust as it skidded to a stop.

Two cars pulled in behind them and some men started running toward their car.

Dave slumped against the windshield, feet splayed out on the hood. He carefully unwound his hand from the clamp. Chris was on her feet standing on the seat and leaning over the windshield.

"Oh, David, David, are you okay?" She was crying and clutching his head at the same time.

Just then one of the men reached them. "Hey, lady, you okay? How about you, mister? What the hell was that all about?" He was a swarthy man with a jowly face that looked a little like a bulldog. He looked up again as he caught his breath and said, "That hombre tried to run you off the road. Say, that was some good driving, lady but you almost put Paco here through the windshield when I had to jump on the brakes." He indicated a slight man with a cigarette drooping from the corner of his mouth who came jogging up to them.

Dave slowly swung his legs over the side of the fender. Two more men came running up. The little group looked expectantly at Dave.

"Did any of you see the gun?" Dave asked, looking from one to another.

"What gun?" asked Chris and another man at the same time. The others wore puzzled expressions.

"The gun, the fucking gun that the passenger was pointing at us." His eyes were filled with fire and he hurt, he maybe even had a cracked rib. He gripped his side, fingers exploring the bruised area. His hand hurt, too where he had held on. "What the hell did you think I yelled Stop for?"

"I'm sorry, David, but I didn't see any gun. I didn't even see the passenger." The rest of the crowd just shook their heads and mumbled.

"Say, what's going on? Are you in some kind of trouble?" One fat man asked.

"No, no. I haven't a clue." Dave just sat and shook his head, leaning on his hands. He slid to the ground. "Thanks for stopping. I don't suppose anybody got a license plate number on that sedan that hit us?" He looked around but was answered by a bunch of headshakes and more mumbles again. "Well, let's forget about it." He walked around to the back of the car and noted a ding in the massive rear bumper, but nothing more. He shrugged, walked around and got in the passenger's seat.

As the crowd reluctantly started back for their own vehicles, Chris slid in beside Dave and closed the door. "Are you really okay, Honey?" She looked up into his eyes, her own dry and smudged. He leaned over and kissed her on the tip of her nose and smiled. As he did, he slid his hand under the seat and moved the gun to his side.

"Let's go. I'm okay and we'll keep a sharp lookout from now on. Those were the same guys who were beside us back in Florida. Drive."

Chris carefully pulled out into the fast-moving traffic, trying to look everywhere at once and drive too. She soon settled down. When they stopped for lunch later that day, Dave called the name on the card and reported what had happened.

He plopped down in the booth of the chain restaurant and leaned over toward Chris. "Know what he said?" She shook her head, finishing her coffee.

"He said, just get the car here, no matter what. When I told him about the top and wheel caps, he just grunted. Can you beat that? He said, forget about the top and covers. Then he said shit a couple of times, asked my location and when did I think we'd be there and hung up." Dave slouched back in the booth, fingers toying idly with a straw.

"What do you figure is going on, Babe?" Dave asked Chris.

She tilted her head, a frown of concentration on her face. "Well, we hired on to deliver a car from Florida to Las Vegas. Then we were almost run off the road back in Florida by two guys you say tried to do it again here in Louisiana. Then last night somebody stole the top but threw it away. Before that, somebody either stole the wheel hub covers or they fell off. You tell me what's going on. Nothing connects. Is somebody after you, me or the car?" She looked baffled. "Was there something about your last job that could be connected? Or something from long ago?"

Dave shook his head. "Who knows?"

Chris sighed. "Let's just deliver the damn car and go home."

The rest of the day passed quietly. They'd made good time into Texas and when the day had ended, they had another five hundred miles under their belts. Their motel was clean, cheap, and had a small Mexican restaurant next door. The food was excellent, real Mexican, and not just Tex-Mex. The tortillas were homemade, and the chili made your eyes water. They drank large glasses of iced tea with mint in it to put the fire out.

That night Dave and Chris slept well and long. As usual, Dave was up at 7:00 AM. He went for a run out of town and along a fence line that stretched along the road. He ran what he figured was about two miles, only having an occasional cow look up and gaze at him for company..

He was catching his breath, leaning on the side of the Lincoln when he noticed the top framework missing.

"Oh, for crissakes," he exploded. Then he sank back against the car with a sigh. What the hell could he do besides sleep in the car? At the rate pieces were missing, he hoped there'd be enough left for them to turn in by the time they got to Las Vegas.

That day, they crossed the vast state of Texas, only stopping for lunch in San Antonio. Chris had never been in south Texas and wanted to see everything. They parked in a parking garage off Broadway and ate at a little cafe along Riverwalk. The sun filtered through the artificially planted trees and the filigrees on the buildings lining the sides of the carefully channeled river. Later they drove by the Alamo, now facing a troop of marauding drug stores and cheap camera and stereo stores. When they retrieved the car from the parking garage, the rear seat cushion was missing. They hardly remarked on it.

Dave was determined to stay awake that night and catch whoever was stealing pieces of the car. When they found a motel that night out on those West Texas plains, Dave deliberately parked the car crossways in front of the door, the whole driver's side visible from the window.

"I'll get the bastard, now," Dave said confidently. "I've got the gun and a clear view of everything."

Chris just snorted.

"I'll take the first watch 'till two or so. When I get too tired, I'll wake you, okay?"

"Sure, whatever," Chris smiled wearily and slid into bed. Dave had all his weapons handy, a six-pack of Coke, a bag of Oreo cookies and two Snickers bars. He'd be so sugar wired that he wouldn't sleep for a couple of days. Hell, when he'd been younger, junk food would see him on non-stop trips cross-country.

The night closed in. He turned the TV off and spun the dial of the built-in radio. Soft country music wafted through the room. The window reflected the grand sweep of stars, moonlight, and the tiny winking lights of airplanes passing overhead. Dave's head nodded just a bit. He jerked himself awake and leaned against the window, trying to draw some strength from the cool glass. He'd already drunk his third Coke and downed a handful of the cookies, yet he still felt drowsy. He settled back in the chair and tried to focus on the dark car in the parking lot.

Chris found him the next morning snoring softly in the chair, his head thrown back. Quietly she looked out the window at the Lincoln. The sun was just coming up and its rouge tint made even the run-down motel look lovely in the breaking dawn. She blinked a couple of times, unsure of what she was seeing.

She shook her head and nudged the sleeping Dave with her foot. "Wake up, oh mighty guardian." Dave made a few noises and tried to settle back into the backbreaking chair.

"Wake up, sleepy pie." She leaned out of the bed and nibbled at his earlobe.

Slowly his eyes came open. Oh, Christ, his back hurt. He was crippled for life. He tried to move but his hands flailed ineffectually at the tabletop, sending empty Coke cans and leftover Oreo cookies skittering in every direction.

"Help," he mumbled. "I can't move. I'm paralyzed!"

"Here, warrior, I'll give you a hand." Chris stood in front of him and grabbed his arms. Slowly and with much grunting and groaning, Dave came out of the chair. He stood there swaying, one hand scratching his butt and the other trying to wipe the sleep from his eyes.

"Well, I guess I kept them away last night, eh?" he managed.

"Yes, dear, but you'd better take a look anyway." They stood side by side at the window, staring into the dawn. The Lincoln was there, the body was there. Even the tires were there. But the doors were missing. Dave and Chris looked at each other and broke out laughing.

Other Books by

Don Kafrissen

- Brothers Beyond Blood
- Long Lost Brother
- Not My Blood
- Missing Pieces
- White Emeralds
- D'Amato's Place
  (Short Story Collection)
- Black Madonna & Other Short Stories
- The Brooksville Terrorist
- *Stories in several anthologies including* Mosaic 2010 & Mosaic 2014

International Digital Book Publishing Industries

About the Author

Even though most authors may hope to write a best seller, it doesn't always work out that way. But Kafrissen was pleasantly surprised when his novel about the Holocaust and its survivors, BROTHERS BEYOND BLOOD began to make some serious sales, first the United States, then Europe and Japan. This was followed up by two more books in that series, LONG LOST BROTHER and NOT MY BLOOD, books that also attracted a lot of attention. Kafrissen has written a number of other popular novels and short story collections including the Dave and Chris Manley Mysteries. GUNFIGHT ON CLEARWATER BEACH is the third book of that series, reintroducing the characters from MISSING PIECES and WHITE EMERALDS, including Chris and Dave's enigmatic warrior buddy, Tom.

"Kafrissen is a multi-level writer," says one reviewer. *"His stories suck you in with action and characterization, but then they make you think and wonder ...."*

Kafrissen is a veteran of the U.S. Navy, and has visited 43 different countries. He's lived in a number places including Rhode Island, Canada, Texas, California, Vermont. He and his wife once lived on a 40' Endeavor sailboat, spending many happy years in the Caribbean. He is a graduate of Cranston High School East in R.I. and Queen's University's McArthur College in Ontario, Canada.

Today Don Kafrissen lives on five rural acres on Florida's West Coast with his wife Diane and their cats. He and his wife built their own house, and are car people, taking part in many car shows and cruise-ins each year with their vintage autos. Don started the Brooksville Writers' Group several years ago, and now enjoys the friendship of many local authors.

For news, other books,
and to contact Don Kafrissen
Go to: http://idbpi.wordpress.com

IDBPI

www.ingramcontent.com/pod-product-compliance
Lightning Source LLC
LaVergne TN
LVHW020522100826
845148LV00010B/1307

* 9 7 8 1 5 7 5 5 0 0 9 7 3 *